ZIPPERED FLESH

Tales of Body Enhancements
Gone Bad!

ZIPPERED FLESH

Tales of Body Enhancements Gone Bad!

Edited by Weldon Burge

Smart Rhino Publications
www.smartrhino.com

First Edition

Zippered Flesh: Tales of Body Enhancements Gone Bad! Copyright © 2012 by Smart Rhino Publications LLC. All rights reserved. Individual stories copyright by individual authors. Printed in the United States.

ISBN-13: 978-0-9847876-0-9
ISBN-10: 0984787607

DEDICATION

For my wonderful family—Cindy, Chris, and Eric.

CONTENTS

ACKNOWLEDGMENTS

Thanks go to Shelley Everitt Bergen for her excellent, creepy cover illustration; to Scott Medina for helping me design the cover and format the interior of the book; to Terri Gillespie for her excellent proofreading skills; to my sister, Sharon Biesecker, for helping design the Smart Rhino Publications logo; and to the members of the Written Remains Writers Guild for their support and encouragement as the project came to life!

I must also point out here that, although most of the stories are original to this volume, three are reprints. Graham Masterton's story, "Sex Object," was originally published in *Hottest Blood* edited by Jeff Gelb and Michael Garrett. Scott Nicholson's story, "The Shaping," appeared in *Unspeakable Horror: From the Shadows of the Closet*, edited by Vince Liaguno and Chad Helder. And John Shirley's "Equilibrium" was published in *REALLY REALLY REALLY REALLY WEIRD STORIES*; John updated and rewrote portions of the story specifically for this anthology.

BOOTSTRAP—THE BINDS OF LASOLASTICA

BY MICHAEL BAILEY

VIRTUAL PARTITION 242 NOT RESPONDING.
ADJUST ARRAY PARAMETERS...

During initial testing on Bill Chevsky, partition 242 had periodically failed over the last few weeks and Victor knew it was finally time to migrate the data elsewhere. He had the five-hundred-terabyte partition ready and waiting in the cloud. It would be simple to replace because soft drives were physically nonexistent, at least from his vantage point, yet the process was cumbersome. Storing biodrives in-house was impractical and too costly; it was much more cost-effective to rent the space at an off-site facility, which he had visited prior to starting the project. As Victor replaced the faulty partition for Bill, he wondered how much of the human mind he was replacing and how much knowledge a single partition contained. It didn't quite work that way, however, because each was useless without the others. The 241 other partitions were figurative puzzle pieces of the Chevsky array, and it would take many more. How large was the mind of man? That was the penultimate question; the ultimate was whether or not cloning could be done on the mind.

The last test Victor ran on Bill had filled twelve petabytes of data, or twelve-thousand terabytes. The transfer was close to completion—or so the system reported before it crashed. The fifty-strand, wide-

1

optical catheter cable at Bill's neck was warm from the gigabits upon gigabits of ones and zeros passing through it per second.

Thirteen years prior, a young student at MIT and his peers had created a company called ImagEnation, more commonly known as the company responsible for founding the Artificial Knowledge Project. Victor had attended the Nobel Prize ceremony in Nepal and could still picture the kid holding up his palmtop computer to the audience. "This device," he had said, "contains the Webster's dictionary, the English language in its entirety," a break for audience applause, "and the complete history of the American People. This is the future of technology. This is the future of education. This is the future of the model U.S. citizen." The screen behind him showed a woman of Mexican descent on a hospital bed with wires connecting to various places on her head, from which acupuncture-like needles protruded. This spider web of wires coupled with a thicker set of cable plugged directly into a similar palmtop computer. When the next slide appeared, Victor laughed. With all of the advanced technology in the world, they were still using slide shows for presentations. The next slide displayed numbers and parabola charts. The next showed the crowd a progress bar, and the next a woman getting "disconnected" from the contraption. The last was a picture of the same woman holding a miniature U.S. flag in one hand and citizenship papers in the other. ImagEnation had programmed a woman to be more American than most Americans.

VIRTUAL PARTITION 242 NOT RESPONDING.
ADJUST ARRAY PARAMETERS...

While moving Bill's data, Victor thought of the Mexican woman and how a part of her psyche had been replaced as easily as swapping a virtual partition—a Mexican programmed as an American thanks to the Artificial Knowledge Project. They had brought her onstage after the slide show and she gave a speech in perfect Americanized English, without a hint of Spanish accent. She gave her testimony on how it had changed her life for the better.

Want to be a helicopter pilot? Victor asked himself as he established the new partition. "Why not," he said aloud when it initialized. *Trigonometry, calculus, advanced theoretical mathematics?* All it took was a little programming, and money. But such things were singular applications. Victor wanted the whole shebang, an operating system, the vessel capable of running programs. Sure, some punk kid from Delaware found a way to store the knowledge and language of the American People onto a compressed two-hundred gigabytes, but no one before had pushed the limits of the human mind. No one had ever attempted to store the entirety of a well-educated mind onto digital storage.

The facility hosting the storage space provided three six-foot-tall racks with the capacity to hold 512 biodrives, and enough power to supply twenty watts to each. This was just the storage, a small part of a larger storage cloud, which replicated to various other data farms around the world for backup and recovery purposes. A forth rack held the server farmstead, an even dozen mega computers, as they were often called, connected and clustered as one. The front display of racks was clean and black and filled with blinking blue and green lights, a beautiful spectacle; the back of the rack was a massive plethora of multi-colored optical and power cables. A generator connected to the multi-AC-controlled room; the device was capable of providing enough redundant, clean power to the building for outage scenarios. The project also required a sizable amount of money. Through a company generically labeled HVS, Human Vitalogy Systems, Victor was able to fund close to two billion dollars in private, short-term investments. He figured the money would last about a year.

ARRAY STATUS HEALTHY.

The display screen reported good news for once. The replacement partition was live and slowly absorbing into the array. It would take about an hour before it would be ready to accept data. Without disconnecting Bill from the programming station, Victor gently woke him. He was merely asleep. All it took was the turn of a knob, and the drugs feeding into his wrists did the rest.

"Bill," he said, and waited for eyes to focus.

"Victor?"

"Did you rest well?"

"Yes. I could sleep for days. Did it work this time?"

Victor sighed, put a hand onto Bill's shoulder, and said, "Almost. Listen, one of the virtual partitions went kaput and I had to suspend data copy in order to replace it. You're still connected, so I can't let you up yet."

The restraints were only a precaution. He didn't want Bill to wake up of his own accord and accidentally roll off the bed. That would be bad.

"I was wondering if you wouldn't mind going a second round. Shouldn't take more than three or four hours."

"What time is it?"

"Two in the morning."

"Monday?"

"Yes, Monday."

"I could use the sleep."

Victor smiled, turned another knob, which shot a dose of Pentithazine through the length of a second catheter, and watched Bill's eyes roll under their lids. In a matter of seconds, his project had returned to REM sleep.

He met Bill Chevsky a few years back while visiting his mother in the hospital. Both Victor's mother and Bill had been diagnosed with lasolastica, one of the incurable cancers, which had adapted over time to the common medicines used to treat other cancers like leukemia, melanoma, and lymphoma. Laso took your life in a few months in most cases, and it quickly took his mother's. Bill wasn't far behind. Victor could already see cheekbones through Bill's semi-transparent skin, the dark shadows under his eyes and the fear of death hidden behind them.

When his mother died, Victor pledged to find a way around the cancer, a way to cheat the incurable disease. It was simple, really, logistically; the process was the complicated part. After the second Gulf War, the United Nations—or Untied Nations, as Victor liked to call them—declared a non-winnable war against human cloning. The war on terror was handled similarly decades before. But his method of fighting was legal, according to the Cloning Laws.

There were five main stipulations of the Cloning Laws, known on the streets as *The Five Cloning Commandments*: (1) a license issued by the Department of Human Modification is required to clone body parts of any nature; (2) cloned animal body parts, not of human nature, may be used to serve either humans or animals requiring medical attention, if such parts are adaptable; (3) cloned human body parts may be used to serve either humans or animals requiring medical attention, if such parts are adaptable; (4) body parts of any nature may never be cloned for monetary gain; and (5) the human central nervous system, thus including the brain, spinal cord, and cranial nerves (retinas excluded), may not be cloned under any circumstances. There were many other facets to the laws, but those were the five basic principles. The Hippocratic Oath was even adapted.

Victor's idea was to clone an entire human body except for the central nervous system—to keep his experiment entirely legal—and then reprogram the original, which would later be transplanted into the cloned healthy version of the diseased or dying body. Sven Morrigan from Norrköping, Sweden, had attempted such a feat a few years prior—minus the reprogramming—but the patient's mind did not properly adapt and the patient was pronounced brain-dead shortly after her body was reanimated. Further studies revealed that the patient's brain had hard-reset, its internal memory and storage wiped clean, in other words. The doctor had rebooted the body, as well as the brain, but the brain was as useful upon reanimation as a reformatted drive, or a Bundt cake, for that matter.

CONTINUE WITH DATA COPY? (Y/N)

"Yes, please."

Victor pressed Y and leaned back in his chair, thinking of Bundt cake.

The copy of Bill Chevsky was at 78%.

He watched the display for the next few hours, adding partitions when needed. Twelve thousand petabytes were used by the time the image reached 87%, an amount of storage he had achieved on his last experiment with Bill, and this included compression. What bothered Victor was that he had reached 91% by this mark on his last run. Had Bill changed that significantly in only a week, enough to warrant such an enormous amount of storage difference? Could possible data corruption be to blame ... aka brain damage? Perhaps bad sectors on drives were similar to damaged neurons within the brain. The thought of defragmenting the human mind sent shivers up his spine because it was highly possible and worth looking into with future research. He made a note of it, realizing he could quite possibly be cloning damaged sections of Bill.

Victor had read articles comparing neuron storage within the brain to the physical storage of biodrives, and they were remarkably similar in nature. "The storage capacity of the human brain is infinite and cannot be set to a numerical storage value," proclaimed a Dr. Moresco from Syria. "Like the universe, the brain is forever expanding." Years ago, a Dr. Birge from Syracuse University had placed such a numerical value, stating that brain capacity ranged anywhere from one to a thousand terabytes, an amount that was quickly disproved. His initial guess was a dismal 3TB. Although he incorrectly hypothesized the storage potential of proteins, the biodrive was born many years later because of his experimental research, using genetically engineered DNA to store data rather than magnetic or metallic medium. Intel had revolutionized the microprocessor not long before by replacing traditional transistors with controlled deoxyribonucleic acids. It was estimated during his time that the brain contained somewhere between 50 and 200 billion neurons, and that each neuron interfaced with thousands upon thousands of other neurons through trillions or possibly quadrillions of synaptic junctions, with each synapse possessing a set numerical value. Long and extremely complicated story short, this equation produced an estimated half to full petabyte of potential data, which was also incorrect. Victor had disproved that theory while researching MLSP, or Molecular Level Storage Potential, while attending Berkeley. His research followed the neuron/synaptic junction equation, but added to it exponentially when his findings proved that ones and zeros could actually be controlled on a molecular level.

VIRTUAL PARTITION 242 NOT RESPONDING.
ADJUST ARRAY PARAMETERS...

A long, drawn-out sigh replaced the silence. Bill's breathing wasn't much louder.

"Partition 242. Again," he told his unconscious patient. "What is with you and partition 242, huh?"

The display read 93%.

"We're almost there, Bill. We're going to do this."

While replacing the partition yet again, he thought of his mother, his reason for the insanity behind the need for this type of accomplishment. Like his mother, Bill's body was going to die. His mind, if that could be saved ...

I could use the sleep, Bill had said to him.

His mother had said something similar just before passing. "I'm taking the long sleep," she had said. The longest sleep possible, one from which she'd never wake. Victor didn't want Bill's last words to be "I could use the sleep" because it was all too familiar.

ARRAY STATUS HEALTHY.

A sigh of relief.

CONTINUE WITH DATA COPY? (Y/N)

"Yes, damn it. Yes."

Life, the waking dream.

Ninety-four percent.

She had looked similar to Bill while on her deathbed, with dark, sunken eyes, pale gray and slightly transparent skin, blue spider web veins underneath feeding the cancer throughout her body. He remembered holding her fragile hand as she looked to him with distant eyes. Her skin, cold and clammy. She had looked past him, Victor knew, to the other side. She could see it, and he knew by her expression that she was afraid of going there alone. Even with those last fighting breaths and her body pumped full of poison, she wanted to live; seeing that only made Victor want to die right there next to her so they could at least be together.

DATA COPY COMPLETE.
CHECKING ARRAY FOR INCONSISTENCIES. PLEASE WAIT...

"Do I have a choice?

He had never gotten this far before.

"Cross your fingers, Bill."

Unconscious, Bill faced the ceiling. Victor crossed Bill's fingers for him. He had fallen asleep happy and was still smiling, anxious about possibly entering a disease-free copy of his body, living again, freed from the binds of lasolastica.

```
DATA CORRUPTION FOUND IN ARRAY.
CORRECTING ... NO ERRORS FOUND.
```

"Well, which is it?"

As if answering him, the screen displayed:

```
IMAGE CREATION SUCCESSFUL.

18,216,369,102,558,196.
```

How large was the mind of man?

For Bill Chevsky, the answer was a little over 18.2 petabytes. Take that number and multiply it by eight, and that's the number of ones and zeros used to portray Bill digitally. Hypothetically, Bill was the first human being with two minds, one physical and the other digital. One of his minds was virtually and quite literally in the clouds, a data storage cloud holding all 18.2PB of him. In terms of psychology, this sort of gave Bill a dissociative identity disorder.

Could it be done? Could the human mind be cloned?

The answer was now yes, and Victor was the first to do it.

He wanted so badly to wake Bill to tell him the good news, but if he did, he'd have to do it twice because he couldn't be disconnected from the catheter cable while conscious. It would most certainly kill him. Instead, he followed procedure and disconnected Bill properly from the computers and from the cloud that now hosted a copy of his mind. Victor turned the knob again to send wake-up juice into Bill's wrists, and he slowly opened his eyes. He yawned.

"So?"

Victor smiled.

Bill cloned it.

"Really?"

"We did it, Bill. You have a digital twin."

"When can we try?"

"Soon. I want to run thorough consistency and integrity checks on your image."

Bill smiled again. Looking at him was like looking at his mother the moment before she died—the eyes cloudy and distant, the smile full of effort and skeptical hope. He didn't say anything, but nodded.

"Tomorrow afternoon."

"Okay."

"You look puzzled."

"Oh ... my mind is going through some loops. Questions, you know? I've been thinking about it for a while. There's technically two of me in the world, right? *Me*," he said, pointing to his chest, "and then me," he said, pointing and looking to the ceiling. "Another me is floating around out there in the data cloud, but I don't know him. I can't feel him. A part of me thinks I should be able to feel that connection somehow. Does that make sense? The version of me that's talking to you is going to die, but the other gets to live. But it's not *me*, is it? I mean, it *is* me, but not *me* me."

The same questions had been haunting Victor's mind.

"This body is going to die. I know that. I'm not going to be a part of it after tomorrow afternoon because my mind—with my actual brain—will be in my new body ..."

"It's a shell, Bill. Your body, it's just a shell and nothing more."

"But you know what I'm getting at, right?"

"Look, what makes Bill Chevsky Bill Chevsky is in here." Victor pointed to his temple. "We've gone round and round about this in our preliminary consults. What we're doing is strange, no doubt, and it's never been done before, but we're taking a good mind from a bad body and we're putting it into a healthy, good body. A new shell. It will still be you in there."

"Can I see him?"

"Before the operation? Of course."

"I mean after."

"You want to see your old body? I'm not sure that would be a good idea, Bill."

"I want to see him."

"Bill ..."

"Promise me, Victor. You owe me that much. If a cloned copy of my mind is going into a cloned copy of my body, I want to at least look into my eyes to know it's no longer me in my dead body, that what's left after the operation is just some ... I don't know, some soulless, brainless husk and nothing more. I don't want a funeral or anyone to know. I want to see that diseased body cremated."

"Everything will be taken care of, I assure you. And please don't refer to your body as a husk. It makes this entire operation seem so Mary Shelly *Frankenstein*. We've come a long way with science since man—or woman in this case—came up with the idea of reanimating life with a donor brain, some metal rods, and a lightning storm. This isn't science fiction. This is life. And your life in this body will end soon and start again in another. From today on, I mean. Everything up until the image was created will be transferred to the new body, of course."

"What does that make me?"

"What do you mean?"

"I mean right now. Right now doesn't matter much, does it?"

"I'm not following."

"This image, it encompasses everything about me, from the moment I was born until the moment you woke me a few minutes ago. Every thought, every learning experience and failure in my life, and everything that makes me who I am today ... that time span of my life is what is on that image. Not now. Now doesn't matter because now isn't on the image you're transferring to my new body. This conversation we're having about this very conundrum—it won't matter much tomorrow afternoon because it won't exist in Bill Chevsky version two. You'll remember it, but the new me never had this conversation. It isn't on the image. Get what I'm saying?"

"I do, Bill, but look—"

"So everything I do from here on is pointless," he said, tears welling in his eyes. "What does that make me?"

"It makes you—"

"Non-important, pointless—"

"It makes you unique, Bill. We've all dreamed as little boys, as adults even, to have a clone. To be in two places at once; one of us to stay home and take care of the chores while the other plays. Am I correct?"

Bill nodded. "That and to be invisible."

"Your situation is a little different, that's all. One of you gets to go out and play while the other, well, passes on."

"I want to look into his eyes tomorrow, Victor, to know that he's not me."

"Bill."

Bloodshot and tired eyes stared back. He was a man clinging to life, a man afraid of waking up from his operation and seeing more than his own lifeless body. Perhaps a man who once believed in souls.

"I want to sleep tonight. I don't want to live any longer than I have to. In fact, I need you to put me under now. Anesthetize me, or dope me up somehow and let me sleep. The thought of a pointless existence will drive me insane otherwise. I want to dream the ultimate dream. I want to wake up tomorrow in my new body. I'm tired of this one. Will you do that for me?"

The last thing Victor said to Bill Chevsky version one: "I will, and thank you."

He was thanking him for more than the opportunity of performing the procedure, what could quite possibly end up being the gateway to a new treatment for patients with terminal conditions; he was thanking Bill for his mother, and for sacrificing his body for the hope of mankind and for the next generation of medicine; for the twelve-year-old girl who will never see thirteen because of the tumor growing on her spine; for the single father who will never see his son graduate because of heart failure; for the newborn born into a life destined for lasolastica or any of the other incurable cancers.

They had started cloning the body prior to the trials. It was a heavy expense, but funding had already covered the body. It was waiting for them in what Victor liked to call "the shop," a facility in the adjacent building. If Bill was anything like Victor's mother, he didn't have long to live. The night, would it be forgiving? Apparently so. He had injected Bill with enough drugs to assist him into a coma, and the next morning Bill's numbers on the electrocardiograph revealed he had survived his final sleep.

Victor recorded the old body vitals and signaled the surgical team. He watched from behind the operating room glass with a select few responsible for funding the project. Not one stayed for the gore, excusing themselves with, "This is excellent work, Victor ... most interesting, but I need to make a noon appointment ..." or similar lines of encouragement to hide weak stomachs. One by one they left him, and soon he was alone, leaning forward in his seat, nose to the glass, eyes moving like a metronome: to and fro, to and fro, to and fro between the health monitors and his patient; the clock on the wall keeping tempo: tick tock, tick tock, tick tock for the next four hours.

The surgery was invasive, to say the least. An ungodly sight. The key was to keep Bill Chevsky alive during the ordeal, something over which Victor had no control as he nervously waited behind glass. The thought of Bill alive as they cut away and removed the skullcap and exposed the membrane—it chilled him; the thought of a man in a coma with eyes still able to see as they detached the retinas, removing most of his face to get to the hidden cranial nerves beneath, cutting away cheekbones, removing the lower jaw, nose and upper row of teeth until there was not much remaining of his head—it repulsed him. A set of surgeons removed pieces of Bill while others worked eagerly to keep the rest of his body alive, injecting medicines, stopping blood flow, suctioning blood spill, and feeding new blood to replace that which was lost during the operation. Bill Chevsky, once a normal looking man, was now a body hacked from the waist up, organs rerouted and placed onto trays out of the way, cables and clamps coming out of a chest peeled open like a banana with the fruit scooped out. They supported the brain before removing the rest of the skull, and then they cut away all remaining and unnecessary soft tissue—as well as bone matter—to expose the central nervous system whole: brain, spinal cord, and cranial nerves. The workspace around them was remarkably clean throughout, despite the mess they had made of Bill's body. And then they unplugged him. Three sets of red-gloved hands lifted out the one thing Victor could not clone because of the fifth stipulation of the Cloning Laws: *The human central nervous system, thus including the brain, spinal cord, and cranial nerves (retinas excluded)* .... They took it out of him and gently placed it onto a stainless steel tray. Bill Chevsky version one was dead. All vitals on the electrocardiogram had flat-lined.

The lead surgeon looked over his mask to Victor and gestured a bloody thumbs-up. Nurses wheeled the massacred body out of the room—a brainless husk, Bill had said earlier. He was right. Victor would be there alongside him to destroy it. Arm-length rubber gloves were replaced on those staying for the second phase of the operation, and they held their arms to the ceiling as they waited for the clone. A doctor rinse-washed the brain and everything connected to it with bottles of clear liquid. She began placing electrical nodes onto it, which would send a minimal amount of current through the exposed central nervous system until transplanted. She finished as the new body was rolled in on a mobile operating table: Bill Chevsky version two.

It was nice to see him whole again.

While they were hacking apart Bill's old body, surgeons in an adjacent operating room had prepared the cloned body for transplantation. Their precision showed; a lack of anything to show would be a better way to phrase it. Only smooth lines were visible where they had made incisions, and they were only visible when the body was flipped onto its side. The entire back of the skull was removed, but would be completely hidden after the piece of bone was replaced and hair grew. Empty eye sockets let in light from the room, revealing that the cranium was empty. Everything else was intact from the face, from what Victor could see from his perspective. The large piece of skull lay next to the body. A straight cut extended from the middle of the back to the base of the skull as a means of entry for the central nervous system. Bill would have a generous scar after they sewed him back together again. Victor wondered about Bill's eyes, and then a nurse walked in with a small cooler, which held the cloned parts of Bill that needed to be installed after the brain, spinal cord and cranial nerves were placed into the body and reconnected. The entire process took them late into the afternoon.

After another thumbs-up, Victor prepared "the shop" for the reimaging process while he waited for the body. Surgery had come a long way in the last fifty years. It was remarkable he could work on him the same day. When they wheeled in Bill version two, it looked as though he were simply asleep on his back, chest rising and falling without the need of a nebulizer. New lungs with auto-inflation/deflation made sure he stayed breathing while an artificial heart kept synthetic blood pumping throughout his body. Various forms of nanotechnology were used to repair damaged tissue and to keep the body in a controlled coma; to quash the coma, it would take only a small electromagnetic pulse to turn off the bots, thus forcing the body to take over.

"Thank you for bringing him to me alive."

"He's a vegetable," said the doctor pushing the gurney, "but a healthy one, at least. The rest is up to you. We all have our fingers crossed."

"We'll get you back," Victor said, patting Bill on the shoulder.

The electrocardiogram displayed a slightly higher than normal heart rate, but blood pressure and pleuth were regular. Bill's image was finishing its final data integrity check while Victor readied the fifty-strand, wide-optical catheter cable and injected Bill with another dose of Pentithazine. The last thing he needed was for the new body to wake up prematurely. Bill's eyes were motionless behind their lids this time. No mind, no REM sleep.

IMAGE STATUS HEALTHY.

18,216,369,102,558,196.

Bill's mind: waiting in the cloud.

IMAGE READY … CONNECTIVITY VERIFIED…

"Ready when you are, my friend. When this is over, we're going out for drinks. But you're buying. Nod if that's all right with you."

Bill's body: toes up.

PROCEED WITH IMAGE DOWNLOAD? (Y/N)

"Fine. I'll buy."

Victor pressed the key with authority.

DOWNLOAD INITIATED…

BYTES COPIED: 1,539,974,021,487

The numbers farthest to the right of the screen were a blur as the byte count jumped at a rate of about 1.5 billion bytes per second. He stared at the number unblinkingly for about ten minutes until the byte count had climbed to a terabyte. It would take another three hours to download the complete image.

BYTES COPIED: 1,028,974,021,487,930

Bill lay there with his mind filling with information: childhood, education, adulthood, sexuality, life experiences, downfalls, and everything else that made Bill Chevsky who he was prior to his body's death; his first time riding a bike, first fight, first kiss, high school, college, marriage, the birth of his daughter, divorce, the death of his mother. It flooded into him as the same thoughts flooded into Victor's mind. What would *his* image look like? How many bytes? How many bad sectors he wished he could erase from memory?

IMAGE DOWNLOAD SUCCESSFUL.

18,216,369,102,558,195.

Three hours had passed, while the span of an entire life had transferred from cloud to man.

CHECKING DOWNLOADED IMAGE FOR INCONSISTENCIES...

Something about the number didn't look right. Hair rose on the nape of his Victor's neck. His stomach tightened. Compared to his notes, it was off by a single digit.

IMAGE SIZE MISMATCH OF 1 BYTE...

"I could have told you that," he said to the computer.

ARRAY STATUS HEALTHY. NO ERRORS FOUND.
IMAGE STATUS HEALTHY. NO ERRORS FOUND.
SIZE MISMATCH OF 1 BYTE ON DOWNLOADED IMAGE.
RETRY COPY? (Y/N)

He didn't have much of a choice. Instead of retrying the copy, Victor first checked the array for inconsistencies, and once more the computer told him the image stored on the cloud was fine, although a single byte larger in size than the downloaded version.

RETRY COPY? (Y/N)

What could one byte matter?
Victor pounded the key this time.

It could be anything—a single one or a zero could matter more than anything!

He watched the screen the entire three hours, rarely moving his eyes away. His leg shook under the table, his palms were sweaty. He was hungry and tired and had to pee, but none of that mattered. He had bitten the insides of his cheeks raw and destroyed a majority of his fingernails by the time the image finished.

IMAGE DOWNLOAD SUCCESSFUL.

18,216,369,102,558,195.

The same damn size. One single byte.

After repeated inconsistency checks on the hosted array image and the downloaded image, the computer greeted him with the same annoying:

RETRY COPY? (Y/N)

"What do you think?" he asked Bill. "It's either going to work, or it's not going to work. If it's the latter, we still have the image stored on the cloud and we can retry downloading using a different machine, or try something else entirely. I'm talking to you like you can actually answer me. I'm losing it. I can't believe I'm talking to myself now and I'm losing it. What would you do if you were me, Bill?"

Bill was as eager as Victor for all of this to work. He'd say screw the single byte and try it anyway. What could it hurt?

He chose no after hesitating over the Y key.

IMAGE COPY SUCCESSFUL.
DISCONNECT BEFORE REBOOTING PATIENT.

Victor disconnected the catheter at the back of Bill's head. It was a strange feeling, knowing he was going to reboot a human being, as if he were some kind of device instead of a living, breathing person. He remembered the term from history class at college. Bootstrapping, they used to say. It was an old term used in computer terminology, when bootstrap buttons were pressed in order to initiate hardwired programs. It derived from the phrase "pulling oneself up by one's bootstrap," which of course was an impossible task. Even before that, the word

16

bootstrap meant "to better oneself by one's own unaided efforts." Both seemed appropriate. Bill required Victor's help to get him out of the mud, and the goal was to better Bill's physical self.

He pressed the button that would normally shoot drugs into Bill's system to wake him up, but since he was comatose, it was simply the first step to rebooting his patient. The second step required the electromagnetic pulse to turn off the nanotechnology in his system. Before doing this, Victor noticed movement behind Bill's eyes. They were shaking back and forth behind their lids. Bill Chevsky was in REM sleep. He was dreaming. He was in there.

Victor's experiment had worked. He had successfully reimaged a human mind.

"Welcome back," he said, pressing the button to send the EMP.

Bill booted, his body jolting as if someone had shaken him awake.

He opened his eyes.

"Bill?"

His patient stared at the ceiling for a moment and then turned to him. Bill cleared his throat and shifted on the operating table. "Did it work?"

Victor smiled.

Bill cloned it.

And then he jolted again on the table and fell flat. He opened his eyes.

"Bill?"

His patient stared at the ceiling for a moment and then turned to him. He cleared his throat and shifted on the operating table. "Did it work?"

Victor smiled.

Bill cloned the smile again.

And then he jolted on the table and fell flat, opened his eyes, and repeated the same process: the same throat clearing, the same shift on the table, the same question of whether or not the experiment had worked. He was on an endless cycle of rebooting.

Victor shook him, tried to snap him out of it, but nothing worked. After the third or fourth cycle, Victor's smile had turned to a look of confusion, then fear. However Victor changed his expression, Bill matched it identically. Soon it became maddening. The jolt and the throat-clearing and the shift and the question—it never ended.

17

While Bill Chevsky continuously attempted the impossible task of pulling himself up by his own bootstraps, Victor checked the display on this monitor because it read something awful.

IMAGE SIZE MISMATCH.

One byte.
Bill cleared his throat.

.

IDOL

BY MICHAEL LAIMO

Money can't buy you love.

The road to happiness is best traveled with material things.

Beauty really is in the eye of the beholder.

Three familiar adages, all making perfect sense in a rather uncommon way to Anna Wesley. She, an only child of parents long lost to the ills of cancer. A store clerk whose limited education and experience afforded her only odd menial jobs throughout life, making it difficult to eke out a so-called living—a lifestyle paltry in its ways. Studio apartment in the burbs. Assemble-it-yourself furniture from the local *Furna-kit* store. A kitchen consisting of nothing more than a dual-top porta-stove and a cubicle refrigerator capable of holding three days of food, at best. Vegetarian, of course.

Happiness, love, beauty. All these *emotions*, instituted through an idolization of Crystal Rivers. Movie star. Pop music icon. *The* Crystal Rivers, whose unerring talents first drew Anna into her fan club. And then the charm she radiated—it made Anna realize how much they were alike. Once Anna discovered their commonalities, she thoroughly researched every existing fragment of Crystal's history in an effort to strengthen her vast knowledge of the life and times of her idol.

Meeting this woman who formulated the materials of her dreams had become an essential endeavor. Her familiarity with Crystal's world—her psychological involvement—prospered beyond a crude, universal obsession. It harbored urgency, whether it be amassing assorted objects of merchandise bearing the image or representation of the lithe blonde, or even a random expression paralleling the icon herself. When modeling herself in an effort to emulate the full spirit and appearance of the pop star, be it through dress or hairstyle or makeup, she made certain to use only those brands that her icon commercially endorsed.

Modeling herself after the object of her adoration didn't exist on a smooth plane of subtleties. It was in Anna's greatest interest not to imitate but to *duplicate* Crystal Rivers to the highest possible degree, thereby garnering an unmatchable measure of self-satisfaction. Of course, Anna's art simply imitated life, and she scoffed at those who insisted that she might actually be the pop star herself—time and time again adoring fans sought an autograph and a handshake from Anna in their quest to rub shoulders with an icon. Illegal impersonation, Anna knew, was a step best left unexplored, although not *every* time did she shun the advances of admiring fans like herself. She'd embrace them, and then slip away into obscurity before the crowd grew too large.

These crazed fans weren't exactly like Anna. No. Indeed, others found pleasure and even occupation impersonating their idols on stage and street: Elvis, Michael, Madonna. But Anna, she derived personal satisfaction in *becoming* the artist Crystal Rivers to the best of her abilities. She aimed to *feel* just as Crystal did, her mind at times drawing upon the innate talents of the pop star, even so much as recalling intimate details of her private past that only Crystal herself would know. Was it possible that clairvoyance played a specific role?

Anna's fixation on becoming Crystal Rivers happened purely through a chance discovery. Anna had never taken part in the institution of face-painting and trendy dress-up that embraced the art of "keeping pace with the masses." Her obsessive behavior had relied solely on the collecting of things that fostered a relation to the one and only Crystal Rivers.

Then, something changed all that.

During one week, on a daily basis, minute to minute in fact, she'd followed the televised happenings of Crystal Rivers' European tour in support of her latest album, *Take What You Need*. Catching a support special on the Celebrity Channel, a piece of raw footage was aired, rocking and adjusting focus as it made its way into the singer's dressing room. It caught Crystal sitting before a mirror, applying makeup. She'd just begun the lip liner, the first of many applications that would transform her into the idol adoring fans knew and loved. *Her face!* The resemblance was uncanny. It was Anna's face ... Anna who'd never worn an ounce of makeup—and to this day had never glimpsed Crystal without her thick blushes, mascaras, and lipsticks. She'd taped the program, and then watched the clip over and over again, frame by frame, as the pop star morphed herself from Anna Wesley lookalike into Pop Icon Crystal Rivers.

Soon thereafter, Anna initiated her transformation into Crystal.

Every cent of her income went to the purchase of cosmetics and apparel. Her hair was dyed to match the most current tint on parade. Her eyes, a shade darker than Crystal's, were lightened through the use of contact lenses. A small rose was tattooed on her shoulder, as well as the freckles and beauty marks that adorned Crystal's arms and chest. Her life savings remedied a variation of breast size, and in a month Anna proudly offered the public 36Cs matching those that Crystal so frequently flaunted.

She took vocal lessons, learned to lip synch Crystal's songs while acting out every dance move. Soon thereafter, she was able to sing every track in Crystal's repertoire, looking up her most recent set list from her tour, dressing up in one of fifteen outfits, and then posing before a mirror and singing along with a karaoke tape.

Uncanny facts came out in Anna's research of her idol's past. The performer was born on the same date, in the same year as Anna. Her parents passed away from the ills of cancer as Anna's had. They worked similar jobs throughout their teen years, each doing her best to make ends meet. The only dissimilarity in their lives was the level of success each had attained by the age of twenty. Perhaps it had been their upbringing; Anna moved in with a foster family in the Midwest. Crystal was raised by an aunt on the shores of California. Anna tried to imagine what would've happened if the opposite had occurred. Would she be singing to sold-out crowds every night? Would Crystal be holding down jobs at the Quick-Mart?

What would happen if they met face to face?

In less than a week, she would find out.

Anna used every cent from her most recent paycheck to book a flight to Los Angeles, three days before Crystal's concert there. In a rare in-store appearance at Borderlands Music, Anna would dress her best to emulate the singer, and then arrive moments before Crystal did and embrace the hordes of adoring fans.

It was an interesting plan. She was certain security would whisk her away, and since she really wouldn't be guilty of any illegal act (she was only dressing up as her idol), the uncanny resemblance would trigger Crystal's curiosity in her look-alike.

It would work.

Two days before Anna's scheduled flight to L.A., Crystal Rivers was involved in a tragic car accident; one too many drinks behind the wheel of her Porsche left her twisted like a ragdoll beneath the dash of the car, an arm and half her leg left behind in an irretrievable pulp. The star went to the ER and then immediately into intensive care, and the public waited for word on her still unreported injuries.

Four hours later, men came for Anna.

They posed as uniformed meter men fixing to check the oil heater in her apartment (it occurred to her only as the rag filled with harsh chemicals was forced over her face that the building was heated by gas). They abducted her. Upon waking six hours later, Anna found herself face to face with her idol.

Crystal Rivers. The car crash had transformed the former teen beauty queen into a Bride of Frankenstein. She lay on an operating table, unclothed, her skin blue and bloated as though it'd been submerged in water for a lengthy period of time. The bruises were abundant, deep bloody blotches that resembled port-wine birthmarks littering her torso and limbs. What remained of them.

Her left leg disappeared at the knee, bandages with black stains covering the severed stump. Her right arm was completely gone, the wound exposed by a series of metal wires holding back the skin at a dozen protracted points. Her face was a balloon, the features lost beneath the dips and dives of her injuries. Her blond hair had turned muddy-brown, an effect of the dried blood still in it.

Up until ten hours ago, Anna had been buried under the lifelong dream to meet her idol; now, she was too repulsed to simply make an approach.

"Anna," a voice said.

She turned and realized that this place was no hospital, but rather a small private room in someone's house, with books on the wall, furniture, a chandelier, a sheet-covered table dressed with medical supplies. A middle-aged man stood before her, dressed in a tennis shirt and khakis, his hands pocketed and fidgeting as if treasuring for change. Peering over a pair of steel-rimmed glasses, he said, "Anna Wesley. Welcome."

"Where am I?" she asked. "What am I doing here?" She felt a hot pulse in her veins that ran to her head, forcing lightheadedness. Everything went hazy, as if she'd just woken from a dream.

The man grinned, lips thin and wet in anticipation. He looked like a boy experiencing his first naked woman. Stepping forward, he reached out and took Anna's hand. "My God, the resemblance is uncanny."

The situation grew more surreal by the moment, and for the first time in years, Anna wanted nothing more than to simply be Anna Wesley. "Why am I here?" she asked again.

"You've always wanted to meet your idol, no?"

She turned to gaze at the unmoving body on the bed. It looked nothing like the pop star, or like herself for that matter. She'd never seen a person so compromised—tubes snaking out from beneath ruptured skin, four computer screens casting green glows, periodic beeps as if communicating in some alien code. The dreamlike feeling began to feel more like a nightmare. "Yes," she finally answered. "But not like this."

"We weren't sure how long she'd live," the man said. "That is why we rushed you here."

She turned to face the man again. His smile dipped into a serious flattening of the lips. He looked as if he'd just heard about the death of a family member, or was about to take on some serious task. Behind him a door opened up and a number of men appeared, those that perhaps had abducted her, Anna thought. Anna noticed a dark splotch on her host's shirt that could have been a remnant of his lunch, gravy or ketchup, but might very well have been blood. Crystal's blood. The men, six in all, surrounded her.

To her immediate right, a blond-haired man wearing a blue leisure suit asked Anna to follow him to a sofa six feet away. She obeyed, settling herself uncomfortably into the paisley cushions. "I find it hard to believe that you kidnapped me just to fulfill my lifelong dream," she said.

The man smiled. "Anna, we did bring you here for a reason. We want you to become, so to speak, the next Crystal Rivers."

Anna's heart expanded with a whirlwind of excitement, adrenaline racing through her body, causing her to tremble. What did he say? Would she really *become* Crystal Rivers? She felt a rush of heat, and used her hand to wipe the beads of sweat sprouting at her hairline. "Are you saying you want me to replace Crystal?"

The man grinned. There was something about his demeanor she didn't trust, as though a flurry of lies waited just beyond his smile, each and every one battling to get out. She looked around the room. The other men surrounded Crystal's body, moving objects about on a table: syringes, scalpels, clamps, and other surgical supplies. What *was* going on here?

"Yes, as a matter of fact we do."

She took a deep breath that burned her lungs. "How did you know about me?"

"Birth records," the man said. He'd been waiting to tell her this, that much was immediately clear. "You and Crystal are twins, separated at birth. Given Crystal's tendency for drink and drug, we knew that someday she'd self-destruct and that we'd need you to replace her. Understand, too many dollars are invested in Ms. Rivers. We're businessmen, and we needed to protect our investment. Like many other Hollywood idols, Ms. Rivers has amassed the very best professionals this planet has to offer—cooks, stylists, personal trainers, and in the case of emergencies, lawyers and doctors. We, Ms. Wesley, are Crystal's doctors. We are here to make sure she is taken care of."

Anna tried a smile. It failed. "Then why am I here?"

Without warning a needle was plunged into Anna's right shoulder. She turned but the pain was severe, paralyzing her in seconds and forcing her to succumb. Her world went hazy, the nightmare now taking over. Two men grabbed her and jammed another needle into her leg, above the knee, injecting her with a clear serum.

"As we said, Ms. Wesley, you are here to replace, to *become*, Crystal Rivers. But only in part. The accident destroyed one of her lungs, a kidney, and her spleen. She needs transplants. The only suitable organs must come from a family member."

"*Christ!*" Anna said, trying to move. Her body was frozen, caught in the grasp of the anesthesia. She looked at Crystal's body, lying in a comatose state and unaware of the horrors about to take place to save her. The horrors that caused Anna's heart to pound for its life. "But she'll never be able to perform! She's missing an arm, a leg!"

The man stood. Two men dressed in white gowns lifted her incapacitated body and placed it on a surgical cart. "Like I said, Anna. Crystal Rivers has the best doctors and surgeons on the planet. And they can perform cutting-edge microsurgical procedures."

The man said something else, but Anna's world went black. It seemed a moment's time passed. When she opened her eyes, she remembered what the man had said, but didn't believe it until she saw the men carrying away her amputated right arm.

Limb transplants.

UNPLUGGED

BY ADRIENNE JONES

When I told my friend Allen I planned to spend a year living alone on the side of a mountain, he didn't respond the way I expected. No concern for my state of mind, no inquiries as to how I was holding up since my wife left. I thought he might suggest I seek counseling before embarking on this Thoreau-like journey of seclusion. Taking a self-indulgent year off work was the kind of thing men in their twenties did, not career teachers of a certain age. Of course, a younger man might take a year off to travel and gain life experience. Me, I wanted the opposite, a defense perimeter away from experiences, an impenetrable bubble of nothingness to curl up in and lick my wounds.

Still, I sort of wanted Allen to talk me out of it. I was feeling sorry for myself, and craved an indication that *someone* gave a crap if I disappeared.

But Allen just scowled at his coffee, shaking his head. "You know about those bears in the Adirondacks that learned to knock on doors? Wouldn't catch me living up there."

"That is the stupidest thing I've ever heard," I said.

"Seriously, I saw it on TV or I read it somewhere, I can't remember. But these bears are getting smart. Evolution, right? If they get hungry enough, they knock on doors and wait for someone to come out on the porch. Then they attack, sometimes in groups. It's freaky, man. Fuckers are climbing up the food chain, so be careful."

That was two months ago. I didn't believe Allen then, and I don't believe him now. But when you live on the side of a mountain, nearest neighbors a mile away, a knock at three a.m. is unsettling. And though I hadn't thought about Allen or his evolved-bear theory in weeks, I was suddenly sitting up in bed, listening to my front door rattle, and picturing a bear crouching alongside the porch.

I climbed out of bed, kicking over a bottle as I stumbled through the dark, my sock now wet with warm beer. I sloshed down the hall to the front door, leaving the lights off as I peeked through the kitchen window, seeing two shadowy figures on my porch. They weren't bears. They were police officers. I recognized the tall, freckled redhead, had seen him on my grocery and beer excursions into town. We were on nodding terms. The other cop was shorter, with a rounded belly. He knocked again and I jumped back from the window.

Opening the door, I blinked, squinting as the big redhead shone a flashlight at me. "Whoa." I backed up. "What's going on?"

He lowered the light. "Sorry to get you out of bed, but we need to search your house."

I thought of the bag of high-quality cannabis I kept in the freezer, and my intestines gurgled. "Um ... why?"

The second cop stepped forward. He was older than the redhead, with graying, brown hair and ruddy cheeks, folksy looking until you saw the eyes. His expression said he'd gladly make you bleed if you even *thought* about pissing him off. "We're pursuing a crime suspect," he said. "He headed up this way. Yours is the only house in the area, we want to make sure he didn't break in here to hide before we move on."

Reasonably sure no one was hiding in my small house, and guessing they'd not be looking for him in my freezer, I let them in.

My cottage had just one small bedroom, a bathroom, kitchen and living area, but the cops tore through with aggressive thoroughness, opening closets, cabinets, and cupboards. I sat in a kitchen chair, watching the tall redhead scour the pantry while the other one went down to check out the basement. The tall guy seemed nervous, his expression tight and flushed, unlike the emotionlessly chiseled cop-face he wore in town.

I heard the other cop stomping up the wooden stairs from the basement, and then he appeared in the kitchen doorway. Ignoring me, he spoke directly to the other officer. "Looks empty, but we'll keep a detail on the property. The others are checking the woods." He looked at me. "You fish?"

I shook my head. "I'm sorry?"

"Fish," he said, casting an imaginary line, then reeling it in. "You've got the pond out back. I'd guess most folks would rent this place as a fishing getaway."

"Ah, right. The pond is nice, but, no, I don't fish. I'm just here to sort out my head. I'm a science teacher in Boston. Took a leave of absence. Life's been a little stressful lately."

They exchanged a glance. The chubby one looked around at the mess, and then raised a brow at me. "Science, huh? Mr. uh, what is your name?"

"Jason Sarno." I held my hand out to shake. He didn't take it.

"Mr. Sarno, would you mind if we took a look at the back of your neck?"

I thought I'd heard him wrong. "My ... my *neck*? What for?"

The ginger cop moved in a slow sidestep behind me as the chubby one edged closer, like they expected me to run.

"Will you or will you not let us look at your neck, Mr. Sarno?"

I glanced over my shoulder. "Yeah, sure. Look at my neck."

He raised his left hand, right hand resting on the gun at his hip. "Put your hands over your head and keep still," he said.

I did what he asked. The officer's cold fingers trailed up the back of my neck, and despite the oddness of the moment, I was self-conscious about my appearance for the first time in weeks. He lifted the mop of hair I'd let grow past my collar. I couldn't remember the last time I'd brushed it. Letting myself go had been intentional, part of my self-imposed exile, but I hadn't planned on other people examining me, poking around my dirty house, invading my disgrace.

"He's clear."

When the fingers were gone, I took a breath of relief, unsure why. What were they expecting to find on my neck? A packet of cocaine?

"You got a phone here?" the shorter one asked.

I shook my head. "I came here to be alone, without a lot of modern conveniences."

The cop huffed, and pointed to the box of empty beer bottles next to the trash bin. "Is beer not a modern convenience? What about electricity? You out hunting your own food, then?"

"No, I meant ... well, this is pretty back to nature for me, coming from the city."

The cop's smirk told me he'd been yanking my chain. "Yeah, I didn't quite figure you for a hunter, seeing you got a pond stocked with trout out there and you don't even fish. I'm guessing your main prey is salami sandwiches." He laughed, throwing his head back. The other cop tried to grin but didn't quite make it, still looking nervous.

"Are we ... done here?" I asked, my face burning. The hangover initially scheduled for sunrise had awoken early and tapped ruthlessly at my temples.

They started for the door. "You see anything, hear anything strange, come out and tell one of the officers," the short one said. "We'll be stationed around your property and the pond. Anyone tries to break in here, you come running. You really don't have a phone?" He paused in the doorway, eyeing me with disdain.

"I don't have a phone. What exactly did this guy do? The one you're looking for."

"Don't you worry about that," he said, and they left the house, climbing off the porch and heading toward my backyard.

"Why are you guarding the pond?" I called out.

They both stopped, turning back. The redhead looked sick and frightened, sweat shining on his skin. "The guy we're after is good at hide and seek. Now, please, just stay inside until we tell you otherwise," he said. "If you need to leave the house, let one of us know. We'll be out back."

They disappeared around the corner of the house. I shut the door and ran to the living room, peering out the back window at the darkness of the woods. Three flashlights danced around the pond area, another two in the woods to the side. I shook my head, rubbing my temples. Moving to the kitchen, I grabbed the bottle of pain pills from the cabinet over the stove, my heart sinking to find only one left. I popped it down with a sip of water from the faucet, knowing it wouldn't do the trick.

Getting back to sleep didn't seem like an option, with cops crawling over my property and the threat of some anonymous perp breaking in. So much for my restful retreat.

I longed to smoke a joint. My nerves danced, fueling the pending hangover's throbbing pulse. I glanced at the freezer. Smoking a joint with a yard full of cops was probably not the best idea I'd ever had. But screw it, I needed it. I could take it in the bathroom and turn the fan on.

I opened the freezer door and something sprang out, knocking me onto my ass. It rolled off me onto the kitchen floor, a shiny lump of flesh, dog-sized and hairless. I crab-shuffled back on my elbows as it unraveled, unfolding itself from a fetal ball, revealing arms, legs, head. The scream that had stalled in my throat found its way out, but the sound was cut short as the thing dove on me, an icy hand clamping painfully down on my mouth.

The eyes looking down on me were yellow with large black pupils, skin pale-green with splashes of turquoise. "Not a sound," it said, and despite the slash of gills on either side of its rubbery mouth, it was the voice of a man.

He released my neck, but hovered over me, a web-fingered hand poised to clamp down again if necessary. "Not a sound," he said again. I nodded.

He stood. One of his cold, slippery hands grabbed my wrist and pulled me to my feet.

As I faced the thing, my body went so still I almost forgot to breathe. It felt instinctual, my primitive mind urging me to become invisible, nonthreatening, like a rabbit freezing stiff at the whiff of a predator.

He was nearly my height, nude, and human looking, despite the odd skin and eye color. Even with the gills, webbed fingers, and what looked like flaps of blue seaweed crowning his scalp, he had a man's shoulders, chest, and abdomen, his navel a blue dent darkening rippled green flesh. I tried not to look at his penis.

"I need some clothes," he said.

I nodded. "Oh, um, okay. My room. I ... they're in my room."

"Show me. And don't try anything." He fanned his hand in front of my eyes, and I gaped at the sharp talons.

31

Shuffling out of the kitchen, we made our way down the hall and into my bedroom, the creature gripping my arm.

When I flicked the light on, he yanked me back, out of the way of the window, nearly pulling my arm out of the socket.

"Ouch!" I fell back against the wall. "Take it easy, the shade is down."

A clawed finger pointed to my dresser. "Clothes. Something dark. Preferably black."

When he let go of me, I dug through my drawers. I was again struck by how normal he sounded, so much that I might have believed this was just a guy in a costume. But all my instincts screamed *other*, *different*. It wasn't just his appearance. His life-force, energy, the very presence of him felt wrong.

When I was six, my father took me walking through the woods and we came upon a dead deer. She hadn't been dead long, no decay or sign of injury, but I still didn't believe it when he said she was sleeping. Something inside me seemed wired to recognize that which is foreign to life, and there's nothing more alien than death. I knew this creature in my room wasn't human, the same way I'd known that deer wasn't breathing.

"Here." I handed him a pair of black running pants and a navy-blue T-shirt.

He got dressed, yellow eyes on me with silent warning. When he'd finished, he sat on the edge of my bed. He remained silent for close to a minute, and in my terror I felt the need to babble. "I don't suppose you'll be wanting shoes." I pointed to his webbed toes, attempting a friendly chuckle.

His blue lips curled in a semblance of a sneer. Bowing his head, he reached back, the claw of his index finger prodding behind his neck. "Damn it, what is *wrong* with this thing," he muttered. His weird face twisted, frustrated; then there was a click and a hiss, like air being let out of a tire.

I jumped back against the wall as his body rippled and pulsed, green skin smoothing to golden tan, gills retracting; the weedy scalp fins elongating and twisting into hair. The rough flesh smoothed and the shifting stopped. Then it was a young man sitting on the bed, wearing my clothes. A young man I recognized.

"You!"

He ran a hand through his dreadlocks and I was pleased to see he no longer possessed claws. "Yeah." He stretched his back, spine cracking. "Me."

"What ... the hell." I stared at him, stunned. His name was Tony. I knew this because I'd heard others greet him at the liquor store where he worked. He'd rung my beer purchases up dozens of times since I moved here, a handsome young guy with a mop of sandy dreadlocks and a perpetual suntan.

I liked Tony; he knew how to mind his business, a sign of professionalism the way I saw it. A liquor store clerk knew better than to comment on your purchases, or the frequency with which you made them, and Tony always rang me up politely, never looking me in the eye or acknowledging that I'd been in there three times already that week. I appreciated it. Even pharmacists weren't so discreet. They always had to add "Don't use that cream internally" or "Stay out of the sun or that rash will spread" while a line of customers pretended not to eavesdrop.

"Why," I started, struggling for words. "Why are you an *alien*, Tony?"

He finished cracking his knuckles and gave me a sour grin. "Oh, I don't know. Shit happens. Jason, is it?"

"Yeah. I didn't think you knew my name."

"Small town," he said, and stood, stretching his legs. "The locals call you Twelve-Pack Jason. How much food do you have in the house?"

I scowled. "I don't know. Not much. Why?"

"Because I need to wait it out here until those boneheads out back give up and leave. Who knows how long that will be, but—OH, no. No, no *no!*"

He grabbed his cheeks as his face rippled, greenish tint surfacing like a neon blush. Then the pulsing, rippling contractions shook his body again, lumps traveling over his visible flesh. A click, the hissing sound, and Tony's features contorted, slipping back into creature form, slick and shiny with gills, dreadlocks back to weedy darkened flaps.

I stared at this thing wearing my clothes, and this time I truly forgot to breathe, clinging to the dresser as a dizzy spell hit. Tony didn't seem to notice, or care, as he was busy punching my bed, his clawed hands balled into fists.

33

"Damn it! Piece of crap! This can't be happening." He straightened up and paced my tiny bedroom, shaking his weird head. "Can't be happening. Not now. Shit."

I held to the dresser, catching my breath. "What's wrong with you?" I whispered.

He made a sound that was likely a laugh but sounded more like a growl. "Oh, gee, what's wrong with me? Not much. Just that I need to leave town stat; this implant is malfunctioning, and I can't go out in public like THIS!" He threw his clawed hands up, showing them to me. He then whirled away, kicking the bed with a frustrated growl.

"What is it for?" I asked. "Your ... implant."

He stopped pacing and tilted his head at me. "I know you drink a lot, but are you dense? You know what it's for, you just saw it work."

"Makes you look human," I said. "So you can blend."

He clapped his hands. "Change of plans, Twelve-Pack. There's someone down in the village who can fix this." He lifted his flaps of scalp weed and showed me the back of his neck where a dime-sized silver plug stuck out like a metallic nipple. "Or he better be able to fix it if he doesn't want an ass kicking."

At first I thought there were black veins spider-webbing out from the implant, but they were very fine wires embedded into his flesh.

"Not that I should blame the manufacturer. When the cops raided my place, one of them whacked a gun on the back of my head. I got away, but he must have damaged the implant. Shit!" He kicked my bed again and I jumped.

"So, are you leaving?" I asked hopefully.

"Well, yeah, I need to get across town. A place called Michelangelo's on Alpine Drive."

"Michelangelo's Body Design? It's a piercing shop."

His shiny green face stretched around the mouth, a smile, I supposed. "You know it, good. You've got a car, right? The jeep outside?"

"You want me to drive you? What about the cops? I mean, I'm terrified of you, don't get me wrong, but that little fat cop gives me the creeps, too."

"He's not a cop." Tony shut off the light and peeked out the window through the side of the shade.

"He looks an awful lot like a cop," I said.

"Well he's not. He's a hunter."

I dared a step closer to alien Tony. "What's he hunt?" I winced.

He held his arms out and did a little twirl. "Guess."

"How did he find you? I mean, I know you've been living here since I moved in, at least two months."

"I've been here three years, and got left alone until now. It's complicated. He's a slippery bastard. Has this new tracker that measures chemical changes in fresh water supplies in the area. If one of us is living nearby, we cause a slight, but very specific, change in the water composition. It's a setback, but we're looking into a way to remedy it."

I sat on the bed, hands on my knees. "One of us? You mean you're not the only one? There are others like you in the world?"

He did a double-take, turning away from the window. "Sorry to fuck up your reality, pal, but there are others like me in this *town*. Which is why I need you to take me to Michelangelo's. I need to see Fat Pierre."

"Is ... Fat Pierre an alien?" I asked.

Tony gave me a sour face. His expressions were becoming more discernible, even in creature form. "No, he's not an *alien*. Fat Pierre's a body modification specialist down at Michelangelo's. He's been working both sides for years. He's trustworthy."

I threw my hands up. "I'm sorry, it's just ... I was picturing some secret underground lab full of scientists in white coats fixing your implant. Not some sweaty tattoo artist in the village."

"Fat Pierre only poses as a sweaty tattooist. Trust me, he's much more. So will you drive me or not?"

"How am I supposed to get you out? They said I have to tell them if I leave the property. They'll see you! They'll probably search my jeep."

His yellow eyes flicked side to side as he thought, finally resting on me. "You got a cooler?"

"Yeah. Why?"

"How big is it?"

I moved to the kitchen and he followed, watching as I pulled my big plastic beer cooler from the pantry. I put it on the floor and looked at him.

He scowled at it, chewing a claw nervously. "I think I can manage that."

"Manage *what?*"

"I can roll myself pretty tight. I'll get in the cooler. You cover me with ice and beer or something. Tell them you're going to the beach. Everyone in town knows you're a drunken slack-ass, they won't question it. Then you can drive me to the body modification place."

I was actually getting annoyed with this guy, gills or not. My hangover pain was starting to take dominance over the shock of having an alien in my house. I just wanted him to leave so I could go to sleep. I'd process the quagmire of his existence later, over a strong cup of coffee. "Why the hell did you come up here, to my house, anyway? Why couldn't you just hide in the woods or something?"

"I was planning to hide it out in your pond. I can stay underwater for hours, but the bastards headed me off. Now will you help me get out of here or not?"

"Why should I? I don't know anything about you. Maybe you deserve to be caught. Maybe you're here to take over the planet and harvest our organs."

"That's brilliant, Jason," he said. "I've got a world domination gig, but I *choose* to work at the liquor store for a shit wage. That makes sense."

I shrugged. "Well, I don't know. You're my first alien. In all the movies, you guys want to kill us or eat us or enslave us."

He held his hand up, fanning out his claws. "Okay then, if that's what you're expecting, we'll do it your way. Tell you what. If you don't help me escape, I'll rip your throat out. Does that work for you?"

I took a step back, but then Tony's yellow eyes widened, and he doubled over, clutching his abdomen. "Oh, come ON!" he shouted.

His body fluxed again, this time into human form, green tint fading to peach, claws retracting. He clung to the kitchen counter, gasping as dreadlocks sprouted like snakes from his scalp. With another long hiss from the neck implant, the creature became just Tony the liquor store clerk again.

And, to my considerable relief, human-looking, crumpled-in-pain Tony was far less intimidating than the green-skinned, claw-flashing version.

When he buried his face in his arms and wept, I was dumbfounded.

"I'm sorry," he sobbed. "I'm just having a really bad day. I ... I really liked this town, ya know? It's quiet. The fishing's good. I have friends here."

I had a blubbering, unstable alien in my kitchen, and though I had no way of knowing if he was the good guy or the bad guy, I was starting to have sympathy for him.

But what if he was lying about the short cop being a hunter in disguise? And even if that was true, what if they had a damn good reason for chasing him, a motivation that ran deeper than "Hey, an alien, catch it!" It was certainly an option that Tony was evil, tears or no tears. This wasn't a movie, as he'd reminded me. In real life, it was entirely possible that villains wept.

But I never did like cops much. And even being a teacher, an authority figure myself, I still possessed my teenage, stick-it-to-the-man attitude on some level. Or maybe I just wanted to think of myself as a free spirit since my carefully crafted life fell apart like a house of cards with one blow. "Free spirit" sounded way better than "drunken slack-ass."

Or maybe I just liked the idea of packing my cooler full of beer. Despite the sunrise warming an amber glow on my window shades, a cold beer sounded real nice right now.

"I'll help you get out of here," I said.

He didn't look up. "I can't compact my body when in human form. There's no place to hide me in your car now."

"You'll probably shift again soon," I said. "I mean, judging by the way things have been happening, right? I'll start rounding up some beach stuff to put in my jeep. When it happens, we'll just load you up and go. I'll bullshit the cops on the way out."

Straightening up, Tony wiped his eyes and studied me. His tanned skin glistened with sweat, dark circles cupping his brown eyes. "Okay," he said. "But no funny stuff. And don't be thinking you'll get me packed up in that cooler and just hand me over to them, like I can't get out and cut your throat. Because I can, I don't need claws for that." He pulled a knife from behind his back. I recognized it as one from the set of steak knives resting on my kitchen counter.

"Wow," I said. "And here I thought we were making friends."

He grinned, holding the knife up a moment longer, and then pocketing it again. "Listen, recluse. I appreciate you helping me, but let's get one thing straight. I am not E.T. You are not Elliott. And there's no spaceship coming to take me back home. I'm an exile, one of thousands rejected and dumped here. And I *will* do whatever it takes to survive. Even if that means killing. Understand?"

I hesitated, and then nodded. "I understand."

He studied me, and some of the tension eased out of his shoulders. He held a hand out and I shook it. He laughed, and it took some of the strain out of his eyes. "You're all right, Twelve-Pack. We could use someone like you playing both sides."

"I have no idea what that means," I said.

He grinned. "Maybe someday I'll explain it to you."

I'd just let go of Tony's hand when the kitchen window shattered.

The dart missed Tony by inches and bounced off the cupboard. Tony ran out of the kitchen and down the hallway. I jumped back as the chubby guy in the police uniform climbed through the shattered window and landed on the floor. Glass crunched as he pushed me aside and stomped off down the hall after Tony, dart gun out in front of him.

I started after them when the front door opened and three more cops, including the tall redhead, plowed in. They surveyed the kitchen and then ran down the hall. I heard Tony scream and the sounds of a struggle, so I ran after them.

I found them in the bathroom, where they had Tony pinned down in the tub, two of them holding his legs as he shrieked and struggled. A dart stuck out of his abdomen, my navy T-shirt soaked with dark blood.

"What are you doing?" I shouted.

They ignored me as Tony tried lunging from their grip. "Give him one more," the fat guy shouted. "He's not going down!"

Tony kicked the dart gun out of the redhead's hands and it clattered across the floor, but the second cop got a shot off and stuck Tony straight in the neck.

He fell back into the tub, jerked twice, and then went still, eyes rolling back as his mouth went slack.

I stood in the hallway, helpless, as they carried Tony's limp body out of the house. The chubby cop eyed me suspiciously. "How long was he in here?"

"He ... he showed himself right after you left the first time."

He moved closer to me, those cold eyes probing, like trying to see a lie printed on my retinas. "Why didn't you alert us?"

I swallowed hard. "He had a knife."

"A knife."

"Yes, a knife, it's in his pocket. Check him if you don't believe me."

"Is that all? Just a knife? He do anything ... strange while you were with him?"

I knew what he was getting at, but strongly suspected that admitting knowledge of Tony's alternate persona would be a very bad thing for me. At best, inconvenient. At the worst, Twelve-Pack Jason would need to be silenced.

"Strange? Well, yeah, he was naked, for starters, and pretty agitated. He made me give him some clothes, and he kept checking the windows. Then you guys came in and shot him with darts."

He stared me down. "That's it? Nothing you want to add?"

I shrugged. "That's it. Isn't that enough?"

"I certainly hope so. You think of anything, anything at all, you call me." He handed me a business card; no name, just a phone number. "You call *only* me. No one else. Got it?"

With that, he left my cottage, slamming the door.

I stuffed the card in my pocket, and then moved in a daze down the hall into my kitchen, frowning at the shards of glass on the floor.

I packed the cooler full of beer and ice, threw a beach chair in the jeep, and headed down the long dirt road toward the village below. When I reached the lake, I pulled in and parked, taking my chair out of the back and setting myself up on the shore with the cooler. I opened a beer and watched the sunrise.

I stayed there until nine a.m., when I was pretty sure the town businesses would be opening up for the day. Then I collected my things, got back in the jeep, and headed toward Alpine Drive.

Michelangelo's Body Design was a little wooden building that smelled like incense and pine-scented floor polish. A bell rang when I stepped inside, my eyes flitting around at the racks of jewelry and glossy photos of tattoo designs pasted along the walls.

A young woman with short platinum hair came out from the back and stepped behind the glass counter. "You need help?" she asked, glancing over at me.

I approached the counter. "I'm looking for a man called Fat Pierre."

She raised eyebrows at me, and I realized how John Wayne it had sounded, so I amended it a little. "A friend told me to ask for him. Does he still work here?"

"Pierre!" she shouted, in a voice so loud it reactivated my hangover, even with three beers coursing through my blood.

A tall, impossibly thin man stepped out from behind a curtain in the back and joined the girl at the counter, eyes on me. He had long, sandy blond hair tied back in a ponytail, a hawkish nose, and a scruffy goatee. "What's up?" he asked.

"This guy was asking for you. Says a *friend* sent him."

"Do I know you?" Though his smile was gentle, the eyes were guarded.

"You're Fat Pierre?" I asked, scanning his thin, gangly body.

"Yeah, that's me. What can I do for you?"

"I need to speak with you. In private."

He frowned at me, then he and the young woman exchanged a glance. He looked back at me and sighed, putting his hands on his hips. "I have no secrets from Adele. Say what you want."

The girl's gaze was hostile now as she studied me, and I thought I saw a yellow gleam in her green eyes, but it could have been the joint I smoked on the beach. I hadn't rehearsed this part, so I opted for bluntness. "They got Tony," I said.

Fat Pierre flinched, only slightly.

I took the business card out of my pocket and placed it on the counter. "This guy, he's the one."

The blond woman glanced at the card, and then started to the back of the store, behind the curtain. Pierre called out to her. "Wait, Adele. Just hold on."

She paused and turned back, holding the curtain, but remained where she was. Her jaw was stiff and she looked ready for a fight, and despite her small frame, I got the feeling she could give a good one.

"What Tony are you talking about?" he asked.

"I think you know," I said. "The guy from the liquor store. He broke into my house. I saw him ... I saw him change. His implant is broken. He wanted me to bring him here, to you, but then they came in and shot him with darts. They took him."

He took his hands off his hips and rested his palms on the counter, taking a deep breath. After a moment, he met my eyes. "What's your name?"

"Jason Sarno. I live up on the mountain."

"Well, Jason Sarno, if you don't want Adele to go back and get the gun she's itching to fire at you, you better tell me what the hell you want. And fast."

I glanced at the young woman, who stood stiff and poised, like a cat about to strike, and then I looked up at skinny Fat Pierre. "I want to help."

"You want to help do *what?*"

"I want ... I want to work both sides," I said.

He scowled. "Where did you hear that term? Working both sides?"

"From Tony. He said he wanted me to."

He stared at me for a long time. He glanced back at Adele, who shrugged, and then he looked back at me. "You better come downstairs," he said. "Hang on."

He went to the front door and locked it, turning the sign around so it read "closed" from the outside, then led me around back, behind the curtain.

I followed Fat Pierre and Adele through a storage room stacked high with boxes and lined with tables displaying body-piercing tools, then through a locked steel door and down a set of stone steps leading to a second door.

Pierre punched in a code, and the door slid open.

I'd moved to the mountain to cast myself away, to deliver myself from the world I'd known, and either disappear completely or resurrect myself into something new.

I followed Fat Pierre and Adele into the vast white room, weaving through tables and cots, some bulky with sleeping aliens covered in sheets. Other aliens sat in chairs, sipping coffee as their yellow eyes followed me, and that's when I knew I'd done it.

The old world was gone, forever transformed. And I was new again.

41

COMFORT

BY CHARLES COLYOTT

The phone rang, and William's heart clenched. The muscles along his ribs seized, squeezing his lungs like a corset, and an ache rolled from his chest down to the fingertips of his hand. He snatched the handset from its cradle before the second ring and, licking a droplet of lukewarm sweat from his upper lip, answered with his standard business-like greeting. Someday, William knew, the phone would ring and bring the worst possible news. It could happen any day, any *minute*. Sometimes, when he lay awake at night, listening to the cavernous wheeze of his mother's labored breathing, he made himself sick thinking about it. One day the wheezing would just ... stop. And then the call would come. The fear had lived in his breast since the age of ten, when Nana had died and woken within him the realization that sooner or later everyone he knew was going to die. Even Mother.

He was so relieved to hear Julia's voice that, at first, he didn't even register what it was that she was saying. While his anxious mind finally did begin to piece together her message in tiny, bite-sized snippets of understanding—the frantic cadence, the sharp tones, the angry sibilant hiss of her S's—he was still shocked at her ultimatum. Yes, he would give the nurse a ring, but no, he would never consider a nursing home. That was out of the question. He would be more than happy to stop off and pick up some perfume on the way home, but if she—Julia—did a better job bathing Mother, then it wouldn't be an issue.

Fifteen minutes after she had hung up on him, William sat with his head in his hands and allowed the truth to wash over him. Julia was leaving him. Just like that, just when he needed her most. Though his eyes burned and were undoubtedly red and swollen, he refused to cry. Not at work. Once he got home, it would be a different story, but here—in his dingy cubicle—he had to remain professional. He composed himself—a quick, dignified sniff, a clearing of the throat, a running of fingers through the hair—and called Dr. Heaton's office. Though he had standing appointments for Mondays, Wednesdays, and Fridays at 5 p.m., he thought that adding in sessions for Tuesday and Thursday might be a good idea for the next two weeks or so, and Dr. Heaton agreed. She also reminded him to take his medication, which he did. The Xanax helped to take the edge off long enough for him to make it through his shift, but he found himself chewing at his fingernails as he drove to his appointment.

Dr. Heaton greeted him at the door and ushered him into her office. She was a good foot taller than he was, but he was used to that; he'd always been mocked for being short, but for whatever reason the fact that she was taller was soothing, somehow. She wasn't a beautiful woman—not like Julia, and not like Mother had been, in her youth—but he always felt a strange attraction to her anyway. Her size was attractive. Her listening was sexy. He sat in one of her overstuffed chairs and waited for her to set her timer before he started in with his problems. There was the bit with Julia, naturally, but the bulk of the session came back, as it usually did, to Mother.

"Julia never understood. Some of the things she said today ... I mean, that stuff doesn't just happen, y'know? I mean, this stuff must have been on her mind for a long time."

Dr. Heaton frowned. "What sorts of things did she say?"

"I dunno ... I mean, she acted like it was just ridiculous for me to want to take care of Mother. She said it was unhealthy. This, from the same person who had me drive to Kansas City twice a week when her grandmother had cancer, y'know? Unbelievable. I mean, really un-friggin'-believable, y'know?"

Dr. Heaton tapped her chin with a pencil, thought for a minute, and said, "Do you think it has something to do with the somewhat ... *unusual* situation that you have at home?"

William blinked and licked a droplet of sweat from his lip. "W-what's so unusual, huh? So Mother's overweight. Is that what you're talking about? There's a friggin' ... a friggin' ... *epidemic* of obesity in this country, okay?"

"Please, William, don't get agitated. I merely meant that maybe Julia wasn't ready to deal with your mother's condition and all the care that it entails. That's a lot to ask of someone, don't you think?"

William worried at his thumbnail. "I dunno. I mean, I never asked her to drive to Kansas City, I'll tell you that for nothing. And y'know, Julia talked Mother into the surgery, anyway."

"Her gastric bypass, you mean?"

"Yeah. I mean, that's when she went downhill. She was heavy before, but that damned surgery is what really screwed things up. I can't tell you how sick she was, that first month or so. Nobody should have to go through that. And no child should have to see their mother like that."

Dr. Heaton glanced up from her notebook in interest. "But you weren't a child, William."

"No, I know that. You think I don't know that? I didn't mean child like that ... I meant it like no *son* should have to see their mom like that, alright? Better?"

The doctor wrote something in her notes and said, "How much does your mother weigh, William?"

William peeled a half-moon-shaped sliver of nail away from his thumb and spit it onto the carpet. "I dunno. I can't exactly weigh her, can I?"

"Is she still mobile?"

"No. God, no. Not since the surgery."

Dr. Heaton took a deep breath, let it out, and said, "Don't you think that your mother might be better off somewhere where she could get the kind of care she needs?"

William fidgeted in his seat. "There is nobody that would take better care of her. Nobody."

After the session, William didn't feel any better. He spent the drive home not really listening to NPR, and pulled into his driveway at 6:30.

As he unlocked the door, he called out a greeting; sometimes, during the day when no one was home, Mother would sit with her nightgown untied in the front, to air out her scar. William didn't want to embarrass her, though he had seen (and cleaned) her scar too many times to count. He heard the faint sound of his mother replying. When he came around the corner to the living room, he hid the small bouquet of flowers he'd bought for her.

"How are you today, Mother?"

The woman shifted her bulk a little to look at her son. "Oh, Willy. Today was a bad one."

William presented the bouquet to his mother, who took the flowers and sniffed at them. "Willy, honey, you didn't have to do that. As I was saying, it was terrible. Laura married that Joe fella, even after he went and tried to run off with that Tina. Can you believe it?"

"No!" he said, feigning interest. He suffered through Mother's daytime TV habits, but it was the one thing about her he never understood. She was a college-educated woman. How could she possibly be interested in soap operas and gossip talk shows?

"Are you hungry? What would you like for dinner?" William said, moving a throw pillow so he could sit beside her.

Mother shifted again. William tried not to think about the way the full-sized sofa looked like a love seat with her in it, but the thought slipped through his defenses. Sometimes, however much he tried, the thoughts came—mean and cruel thoughts about Mother—and they made him sick. She looked up at him with her kind eyes, and he wanted to cry.

"Is Julia coming back for dinner?" she asked.

"No, Mother."

"She seemed cross earlier. I hope it wasn't something I did ..."

"No, Mother, of course not. When did she leave? Did she change you before she left?"

Mother hated having to talk about that, but it was necessary. Once she lost the ability to walk herself to the bathroom, she had to use bedpans. After her weight kept steadily increasing, William had to devise other solutions because she couldn't move enough to use the pans. She hated the adult diapers, but William didn't know what else to do.

"She left around 4:30, I guess."

46

"And did she change you?"

"Yes, yes. Sure. Is everything alright with you two?"

"Yeah, Julia just had to go back to work for a bit. She's got a deadline coming up and they want her to get it finished up."

His mother seemed satisfied with his lies, so she patted his knee and turned her attention back to the television. Wheel of Fortune was on, and that was her favorite game show. As he rose and made his way to the kitchen, she said, "Why don't you just make something quick and easy? What about spaghetti? We haven't had spaghetti in a while."

He went to the kitchen and put a pot of water on the stove to boil. He leaned against the counter and pressed his hands tight against his mouth, just barely catching himself as a sudden sobbing wracked his body. He slid down to the floor and let the tears come. He thought about Julia, about their wedding—Mother had been there, beautiful in a pastel green dress, back when she was still walking. He thought about buying their first home together, and how the kitchen—this kitchen— used to always smell like vanilla and fresh-baked cookies and ... and *her*. Julia was the vanilla and the cinnamon and the spice. Now the kitchen smelled like stale urine, like the rest of the house.

William took a deep breath and wiped the stinging tears from his eyes. He still wept as he carried out the trash, telling himself that getting rid of the offending bag would improve the smell. It made no difference. He cooked their noodles in silence, stopping to wipe his eyes every so often. The sauce would not be some doctored creation, as it was when Julia cooked. Instead, it came straight from the jar; neither of them would notice. He carried the plates into the living room, sat beside Mother, and ate from a TV tray. A mindless primetime detective show droned on, and with it the ragged sounds of Mother's breathing.

She drifted off sometime before ten o'clock. William had changed her, and helped her brush her teeth (it was nothing compared to the ways she had cared for him for all those years), and turned the channel to Jay Leno, her favorite late-night show. He did the dishes and balanced his checkbook. And when she was asleep, he kissed her damp forehead, took another Xanax, and went to the bedroom to call Julia.

She answered on the second ring.

"What do you want, Will?"

He stopped chewing the nail of his pinkie finger long enough to say, "I want you to come home, Jules ... I love you. Whatever this is, we can work it out, y'know?"

There was no response. He checked to see if the call had dropped. It hadn't. Finally, she sighed. "Will, I've really tried. I have. And I really did love you ... but I can't live like that anymore."

"What do you mean, 'did'? Huh? What's that supposed to mean? You don't love me anymore, is that what you're trying to say?"

He heard her inhale. Pause. A forceful exhale. He could imagine her somewhere, in the dark, a cigarette perched in the V of her fingers. She'd quit when Mother had to move in with them. She had to, with Mother's respiratory problems.

"No," she said. "And even if I did, I think I'd be tired of always coming in second place to your mother."

"She's sick, Jules."

A bitter chuckle. "Will, that woman will outlive us both."

William swallowed his anger and looked at the vacant half of his bed. "So that's it, then? You won't come home?"

"It's not my home anymore, Will. I'm sorry. I have to go. Good luck."

He considered calling her again. Begging. Promising to put mother in a home ... anything, just to have her back. Instead, he took two more Xanax. Women would come and go, but family—

He jolted awake, his phone ringing incessantly. As he answered, he glanced at his clock—11:49 a.m. It was Krieger on the phone—a pockmarked, officious little schmuck from HR. Was there something wrong with William's health, he wondered, that could make him almost four hours late for work? Didn't he know he was letting his "team" down by not being there? William apologized profusely. He showered, shaved, and was halfway out the door before realizing that he still had to change Mother.

By the time he got to work, everyone in his department was off to lunch. He needed to call the nurse to check in on Mother, but with everything that was going on, he thought it wiser to look busy for his coworkers whenever they came back. He could call the nurse later. With everyone gone to lunch, the building was quiet. William relished the silence, and found plenty of work to keep his mind and his hands busy. He rolled through processing his first seven claims—going into the files, correcting them, calling the providers to confirm—and was looking over his eighth when Potts called him to his office. Mr. Potts, William's immediate supervisor, had spoken to Mr. Krieger and the two of them were very concerned with William's performance. Didn't William realize the kind of bind he was leaving his "team" in? William apologized, but Potts just kept staring at him. By the time he was allowed to return to his cubicle, William needed another Xanax. He struggled through another four claims, but his heart wasn't in it. When he left for his appointment with Dr. Heaton, he could feel his coworkers staring at him. He could hear them whispering, but he couldn't make out what they were saying. His shirt was soaked through with sweat by the time he reached his car, and his hands shook when he tried to slide the key into the ignition.

In the safety of Dr. Heaton's office, he ranted about the way that work made him feel. He asked if he needed a stronger prescription, because the pills just weren't doing it for him anymore. He told the sympathetic doctor about his conversation with Julia, and about the end of his seven-year marriage. And, in a moment of acute weakness, he told Dr. Heaton that he was in love with her.

Dr. Heaton looked up from her notebook, cleared her throat, and said, "Tell me more about that." William did. He told her how safe he felt with her, and how wonderful it was to have someone to listen to him. He told her that she was beautiful (a lie, but one born out of kindness), and that he often thought about her, at night, when he was alone (a truth, though a recent one). And as he talked he slowly began to realize that Dr. Heaton's features had not changed. There was no grand blooming of emotion, no welling of grateful tears, no swooning from his romantic confessions.

"I think," she said at last, "that you're feeling very lonely, William, and very vulnerable. And I think that's very understandable. It's important to remember, though, that our relationship is a professional one. And it would make me more comfortable if you could keep that in mind in our future sessions."

The wind had taken a cold turn while he was inside, and William drew in upon himself for warmth as he shuffled back to his car. He got in and started the engine. The radio blared the voice of a cheerful D.J. raving over the customer service he'd received from a local flooring outlet. William turned the radio off. He punched the dashboard until his fists ached, and cursed himself for being an idiot. *In our future sessions*, she'd said. Like he could ever look her in the eyes again. Like he could ever come back without thinking about the things he'd said, and the way she'd batted him aside like a gnat. He cursed loudly, scaring an elderly homeless man on the sidewalk, and drove away from Dr. Heaton's office. He did not look back.

He opened his front door with the familiar greeting. He received no response. In a panic, William rushed around the corner to find Mother sleeping, slack-jawed, on the couch. He got a paper towel to wipe her chin, and gently shook her awake.

"Willy? Where were you? I was so worried ... I was all alone. Willy, I didn't know when anyone was going to be back." She started coughing, a thick, wet cough.

William ground his teeth. *I forgot to call the nurse ... Jesus Christ, I forgot the nurse!*

"Mother, I'm so sorry. There must've been a mistake. I'll get the nurse, okay? How are you feeling? That cough sounds terrible."

"Oh, Willy ... my sweet Willy ... I'm alright now that you're here."

After William changed Mother and got her cleaned up, he made a meatloaf. While it was in the oven, he called Lois Gilder, Mother's nurse, and set up times for her to stop by throughout the day whenever William was at work. He'd asked Mother about her nurse when she moved in, but she waved off his questions by saying, "Oh, you know how doctors are. They're just fussin' over my scar on account of how it hasn't healed up right. Everything's fine."

He picked at his dinner, still sick inside that he'd forgotten Mother, that he'd been so selfish. He helped Mother get ready for bed, scrubbed the stains out of the laundry, and went to his bedroom. He curled up into a fetal position under the sheets—appreciating the dark and the closeness—with his cell phone pressed to his ear. The Trident National automated switchboard picked up, and he dialed the appropriate mailbox. After Potts's generic recorded message, William said, "Hi, Mr. Potts. Um, I'm really sorry but something's come up with my mother's health, and ... she needs me. So I can't come in tomorrow. I might not be in on Friday, either. I'll let you know. I'm really sorry."

Nurse Gilder came at noon the next day. After checking Mother over and helping to give her a sponge bath, she took William aside.

They went into the kitchen, and William offered her an iced tea. When she refused, William continued to pour a glass for himself.

"I know what you're going to say, and you can forget it. I'm not sending her off to die in some nursing home somewhere," he said with a calm in his voice that he did not feel.

"Oh, the time for that is passed, Mr. Baker. I honestly don't know how we could get your mother out of this house, short of knocking down a wall."

William frowned. "Y'know, that kind of talk isn't necessary, alright? We both know that Mother's overweight. There's no reason to be cruel."

Nurse Gilder said, "I'm not being cruel, Mr. Baker. I'm being practical. Your mother must weigh between six and seven hundred pounds. She should have been in a home long before now, but, at your insistence, she's stayed here. Now it's too late."

William was stunned by the pronouncement, but he said, "Well, it's not like you can do anything that I can't do. I'm her son. Do you mean to tell me that you think you could care for my mother more than I do?"

The nurse looked down at her hands and said, "Mr. Baker, your mother's problem is not about obesity. Your mother has cancer."

"What the hell are you talking about?"

Nurse Gilder took a deep breath and said, "They found the tumor when they opened her up for her bypass. She didn't want to alarm you."

William was speechless. He was vaguely aware of his jaw quivering. Then the nurse was speaking again. "She declined treatment. It probably wouldn't have helped anyway ... her tumor is inoperable and, clearly, growing at an uncontrollable rate. She should have lost some weight after the bypass, but ... it's the cancer. I've seen it more times than I'd ever care to. Once the air hits it, it's like wildfire. She said she just wanted to be home, with you. I can give you antibiotics for her upper respiratory infection, but I have to warn you ... I wouldn't expect her to last more than a month."

The glass slid from William's fingers and shattered on the tile floor, but it was William who felt as if he were falling. Nurse Gilder walked him through some care instructions, things to do to keep his mother comfortable, but none of it registered with William. Everything was fuzzy and disconnected, and his pulse thrummed in his head, making him feel nauseated.

He left the nurse to find her own way out and sat beside Mother on the couch. She patted his hand. He leaned against her, gingerly, and closed his eyes.

Two weeks later, a package came in the mail. Inside, a letter read that Trident National regretted to cancel Mr. William Baker's employment contract. The box contained the contents of his desk—push pins, paper clips, a picture of him with Julia. He threw it all in the trash. The phone rang later in the day, and he listened to Dr. Heaton's message. She hoped that things were going well, and wondered why he hadn't been coming to appointments.

On the following Thursday, William tried to call her back. It was after hours, though, and he only got her machine. He did not leave a message.

Over the following four days, he called Julia twelve times. He was answered one week later when a thick manila envelope was hand-delivered to his door. He threw it in the trash.

Through it all, he had Mother. She woke and ate and slept and needed changed. It was reliable, a stable routine. It was comforting. On a Monday night in early November, William woke in a cold sweat and stumbled to the kitchen for a glass of water. He drank the water and refilled the glass when something struck him suddenly—the silence. There was nothing in it, nothing at all.

He walked slowly into the living room and stared at the unmoving shape on the sofa. He crept closer and knelt by her side, but he didn't have to put his head to her chest. He knew. There was no more rattle, no more wheeze. He took her hand; it was still warm and soft. He kissed it, gently, and wiped the tears from his cheeks one-handed. Somewhere in the distance he heard a siren, and he thought about calling 911. He thought about what would happen when they found her.

He would never call, he knew that. He couldn't stand the thought of them coming in, making whatever snide remarks they would make behind his back. He couldn't stand the thought of a world without her. William sat on the floor beside Mother and held her until the first rays of dawn crept through the curtains. When he woke, he was curled up in a ball at his mother's feet. His jaw ached from sucking his thumb.

He rose awkwardly, his body aching, and looked at the alien landscape of the room. Nothing here held any meaning anymore. It was no longer his house or his life. All of that was past, a failure, and better left forgotten.

In the bedroom, he found a basket with Julia's old craft materials inside. She had flirted with sewing for a month or so before admitting that she liked the idea of mending things more than she liked actually working at them. William carried the basket back with him to the living room. He took a pair of orange-handled scissors from the bottom of the basket and used them to cut away Mother's nightgown. He washed her carefully, tenderly, with a soft cloth, soap, and water, and brushed her thin hair until it shone in the dim light. He took the old bouquet he'd given her and spread the dried flower petals around her on the sofa, arranging them just so.

After a lengthy shower, William did what needed to be done. It wasn't pleasant, but he had become used to that, caring for Mother. In the scheme of things, it really wasn't as bad as changing her had been; the scissors were surprisingly sharp, and her scar parted eagerly. He took out the cancer that had killed his mother, tied it up in a garbage bag, and, with considerable effort, dragged it out to the trash cans by the sidewalk. On his way back to the house, he had the briefest moment of doubt, but that was the way the old William thought, and Willy knew that way was a path to failure.

Inside, he locked the doors and closed the blinds. He undressed, and patiently folded his clothes before dumping them into the trash. And then he returned to his Mother. Gently, carefully, lovingly. Inside the soft, warm darkness of her body, Willy did his best to stitch up Mother's scar. It was enough. William closed his eyes, relishing the safety and security he felt around him. In the primordial comfort of Mother's womb, William began to doze, content. And in the twilight realm of his somnolent consciousness, a shuddering twitch from cooling muscle tissue signaled a transformation. Willy smiled in the darkness as his world heaved around him with the cavernous wheeze of new life.

YOU WITH ME

BY CHRISTOPHER NADEAU

They met in a sports bar. Sarah hated sports, but was told you could meet men there—and you could, if you liked sports, too.

Arnold was different; he didn't like sports either. He said he'd only stopped in to take the edge off after a particularly brutal day at work at the hospital. He was a blood tech and there'd been a horrible seven-car pile-up on I-94 that day. The doctors were typically demanding and unconcerned with his issues.

She could relate. As an executive assistant, she often endured shitty meetings with shitty people. Arrogant assholes and bitches that looked down their noses at her while simultaneously expecting her to solve all their problems. This bar was the perfect place to fade into the background and forget how much she hated the weekdays.

Arnold was the first guy to approach her since she'd started coming to the bar three months previously. He was attractive, not a hottie or anything, but he had a certain earnest boyishness she found very appealing. Especially when comparing him to the cocky Alpha Males and their Beta sycophants with whom she was surrounded at work ten hours a day.

Their ensuing romance consisted of lots of trips to museums, where Arnold displayed an unusual fascination with representations of human anatomy, and rendezvous at ye olde sports bar. She was fine with that. After having undergone emotional abuse from her ex, an aloof situation based on mutual enjoyment had an immeasurable appeal.

It was during one of their sports bar nights that he shared his views on death with her.

"It doesn't have to be the end, you know," he said between sips of Coke. They always started with Cokes before switching to something harder. It was their thing.

"I didn't think you were religious." She gazed around the room at cuter, more dynamic guys who didn't obsess over the way breasts were represented in Renaissance artwork. Was she growing bored with this sweet but odd man?

Arnold laughed in his snorting, hiccupping way. "Religion is just man's way of wrapping the comfortable around the absurd." He took a final sip from his glass and set it down, eyes wide, mouth twitching. "Know what I mean?"

To her, he looked like a child who had to go to the bathroom but didn't know how to ask. She later realized that this was the moment she lost interest. She didn't want to hurt his feelings by saying something to the effect of, "You've grown tiresome. See ya." Instead, she nodded knowingly, prompting him to continue his tirade.

"There are ways to preserve life." He glanced at a muscular man in a tight polo shirt, his lip curling in a display of contemptuousness. "Not that everyone *deserves* to live forever."

"Why would anybody want to?" She looked at him, and then felt a shiver along her arms. Sometimes Arnold's intensity, particularly in his eyes, was downright disturbing. "Living forever while everyone around you dies? Wouldn't that suck?"

He smiled. "Not if you could take all the people that matter with you."

She frowned and lapsed into uncomfortable silence as he started complimenting her body parts, especially her feet and hands. She forced a smile and endured his comments until the night concluded, at which point she swore they would never see each other again.

A year later, she'd awake strapped to an operating table in a place that reeked of ammonia and mildew.

He floats in and out of her vision and consciousness, smiling down at her, sometimes frowning at something she can't see, clapping and singing to himself. She wants to get free, to kill him or at least cause him as much pain as he's caused her.

She wants to go home.

"Don't cry," he says in a tone that is meant to sound soothing. "I'm here with you."

Doesn't he understand that's why she's crying? How can someone be so crazy, so disconnected from reality? Why won't he just let her go and why can't she feel her hands?

"I missed you," he says. "Did you know that?"

She tries to say, "I don't *care*, you freak," but she can't speak. Does anything work on her anymore?

What she really wants to know is how long she's been here. For all she knows, it's only been a few hours—but it could have been days.

"At first, I didn't understand why you'd stopped seeing me." He speaks from somewhere near but out of her line of sight. "I wondered what I could have done wrong. Who wouldn't?"

She feels herself going in and out. Sleep is not an option, but how much longer can she resist its comforting pull. Besides, she knows he does awful things to her when she sleeps.

She's not sure she wants to know what they are.

"I thought about it for months!" A scraping sound, metal against metal, over and over. "Even when I dated other women, I couldn't stop wondering what I'd done wrong with you."

Footsteps, light but determined, growing ever nearer. "Then I remembered our final conversation."

His face appears, looking down at her, filling her entire universe with lunacy and unpredictability. "Do *you* remember what we talked about?"

She blinks, trying to force herself to remain awake. Of course she remembers. It was why she stopped dealing with his crazy ass.

"I bet you *dooooo*," he says in sing-song fashion.

He smiles down at her, a tiny bubble of spittle forming in the corner of his mouth. His brow is coated in sweat and his face is red.

But it's his eyes she can't avoid. Although they look right at her, they seem focused on something else, something only they can see.

Arnold starts rambling about life and death and preserving what matters. She tries to focus on his words, but she's so damn drowsy. She hears him babble about an epiphany that occurred soon after they stopped dating. Some bizarre realization based on his stupid theories about immortality. Somehow he thinks she was responsible for this experience, an opinion that seems to have prompted his abduction of her.

She hears that grinding metal against metal sound again. She tries to turn her head to see what he's doing, but everything goes black.

Someone speaks gibberish and moans incessantly. She tries to tell the voice to shut up so she can get some sleep. Her eyes refuse to open, proving just as uncooperative as her mouth. She hears classical music and thinks back to the art museum and Arnold's off-key humming as they shuffled from gallery to gallery. Sometimes he would stare at certain paintings and other times he'd start going on about the limbs and how real the skin and eyes looked.

She remembers how Arnold's interest in her seemed purely analytical. He would often compare what he admired in the paintings to what he saw on her body. She kind of liked that then; it made her feel unique without feeling obligated to put out. She knew it was a doomed relationship, but she was too busy enjoying the moment to care.

She isn't enjoying the moment now.

The mush-mouthed, moaning person won't shut up. It's so fucking annoying. She just wants to get a little more sleep and then maybe she'll be able to figure all this out.

"It's a bit hard to understand what you're saying right now, hon," Arnold says.

The mumbling and moaning stops and she realizes it was her.

"If you're wondering why you can't talk," Arnold says, "It's because your mouth is filled with gauze and your tongue is, umm, in a jar." More of that metal-on-metal scraping sound. "Please don't try to yell. You'll just start bleeding again, and we don't want that, do we?" *Scrape-scrape.* "And crying just upsets me."

58

She has no idea if Arnold is still talking. She leaves this place, drifts far away into a safer, more logical realm of existence where she still has a tongue and can move her arms and legs. She's back on the day she met Arnold in the sports bar, only this time she notices things she didn't consciously realize before.

He's been watching her all night. Not only that, he seems to take a sip from his glass each time she does, their motions synchronized to a degree that would be enviable among clockmakers. She knows there are better-looking women in the bar, but she's the only one he seems to notice. That should make her feel really good about herself. She feels removed, isolated from everyone else, perhaps even preserved for something best left undiscovered.

She also notices him writing in a small notepad. No, not writing. *Sketching.* His hand is moving about too freely to form letters. Is he drawing her?

Here comes the moment where he gets up and heads over to talk to her for the first time. She's nervous but looking forward to it just like last time, only this time she notices something odd about his walk. He doesn't so much saunter as shuffle, as if weighed down by something in the middle of his body. And his skin. Was it really that pale and splotchy?

When he sits down, she wishes she could say, "What are you?" but that's not how it happened in the past.

He still has the little sketch pad in his hand when he sits across from her, smiling his seemingly harmless smile. This time she takes special notice of the scribbled design on the page moments before he puts it in his jacket pocket. It looks like an octopus with a human head. The head looks like Arnold's.

Scrape-scrape.

She returns to the present, still unable to move or speak.

She hears Arnold, but his voice is too muted, too far away, to be understood. She blinks. His face looms over her, wearing an expression dripping with worry.

"Not much time left," he says. "I have to move around a lot for obvious reasons." *Scrape-scrape.* "This isn't going to be my best work, I'm afraid, but it will have to do."

He squints down at her, cocks his head to the side. "What? You still don't get it? That's disappointing."

She feels tears stinging her eyes and blinks them away. This isn't really happening. This is just some sleep-deprived dream based on her guilty feelings about dumping Arnold so unceremoniously.

"You're not the first, you know." *Scrape-scrape.* "That doesn't mean you're not special. I love you just as I love them."

You don't love me at all! her mind screams. *Love to you is just another way of expressing the need to control and destroy!*

Arnold leans over and kisses her forehead, lingering there for a moment with his cold, dry lips before raising his head. "The best parts of you will always stay with me."

His shirt falls open at the chest and she feels her grip on reality dropping away, as if falling from a high rooftop. Arnold frowns and follows her gaze to his chest.

"Darn, that was supposed to be a surprise." He quickly buttons his shirt and steps away

Scrape-scrape.

She tries to convince herself she didn't see ... what? It isn't physically possible. No medical procedure exists to do that. She must be slipping away.

She's okay with that. Anything to end this. Anything to never have to hear Arnold's tuneless humming and that awful metal-on-metal scraping sound. Why doesn't God intervene and take her life? Hasn't she suffered enough?

"I must admit, I'm a little jealous."

She shivers, all hope that Arnold was gone diminishing. He'll never leave. He apparently has a mission.

Scrape-scrape. "Do you finally remember what you said to me the last time we saw each other? You said being immortal while everybody else dies around you was pointless." *Scrape-scrape.* "You inspired me that day. I wanted to tell you all about it, but you had moved and there was no forwarding address. You never called."

She hears a hint of resentment in that last part and shivers yet again.

"I wanted to include you, sweetie, because you were the one that opened the floodgates."

60

Oh, God, she thinks. *OhGodOhGodOhGod, no!*

"I knew I'd find you again some day, so I kept busy."

Please God, please don't tell me this is happening because I stopped seeing him!

There was a voicemail message, a weird one that made absolutely no sense no matter how many times she replayed it before sending it to the Land of Deleted Oddities. It was from Arnold, two weeks after they'd parted company at the sports bar. She was taking a shower when the call came in—so, technically, she hadn't avoided his call, although she would have if she'd seen it on the screen of her cell phone.

It took her a few minutes to work up the nerve to listen to the message:

> *Hi, sweetie. Haven't heard from you or seen you lately. Hope everything's good with you. I miss our museum trips. I know you do, too. I've been working on something lately after what you said, and I can't wait to show you! I used to be afraid of life because it's temporary, but you opened my eyes to so many ... what I mean is, I think I might be falling in ... okay, I promised myself I wouldn't ... It's just that there are so many people out there that don't GET IT! Love can last forever. Oops, did I just say ... well, okay, cat's out of the bag! I want you with me ... always. See you soon.* (Muffled sound in the background, like screaming, and the call ends)

She and her friends had a good laugh at that one. What a creep, they said. Such melodrama, one friend added. An obvious virgin, another agreed. Arnold was the subject of one more conversation during someone's birthday party, and then summarily forgotten.

Arnold tells her there were others, both before and after her. Loves that didn't work out for different reasons, although he seems convinced the core reason is the lack of permanence. He tells her he's solved that little conundrum. Arnold says he always knew he was special.

"I'm only the first," he says. "There will be many more."

She manages a "*Wha-wha-wha*" sound, the closest thing she'll ever make to words again in her life. Somehow, Arnold understands.

"It was when you said you didn't know I was religious." He reaches out and strokes her hair. "Remember, sweetie?"

She nods, unsure what that has to do with anything.

Arnold shrugs, gazing down upon her with that smitten look that makes her want to projectile vomit. "I never was. Never even opened a Bible. But then I started wondering if you were using secret code. So, I opened it and I found what you were talking about. People used to be immortal until we sinned against God."

Her eyes widen. Now she understands. Oh, God, now she understands too well.

"Sure, it's silly to believe it happened just as written, but it didn't matter. You believed in me." He starts crying. "Somebody finally got me."

If not for the missing tongue, she could talk to him in placating, appealing tones. If she could move her arms, she could stroke his face and make him believe she was okay with all of this. But she can't do anything except mumble and stare up into his insane eyes, wide and filled with longing.

"We're going to be so happy," he says. "All of us."

He opens his shirt to reveal the full extent of what she's only glimpsed previously. She tries to scream and thrusts her head forward. She hears Arnold asking her what's wrong. She tries to look away, to escape into her mind like before, but it doesn't work this time.

She stops and stares at him, repulsed and fascinated. His chest is covered with extra skin and eyes and mouths sewn into his flesh. Women's eyes. Woman's mouths. Breasts. His "loves." Her eyes roam up and down his disfigurements, past holes oozing pus, past rejected transplants in various stages of decay and decomposition. The stench of putrescence and disease, of what he's become, now fills her nostrils and burns her eyes. She notices Arnold swaying back and forth, his face drenched in feverish sweat.

Slowly, her gaze moves upward until she looks into his gleaming eyes. He tells her not to worry.

"You're going to go right here!" He points with a trembling finger.

She glances down at the currently unoccupied spot directly above his heart and then back into Arnold's grinning face.

"I love you most of all."

THE SHAPING

BY SCOTT NICHOLSON

"One in a hundred."

"I've heard more like one in eighty."

"Possibly. Still, my chances are much tougher than yours. Haven't you heard the saying, 'Painter's plenty, one in twenty?'"

"Poppycock. The odds are better than that for gaining entry into the Areopagan Skyfleet."

"Arn, what do you care? You wouldn't be selected if the odds were one in two," a scornful voice interjected from a nearby bunk.

Ryn put his pillow over his head. He had heard the same arguments nearly every night for two weeks. It had started out as good-natured ribbing, one or two voices reverberating down the long halls at bedtime. But as the day of the Trials approached, everyone was getting on edge. Now nearly four dozen voices were buzzing at once, and probably many times that in the other sleepless rooms that littered the sprawling grounds of the Akademeia. The room smelled of stones and sweat and fear.

Fools all, thought Ryn. This was time for concentration, self-reflection, and meditation. This was a time to scrutinize the mirror, to reach deep and tap into hidden wellsprings. To probe the pleasures and pains and all else that was kept buried. But he supposed each artist had his own methods.

Arn, for instance, was a painter. Such a crude and callous field might call for blustering. Why should Arn care about the inner nature when he only reproduced the external? He worked on a flat surface, in two dimensions. No inner truths to reveal. Arn, and all other painters, were tricksters and illusionists.

And poor Soph in the next bunk, prattling on about metaphors and misplaced modifiers. As a novelist, Soph had no discoveries to make, no secrets to unveil. The words already existed. All he had to do was arrange them. True, writing was a precise craft, but Soph could make revisions at any time. But Ryn was a sculptor. He had no such luxury.

Soph's voice came to him through the clamor. "Ryn? Ryn?"

Ryn lifted the pillow from his head. He turned toward Soph, the sackcloth blanket rasping his skin. "What?"

"What are you thinking about?"

"What else?"

"Are you afraid?"

Ryn searched inside the dark alleys of his head and heart. He knew himself well. He believed he had to, if he was to be selected.

"No," he said. "I just want it to be over." He tried to make out Soph's face in the half-light, but saw only his fuzzy, crown-wreathed shadow in the next bunk.

The windows were small slits set high in the walls, allowing only slivers of meek moonlight to penetrate the dormitory. Rumor had it that the windows were narrow so that no one could escape, but conjecture was a favorite pastime at the Akademeia. Ryn didn't think anyone would leave after being allowed inside the gates. At least, no one would leave as a failure.

After a moment filled with distant shouts and forced laughter, Soph said, "I'm afraid, a little."

Ryn nodded in sympathy, the blanket scratching his cheek. He knew Soph could not see him, but the gesture was reflexive. He reprimanded himself for succumbing to an involuntary movement. One wrong move might prove costly tomorrow.

"Listen to that idiot Fen, bellowing about his coming glory," Soph said. "One would think that a tenor would rest his voice the night before the Trials. What if he should crack during a critical *glissando*?"

"They say confidence is important. And Fen lacks none of that."

66

"But I heard one in sixty for tenors. Surely room for self-doubt in anyone, even the megalomaniacal. Or perhaps I should say 'insolent.'" Soph had a habit of revising as he spoke.

The dormitory had grown quieter as the apprentices one by one ducked into the solitude of worry. The distant sounds of Athens washed through the windows, jetcars and electronic chatter and other civilized white noise. A few students still carried on, performance artists hiding their stage fright behind brash ripostes. Ryn whispered the question that was on everyone's mind. "What do you think of your chances?"

"I believe mine are among the worst," Soph said almost cheerfully, as if having the fear exposed made it powerless. "Certainly over one in a hundred. So many try for it, you know. That's why it's called popular fiction."

"Are you satisfied with your portfolio?"

"I believe it's the best I can do at this stage of my career. There's always room for improvement, but now is as good a time as any to see if I survive the cut. I'd hate to waste another dozen years. What about you?"

Portfolios varied for the different fields. The performing artists were judged periodically, on mysterious criteria known only to the Evaluators. But the grading in every field was esoteric and subjective. That was one of the more maddening aspects of the Trials, the one that brought dampness to the palms and moth wings to the belly.

"I am satisfied," Ryn said. "My minor pieces are solid and noncontroversial, a blending of gothic form and baroque detail. But I believe my magnum opus gives me an edge."

"Your rendering of Medi. It's one of the best in the gallery."

As it should be. Ryn knew every finely crafted inch of Medi's flesh, every pore and follicle, down to the tiny bas-relief scar on Medi's knee where he had fallen as a youth. Ryn had spent many nights exploring that skin, the narrow ridges and the taut dancer's muscles and rippling buttocks and angled cheeks. The slight slope of the Romanesque nose, the graceful eyebrows, the smooth plane of the brow, the gently bowing lips. He knew Medi inside and out.

And he had captured Medi perfectly, in gleaming calcite pirouette, a dancer whose soul aimed toward the heavens even as the body remained captive to gravity. A figure so light-footed that any material would prove too clumsy at reproduction. Yet Ryn had accomplished a miracle, giving wings to the earth-bound. He visualized the sculpture. His proud heart swelled against the molten bands of emotional pain.

Soph interpreted the silence as if he had read Ryn's mind. "You're thinking of him, aren't you?"

Ryn swallowed, trying to plunge the thickness from his throat. "It's hard for me. Especially now, when I need to focus my energy toward the Trials."

"Don't blame yourself. Dancers need attitude."

"You've managed to adopt a novelist's reserved facade without becoming cruel. Arn is expressive, but not brutish. And I like to think I've played the starving artist to perfection."

Ryn ran a hand over his ribs like one of the musicians might strum a zither. Perhaps he should have been a string musician. He heard they were in high demand. One in ten, perhaps.

"Performing artists are probably evaluated more heavily on their attitudes," Soph said. "Medi thinks being aloof and arrogant is best for him. Besides, they say emotional tension detracts from performance."

Ryn tried to change the subject. "Do you think it's as difficult at the Technical Schools?"

"Certainly not. Those who are culled from the Skyfleet have plenty of options. Engineers and mathematicians and geologists are needed on every chunk of rock in the galaxy, it would seem."

"What about Spirit Officers?"

"The odds are one in three. And even the failures there are allowed to make other career choices. They can be gardeners or philosophers."

"But we have no options," Ryn said, without bitterness.

"That's what brought us to the gates as children. That's why we capture the public imagination."

"They envy our talent."

"Or hate us for it."

Suddenly Medi's voice erupted from the far dark end of the hall. "Sweet dreams, you poets and songbirds and shapers. Tomorrow will give rest to your noise." Ryn wondered if the words were for him alone, or if Medi was only rehearsing.

A Mentor pounded on the window bars with a cane. "Quiet down in there," came the deep, commanding voice. The smattering of conversations broke off.

They waited until the receding footsteps were swallowed by the walls. "Talent," whispered Soph, mostly to himself.

"What?"

"Talent. It's not a natural blessing. It's beaten out from inside, just the way you beat the beauty out of a chunk of stone and I wring the meaty juice out of the alphabet."

Just as love is, thought Ryn. *Everything about us is shaped.*

The atmosphere was thick, as if a blanket of anxiety were spread across the room, a smothering and irritating fabric that would afford little sleep. Beneath it, bundled and shivering hot, the students lay with their dreams and frail hopes and attitudes.

The portfolios were submitted and graded. All that remained was to stand in front of the Critics and practice your art before those solemn gray faces. And before the eyes of the crowd, those plebes lucky in the lottery in live attendance, the others watching via videoscreen.

Even across space, in Areopagan colonies and ships, the Akademeia's performances would be viewed, discussed, gambled on, savored.

"Good night, Ryn." It sounded like a goodbye.

"Sweet dreams." Ryn rolled into his coarse covers and balled himself into a knot of exhausted lonely fear, searching for the mirror inside his head.

The dawn was an orange glory. A breeze swept down the stone streets of the Akademeia, carrying the dust of the crumbling Acropolis around the ankles of the milling students. The air smelled of figs and olives and salt. On the distant hills, the heaps of fallen walls and stunted columns jutted from the greenery like teeth.

His knowledge of the world beyond the walls was secondhand, coming from secrets that slipped through the narrow cracks in the masonry. Maybe he could discover which of the secrets were true. If selected, Ryn could walk among those fabled ruins, caress the faded Doric splendor, and sit on the ancient bleached bones of acroteria.

If selected, he could go among the citizenry of Athens, esteemed by the plebes and publicans and Skyfleet pilots on shore leave. He could cross the bustling city, with crowds parting in reverence, jetcars halting to allow him passage, admirers throwing flowers from balconies to provide a carpet for his bare feet.

If selected.

Excitement charged the air, flitting over his skin like soft bumblebees and hummingbirds. He touched his cheek, and his skin tingled from his own electricity. He turned from the faint hills with their broken cities and joined the others.

The forum was bloated with students, the performing artists in gay extravagant robes, the poets in rags, the musicians in tight masculine stockings with their instruments clasped to their chests like lovers. Everyone was chattering brightly, as if the sun had purified their fears.

Not a single Mentor was among them. No Evaluators showed their waxen skin. The audience had been admitted in the early hours so as to provide no distractions. Ryn saw Soph among the crowd and hailed him.

Soph came to him, smiling, full of summery confidence.

"So, you're a sentimentalist?" Ryn pointed at Soph's hands.

The novelist flushed slightly. "Ink and wood pulp. I'm aiming for the intimate touch. And look ..." Soph waved his quill toward the blue ocean of sky. "No eraser."

"Nice props."

"I've seen a horde of other novelists, with their videoscreen keyboards under their arms, looking smug and distant. But others have only a stylus and wet clay tablets. Who knows which is more highly regarded?"

"I suppose it depends on the weight given to tradition. I thought of clay myself, but I don't have time for modeling or waste molds. And metal casting is out of the question. What do they expect in fifteen minutes?"

"Don't forget that they are judging attitude more than product. Fifteen minutes is long enough. It will seem like years."

Two other sculptors shoved past Ryn, their tools clanging inside canvas bags. He watched them disappear into the crowd. "Do you have your performance planned?" he asked Soph.

"I've done a rough draft in my head. But I've left enough room so that I can show a little spontaneity. What about you?"

Ryn shook his heavy satchel and shrugged. "I have my tools, a small cube of marble, a block of mahogany, some bronze wire. And I've got a few ideas, but nothing set in stone."

Soph winced.

"Don't worry," Ryn said. "Verbal clichés are only dangerous in your field, not mine."

"So you're going to wing it? Or should I say, 'be spontaneous'?"

"I'm trusting divine inspiration."

"I always knew sculptors had rocks in their heads."

They smiled at each other with false brave faces, only minutes away from judgment. The Trials would soon be over. The Trials—

Shouts erupted from a neighboring group. An ebony-skinned painter was flapping his arms with a flourish, his palette and easel slung across his broad back. Other painters gathered around him, as if to soak up charisma by osmosis. Arn was among their number.

"I'm putting my faith in ochre," the dark painter blustered. "You can have your cadmium yellow and lemon, even your mustard. For me, it's ochre or die."

Some of the heads bobbed in agreement. The speaker made a sword stroke with his arm. "And broad swathes. Nothing timid."

A murmur ran through the circle of painters. Ryn could almost smell the competition. According to rumor, work wasn't directly compared. Some years, three or even four were said to be selected in each discipline. Other years, none. But ambition was a vital part of attitude.

Ryn turned back to Soph. "They fear the Critics."

"Don't you?"

"I think I can please them."

"At least your Critics have human faces. I've seen them in the streets, heads stooped and necks hunched into long black robes, their wrinkled skin and tight lips as frozen and severe as if you had carved them in your marble. But I'm at the mercy of Editors, who are hidden behind panels and are never seen by mortal eyes. I will not have the advantage of seeing their reactions, a raising of an eyebrow or a twitch of the lip that might signal approval."

"Three invisible thumbs up or down. But maybe that's better. A blind rejection rather than visible scorn. Far more painless, I would think."

"Painless to the flesh, but not the spirit."

"Pain is essential to an artist. The pain of creation, of giving birth, the torture of the imagination, the agony of searching for some kind of useless inner truth." Ryn thought again of Medi. *Pain. Maybe that was Medi's gift to me. His way of shaping me.*

"Maybe you should have been a philosopher," Soph said.

"And be sweeping the streets? I'd rather take my chances here."

A bass foghorn blared, the long low note echoing off the hills and towering walls. Time for assembly.

Ryn and Soph bid each other luck and farewell, and then Ryn pushed through the throng to the Hall of Sculpting. He was at first pleased to see only twenty or so other sculptors. But that might not mean anything, if odds were one in fifty.

The limestone of the steps was cool under his feet, the rock worn smooth by all those who had faced the Critics throughout the centuries. Ryn studied the other sculptors standing alertly, with their strong, scarred fingers and dense forearms, trying to guess what materials were hidden in their bulky satchels. A hand fell on his shoulder. He turned awkwardly, unbalanced by the weight of his satchel.

"All grace forgotten, Ryn?" Medi said, even at this late moment steel-jawed and sneering. His face was inches away. He was wearing a taut body stocking, blazing red. His muscles ridged out along exquisite flesh.

Ryn tried to look away. "Shouldn't you be at the Hall of Dancing?"

Medi performed a quick, airy shuffle. "Plenty of time for one with clever toes."

"You were always confident, Medi."

"I will be selected even if the odds are one in a thousand. And you should have the same attitude. Don't let them touch you."

"So you win by hurting? Is pain a talent, an art?"

Medi's eyes narrowed, his irises as cold as obsidian. Ryn wondered how he had ever found softness in Medi, the quality that had brought Ryn's best sculpture to life. But that Medi would float forever in the gallery, the false Medi that was held aloft by the invisible wires of dreams, a fleeting impression captured in alabaster and feathered by loving hands. The sculpted Medi would live eternal, withstanding the withering countenance of critics. He wondered if the real Medi would be so fortunate.

"Embrace the pain. It only makes you stronger," Medi finally said. "Besides, dancers must travel light."

"No matter the expense?"

"Sentimentality is a risk. The odds for dancers are said to be one in eighty."

"You were the one of one to me. Isn't that enough?"

"When you stand before the Critics, you stand alone." Medi's features relaxed. Ryn wondered if the great Medi had suffered a moment of doubt.

Suddenly Medi grabbed him and kissed him hard on the mouth, then slipped athletically into the crowd. The massive oaken door swung open and the students moved forward. Blood was just returning to Ryn's lips as he stepped under the high, hushed arches into the Hall of Sculpting.

The foyer was cool and dark. Waiting was the worst part. No one spoke. None wanted to be first or last.

A smaller door, ornamented with ceremonial figureheads and alloy symbols, opened on heavy hinges. An Evaluator summoned the first performer, then, minutes later, the next. Finally, after a stretch of time that seemed longer than his entire twelve years at the Akademeia, Ryn's name was called.

He stepped through the door, and the Evaluator led him to a table in the center of an open room. The Evaluator then shuffled offstage, the soft rustle of his robes the only sound. Not a crumb remained from the previous performance.

The room was much like the architecture Ryn had built in his mind from the bricks of rumor and the mortar of imagination. He stood beneath a bank of arc lamps, under which no error would go undetected. He saw the outline of the Critics, three forms seated on a dais just at the edge of shadow. He risked a glance behind him and saw the black mirror. A thousand unseen eyes were fixed on his back. He blinked into the lights, trying to spot the camera that was beaming his performance across the galaxy.

He looked for the eye of the vaporizer that would turn his flesh to dust if he were rejected.

Then he faced the Critics. He calmly placed his satchel on the table and opened it. Ryn took out his mahogany and marble, and then quietly spread out his tools.

He waited for divine inspiration. Medi again. Medi, always. Inspiration came.

"You have seen my work," Ryn said, his voice swallowed instantly by the dead air of the room. "By that alone I should be judged."

He didn't know if speaking was acceptable. But it was his performance, after all.

"But the work itself has never been enough," he continued. "We aren't allowed to merely produce icons that reflect all that is gallant and fragile and terrible about the human race. We also must wear it like skin, harbor it in our flesh, pump it in the vintages of our veins. The art must become our lives."

He picked up his garnet paper, which he used for polishing stone, and rubbed the back of his hand until the skin peeled. He looked up at the Critics, their faces slowly taking shape as his eyes adjusted to the dramatic lighting.

He held his riffler rasp to the light, turning it so that all might see its wicked pits.

"You ask us to seek the truth for you, because you haven't the courage to do it yourselves."

He drew the rasp across his forearm like a cellist drawing a bow, leaving a raw streak of pink in his flesh. He held the wooden handle of his skew chisel in his other fist, testing the edge for keenness. A small seam of crimson flared across his thumb. Quickly, he crisscrossed the blade against his shoulders, and his gown fell around his feet. Stipples of blood rose around his collarbone.

Out of the corner of his burning eye, Ryn saw an Evaluator step from the dark wings. For a moment, he was afraid that he had committed some blasphemy, that he wouldn't even be allowed the honor of a public immolation. He paused, a tool dripping in each hand.

The Evaluator cocked his head, as if heeding an invisible voice, then stepped back and once again merged with the shadows.

Ryn picked up his steep-angled fluter and ran it along his thigh, digging out a strip of meat that curled and fell to the granite floor. He felt no pain. He was drugged by his creative juices, caught in revelation and discovery, lost in the shaping.

He brought the fluter to his cheek and pressed open what he hoped was a graceful red curve. With his other hand, he dropped the rasp and gripped the metal shank of his flat chisel and ran it across his stomach. The blade penetrated, and a gray intestine ballooned from the wound.

He could make out the Critics' faces now, harsh and immobile and impassive. Not a nostril flared, not an eye flinched. Those were the stolid faces of legend, as stony as godly busts.

"You need someone to reveal the inner beauty, because the outer is so commonplace," Ryn gasped. "You need someone to show you what it means to be human. Because you don't dare look inside yourselves."

Ryn erupted in a frenzy, the blades and chisels and awls flashing in the light as he used each tool to its fullest potential and then replaced it with the next. As he whipped at his skin, as he explored his meat, as he lovingly sculpted himself, he thought of Medi, twirling, giving the performance of his life, and Soph, with only words to save him.

Ryn flensed his biceps and flayed his forehead and claimed his own scalp and ran his gouge into the gristle of his joints. Still not a sign from the Critics, no nod or blink. Surely his fifteen minutes were nearly over. But he had not been vaporized.

Ryn continued with his carving, fascinated by how the meat yielded as easily as wood. And he didn't have to worry about cutting against the grain or fighting burls and knots, or discovering a flawed grain as one might encounter in granite. He lifted his pickax and worked it against his abdomen to free his burgeoning bowels. He dropped the pickax to the floor and it bounced away with a dull metallic clatter.

There was no more Medi, no thoughts. Only pain, sacrifice, and art. Only the shaping. He picked up the bull point and placed the blunt chisel against his chest. He raised his hickory mallet with effort, the handle slippery with blood. He was about to summon his strength for a final revealing blow when he saw movement on the dimming edge of his awareness.

The Critics were standing.

Would they take him as a boy, or love him as a man?

Ryn swayed, glaring into those gray wizened faces and dark marble eyes, waiting for them to raise their arms and tilt their thumbs toward the stone floor, waiting for them to signal the merciful vaporizer.

But they didn't. They brought their wrinkled hands together, woodenly at first, then faster. They were applauding.

And smiles creased their faces, unheard-of smiles!

The pain ripped through Ryn's velvet curtain of rhapsody as he sagged against the table and looked gratefully at the Critics. Thin hot fluid streaked down his face and he thought it was only more blood. But the fluid made his ruined cheeks sting as it rolled across the ditches in his face.

Tears of joy.

He was selected.

The sculpted Ryn would live eternal.

SOMETHING BORROWED

BY J. GREGORY SMITH

Malibu, California: Unlimited Potential Retreat Clinic

"Needles? Goodness no, they don't bother me." Maud Spitfire drew her full lips into a perfect smile. Her Wedgwood-white teeth should have had their own wattage rating. "You leave that right there, but I don't think you need to worry about bees here, Mr. Getty."

Getty put the auto-injector on the glass table top. "It's a serious allergy. But this can get uncomfortable in my pocket."

"I get that reaction from men all the time. And they're not all carrying hypos, if you get my drift."

How could he miss it? Might even be true, despite her age—old enough to be his mother. "Thank you for agreeing to see me on such short notice."

Almost as short as her skirt. She'd never see fifty again, but looked frozen in time at thirty-two—and ten times better looking than most ladies on the best day of their lives. Her platinum hair could have been the real thing and, if he hadn't known to look, he couldn't tell which eye had been replaced.

"Anything for Invincible Studios. I've been dying to work with them ever since Herm took over." She touched his thigh under the table.

Considering she hadn't worked for years, he wasn't surprised. Fan conventions may have helped float the fantasy, but she was hungry for a new shot. He felt her fingers tremble on his leg. "Mr. Blankwater regrets he couldn't be here himself, but he's personally supervising the wrap on a project in Israel."

She pulled back her hand and gave a dismissive wave. "It's that personal attention he gives any project that makes me want to work with him."

That and your career in the toilet. At least she didn't sound like she'd want to get him on the phone. Getty had some dummy lines set up, but better not to have to use them. She was sharper than she let on. "I think you'll love the part he has in mind for you."

She flashed another gleaming smile. "This is so sudden. He seems like he forgot about my body of work."

"Who doesn't know the Quasar series? Your 'Zora' is a household name. The final episode was the best."

"I know." She'd winced at the word "final," but puffed up at the compliments.

"Mr. Blankwater said to tell you he appreciates starting off here with a face to face." Getty feigned an awkward pause. "Well, with me as his surrogate. He needs to know first if you are interested."

"Tell me more." She patted his arm, perhaps pretending it was meant for this Blankwater character. Getty needed to steer this back to her before he ran out of background research.

Getty looked around to confirm they were alone. He needn't have worried. A decade of five-star seclusion, where stars recovered from various surgeries, made hiding here second nature, Getty figured. They sat on a balcony overlooking the Pacific.

"Off the record, Mr. Blankwater has acquired the rights to produce all-new features based on the Quasar franchise."

She sucked in her breath like he told her she just won the lottery. *Wait, she's already rich.* This *was* her lottery.

He nodded and put a finger to his lips. "Of course, you are one of the first people he mentioned, but he's understandably concerned the news will leak."

"Of course. We can work out the business end. That's what I have people for."

Not lately.

"Certainly. Now you understand why we needed to see you in person. When we heard you were here, we were worried."

"Oh that. As you can see, I'm fit and firm. I was only out here for the spa experience and hair. They're quite full-service, and so discreet."

If she knew the size of the hole in their security a few grand could buy, it'd wrinkle her botoxed forehead.

"Very good. Now in this sequel, Zora is going to be headlined. She's become Queen of the Quasar Confederation," Getty saw her sit up ramrod-straight. Getting into character, no doubt.

"Yes?"

"And, despite most of her subjects' adoration, one planet has become suffused with epidemic callousness that threatens to subvert the entire Quasar System."

"How so?"

That faraway look in her eye told Getty he was speaking directly to Queen Zora herself.

Time for a royal wake-up. He tried to remember the script they gave him. "The population of Surgican, that's the planet, has divided into Master and Slave. Really, the Haves and the Won't Have for Long."

Confusion pulled "Zora" a little closer to Earth. "I don't follow."

"See, the slaves are used as spare parts to maintain the rulers. They mean to live forever by harvesting whatever organs they need, right from the Haves. Sick, huh?"

Outrage boiled out of her face, exaggerating its effect on parts not paralyzed with Botox. Her nose twitched like a rabbit and her hands shook like they were palsied.

"Who the hell are you?"

"Think of me as kind of a repo man."

"What?"

"How about, I'm a friend of your sister?" He watched her eyes for a reaction. Her head snapped back.

"Rena is dead!"

She was a better actress than he'd thought. They said she would lie, but he was impressed by her intensity. "Then she's a high-paying ghost."

"She died in an accident soon after she donated her kidney to me. Mother said—" She stood up and anger tinged her cheeks scarlet. "Why I am telling you this? Get out of here right now, you sick—"

"Donated?" He'd expected her to put up a fight. She was getting too loud for his comfort. "And the eye?"

She shook her head. "That was from the eye bank. Wait. How do you know these things?"

Her body language told Getty she was close to panic. Her gaze darted for a way past him. Not a chance. She inhaled for a theater-worthy scream.

Getty uncapped the auto-injector and plunged it into her thigh. He covered her mouth with his other hand and ignored the pain when she bit down on the meat of his palm.

Her body began to relax, but her eyes remained open.

Getty eased her into her chair. She sat like a warm stature. He lifted one arm and it stayed when he released it. "You're kind of like a posable Barbie."

He retrieved a wheelchair from the bedroom and half expected it to have her name on the back.

He punched a number into his phone. "Oh, sorry, I must have misdialed. These gadgets get smaller all the time, don't they?" He hung up and gave the guard time to clear his way. Shouldn't take long to get those cameras to blink.

Getty loaded her onto the wheelchair and arranged her limbs. He pulled her lips into a smile, but it looked like a fleshy clown grin. He pushed her cheeks back more or less to where they were. "You get to keep the eye. *I* probably wouldn't be so generous."

Getty hoped the hour traffic jam on the Pacific Coast Highway wouldn't hurt his plans. All he'd been told was that the drug would give him "plenty of time," which grated on his craving for meticulous detail on a job.

The doctor's condescension had raised his blood pressure enough for him to skip it.

Not the money?

That, too.

He brought duct tape in case Maud came around, but he'd have to stuff her in the trunk and avoid HOV lanes if that happened.

As it was, she reclined in the front seat next to him in a posture of slumber. He wanted to see her in case she moved. It wouldn't do to get attacked while he was watching Elephant seals mating on the beach or whatever.

He pulled into San Diego just before midnight. Maud hadn't moved, but the only reason her eyes were closed was because he pulled the lids down himself. That was one detail the doctors (if that's what they really were) shared with him. Otherwise he'd need to put drops in her eyes every fifteen minutes. Getty made the assumption Maud wasn't unconscious and could hear, so he stuck to whistling.

The metal gate rolled up when he approached, and he drove in. At least he knew he had the right place.

He didn't like it when the door came back down, cutting off his escape. Then again, he didn't need prying eyes watching him offload his cargo, either.

One of life's little risks, that's all. He had fifteen rounds in his nine and a vest on to discourage last-minute renegotiations.

Three figures stepped into view. They were dressed like doctors, in scrubs and everything. He recognized the short one. He called himself Garcia.

"You're late." Garcia tapped his wrist like Getty didn't speak English.

"Sunset traffic on the PCH. She hasn't moved a muscle other than to breathe. What was that stuff?"

"It'll wear off soon." Garcia motioned to the other two. One rolled up a wheelchair and the other opened the car door. "She put up a fight?"

"Not really." His palm had turned purple where she bit him.

Garcia looked worried. "Did you hit her in the body? Near the liver or the kidneys?"

"Not even in the haggis. You're paying for a pro. She's fine as long that stuff isn't harmful."

"Then your bonus is safe." Garcia looked relieved, but Getty felt a flush creep up his neck. Clients didn't usually get under his skin like this. He held out his hand. "Let's see it."

If they were going to pull anything, this was the time. He listened for any threatening sounds.

Garcia walked to the back of a car and opened the trunk.

Getty hated how exposed he was in the middle of this garage. No choice right now. He rested his right hand on his hip and hooked his thumb under his shirt so he'd be able to make a clean draw.

Garcia stepped back around with a briefcase. Getty watched the other hand, empty. His gaze flicked to the other two men, who watched him but remained with Maud, whose only response was marked by a single tear's march down her flawless cheek.

Garcia handed the case over and Getty crouched on the floor to open it up. No explosions. Good. He saw the right number of stacked hundreds. Better.

He looked up at the men in green scrubs like a lion guarding a kill. They stood by with placid expressions.

Getty lifted the cash and saw the glint of the twenty gold bars. He took one out and relished the heft. He took a piece of ceramic from his pocket and rubbed it on the bar.

Real.

"So we're done, yes? Good job and good luck." Garcia strode toward the red button to let Getty out.

This was the part where he got into the car and put a couple thousand miles between him and them.

But his skin was crawling. The day he stopped listening to his instincts was the day he retired (or got killed.)

"Hang on." All three turned to him.

He lowered his voice so Maud wouldn't be able to hear him even if she was conscious. "What are you going to do with her?"

Garcia's face reddened like he'd been slapped. "We've discussed this already."

"You told me her sister is alive. That Maud and her mother went batshit crazy and allowed doctors that Mom brought from Mexico to take parts out of Rena to give to Maud, just so she could prosper and become a big star."

"Your memory is excellent. Now—"

"Not yet. I'm no doctor, but you said Rena was sick. Needed a kidney and wants her old one back?"

"That's right." Garcia folded his arms across his chest.

"Fair enough. I know Maud can live with dialysis, but you said something else."

"Did I?"

Getty pointed to his own head. "Memory? You mentioned the liver. Rena needs one of those too?"

"Not your concern." The condescension was back.

Walk away.

"Beg to differ. I need to know which shoulder to look over when this is done, since I'm an accessory. You can't live without a liver, I know that much."

Garcia closed his eyes. Getty stared at the man's face and wondered if the cheesy mustache was glued on. Garcia opened his eyes and smiled. "One moment." He scurried over to the other two.

Getty half expected them to break their huddle with guns blazing. But they didn't look like shooters, and he'd make them sorry if they tried.

Garcia approached Getty with his hands out.

"Since these are unusual circumstances, we'll share more than we thought initially prudent."

"Go ahead."

"We work for a group of physicians who operate, shall we say, outside of the conventional framework."

"No shit."

"Unlike our less-ethical colleagues, such as the ones who abused our client, we seek to rectify the mistakes while exploring opportunities to expand mankind's knowledge."

Head this off before it becomes a lecture.

"For a price. But I'll skip the slippery slope arguments."

"And we shall dispense with those about glass houses."

"Touché."

Garcia touched his mustache. "Miss Rena has suffered her entire life. We've only recently been able to recover her from the virtual prison her late mother imposed. She's an identical twin in name only, due in part to the accident that paralyzed her, not to mention the appalling lack of nutrition during her formative years."

"Look, you don't need to cue the string music. Things are tough all over. I need to know if I'm part of a murder rap. That's outside the scope of work."

83

"Ms. Maud will be quite fine."

"Fine with no liver?"

"We aren't going to take her liver."

"Tell me, are you certain Maud knew what her mother was doing? And that Rena is alive? She sounded convincing." Getty had to rely on Garcia's word that there was a Rena who was footing his bill. As long as the money was good.

"Mr. Getty, what do you care? I should think a conscience would qualify as a hazard in your line of work."

Getty had to give him that one. Maybe it *was* time to retire.

Getty picked up the case and entered the car. The two men with Maud rolled her out of sight. "*Now* we're done." He slammed the car door and leaned out the window. "But I'm going to be watching. If Maud disappears, you're going to pay the price for putting heat on me. Are we clear?"

"If you want proof, we'll see you get all you need."

Whatever that meant.

Nine Months Later—Outside the Peacock Auditorium, Los Angeles

Getty checked his watch and skimmed the *Daily Variety* review.

Comeback of the Year?

by Myron Byron

Maud Spitfire, known to most as "Zora" in the timeless *Quasar* films, has managed to resurrect her fading career following a freak accident that robbed her of the use of her legs.

Undaunted, she emerged determined to reinvent herself, and has completed the transformation from sci-fi sexpot to the most refreshing comedy act in a generation. In *We're not Zora*, Spitfire's one-woman act comes across as something dreamt by Walt Disney's twisted clone. Not since the Smothers Brothers has an act worked in the "Mom liked you best" theme so effectively.

While we must admit a degree of disappointment at the veil of secrecy with which Spitfire now enshrouds her life, we concede she's earned the right to be as diva as she wants with this fearless tour de force.

Getty tossed the paper aside and crossed the street. The line had started to move and he didn't want to miss the beginning. The "anonymous" card and envelope with ticket left on his windshield had warned him not to be late.

Getty sat in the front row and stared at the pitch-black stage. The music built around the audience; it made him think of a funeral dirge sped up to sound more like calliope music.

You're too close. This could be a trap. He'd already been too careless, but he might as well see this through. Besides, his eyes weren't what they used to be and he wanted to be sure.

He didn't think they'd come at him directly, so he wasn't carrying any weapons or other suspicious items. If they thought of setting him up with the cops, they were in for a surprise. And it wouldn't be the last. He'd find every one of them later.

A pencil-thin spotlight hit the stage and slowly widened to reveal a table covered with a black cloth. Behind the table sat a woman, staring out into the crowd.

He recognized Maud at once. So, she really was alive. Maybe Garcia and friends had been sufficiently frightened of him that they felt compelled to show him they hadn't hurt her. Not more than what they'd promised, anyway.

Maud's face showed some of the years her Botox treatments had staved off, but she was still beautiful—though the sadness that had cracked through her drugged façade might never have left, it was so etched in her features. The spotlight continued to widen and illuminate the rest of the stage.

The white light crept down her ample chest and he saw the blond hair first. Soon he saw the face and torso of what looked like some sort of animatronic ventriloquist's dummy seated at her hip. The dummy wore a T-shirt that read: "Molly Made."

"Molly" looked just like a scaled-down version of Maud. And she was so realistic. Too realistic. When she looked around, he noticed just one blue eye moved, like the other one was fake. Only that would mean—

The house lights came up. Getty knew how a kitchen roach must feel.

"Molly" turned her head to scan the audience. Maud remained still.

Getty tried to look past the painted lines on Molly's face. The eye that moved glittered, and the gaze rested right on him.

Then she winked.

It couldn't be. "Rena?" He mouthed the name.

She stuck her tongue out at him. The audience cheered and he felt gorge rise in his throat.

Rena spoke in a deep, rasping voice and pointed a small arm in his direction. "What a surprise. Sweaty Getty who kidnaps betties."

Getty's heart hammered in his chest. He staggered to his feet and ignored gripes from seated patrons.

Maud snapped into motion. Her eyes bulged, as did her throat when she screamed. "Kidnapper! Somebody get him! Look what he made them do to me!"

Getty stared at Maud, who started to roll the oversized wheelchair backward.

"No!" and Rena leaned forward and grabbed the edge of the table. The momentum of the chair won the tug of war and the table toppled with a loud slam.

Getty felt rooted to the floor. The audience erupted in puzzled murmurs, apparently torn about whether this was part of the act or not.

Getty knew, and now the illusion of an elaborate dummy evaporated when Maud yanked up her shirt.

Scars like railroad tracks ran wide across Maud's torso, revealing ropy pink lines of healed flesh where Rena's torso had been fused with her sister.

Random pictures of anatomy books flashed through Getty's mind and he pictured the liver and kidney in Maud now working for two.

We aren't going to take her liver ...

Rena screeched and pulled down the shirt. "You'll ruin everything, you selfish ..."

Some people in the audience screamed, others laughed, and chaos reigned.

Maud tried to pull it up again and Rena let go to punch her sister in the face. Rena's small fist just reached Maud's chin and her sister's head snapped back, reminding Getty of Maud's reaction at the clinic.

She really hadn't known. She'd thought Rena was dead.

Maud wrapped her hands around her smaller sister's throat and began to throttle her.

Rena clawed Maud's arms and legs and made a horrible mewling sound.

"Stop them!" Getty heard a voice from off stage. The women's flailing arms caused the chair to rotate like it was on a turntable.

"Get out of my body." Maud tugged and pushed Rena.

Getty heard a wet tearing sound.

"You stole my life."

Getty saw stage workers flood onto the stage and try to restrain Maud only.

They don't understand. They think Maud has gone berserk on a dummy. He didn't think it was funny, but Getty started a high manic laugh that told him to get out of there before he lost his mind.

The last thing he saw before running over an usher on his way out was blood coming from under Maud's shirt.

Four Weeks Later

Getty sat in the warm spring air in Balboa Park near the Fleet Science Center. Parents with kids in tow wandered along the paths and into the museum. Young people jogged by. Even the air tasted clean and sweet today.

He'd miss the park maybe most of all. He doubted this town would miss him, but that was all right. That was the point. Not to be missed.

He wondered of anyone would mourn the Spitfire sisters. From what he'd heard, they seemed to lose the will to live and their bodies barely put up a fight against the infection.

At least they'd had the decency to bury them in separate plots.

He gazed at his newspaper.

San Diego Union

Still No Clues in Deadly Doctor Triangle

Police maintain they still have no suspects in the bizarre triple homicide of three foreign-born surgeons found last week in a San Diego apartment. The victims were apparently poisoned; however, toxicology reports have not confirmed this.

The *Union* has uncovered that all three victims had lost their licenses to practice in their respective countries, but so far no criminal motive has been determined concerning their presence in the United States. There appears to be no connection between each of them.

Police will not confirm the rumor that several gold bars were found in plain sight at the scene, but, if true, that would cloud robbery as a potential motive.

"Not for money." Getty watched a pigeon peck at a single piece of popcorn lodged in a crack in the sidewalk. "Nor love either, that's for sure." He leaned toward the near-tame bird and whispered, "When did things get so complicated?"

EQUILIBRIUM

BY JOHN SHIRLEY

He doesn't know me, but I know him. He has never seen me, but I know that he has been impotent for six months, can't shave without listening to the news and TV at the same time, and sometimes mixes bourbon with his coffee during his afternoon break. And is proud of himself for holding off on the bourbon in the afternoon.

His wife doesn't know me, has never seen me, but I know that she regards her husband as "something to put up with, like having your period"; I know that she loves her children blindly, but just as blindly drags them through every wrong turn in their lives. I know the names and addresses of each one of her relatives, and what she says to her brother Charlie's photograph when she locks herself in the bathroom. She knows nothing of my family (I'm not admitting that I have one), but I know the birthdays and hobbies and companions of her children, the family of Marvin Ezra Hobbes. Costarring: Lana Louise Hobbes as his wife, and introducing Bobby Hobbes and Robin Hobbes as their two sons. (Play theme music.)

I know Robin Hobbes and he knows me. Robin and I were stationed together in Honduras. We were supposed to be there for "exercises," but we were there to help train the anti-insurgent troops. It was a couple of years ago. The CIA wouldn't like it if I talked about it much.

I'm not the sort of person you'd write home about. But Robin told me a good many things, and even entrusted a letter to me. I was supposed to personally deliver it to his family (no, I never did have a family ... really ... I really didn't ...) just in case anything "happened" to him. Robin always said that he wouldn't complain as long as "things turn out even." If an insurgent shoots Robin's pecker away, Robin doesn't complain as long as a rebel gets *his* pecker blown away. Doesn't even have to be the same rebel. But the war had no fairness, no ethic of reciprocity. It remained for me to establish equilibrium for Robin.

Robin didn't want to enlist. It was his parents' idea. It had been raining for three days when he told me about it. The rain was like another place, a whole different part of the world, trying to assert itself over the one we were in. We had to make a third place inside the first one and the interfering one, had to get strips of tin and tire rubber and put them over our tent, because the tent fabric didn't keep out the rain after a couple of days. It steamed, in there. My fingers were swollen from the humidity, and I had to take off the little platinum ring with the equal ($=$) sign on it. Robin hadn't said anything for a whole day, but then he just started talking, his voice coming out of the drone of the rain, almost the same tone; almost generated by it. 'They're gonna start up the draft for real and earnest,' my Dad said. 'You're just the right age. They'll get you sure. Thing to do is, join now. Then you can write your own ticket. Make a deal with the recruiter.' My Dad wanted me out of the house. He wanted to buy a new car, and he couldn't afford it because he was supporting us all, and I was just another expense. That was what renewed my Dad, gave him a sense that life had a goal and was worth living: a new car, every few years. Trade in the old one, get a whole new debt. My Mom was afraid I'd be drafted, too. I had an uncle was in the Marines, liked to act like he was a Big Man with the real in-the-know scuttlebutt; he wrote us and said the Defense Department was preparing for war, planning to invade Honduras, going to do some exercises down that way first ... so we thought the war was coming for real. Thought we had inside information. My Mom wanted me to join to save my life, she said. So I could choose to go to someplace harmless, like Europe. But the truth is, she was always wet for soldiers. My Uncle Charlie used to hang around in his dress uniform a lot, looking like a stud. She was the only woman I ever knew who liked war movies. She didn't pay attention during the action parts; it wasn't that she was bloodthirsty. She liked to see them in uniform, dancing with the girls at the USO, displaying their stripes and their braid and their spit and polish, marching in step with their guns sticking up ... so she sort of went all glazed when Dad suggested I join the Army, and she didn't defend me when he started laying the guilt on me about how I was leeching, I wasn't getting a job—and two weeks later I was recruited and the bastards lied about my assignment and here I fucking am, right here. It's raining. It's raining, man."

"Yeah," I said. "It'd be nice if it wasn't raining. But then we'd get too much sun or something. Has to balance out."

"I'm sick of you talking about balancing stuff out. I want it to stop raining."

So it did. The next day. That's when the rebels started shelling the camp. Like the shells had been waiting on top of the clouds and when they pulled the clouds away, the trap door opened, and the mortar rounds fell through ... rain gone, gotta have equilibrium, balance it out, so here comes an attack.

Immediately after something "happened" to Robin, I burned the letter he'd given me. Then I was transferred to the Fourth Army Clerical Unit. I know, deeply and intuitively, that the transfer was no accident. It placed me in an ideal position to initiate the balancing of Equilibrium and was therefore the work of the Composers. Because with the Fourth Clerical, I was in charge of dispensing information to the families of the severely wounded or KIA. I came across the notice to inform Robin's parents of his condition, and I destroyed it. His parents never knew, 'til I played out my little joke.

Jokes are always true, even when they're dirty lies.

I juggled the papers so that the badly injured Robin Hobbes, 20 years old, would be sent to a certain sanitarium, where a friend of mine was a Meditech who worked admissions two days a week. The rest of the time he's what they call a Psycho Handler—a Psych Tech. My friend at the sanitarium likes the truth. He likes to see it, to smell it, particularly when it makes him gag. He took the job at the sanitarium with the severely brain-damaged eighteen-year-olds who bang their heads bloody if you don't tie them down, and with the demented older men who have to be diapered and changed and rocked like babies, and with the children whose faces are strapped into fencing masks to prevent them from eating the wallpaper and to keep them from pulling off their lips and noses—he took the job because he *likes* it there. He took it because he likes a good joke.

And he took good care of Robin Hobbes for me until it was time. I am compelled to record an aside here, a well-done and sincere thanks to my anonymous friend for his enormous patience in spoon-feeding Robin Hobbes twice daily, changing his bedpan every night, and bathing him once a week for the entire six months of detainment. He had to do it personally, because Robin was there illegally and had to be hidden in the old wing they don't use anymore.

Meanwhile, I observed the Hobbes family.

They have one of those new bodyform cars. It's a fad thing. Marvin Hobbes got his new car. The sleek, flesh-tone fiberglass body of the car is cast so that its sides are imprinted with the shape of a nude woman lying prone, her arms flung out in front of her in the diving motion of the Cannon beach towel girl. The doors are in her ribs, the trunk opens from her ass. She's ridiculously disproportional, of course. The whole thing is wildly kitsch. It was an embarrassment to Mrs. Hobbes. And Hobbes is badly in debt behind it, because he totaled his first bodyform car. Rammed a Buick Marilyn Monroe into a John Wayne pickup. John and Marilyn's arms, tangled when their front bumpers slammed, were lovingly intertwined.

Hobbes took the loss and bought a Miss America. He is indifferent to Mrs. Hobbes's embarrassment. To the particularly astringent way she uses the term *tacky*.

Mr. Hobbes plays little jokes of his own. Private jokes. But I knew. Mr. Hobbes had no idea I was watching when he concealed his wife's Lady Norelco. He knew that she'd want it that night, because they were invited to a party, and she always shaved her legs before a party. Mrs. Hobbes sang a little tuneless song as she quested systematically for the shaver, bending over to look in the house's drawers and cabinets, and *behind* the drawers and cabinets, peering into all the secret nooks and burrow places we forget a house has; her search was so thorough I came to regard it as the product of mania. I felt a sort of warmth, then: I can appreciate ... thoroughness.

Once a week, he did it to her. He'd temporarily pocket her magnifying mirror, her makeup case. Then he'd pretend to find it. "Where any idiot can see it."

Bobby Hobbes, Robin's younger brother, was unaware that his

father knew about his hidden cache of Streamline brand racing-striped condoms. The elder Hobbes thought he was very clever in knowing about them. But Dad Hobbes didn't know about me.

Marvin Hobbes would pocket his son's rubbers and make *snuck-snuck* sounds of muffled laughter in his sinuses as the red-eared teenager feverishly searched and rechecked his closet and drawers.

Hobbes would innocently saunter in and ask, "Hey—you better get going if you're gonna make that date, right? What'cha looking for anyway? Can I help?"

"Oh ... uh, no thanks, Dad. Just some ... socks. Missing."

As the months passed, and Hobbes's depression over his impotence worsened, his fits of practical joking became more frequent, until he no longer took pleasure in them, but played his practical jokes as if they were some habitual household chore. Take out the trash, cut the lawn, hide Lana's razor, feed the dog, play a joke.

I watched as Hobbes, driven by some undefined desperation, attempted to relate to his relatives. He'd sit them at points symmetrical (relative to him) around the posh living room; his wife 30 degrees to his left, his youngest son 30 degrees to his right. Then, he would relate a personal childhood experience as a sort of parable, describing his hopes and dreams for his little family.

On one occasion, he said, "When I was a boy, we would carve out tunnels in the briar bushes. The wild blackberry bushes were very dense around our farm. It'd take hours to clip a good tunnel three feet into them with the gardener's shears. But after weeks of patient work, we snipped a network of crude tunnels through the half-acre filled with brambles. In this way, we learned how to cope with the world as a whole. We would crawl through the green tunnels in perfect comfort, but knowing that if we stood up, the thorns would cut us to ribbons."

He paused and sucked several times loudly on the pipe. It had gone out ten minutes before. He stared at the fireplace where there was no fire.

Finally, he asked his wife, "Do you understand?" Almost whining it.

She shook her head, eyebrows raised. Annoyed, jaws bruxating, Hobbes slipped to the floor, muttering he'd lost his tobacco pouch, searching for it under the coffee table, under the sofa. His son didn't smile, not once. His son had hidden the tobacco pouch. Hobbes went scurrying about on the rug looking for the tobacco pouch in a great dither of confusion, like a poodle searching for his rawhide bone. Growling low. Growling to himself.

After one of these family communication sessions failed, he would give up and go off muttering to the garage, to putter about with his hobby: restoring antique vacuum-tube radios. (He sold them to collectors, on eBay.)

Speculation as to how I came to know these intimate details of the Hobbes family life will prove as futile as Marvin's attempt to relate to his relatives.

I have my ways. I learned my techniques from other Composers.

Presumably, Composers belong to a tacit network of free agents the world over, whose sworn duty is to establish states of interpersonal Equilibrium. No Composer has ever knowingly met another; it is impossible for them to meet, even by accident, since they carry the same charge and therefore repel each other. I'm not sure just how the invisible Composers taught me their technique for the restoration of states of Equilibrium. But that's not quite true; I *am* sure as to how it was done—I simply can't articulate it.

I have no concrete evidence that the Composers exist. Composers perform the same service for society that vacuum tubes used to perform for radios and amplifiers. And the fact of a vacuum tube's existence is proof that someone must have the knowledge, somewhere, needed to construct a vacuum tube. Necessity is its own evidence.

Now picture this: Picture me with a high forehead crowned by white hair and a square black graduation cap with its tassel dangling. Picture me with a drooping white mustache and wise blue eyes. In fact, I look a lot like Albert Einstein, in this picture. I am wearing a black graduation gown, and clutched in my right hand is a long wooden pointer.

I don't have a high forehead. I don't have any hair at all, anymore. No mustache. Not even eyebrows. I don't have blue eyes. (Probably, neither did Einstein.) I don't look like Einstein in the slightest. I don't own a graduation gown, and I never completed a college course.

But picture me that way. I am pointing at a home movie screen with my official pointer. On the screen is a projection of a young man who has shaved himself bald and who wears a tattered *Army* uniform with a Clerical Corps patch on the right shoulder, half peeled off. The young man has his back to the home movie camera. He is playing a TV-tennis game. This is one of the first video games, old school. Each player is given a knob that controls a vertical white dash designating the "tennis racket," one to each half of the television screen. On a field of blank gray, the two white dashes bandy between them a white blip, the "tennis ball."

With a flick of the knob, snapping the dash/racket up or down, one knocks the blip past the other electronic paddle and scores a point. Jabbing here and there at the movie screen, I indicate that the game is designed for two people. I nod my head sagely. But this mysterious young man manipulates left and right knobs with both hands at once. (If you look closely at his hands, you'll note that the index finger of his left hand is missing. The index finger of his right hand is missing, too.) Being left-handed, when he first began to play himself, the left hand tended to win. But he establishes perfect equilibrium in the interactive poles of his parity. The game is designed to continue incessantly until 15 points are scored by either side. He nurtured his skill until he could play against himself for long hours, beeping a white blip with euphoric monotony back and forth between wrist-flicks, never scoring a point for either hand.

He never wins, he never loses, he establishes perfect equilibrium.

The movie ends, the professor winks, the young man has at no time turned to face the camera.

My practical joke was programmed to compose an Equilibrium for Robin Hobbes and his family. Is it Karma? Are the Composers the agents of Karma? No. There is no such thing as Karma: *That is why the Composers are necessary.* To redress the negligence of God. We try. But in establishing the Equilibrium—something far more refined than vengeance—we invariably create another imbalance, for justice cannot be precisely quantified. And the new imbalance gives rise to a contradictory inversity, and so the Perfect and Mindless Dance of Equilibrium proceeds. For there to be a premise, there must somewhere exist its contradiction.

Hence, I present *my* clue to the Hobbes conundrum, encrypted in a reversal of the actual situation.

In the nomenclature of the Composers, a snake symbolizes an octopus. The octopus has eight legs, the snake is legless. The octopus is the greeting, the snake is the reply; the centipede is the greeting, the worm is the reply.

And so I selected the following document, an authentic missive—a true story, in every detail—illicitly obtained from a certain obsessive cult overseen by the Composers. I mailed the document to the Hobbes family as *my* clue, offered in all fairness. It was the inverted foreshadowing. It read as follows:

My dear, dear Tonto,

You recall, I assume, that Perfect and Holy Union I myself ordained, in *my* dominion as High Priest—the marriage of R. and D., Man and Wife in the unseeing *eyes* of the Order, they were obligated to seek a means of devotion and worship, in accordance with their own specialties and proclivities. I advised them to jointly undertake the art of Sensual Communion with the Animus, and this they did, and still they were unsatisfied. Having excelled in the somatic explorations that are the foundation of the Order, they were granted leave to follow the lean of their own inclinations. Thus liberated, they settled on the fifth Degree in Jolting, the mastery of self-modification. They sought out a surgeon who, for an inestimable price, fused their bodies into one. They became Siamese twins, the woman joined to his right side. They were joined at the waist through an unbreakable bridge of flesh. This grafting made sexual coupling, outside of fondling, nearly impossible. The obstacle, as we say in the Order, is the object. But R. was not content. Shorn of normal marital relations, R.'s latent homosexuality surfaced. He took male lovers and his wife was forced to lie beside the copulating men, forced to observe everything, and advised to keep her silence except in the matter of insisting on latex condoms. At first this stage left her brimming with

96

revulsion; but she became aware that through the bridge of flesh that linked them she was receiving, faintly at first and then more strongly, her husband's impressions. In this way, she was vicariously fulfilled and, in the fullness of time, no longer objected when he took to a homosexual bed. R's lovers accepted her presence, as if she were the incarnate spirit of the frustrated feminine persona that was the mainspring of their inner clockwork. But when their new complacency was established, the obstacle diminished. It became necessary to initiate new somatic obstacles. Inevitably, another woman was surgically added to the Siamese coupling, to make it a tripling, a woman on R.'s left. Over a period of several months, and after the proper blood tests, more were added to the surgically fused group. Seamless cosmetic procedures and the most intricate mysteries of internal surgery were employed. Today, they are joined to six other people in a ring of exquisite Siamese multiplicity. The junctures connect in a circle so the first is joined to the eighth, linked with someone else on both sides. All face inward. There are four men and four women, a literal wedding ring. (Is this a romantic story, Tonto?) Arrayed as they are in an unbreakable ring, they necessarily go to great lengths to overcome practical and psychological handicaps. For example, they had to practice for two days to learn how to collectively board D.'s Lear jet. Four of them, usually the women, ride in the arms of the other four; they sidle into the plane, calling signals for the steps. This enforced teamwork lends a new perspective to the most mundane daily affairs. Going to the toilet becomes a yogic exercise requiring the utmost concentration. For but one man to pee, each of the joined must provide a precisely measured degree of pressure. ... They have been surgically arranged so that each man can copulate with the woman opposite him or, in turns, the man diagonal. Homosexual relations are limited to one coupling at a time since members of the same sex are diagonal to one another. Heterosexually, the cell has sex simultaneously. The surgeons have extended the relevant nerve ends through the links of flesh so that the erogenous sensations of one are shared by all. I was privileged to observe one of these highly practiced acrobatic orgies. I admit to a secret yen to participate, to stand nude in the center of the circle and experience flesh-tone piston-action from every point of the compass. But this is below my Degree; only the High Priest's divine mount, the Perfect and Unscrubbed *Silver,* may know him carnally. ... Copulating as an octuplet whole, they resemble a pink sea anemone capturing a wriggling minnow. Or perhaps interlocked fingers of arm wrestlers. Or a letter written all in one paragraph, a single unit. ... But suppose a fight breaks out between the grafted Worshippers? Suppose one of them should die or take sick? If one contracts an illness, all ultimately come down with it. And if one should die, they would have to carry the corpse wherever they went until it rotted away—the operation is irreversible. But that is all part of the Divine Process.

Yours very, very affectionately,

The Lone Ranger

Mrs. Hobbes found the letter in the mailbox and opened it. She read it with visible alarm and brought it to her husband, who was in the backyard, preparing to barbecue the ribs of a pig. He was wearing an apron printed with the words DON'T FORGET TO KISS THE CHEF. The words FORGET TO were almost obliterated by a rusty splash of sauce.

Hobbes read the letter, frowning. "I'll be gosh-darned," he said. "They get crazier with junk mail all the time. God-darned pornography." He lit the letter on fire and used it to start the charcoal.

Seeing this, I smiled with relief, and softly said: "Click!" A letter for a letter, Equilibrium for the destruction of the letter Robin Hobbes had given me in Honduras. If Mr. and Mrs. Hobbes had discerned the implication of the inverted clue, I would have been forced to release Robin from the sanitarium, to the custody of the Army.

When the day came for my joke, I had my friend bring Robin over to my hotel room, which was, conveniently, two blocks from the Hobbes' residence.

It should be a harmless gesture to describe my friend, as long as I don't disclose his name. Not a Composer in fact but one in spirit, my Meditech friend is pudgy and square-shouldered. His legs look like they're too thin for his body. His hair is clipped close to his small skull and there is a large white scar dividing his scalp, running from the crown of his head to the bridge of his nose. The scar is a gift from one of his patients, received in an unguarded moment. My friend wears thick wire-rim glasses with an elastic band connecting them in the rear.

Over Robin's noisy protests, I prepared him for the joke. To shut him up, I considered cutting out his tongue. But that would require compensating with some act restoring equilibrium that I had not time to properly devise. So I settled for adhesive tape over his mouth. And of course the other thing, stuck through a hole in the tape.

Mr. Hobbes was at home; his Miss America bodyform car filled the driveway. The front of the car was crumpled from a minor accident of the night before, and her arms were corrugated, bent unnaturally inward, one argent hand shoved whole into her open and battered mouth.

Suppressing sniggers—I admit this freely, we were like two twelve-year-olds—my friend and I brought Robin to the porch and rang the doorbell. We dashed to the nearest concealment, a holly bush undulating in the faint summer breeze.

It was shortly after sunset, 8:30 p.m., and Mr. Hobbes had just returned from a long Tuesday at the office. He was silent and grumpy; he'd spent time commiserating in the driveway with his abused Miss America.

Two minutes after our ring, Marvin Hobbes opened the front door, newspaper in hand. My friend had to bite his lip to keep from laughing out loud. But for *me*, the humor had quite gone out of the moment. It was a *solemn* moment, one with innate dignity and profound resonance.

Mrs. Hobbes peered over Marvin's shoulder, electric shaver in her right hand; Bobby, behind her, stared over the top of her wig, something hidden in his left hand. Simultaneously, the entire family screamed, their instantaneous timing perhaps confirming that they were true relatives after all.

They found Robin as we had left him on the doorstep, swaddled in baby blankets, diapered in a couple of Huggies disposables, a pacifier stuck through the tape over his mouth, covered to the neck in gingham cloth (though one of his darling stumps peeked through). And equipped with a plastic baby bottle. The shreds of his arms and legs had been amputated shortly after the mortar attack on Puerto Barrios. Pinned to his chest was a note (I lettered it myself in the crude handwriting I thought would reflect the mood of a desperate mother.) The note said:

PLEASE TAKE CARE OF MY BABY

SAWBONES

BY L. L. SOARES

There was the initial shock of waking up in a strange place, followed by the realization that he was strapped down to the bed. Not exactly the most pleasant of awakenings. The anesthesia was dissipating slowly.

"Are you awake?" the voice said, filtered through the fog in his brain. He saw, as if through a fish-eye lens, a face hovering above him.

Paolo Searle struggled with the bonds, and a hand rested on his shoulder.

"Don't freak out," the voice said. "You're in good hands here."

His vision focused, blurred, and focused again.

"I'm Dr. Raymond," the voice said. "The surgery was a success."

Dr. Raymond. It sounded familiar at least. They must have pumped him full of some high-test elephant tranquilizer, considering how tough it was for Paolo to return to the land of the living. Dr. Raymond was the guy you went to when you needed to keep it off the books. Dr. Raymond was the epitome of discretion.

"You did it?" Searle asked, coming back to his senses.

"Yes," the doctor replied, clearly happy that Paolo was coherent again. "I thought I was going to have to sedate you again."

"No, I'm fine. I think."

"Good, good. I'm sorry about the straps, but you would have been more than a handful if you had freaked out unrestrained. I did it for my own safety, as well as yours."

"I understand."

"This was a very unusual request," the doctor said. "I hope you're happy with the results."

"I'm sure I will be," Searle said.

The doctor then started unstrapping him from the table.

"This is going to take some getting used to," the doctor said.

Searle sat up and instantly felt severe pain in his arms. He could barely move them.

"I think someone needs more morphine," Dr. Raymond said when he heard Searle groan.

Back at the apartment, his arms were sore as hell, but that was to be expected. He took off his jacket and noticed the sleeves were already split down the middle. He stood in front of the full-length mirror and admired the craftsmanship.

Ridges of exposed bone on each forearm, from just below the elbow to just short of the wrist on each arm. Like two shark fins. The left arm, sharp and serrated like a saw. The right, honed to razor sharpness. Both were formidable to look at.

They had been his own idea. No other doctor would have even considered the operation. But Dr. Willard Raymond was no typical doctor. He was open to some very wild things, *if the price was right.*

He remembered the initial consultation. Dr. Raymond had never uttered the word "crazy." He just nodded his head as Paolo explained what he wanted.

The skin around the bone fins was caked in bandages. It hurt just to move. But in a few weeks, he would be as good as new.

They're going to be beautiful, Searle thought as he admired himself in the mirror. *Fucking beautiful.*

He learned the hard way how dangerous they were. How careful he had to be at all times. It was so easy to cut himself if he wasn't careful. When his modifications had healed enough for him to become comfortable with his new additions, Searle hired two prostitutes and brought them back to his apartment.

One was named Esmeralda and the other was Aggie, from what he could gather from the conversation they were having on the elevator ride up to his loft. He had picked them because they were pretty and they were huddled together. Something about them said "package deal," and he was in the mood for a threesome.

"Make yourselves at home," he told them, as he went to get the wine from the refrigerator. He rarely brought hookers to his home. There were motel rooms for that sort of thing, but he was finally starting to feel like his old self again, and it was time to celebrate.

As they drank and turned on the television, he went into the bedroom and changed into a blue silk robe with big, loose sleeves and then went out into the living room to invite them to join him.

He watched them undress, but kept his robe on. He didn't want to give away the surprise too soon. He held one on the bed and pressed the tiny switch with his tongue that released a venomous fang (another enhancement courtesy of Dr. Raymond), and bit her on the neck. The poison was slow-acting and would take a few hours to kill her, but in the meantime, she would be in a paralyzed state, a captive audience. Then he turned his attention to the other one.

The other one, Esmeralda, was so busy drinking that she didn't notice what was going on. Paolo threw her down upon the bed and held her wrists tightly as he fucked her. He kept his robe on. She pretended to enjoy it, looking to Aggie who rested on the pillows with a blank look on her face.

"What's up with you, Aggie?" she asked. "Why don't you join in?"

Paolo held both her wrists above her head with one hand and grabbed her face with his free one. He turned it to face him. "Is your name really Esmeralda?"

"Yes," she said.

"That's a beautiful name," he said. "It sounds like a Russian princess."

It's then that he let go of her and rose up on top of her, letting the robe slip to the floor, revealing the sharp edges of the boney knives protruding from his forearms. With the serrated one, he pressed down gently on her throat, just enough to draw blood from a series of pin pricks and keep her from struggling, and he kept thrusting until he was about to come. Then he switched arms and sliced off her head with the other, sharper blade. It cut through her neck muscles and spine effortlessly, much easier than he had expected, and her head dropped to the carpet, her neck bathing him in blood. The action had caused all of her muscles to contract, and her vagina closed tightly around him for a moment, squeezing every last drop from his orgasm. *The ultimate donkey punch.*

He turned to Aggie with a grin on his face, now dripping with blood. He could tell she wanted to scream, but the venom kept her frozen.

"Aren't they beautiful?" he said, displaying his arms. They had healed nicely. "I am a work of art, no?"

She could not even nod her head.

He tossed Esmeralda's body, which had stopped convulsing beneath him, to the floor, and then turned his attention to the other girl.

"Aggie, is it?" Paolo said. "I'm guessing your real name is Agnes?"

She stared at him.

"A dignified, old-fashioned name," Paolo said. "I think it's a shame you go by Aggie. That sounds like the marbles we used to play with on the playground as children. Don't you think?"

He raised his arms and then made short work of her. It was interesting to see how much damage the blades could create. He tested them to see how much effort it took to do the things he wanted. All in all, it was a nice way to try them out—on the flesh of two people who would probably never be missed. The way they'd been huddled together on the rainy night when he found them, it made him think they were the only friends each other had in the world.

Now they would be together in heaven.

He raised his arms and then made short work of her. It was

Lucy woke with a start. It was a nightmare about Aggie, and it seemed so real that she found herself hyperventilating. Her heart rate was going a mile a minute. She hadn't had such a vivid dream in years.

No doubt it was guilt. She hadn't seen her sister in months, and hadn't done a very good job of keeping tabs on her. Part of her wanted to stay strong and keep administering the tough love that she vowed she'd adhere to. There was nothing else she could do for Aggie. She just couldn't be an enabler anymore. But, at the same time, there was that sisterly bond. And more than that, they were twins. No matter how differently their lives had turned out, they still had an attachment that predated their birth.

Lucy slowed down her breathing. She got out of bed, realizing yet again that she was alone. She and Armand had broken up only a week ago, and she still missed the way he'd hold her in her sleep. That sense of loss wasn't about to go away any time soon. She just hated sleeping by herself. It didn't happen very often. Even when she was a kid, there had been Aggie. They shared the same bed until they were teenagers and they finally wanted separated beds. Their parents had never gotten a big enough place to give them separate *rooms*.

I have to find her, Lucy thought, walking down the hallway to the kitchen. Just to keep an eye on her. Make sure she's all right.

There was a bottle of port on the counter near the microwave. Lucy pulled out the reusable cork and took a long swig. It wouldn't be long before she was relaxed again and heading back to sleep.

"I haven't seen her," the girl with the black eye said. Her name was Mandy. Lucy remembered her from last time. She wondered how long this girl had been on the streets. She seemed young, but didn't quite look it. There were so many lost souls floating around the city.

Lucy was going to ask about the eye, but then decided not to. What was the point?

"What about the other one?" another girl said.

"Huh?" Lucy turned to her. But the girl was talking to Mandy.

"The other one. The one she was always with. The sisters."

Mandy looked at Lucy and grimaced.

"What's she talking about?"

"Aggie found a friend. They used to score dope together," Mandy said. "They were always together. Girls used to call them 'the sisters.'"

That hurt. It made Lucy realize that, even though she'd pushed Aggie out of her life, her sister had gone and found someone to replace her. Suddenly, it all rushed back to her. The intervention with the family, the refusal to help her out anymore, the list of grievances. Lucy had participated against her better judgment. She hated being a part of such a thing. But they'd all convinced her it was the only way to really force Aggie to get back on her feet again. The girl was just spiraling deeper and deeper into the abyss, and there was nothing else they could do to stop her descent.

But Lucy was almost certain that pushing her away would just make her fall all the faster to the bottom. Now, she knew she was probably right.

"You know, when I first saw you, I thought it was her," the other girl said. "You look just like her. I thought she'd gotten all cleaned up and got some nice clothes. That she'd picked herself up."

"We're twins," Lucy said. "It makes sense."

"For a moment there, I had a twinkle of hope. That she'd gotten her life back together. That maybe there was a chance for me, too."

Lucy looked at her. The other girl lowered her eyes.

"So much for that," Mandy said. She lit another cigarette. "Honestly, I haven't seen her in a couple of days. I'd tell you if I had."

Lucy gave them both twenties for their time and went back to her car. She'd asked any girls on the strip who looked familiar, but they all had the same story. They hadn't seen Aggie for at least a day or two. And they hadn't seen the girl they called her "sister" either, some girl named Esmeralda.

Sister, Lucy thought. *I'm her fucking sister.* And I wasn't able to protect her, yet again.

There was a good chance Aggie was somewhere, high as a kite, huddled in some dark crack den, oblivious to the world, but alive.

But Lucy doubted it.

It was that dream. That vivid dream. She was sure Aggie was dead. Either way, she needed to know for sure.

Paolo was working.

Normally he would have taken the sniper route and picked the guy off from a distance, but something about his new weapons made him want to get up close and personal. He wanted to feel the flesh ripping apart. Get some blood on him. Get sloppy.

He knew this was bad. That in his business, it was a dumb move to get so close to his prey. But he couldn't control himself.

Besides, a mutilated corpse was a bigger message to strike fear in people's hearts than any clean gunshot. It would tell any would-be smart guys to back the fuck off. Cross Johnny Swayne and this was the kind of thing that happened to you. You got filleted like a fish dinner.

Paolo grabbed the guy near the docks, hauling him into the alleyway. Before the guy even knew what was happening, Paolo had ripped his belly open, and then sliced his throat. The messy remains hit the pavement and Paolo was already out the other end, in his car, high-tailing it as far away as he could get.

His adrenaline was pumping to such a degree he thought he could explode all over the dashboard. Shooting someone had *never* felt like this. He could have been a robot, pulling a trigger. But this was different. This was a lion stalking its prey and bringing it down. This was visceral and real and satisfying. Like great sex or a good meal.

Everything that told him this was wrong was overridden by the instinctual certainty that there was nothing more *right*.

All that money he had made from past jobs. He didn't have any hobbies. He didn't have any extravagant needs. He didn't need a top-of-the-line car or a penthouse apartment. And there was no one else to share it with. No one else to lavish it on. No one who ever stuck around for very long.

So, to stave his boredom, he started getting into body modification a few years ago. First it had been the usual stuff, the tattoos and piercings. But the thrill of those didn't last long, and they didn't *add* anything substantial to him. They didn't make him any better. Any more dangerous.

Then he'd gotten some more pragmatic alterations. Like the retractable fang that worked like a charm if he got close enough. He was a human rattlesnake. A gaboon viper. *A king fucking cobra.*

And now he had some other delightful toys to go with the set.

"I saw her with some guy," the platinum blonde said. Her roots were growing out and they were dark, clashing with the dye job. "Her and the other one."

"This was three nights ago?"

"I think so," the blonde said. "I lose track, sometimes."

"Had you ever seen him before?"

"Yeah, he comes out here a lot. A lot of the girls have been with him. Even me. He's an intense son of a bitch, but I don't think he ever really hurt any of us. Not badly, anyway."

"Where did he take you?"

"With me, it was a motel room. Likely the same with them. He didn't take anyone to his place very often. Maybe once in a while. But I don't think he wanted to get his home dirty."

"If you saw him, would you recognize him?"

"Sure," the blonde said. "I told you I fucked the guy. I seen his face up close."

"Will you call me if you see him again?" Lucy asked. "I just want to talk to him about my sister. I just want to find out if he knows anything. You're the only one who saw her before she disappeared."

"Yeah," the girl said. She wore a big white, fake fur coat that had lots of stains on it. It made her look like a dirty stuffed animal.

Lucy noticed that a lot of the girls had cell phones. No matter how destitute they got, they always had phones. Probably unregistered numbers that couldn't be traced to anyone. They were supposedly pretty easy to get. It was funny how cells were everywhere these days. Like a virus.

"Thank you," Lucy said.

Then she drove another block down, to ask more questions. To try to find more clues. To find any breadcrumbs she could that revealed the trail Aggie had taken away from her.

"You're getting too messy," Johnny Swayne said. "I want to leave a message and you leave behind a blood bath."

"It ramps up the fear," Paolo said. "Keeps people in line. They'll think twice before they cross you."

"It's getting so I don't need the extra attention. It's making everyone real antsy."

"So what are you saying?" Paolo asked, sitting in front of the big man's desk, feeling the bone blades on his forearms rubbing up against the leather of his sleeves, slowly cutting through.

"I'm saying to tone it the fuck down," Swayne said. "I'm saying to lay low for a little while and give things a chance to go back to the way they were."

"What about work?"

"You'll get more work when you learn some self-control," Swayne said.

Paolo got angry at that. He got up from the chair.

"Like I said, lay low for a bit," Swayne said. "I'll call you when I need you."

Paolo said nothing as he left the room. He went outside and lit a cigarette. It was starting to rain again. It had been raining on and off every day, all week, and he was getting sick of it.

I need to get out of this city, he thought. I need to go someplace where people would appreciate what a man like me can do.

In the middle of the night, he woke up, startled. He'd had a nightmare. About that hooker, the one he'd given the poisoned hickey to, the one who watched as he decapitated her friend. What was her name again? Maggie? He didn't remember.

Of all the people he'd killed over the years, all the blood that was on his hands, why would he think of some nameless skank he'd picked off the street for one night of fucking and slicing? And why the fuck was this *nobody* in his dreams?

He usually slept like a baby on Ambien. Without a care in the world.

And why was he out of breath, with his heart racing?

At least it didn't take him long to get back to sleep.

"That's him," the blonde said.

She'd called Lucy and told her where to meet. It was raining again. Lucy was in her car at the time, making her rounds, and she was close enough to get there quickly.

"You sure that's the guy?"

"Yeah. He likes to look the girls over. He gets out of his car and checks them out. He's picky like that. I'm surprised, though. He usually doesn't come looking this soon after the last time. There's usually a break in between. I get the idea he doesn't like to shop much."

The guy across the street was wearing an oversized leather jacket that looked odd on him. He was chatting up some young-looking thing in a beehive hairdo. You could tell it was a wig, but she had a *look* at least. The bitch was trying to be a street-corner Amy Winehouse.

They both went to his car. He wasn't a gentleman and didn't open the passenger side door for her.

She was snapping gum and Lucy could almost hear it from where she stood.

Lucy paid the girl who called her. She then got into her car and followed the man to a motel. She tailed him when he dropped the girl off at the street corner where he'd found her, and then Lucy followed him home.

She saw the building he went into. She waited awhile, and then she went home herself.

The next night, when he arrived home, she waited for him, sitting on the stairs. She looked up when he approached.

Her. The girl he'd killed that night.

Aggie. That was her name. Agnes.

It all came back to him now, thanks to the dream, and now this. He knew she was a ghost, that she probably wasn't real, but he held the door open for her anyway. She was dressed similarly to what she'd worn the night he brought her home. She didn't say anything as they took the wooden elevator up to his loft. He just stared right at her, and she stared back.

When they got to the right floor, he lifted the carriage and she slipped out.

"So," he said. "You're haunting me, now?"

She smiled and nodded her head. No reply.

He'd killed some of the biggest swinging dicks in town, some of the most hardcore bastards you could meet, and he didn't blink an eye. Didn't break a sweat. And now this sad little thing was going to throw him off his game. Put some kind of fright into him.

It almost made him laugh.

"So, can you enter my home if I don't invite you in?" he asked. "How does it work?"

She didn't respond. Just stood there at the threshold.

"C'mon in," he said.

He poured her a glass of wine, and she seemed real enough as she took it from him. Maybe she was tangible after all.

Maybe he'd be able to kill her all over again.

Although this time, he'd *really* let loose.

"So how does this work?" he asked again. "You're here to freak me out for killing you. To make me regret what I did? To scare me? I know you're not real. I dumped your body myself."

An odd emotion flickered in her eyes.

"Well, lady, I don't scare. I ain't afraid of anything, not even you."

She drank her wine in silence.

The way she didn't say a word really seemed to bother him. And though he claimed he didn't know fear, she could see the fear in his eyes. For someone who was so dangerous, he sure was quick to believe that she was a ghost or some kind of spirit of retribution. He didn't even consider the fact that she could be a living, breathing human being that just happened to look like a woman he killed. The thought hadn't even crossed his mind.

"I don't know what you've got planned for me," he said. "But why don't we have a little fun first? Might as well fuck if you came all the way here to see me."

She thought about this for a few seconds, then nodded her head.

He led her to the bedroom.

There was a bathroom adjoining the bedroom, and he went there for a moment. She just stood in the middle of the dimly lit room, waiting for him.

She looked at the bed. This was probably the bed he'd fucked her sister in. The one he'd *killed* her in. For some reason, she was sure it hadn't been in a motel room. It had been *here*. And she knew that he'd done it. He'd admitted it to her face without a second thought.

He came out, dressed in a robe with big sleeves and saw her standing there, waiting for him.

"Get comfortable," he said. "Get out of those things."

She hesitated.

"If you can drink wine, then you can do this. Can't you?"

She started to take off her clothes. He stretched out on the bed and watched her. He seemed spellbound by her movements, like he'd never seen someone getting undressed before, like he was a child watching an especially fascinating magic trick.

There was a scar down her belly. It started between her breasts and went all the way down to her pubic mound. He hadn't noticed that the first time he killed her. Then again, maybe it was a remnant from what he'd done to her, back when she was alive.

"I never did it with a ghost before," he said. He couldn't hide his enthusiasm.

She smiled at the sheer childish innocence of his reaction. It caught her off guard. He wasn't acting at all like she thought he would.

"Come here," he said, patting the bed in front of him.

She slowly approached the bed.

He grabbed her wrist and pulled her down toward him. Then she was on her back and he was straddling her, holding her wrists down as he fucked her. He opened the robe and threw it off. He was above her like some kind of vulture, but instead of wings there were scythe blades of bone.

He seemed so damn proud. Like a peacock in all its glory.

"I am going to kill you," he said. "Just like last time, except even worse. And if you show up here again, I'll do it again. And again. And you'll rue the day you ever came to haunt me."

She reached up and touched her scar. She pressed down on it, and there was a seam. He watched with curiosity as she grabbed the edges and opened her skin like a coat.

Her intestines darted out of her like giant serpents. Two ends grabbed his wrists, keeping the blades away from her. He struggled, but the fleshy tubes were too strong.

A third abdominal serpent wrapped around his throat, constricting like a python, snapping his neck in an instant. He didn't even have time to think about what was happening to him as it squeezed the life out of him. Then her intestines threw him to the floor.

His arms were spread out at his sides, playing the vulture even in death. His glassy eyes stared up at the ceiling, lifeless, and a mixture of blood and drool oozed from his mouth.

It had all happened so quickly. She hadn't given him a chance to fight her off, to slash at her with those blades of his. It had all been fast and efficient—and final.

Lucy coaxed her intestines back into her abdomen and closed the seams. Once again, they sealed and became the scar.

She slowly dressed, staring at his corpse.

It didn't bring Aggie back, but Aggie was a lost cause anyway. She was bound to have died one way or another, probably after some final drug binge. Even so, she didn't deserve to be killed by this guy, carved up like a Thanksgiving turkey.

Her only regret was that he'd interrupted their fucking for his big revelation, that she'd killed him before she'd had a chance to climax. Now she'd have to go home and finish herself off.

WHIRLING MACHINE MAN

BY AARON J. FRENCH

The Jeffrey Hogan case had been all over the local news, with various stories being run on a poor kid who had come stumbling out of the woods, white-haired and drooling, with a great deal of his teeth missing and his tongue cut out ...

That was the most horrifying part of the whole thing—at least in my opinion—the bloody, gaping hole in the center of his face. I had the unfortunate pleasure of viewing it in the medical photos in his case file.

His parents found the eleven-year-old boy sitting in a puddle of his own excrement on the kitchen floor. Jeffrey was wide awake, staring into midair—a condition he maintained thereafter, even once they got him to St. Mary's Memorial Hospital. Even now up in the Serene Hills mental facility, where, presumably, he'll be spending the remainder of his days.

I want to tell you also that the Hogan case ended my P.I. career, failure though it might've been, and to this day I hold a position at the Department of Motor Vehicles, sitting on my ass issuing license plates and I.D. cards. Not the most exciting work, but digging in the Hogan case produced a desperate need in me to feel *safe*.

That's what my DMV job is: safe.

Way I saw it, if I didn't procure some safety—and fast—I was

115

liable to end up in Serene Hills right along with Jeffrey. Because there will always be that empty space where my right arm used to be … antagonizing me with its absence. Simple things like riding a bicycle—unless I decide to get fitted for the prosthetic, and them things ain't cheap—will forever remain unavailable to me. That's something I have to live with. But allow me to fill in some of the details so you can have a better understanding.

I don't recall the exact day Maria Hogan came into my office, but I do know it was some time after the hubbub surrounding her son had died down. The county gazettes had pumped several weeks' worth of sensationalism onto their front pages at her son's expense, but had since returned to running their usual drivel. I had pretty much forgotten about it, and so when the tired-looking blonde with large breasts and larger hips appeared opposite my desk, it took me by surprise.

I recognized her from the news reports, but now she just looked terrible. I said, "Please, have a seat," and signaled to the vacant leather chair; nodding, she installed herself accordingly.

"My name is—"

"I know who you are."

She blinked. "You know what happened to my son?"

"I do."

"You know where he is?"

I presumed she meant Serene Hills, so I nodded. "What can I do for you, Mrs. Hogan?"

She was quiet a moment. Then: "I want you to find who did this to Jeffrey."

"Ma'am, the police are doing their best—"

"No, they're not." There was a flicker of ferocity in her eyes that I found briefly attractive. "Jeffrey can't speak and he won't write, and the cops must've combed through the woods behind our house two dozen times, and nobody knows a single thing, and I know—I just *know*—that it's gonna fall off their radar soon. They're gonna box up my baby's case file and go about their business."

She ended with a burst of emotion, and I sat there feeling

awkward while she wept in her hands. I lit a cigarette and Maria Hogan raised her face to glare at me, but I didn't care: I needed the nicotine.

"Mrs. Hogan," I began, "I understand all of your concerns, but I'm just not sure what I can do about it. From what I've heard there are absolutely no leads, no motive, no evidence, and no blood in the forest. They've got nothing, which means I'll get nothing. I'm sorry, but it is what it is."

She arched her eyebrows. "I thought you ran a business here?"

"I do, it's just—" I blew smoke out my nose. The truth was that I was scared. And not just scared: *horrified.* I couldn't imagine the kind of person who could remove an eleven-year-old kid's tongue and teeth, and didn't want to, either.

Sensing my distress, she said, "I'll let you in on a secret."

"I think you'd better go to the police if you have new information." Watching my own ass was something I excelled at, thankfully.

But she tossed her head. "Nope, they won't listen, not to this. I can only tell someone who has an open mind." She glanced at the nameplate on my desk.

"Morgan Summers, and call me Morgan," I said. "I suspect I have an open mind, but—"

"The person who did this to Jeffrey lives in a cabin in the Mintano Wilderness behind our house."

My eyes widened. "You told that to the cops?"

"No ... it's not really there—not physically."

"What?"

She sighed, struggling with the words. "I've never actually seen it. Only Jeffrey saw it. He saw it a few times. He said a mad scientist lived there."

I chuckled. "Yes, I did hear something in the news about your son having *strange* episodes in the woods."

"I told them that. And you know what, my word returned to me void. That's why I didn't tell the police about the cabin."

She reached in her flower-patterned handbag and withdrew a small manila envelope, the kind of thing in which you might receive a piece of jewelry in the mail. She placed it on the desk and slid it over to me. Stamping out my cigarette, I picked it up and opened the flap.

"I found that lying on the back porch when I went outside this morning."

I frowned at her. "Does your husband know you're here?"

She didn't answer. I knew it was probably evidence that I was potentially contaminating, but I was too intrigued now not to proceed.

The first object I pulled out was a small gold, old-style key; the second, a folded sheet of paper; the third, a small hunk of metal that I thought was just metal, until I realized there were several human teeth wedged into it.

"Jesus!" I shrieked, dropping the object. "Are those ..."

"Yes. They're Jeffrey's." She picked up the sheet of paper and unfolded it. "This's a letter intended for him." She read:

To the one speaking for the dead:

I realize you experienced great pain and suffering during your transformation. But still I do not understand your departure from the lab. I warned you that crossing over would be ... uncomfortable. Of course there was physical pain. Illusory though it may have been, I know it seems very real in the moment. But it is for the good of science. We're pioneering a new frontier. I'm enclosing a key, so that you might return to the lab at your leisure, as well as a portion of the prototype in hopes that looking upon it might entice you back.

Yours,

The Amputator

Maria Hogan put down the paper, looked at me. I wasn't sure if she was giving me shock, disbelief, or just plain rage. "Well?" she said.

"Totally nuts. I think you need to pack up your stuff and take it over to—"

"No ... No! You're not getting it." She slammed her palm down on the desk. "Even if they did hear me out, they wouldn't believe any of it, which means they won't look in the right places, which means nothing will happen. Which means this bastard"—she waved the paper—"goes free."

"I'm not sure I believe you," I said. "All I know is that several human teeth wedged into a metal harness are lying on my desk. I have half a mind to call the police myself. The D.A. is a close friend of mine, and so are a number of boys on the force."

She sat back, her eyes going cool as she reached into her bag a second time. "Guess I should make this more worth your while, huh?" She dug out her checkbook and pen, leaning on my desk to write, glancing at my nameplate again. She tore off the check.

I took one look and had to light another cigarette. "That's a lot of zeros," I said. "You have this kind of money?"

"My husband does."

"Does he know you're here?"

"What does that matter? He's sunk so far into his morbid funk after what happened to our son that I'm not sure he'll pull out of it. Besides, he knows about the hidden cabin. Jeffrey told us both."

I smoked and sighed and felt like something like a rusty railroad spike was being dug into my side. My salary at the time was measly to say the least, and I'd even had to let my secretary go in order to maintain the business. I desperately needed money.

I thought: What's the worst that can happen? I take the key and rummage around in the Mintano Wilderness, find nothing and come back empty-handed, then tell her I told you so, take the money, and run off to Cancun. Piece of cake.

But, of course, there was the whole conscience thing, not to mention the possibility, be it slight, that she was telling the truth—in which case I could find myself face to face with some psychotic criminal. But even that had its egoistical perks. And it wouldn't be the first time I had squared off against something violent. I'd been in the private investigator business for over eight years, and had seen my share of fights.

I took a long, deep drag on the cigarette and sat back in my chair. "I'll take your case, Mrs. Hogan, but on one condition."

She brightened. "What?"

I flipped the check with my index finger. "I'll be cashing this *before* I get started, which is not my usual policy, but what you're asking for is

119

dangerous, could even get me into trouble with the City if they found out I'm withholding evidence on an open case. That means I'll have to use some of this money to pay off cops and detectives in order to get my hands on the file. Understand?"

She nodded, smiling. She seemed extraordinarily relieved, and I even noticed a portion of her weariness evaporating. "Do what you need to do," she said. "And thank you, Morgan."

"You can thank me once we get through this without landing our balls in the grinder."

She made a face, and I nearly burst out laughing. Leaning farther back, I kicked my boots up on the desk, closed my eyes and smoked, and said in my best Perry Masonesque voice, "Now, Mrs. Hogan, tell me everything you know about the incident involving your son."

I waited in the rain at 10th and 63rd, secreting myself under the awning of an Italian bistro. My long coat was drenched, but I kept wrapping it tighter, hoping to preclude the chill. The cars on 63rd moved spectrally through the mist, flinging water from their tires, their headlights looking like passing souls.

When Detective Browning pulled alongside the curb in his sharp blue Pontiac with the white roof, windshield wipers flapping, I pushed through the rain and slipped in the passenger door.

"Summers," he said.

"Howdy, Robert." I took this opportunity of dryness to light a cigarette. Smoke filled the cab, but I knew Rob didn't care—he customarily chuffed cigars in the damn thing.

"I'm going 'round the block," he commented.

"Why?"

He said nothing, but piloted the Pontiac into the storm of souls. He was a larger man, nearly twice my size, with rubbery skin and a face like a grizzly bear. His meaty forearms, poking out the sleeves of his coat, bristled with black hairs, and his muscles tightened as he manipulated the wheel.

I had expected him to hand over the file, for me to pay, and then to be on our ways. It was how things had worked in the past. But now he was weaving through city blocks sluiced with rain, and there was something tense about him.

I chose not to speak until we reached our final destination: a nondescript alley behind this Chinese restaurant I'd been meaning to try. I thought of having lunch there and taking a cab back to my car.

"What's with the secrecy?" I asked. Rain drummed on the roof of the car. "It's not like we haven't done this before."

He shifted his bulky weight and the Pontiac squeaked on its axles. His weary brown eyes observed me. "This one's different, Summers," he said. "Not to say it's high priority, but just that it's ... different. Which is strange because nobody even died. Yeah, some eleven-year-old kid got assaulted, but last week we found a teenage girl in the dumpster with a hot curling iron shoved up her—and you don't hear diddly about that."

I grimaced. "Jesus."

He waited, took a deep breath, and then continued: "Yeah. Well, this Hogan case's got some weird vibes about it. Everyone down at the station is going bonkers. But there ain't a thing to go off of, so they're all staying away from it. Not to mention the Jeffrey kid is completely nuts now, and his folks are right up there with him. Plus the media's been all over it, don't ask me why. There are even rumors of one of those *Unsolved Mysteries* shows running a spot on it. Christ, and because of this brouhaha, the chief and other detectives, not including myself, are hell bent on getting it solved, or at least putting it down to rest. Yet they won't touch it! I think they just wanna believe the Hogan kid sheared his own tongue with a pair of scissors and knocked his teeth out with a rock. Meh. Who knows what really happened."

He was silent. The back door of the Chinese restaurant opened and a thin Asian man dressed in white, carrying a trash bag, moved past the Pontiac. He glanced at us, knit his brows, then continued walking.

Rob grunted, withdrew a sealed manila folder from his coat. He smiled, showing coffee-stained teeth. "Thanks for letting me bitch."

I took the folder. "Don't mention it. And thank you." I handed him the envelope containing his payment.

He nodded, disappeared it into his coat, but he still seemed worried.

"Listen," I said. "The worst that can happen is we get caught, at which point I'll contact the Chief Deputy District Attorney myself and get things straightened out. Howels and I go way back, so don't fret.

Everything's gonna be okay."

This placated him. He smiled and nodded again. "Want a lift back?"

"Nah, I've been wanting to try this place." I hooked a finger toward the restaurant and got the passenger door open. The sound of rain emerged like a roaring beast. I flicked the last of my smoke into its gullet.

As I closed the door, he said, "Hey, Summers?"

I peeked my head back into the cab.

"Take care on this one. Something different about it. Got some bad vibes. I'd hate for *either* of us to get in trouble."

I nodded, thanked him again, closed the door, and watched him coast away. Then I went into the restaurant and ordered egg foo yung.

Later, back at my apartment, I uncorked a bottle of merlot and sat at my kitchen table under the harsh glare of the fluorescents and sipped, smoked, read. Inside the case file there were several stacks of photographs, the police reports, medical reports, some statements given by neighbors and the boy's parents.

I read through everything, fueled by the wine and the increasing darkness outside the window. The medical reports I found significantly disturbing. The doctors were baffled as to *how* Jeffrey Hogan's teeth and tongue had been removed, with not a single tear appearing in the flesh or gums of his mouth. There were no signs of trauma, which there would've been if the tongue had been yanked out. It had been removed cleanly, as if by a master surgeon.

The photos mostly showed long swaths of empty wilderness and rows of standing pines. One showed the disgusting puddle of excrement in which the boy had been found. Various photos documented the extent of his wounds, some grisly close-up shots of the severed tongue and the vacant teeth.

Finally—having pushed through innumerable chills and waves of unease—I got around to the statements given by the parents. Maria Hogan seemed the most adamant on the subject. Her statements made up seventy-five percent of the report. She went into explicit detail about several previous incidents in which Jeffrey had had unusual experiences in the woods.

The officer conducting the interview had jotted in his notes that Mrs. Hogan "appeared slightly unnerved, and although her story seemed fabricated, there was an aspect of sincerity about her. She believed she was telling the truth."

The first time Jeffrey claimed to hear sounds and see lights coming from the Mintano Wilderness was a year or two before the incident. According to Mrs. Hogan, he had been in the backyard playing in the grass for most of the evening while she had been washing dishes and cleaning the kitchen. At one point, she glanced out the window and didn't see him, but figured he was merely playing around the side of the house.

Later, he came in the back door looking pale and shivering with fright. When asked about it, he claimed he had followed some "whirling machine man" into the woods, where he saw a ghost weaving in and out of the branches.

Maria, disturbed, put her son to bed, thinking he was coming down with something. Over the next year, however, Jeffrey claimed again to have contact with a "whirling machine man" and to have seen more spirits or ghosts in the trees. Maria grew unsettled, but when he came with his story a third time, she started to think it was merely his imagination, that he was playing a child's game.

The boy's father, Henry Hogan, when told of Jeffrey's claims, dismissed them as mere imaginings and told his wife not to worry about it. His statement in the report consisted of two meager paragraphs in which he stuck to his belief that the boy had imagined it. He felt, begrudgingly, that Jeffrey had somehow done it to himself—though why and for what purpose, he had no idea.

In the final incident leading up to the terrible night when Jeffrey lost his tongue and teeth, as reported by Maria Hogan, Jeffrey didn't show up for dinner. Maria was alone in the house; her husband had been working late at the office. Placing Henry's plate in the oven to keep warm, she stuck her head out the window and hollered for Jeffrey. When he didn't come, she put on her coat and went outside.

She'd only gone a dozen feet into the trees when she became enshrouded in a light mist, such as forms after a heavy rain. She pierced through the mist and found her son kneeling on the spongy forest floor, his hands clasped before his chest in prayer. A bulky shape crouched on a network of roots before him. At first, in her fanciful mind, the thing was a goblin or a squatting gnome. But, as she got closer, she saw that it was a conglomeration of metal slabs leaning around a thick wooden pole, with a series of old tubing hooked one to the other. Draped over this bizarre pile of junk was something long and stringy that resembled human hair.

She touched her son on the shoulder. He opened his eyes. He was shivering. When she asked him what he was doing, he pointed toward the junk pile and said he was speaking with the machine man, who had showed him the "hidden cabin" in the woods.

Unnerved, she picked him up off the ground and led him back through the mist, through the backyard, and back into the house, seating him at the dinner table. They spoke no more. When Jeffrey's father came home and Maria told him what happened, Henry said that the boy had probably assembled the old junk to play with. But he agreed it wasn't safe, and assured her he would get rid of it in the morning.

However, when morning came, he searched the forest and found no sign of the junk heap. Maria even led him to the exact spot, but they found only an empty space on the roots. They told Jeffrey he wasn't allowed to play in the Mintano Wilderness anymore, and Jeffrey accepted this new limitation agreeably. But, one week later, they woke to find him submerged in his own feces on the kitchen floor, with a hole in the center of his face.

I had reached my limit at this point and put the file down, lit a fresh cigarette, and poured another glass of wine. Glancing at my wrist watch, I saw it was nearly midnight. The city lights twinkled in the darkness through my fourth-floor apartment window. I thought of what I had read, recalling the grisly photos and the "machine man." My thoughts then wandered to the letter Mrs. Hogan had showed me, an absurd item signed by someone calling himself "The Amputator." I shook my head and blew smoke—it all seemed crazy.

Reaching into my pocket, I took out the small antique key Maria had given me—the key to the lab, according to the letter which had been left on her porch. Luckily, Mrs. Hogan had agreed to keep the strange metal piece with the human teeth wedged into it. I wasn't able to have something like that in my house. Yet, I stared at the key for a long time, wondering where it came from.

I called it quits and retired to bed, but I couldn't fall asleep. I kept seeing visions from the case file—the junk heap, the swirling mist, the lights in the woods, the empty cavities where teeth should have been.

Eventually I dozed off, but the sleep was poor due to nightmares. I awoke in the middle of the night to a scratching sound coming from the wall. I sat up in the darkness, trying to *unhear* the sound, convinced it was some mental remnant from my nightmare. When it didn't stop, I got out of bed and flipped on the light.

The sound came from the opposite side of the west wall. Mine was the final-most apartment on the fourth floor, which meant that, unless it was a bird, the sound-maker was hovering in midair or perched precariously on the building ledge.

I moved closer, saw that the scraping was accompanied by an indentation that moved correspondingly along the wall, as if something on the other side was *digging* through the bricks and plaster, the sharp tip poking through to this side into my room. Of course that was ludicrous. Still, I watched in awe as the impressing groove moved up and down the wall, scribbling like a pen.

After several minutes of watching, the sound stopped, and I stood staring at the words etched onto my wall.

The Amputator

I tried blinking them away, but they wouldn't vanish. At length, I grabbed my blanket and pillow and went into the living room, turning on the TV and the lights, smoking and drinking more wine until I fell back asleep. This time, sleep was dreamless, and in the morning the words on my bedroom wall had disappeared.

I called Maria Hogan.

"Mrs. Hogan? Morgan. I finished reading your son's case file."

"And?"

"And ... I'm starting to think maybe you're telling the truth."

A pause, then a sigh. "That's a relief. So you'll go?"

I knew what she meant. She meant go into the Mintano Wilderness and search for this lab mentioned by The Amputator in his letter.

"I'll go," I said. "But first I'd like to speak to your husband."

"No. He doesn't know about the letter."

"Can't we inform him?"

"I'd rather not. He seems so fragile lately. His belief that Jeffrey did this to himself is the only thing keeping him sane."

"I'd like us all to be in on this."

A longer pause this time. "Okay, he's here right now. I'll go and tell him, if you want to stop by."

"I'll be right there."

She gave me the directions and then I hung up the phone. I donned my coat and pistol and thrummed down the stairs, out into the overcast morning.

Henry Hogan sat in the armchair in his living room, staring out the window toward the dirt road leading to the highway, which I had piloted my Honda Civic up not five minutes before. He held a coffee mug and had a section of the newspaper spread on his lap. He wasn't reading or drinking, just staring straight ahead.

When Mrs. Hogan had answered the door, she invited me in and then leaned her blond head beside my ear. "It wasn't easy, but I told him," she whispered. "I showed him this, too." She held out the metal piece with the teeth wedged into it.

I walked over to the armchair. "Mr. Hogan? I'm Morgan Summers. You're wife hired me to—"

"I know why she hired you." His voice was gruff. When he flicked his eyes at me, they appeared weary and drawn. "Don't expect to find anything. There's nothing there. She made it all up. No hidden cabin, no laboratory. Jeffrey went nutso, plain and simple. The rest, well ... mothers get awfully attached to their children."

"Stop being a jerk!" Maria snapped.

Henry sighed and his whole body seemed to deflate in the dirt brown suit he was wearing. He looked so small, so defeated to me, shrunken, like a sailor drowning at sea, going down with his ship. I

126

immediately understood there was nothing to be gained by speaking with him.

"All the same," I said, cultivating my most neutral, most tension-dissolving voice. "Since she did hire me, I'm going to have a look behind your home."

"Cops been all through there," he muttered. "You won't find nothing."

I didn't deign to respond to him. I simply bowed slightly, and then turned and headed over to Maria. She looked on edge, arms crossed, chewing on her lip. "Satisfied now?" she said.

"I am actually, thank you. I'd like to see the spot."

She nodded and led me through a narrow hallway lined with framed photographs, which I glanced at as we passed, catching Jeffrey's baby-blue eyes staring back at me.

"We found him here," she said as we entered the sizable kitchen. The floors were smooth and made of wood; a kitchen island encompassed the center of the room; the countertops, fridge, and sink were all made of stainless steel; and several rows of oak cupboards adorned the wall.

Next to where Mrs. Hogan stood, a dark spot about four feet in diameter stained the floor. I recalled from the case file that Jeffrey had sat in a puddle of his own excrement all night. I was slightly nauseated. "What exactly is that stain?" I asked. "Is it …?"

"Most of it," she said. "Blood, too. And something else, something the investigators said they're unsure of—add that to a hundred other things they're unsure of." The bitterness of her tone cut into the kitchen air. "They said it would come out, but it didn't. And no matter how much I scrub and mop, the stain remains. I've given up."

I then told her I was ready to go into the Mintano Wilderness. She nodded and I followed her through the adjacent back door. The wall of trees and bushes seemed to rear itself forward right up to the back of the house. The density of the foliage was astounding, like an encroaching tsunami of leaves and branches that was going to crash into the porch at any second.

"Jesus," I said. I reached into my pocket to retrieve my pack of cigarettes.

"The City has made a significant effort to preserve this section of the Mintano Wilderness. All the houses in this area border it. I believe there's a bike path winding through it, several hiking trails ... the rest is feral nature."

"Amazing," I said. And I meant it.

She turned and started toward the house. "Guess I'll leave you to it." She stopped on her way, glancing at my cigarette. "Make sure you dispose of that properly."

I nodded. "You got it, ma'am."

She started walking, and then stopped again. "Thank you, Morgan. My husband ... he ..."

"It's okay," I said. "I understand this has been hard on both of you. Besides, I'm doing my job, and ..." I suddenly recalled the scratching sounds of the previous night, and the pair of words that had magically appeared on my bedroom wall. "I have my own reasons for checking this out."

"Oh?" There was a pause, and I knew she wanted to ask what they were. But instead, I just turned and headed across the grass, denying her the opportunity. In no time, I had been swallowed by the darkening wilds.

When I came across the first letter—the *A*—I gazed long at it, questioning the reliability of my physical senses. I did drink and smoke a lot. But by the time I spotted the lowercase *R* on the oak trunk—the collection of the seven letters coalescing into the word *Amputator*—I was pretty much convinced I was crazy.

I stayed for a while with the R letter, leaning against the tree. I smoked a cigarette or two, making sure to bury the butts properly. Finally, I summoned the nerve to continue, telling myself I had to play out this movie to the end.

I hadn't gone more than twenty paces when the mist appeared, the air hanging beneath the branches swirling and churning. I was soon meandering in the thick of it, groping blindly, certain I was getting increasingly lost.

The mist grew thicker and I saw shapes materialize out of the softly swirling gas. Abstractly humanoid, they bent through the network of branches, weaving in and out of the treetops, bodies elongating and stretching like taffy, and then shrinking down to their original size.

I stopped to admire the apparitions—ghosts, spirits, whatever they were—magical with their yawning mouths and hollow eyes. I felt a storm of emotions rising within me, admonishing me to release whatever resistance I was harboring as to whether or not this was real—to just accept it.

I forged ahead through the bluish mist, like some kind of hero from a fantasy novel. The spirits of the dead drifted around me until, at last, I spotted the ominous cabin in the distance. I climbed the series of terraces leading to the grassy eminence and headed for the front porch.

It wasn't very large, about the size of any other cabin you might find in the woods. Except that it was only one story, which seemed odd, especially since this person—The Amputator—was supposedly conducting full-scale scientific experiments in there.

I drew my pistol. The weight of it, the cold of the steel, felt good, comforting. Each step had me sinking a little more into the soft, mulchy loam. The porch boards creaked and crumbled beneath my feet, and I glanced behind me and noticed the mist had stayed back in the trees. I was grateful.

I felt in my pocket for the key. Was I just going to walk in the front door? Perhaps a little audacious, so I did a quick beat around the perimeter, searching for other doors and openings. Finding none—only more darkened windows, begrimed to the point of opaqueness—I returned to the front, withdrew the key, and approached the door. Unlocking it, I pushed the door creakingly open and gripped the handle of my pistol as I entered.

I immediately cursed myself for not bringing a flashlight. The darkness was so thick that I could only see the faint outlines of objects and the dim wood surfaces of walls. The further I went into the cabin, the greater my fear became. My breathing accelerated, my heart pounded like a hammer, and I began to sweat.

I emerged from the hallway into a spacious room. My eyes adjusted to the dark and I could see hulking mounds all along the floor that I presumed were pieces of furniture—a mirror, reflecting back the silvery blackness; even gossamer webs clinging to the higher corners and ceiling.

In the center stood another large shape, still as lake water on a windless day. I approached with my fingers raised and extended. I felt drawn to it, and when I got close enough, I touched the surface, which was cold and hard, like touching the skin of a reptile. As I moved my fingers higher, I felt harder surfaces—most likely metal, as well as rubber tubing and looping chains—and higher still, I felt something like stringy human hair. Suddenly, I knew this was the strange "machine man" before which Jeffrey Hogan had been found kneeling. As my fingers neared the top, I somehow sensed it was going to move. In a panic, I raised the pistol.

It came jerking to life with a tremendous burst of motion that swept the darkness along with it. I dashed to my left, back around, and then whirled, flailing the pistol butt. The machine man was quicker. It resembled some kind of idol or tribal totem pole as it danced around me like the Tasmanian Devil of cartoons. A dark hunk arced out and down from the top of the pole, crashing onto my head with the weight of a tree branch. I screamed as it crushed me to the floor—then I was hit again, and my vision dimmed. I felt myself hurled into a place of emptiness.

Then the world abruptly winked out.

When I came to, dreamy, gauzy ribbons of blue and white, like the auras of planets, swam before my eyes. My body weighed a thousand pounds. I attempted to move my limbs but was met with strong resistance. And something else ... some foreign metallic element that was connected to me, that permeated whatever parts of my organism I could still register.

I managed to re-illuminate the world through the faculty of sight. Darkness and blues and whites bled away. I saw that I was strapped with metal bands into a corrupt wood chair, like an antiquated electric chair. The room around me was crowded with huge pieces of buzzing, bulky scientific equipment, which my fuzzed-out mind could only begin to comprehend. Lights, computer monitors, keyboards, EKG readouts.

"You're not the boy," said a voice. "But you will have to do."

It was not a pleasant voice.

I blinked again and saw a grotesque being standing over me. I knew at once it was The Amputator. He was tall, lanky, and wiry like a weasel, with beady eyes and a scraggly beard. He wore a stained white lab coat; greasy spectacles clutched his face. Behind him was a storm of misty spirits, like those I had encountered in the Mintano Wilderness.

"How do you feel?" he said.

"I—" But I could not speak. I felt crazy, delusional, nothing made sense anymore.

"Speechless," The Amputator murmured. He eyed me suspiciously. I didn't like the intent of his gaze—it was as if a giant rat was considering whether or not I'd make a good meal.

"The left side of his brain has been successfully quarantined," he continued. He turned to his right, speaking to someone in the darkness. "Bring me the mediumistic rod."

The furious totem-pole machine man came whirling into view. The shock of seeing it this close up and under the harsh yellow lights sent me into convulsions. My soul felt like it was going to jump out of my flesh.

The Amputator accepted a long copper rod from the automaton, that terrible assembly of wire and tubing and metal with a flat head of long, dark, horse-like hair. As it spun away into the blackness, I thought of Robby the Robot, a fictional character from a movie I'd seen as a child called *Forbidden Planet*. The bulbous, robotic humanoid machine in that movie scared the pants off me as a child. Seeing this weird totem thing now recovered the same childhood fear.

The Amputator leaned over my right side. As I followed him down with my eyes, I began to scream, and my hoarse cries echoed about the room. My body shook and sweat saturated my brow. I was convinced I was dying—had died—*would* die.

"Calm yourself," The Amputator said.

But I couldn't. Where my arm used to be now extended a bloody metal appendage, looped with silvery wires and colorful blinking lights. It pulsed inwardly with a glowing orange fire, as though it had a heartbeat. The fibrous metal materials of which it was composed stretched up to my right bicep, where the sleeve of my shirt had been cut away. The appendage itself was neatly *squashed* into the flesh of my arm.

I thought I would never stop screaming.

Very carefully, he placed the rod in my hand, and the fingers closed of their own accord, clutching it like a baton. The Amputator moved aside, and the misty wall of spirits moved forward.

Without warning, the metal bands retracted with a snap and I was free. Yet, suddenly, I was yanked forward by the metallic arm which was now flailing and jerking, swinging the copper rod like a conducting baton. My teeth clenched and sweat poured down in my eyes. I was nearly blind as my feet, led by the insane metal arm, drew me out of the chair.

I began walking across the floor, while the swelling blue orb of spirits moved closer. The Amputator tracked my progress, a greedy little figure at my right. Opposite him spun the madly whirling totem, which, I now realized, was functioning as his assistant.

"It's working!" he cried. "They are bending to his will! Embrace them, you fool! Embrace them!" He slapped me on the back, hard, and I pitched forward, almost falling onto my face.

Abruptly, the wall of spirits was before me, flowing around me, enveloping me, pressing close. I could make out their hollow eyes and gaping mouths as they darted about like guppies in a fish bowl. I sensed music from somewhere, a simple melody, but soon I was blind and lost, the laboratory obscured in the churning blue cloud.

The Amputator's voice rose above the madness. "Do not fight it! Open yourself up to the experience—for the good of science! The body enhancement I implanted in you will *bind* you to them, so long as you do not resist. Let go, let them ferry you away!"

I almost laughed, for I was well beyond fighting, resisting, or anything else. I'd collapsed inwardly into a state of true madness. I saw only the misty spirit storm and furious thrashings of my metallic arm, and I heard only the weird discordant music and the excited ravings of The Amputator.

"Into the higher spiritual worlds!" he shouted. "Go! Let yourself dissolve into the ether!"

I felt so sick I thought I would faint. But, just at the last moment before I went down, I felt a flurry of spongy limbs, like tongues, gather me up, lift me. The sensation was something quite magical, an inner burning of faith, desire, devotion, longing—as though I were caught in religious reverie.

I evaporated into the ether.

I saw a flash of a world made of pure light, where I could make sense of nothing. But this was swiftly taken away and then I was lying under some trees behind the Hogan house, sprawled in the dirt, my arm bleeding.

I opened my eyes and moaned, when suddenly I was whisked away again and given a glimpse of myself lying face down on the sidewalk in the city with blood oozing from my arm, a shocked group of civilians standing around me.

Then sirens, visibar lights, stomping boots, and someone giving orders, then a gurney ride, an ambulance, then white walls, white coats, white doctors, and white nurses.

My next memory was of Detective Browning standing beside my hospital bed, questioning me about my experience in the Mintano Wilderness. I told him everything. And so he looked at me like I was nutso, but said he would be the one handling my case, so not to worry. He would check things out.

Meanwhile, he told me to take care of myself.

As he turned and vanished through the doorway, replaced by a dutiful nurse, I let my eyes sink closed, let my heart follow, and then descended into a deep, deep, dreamless sleep.

About a month or so after things died down, I was able to leave the hospital and return to my job and my office. Maria Hogan stopped by to see me. She apologized for getting me involved in this mess, and said she hoped I wouldn't end up like her son.

I assured her that I wouldn't.

She seemed very happy that I, too, had experienced whatever it was that lurked behind her house. She said it made her feel less crazy. Nonetheless, she and her husband were planning on moving soon. I told her that was a good idea.

She offered to pay me more money, even though I hadn't necessarily satisfied her or conclusively solved her son's case. I had satisfied some things. My missing arm was testament to that.

I accepted the money without hesitation.

The police, led by Detective Browning and backed by Chief Deputy District Attorney Howels Wates, combed the Mintano Wilderness repeatedly again, exhausting a ton of resources, but they never found the hidden cabin. They never found The Amputator, either. Because of this, my credibility as a professional—hell, as a *sane human being*—went down the tubes. People gradually stopped talking to me, stopped seeking me out. I lost my law enforcement connections.

This wasn't the only reason I resigned from P.I. work, but it certainly added to the load. I closed down my office, packed up my things, and retreated to my apartment. Several months later, I came on at the Department of Motor Vehicles and have been there ever since.

At the start of this, I spoke of needing safety after my experiences, which I have obtained. But, the absence of my right arm is a constant reminder of those things under the veil of reality that I would like to forget. Perhaps if I save up the money to acquire a prosthetic limb, that will serve to complete my forgetting process. Although, even then I fear the name of that terrible, unknowable entity will remain etched onto the fabric of my consciousness, as it was once etched fleetingly, supernaturally, and indescribably on my bedroom wall ...

The Amputator

SEX OBJECT

BY GRAHAM MASTERTON

She sat against the foggy afternoon light, perched straight-backed on the black Swedish chair, her ankles crossed. She wore a perfectly tailored Karl Lagerfeld suit and a black straw hat and her legs were perfect, too.

Dr. Arcolio couldn't see her face clearly because of the light behind her. But her voice was enough to tell him that she was desperate, in the way that only the wives of very, very rich men are capable of being desperate.

The wives of ordinary men would never think about such things, let alone get desperate about them.

She said, "My hairdresser told me that you were the best."

Dr. Arcolio steepled his hands. He was bald, dark, and swarthy, and his hands were very hairy. "Your hairdresser?" he echoed.

"John Sant'Angelo ... he has a friend who wanted to make the change."

"I see."

She was nervy, vibrant, like an expensive racehorse. "The thing was ... he said that you could do it very differently from all the rest ... that you could make it real. He said that you could make it *feel* real. With real responses, everything."

135

Dr. Arcolio thought about that and then nodded. "This is absolutely true. But then I'm dealing with *transplants*, you understand, rather than modifications of existing tissue. It's just like heart or kidney surgery. We have to find a donor part and then insert that donor part and hope that there's no rejection."

"But if you found a donor ... you could do it for me?"

Dr. Arcolio stood up and paced slowly around his office. He was a very short man, not more than five-foot-five, but he had a calmness and a presence that made him both fascinating to watch and impressive to listen to. He was dressed very formally, in a three-piece chalk-stripe suit, with a white carnation in the buttonhole and very highly polished oxfords.

He crossed to the window and drew back the curtains and stood for a long while staring down at Brookline Place. It hadn't rained for nearly seven weeks now, and the sky over Boston was an odd bronze color.

"You realize that what you're asking me to do is very questionable, both medically and morally."

"Why?" she retorted. "It's something I want. It's something I *need*."

"But Mrs. Ellis, the operations I perform are normally to correct a physical situation that is chronically out of tune with my patients' emotional state. I deal with transsexuals, Mrs. Ellis, men who have penises and testes but who are psychologically women. When I remove their male genitalia and give them female genitalia instead ... I am simply changing their bodies in line with their minds. In *your* case, however—"

"In my case, Doctor, I'm thirty-one years old, I have a husband who is wealthier than anybody in the entire state of Massachusetts, and if I don't have this operation then I will probably lose both him and everything I've ever dreamed of. Don't you think that falls into exactly the same category as your transsexuals? In fact, don't you think my need is greater than some of your men who want to turn into women simply because they like to wear high heels and garter belts and panties by Frederick's of Hollywood?"

Dr. Arcolio smiled. "Mrs. Ellis ... I'm a surgeon. I perform operations to rescue people from deep psychological misery. I have to abide by certain strictly defined ethics."

"Dr. Arcolio, I am suffering from deep psychological misery. My husband is showing every sign of being bored with me in bed and, since I'm his fifth wife, I think the odds of him divorcing me are growing steadily by the minute, don't you?"

"But what you're asking—it's so radical. It's *more* than radical. And permanent, too. And have you considered that it will disfigure you, as a woman?"

Mrs. Ellis opened her black alligator pocketbook and took out a black cigarette, which she lit with a black enameled Dunhill lighter. She pecked, sucked, blew smoke. "Do you want me to be totally candid with you?" she asked.

"I think I *insist* on your being totally candid with me."

"In that case, you ought to know that Bradley has a real thing for group sex ... for inviting his pals to make love to me, too. Last week, after that charity ballet at Great Woods, he invited seven of them back to the house. Seven well-oiled Back Bay plutocrats! He told me to go get undressed while they had martinis in the library. Then afterward they came upstairs, all seven of them."

Dr. Arcolio was examining his framed certificate from Brigham and Women's Hospital as if he had never seen it before. His heart was beating quickly; he didn't know why. Wolff-Parkinson-White syndrome? Or atrial fibrillation? Or maybe fear, with a subtle seasoning of sexual arousal? He said, as flatly as he could manage, "When I said candid ... well, you don't have to tell me any of this. If I *do* decide to go ahead with such an operation, it will only be on the independent recommendations of your family doctor and your psychiatrist."

Mrs. Ellis carried on with her narrative regardless. "They climbed on top of me and all around me, all seven of them. I felt like I was suffocating in sweaty male flesh. Bradley penetrated me from behind; George Cartin penetrated me from the front. Two of them pushed themselves into my mouth, until I felt that I was choking. Two forced their penises into my ears. The other two rubbed themselves on my breasts.

"They got themselves a rhythm going like an Ivy League rowing team. They were roaring with every stroke. *Roaring.* I was like nothing at all, in the middle of all this roaring and rowing. Then the two of them climaxed into my mouth, and the other two into my ears, and the next two over my breasts. Bradley was the last. But when he was finished, and pulled himself out of me, I was dripping with semen, all over me, dripping; and it was then that I knew that Bradley wanted an object—not a wife, not even a lover. An *object*.

Dr. Arcolio said nothing. He glanced at Mrs. Ellis, but Mrs. Ellis's face was concealed behind a sloping eddy of cigarette smoke.

"Bradley wants a sex object. So I've decided that, if he wants a sex object, I'll *be* a sex object. What difference will it make? Except that Bradley will be happy with me and life will stay the same." She gave a laugh like a breaking champagne glass. "Rich, pampered, secure. And nobody needs to *know*."

Dr. Arcolio said, "I can't do it. It's out of the question."

"Yes," Mrs. Ellis replied. "I knew you'd say that. I came prepared."

"Prepared?" Dr. Arcolio frowned.

"Prepared with evidence of three genital transplants that you performed without the permission of the donors' executors. Jane Kestenbaum, August 12, 2007; Lydia Zerbey, February 9, 2008; Catherine Stimmell, June 7, 2008. All three had agreed to be liver, kidney, heart, eye, and lung donors. Not one of them had agreed to have their genitalia removed."

She coughed. "I have all of the particulars, all of the records. You carried out the first two operations at the Brookline Clinic, under the pretense of treating testicular cancer, and the third operation at Lowell Medical Center, on the pretext of correcting a double hernia."

"Well, well," said Dr. Arcolio. "This must be the first time that a patient has *blackmailed* me into carrying out an operation."

Mrs. Ellis stood up. The light suddenly suffused her face. She was spectacularly beautiful, with high Garboesque cheekbones, a straight nose, and a mouth that looked as if it were just about to kiss somebody. Her eyes were blue as sapphires, crushed underfoot. To think that a woman who looked like this was begging him to operate on her, *bullying* him into operating on her, was something that Dr. Arcolio found incredible, even frightening.

"I can't do it," he repeated.

"Oh, no, Dr. Arcolio. You *will do* it. Because if you don't, all of the details of your nefarious operations will go directly to the district attorney's office, and then you will go directly to jail. And with you locked up, think of all those transsexual men who are going to languish in deep psychological misery, burdened with a body that is so chronically out of tune with their minds."

"Mrs. Ellis—"

She stepped forward. She was threateningly graceful, and nearly five inches taller than he was, in her grey high heels. She smelled of cigarettes and Chanel No. 5. She was long-legged, and surprisingly large-breasted, although her suit was cut so well that her bosom didn't seem out of proportion. Her earrings were platinum, by Guerdier.

"Doctor," she said, and for the first time he detected the slight Nebraska drawl in her undertones, "I need this life. In order to keep this life, I need this operation. If you don't do it for me, then so help me, I'll ruin you, I promise."

Dr. Arcolio looked down at his desk diary. It told him, in his own neat writing, that Mrs. Helen Ellis had an appointment at 3:45. God, how he wished that he hadn't accepted it.

He said, quietly, "You'll have to make three guarantees. One is that you're available to come to my clinic on Kirkland Street in Cambridge at an hour's notice. The second is that you tell absolutely nobody apart from your husband who undertook the surgery for you."

"And the third?"

"The third is that you pay me a half-million dollars in negotiable bonds as soon as possible, and a further half-million when the operation is successfully completed."

Mrs. Ellis nodded the slightest of nods.

Dr. Arcolio said, "That's agreed, then. Christ. I don't know who's the crazier, you or me."

In the dead of February, Helen Ellis was lunching at Jasper's on Commercial Street with her friend, Nancy Pettigrew, when the maitre d' came over and murmured in her ear that there was a telephone call for her.

She had just been served a plateful of nine Wellfleet littlenecks with radish-chili salsa and a glass of chilled champagne.

"Oh ... whoever it is, tell them I'll call back after lunch, would you?"

"Your caller said it was very urgent, Mrs. Ellis."

Nancy laughed. "It isn't your secret lover, is it, Helen?"

The maitre d' said, soberly, "The gentleman said that time was of the essence."

Helen slowly lowered her fork.

Nancy frowned at her and said, "Helen? Are you all *right?* You've gone white as a sheet."

The maitre d' pulled out Helen's chair for her and escorted her across the restaurant to the phone booth. Helen picked up the receiver and said, "Helen Ellis here," in a voice as transparent as mineral water.

"*I have a donor,*" said Dr. Arcolio. "*The tissue match is spot-on. Do you still want to go through with it?*"

Helen swallowed. "Yes. I still want to go through with it."

"*In that case, come immediately to Cambridge. Have you eaten anything or drunk anything?*"

"I was just about to have lunch. I ate a little bread."

"*Don't eat or drink anymore. Come at once. The sooner you get here, the greater the chance of success.*"

"All right," Helen agreed. Then, "Who was she?"

"*Who was who?*"

"The donor. Who was she? How did she die?"

"*It's not important for you to know that. In fact, it's better psychologically if you don't.*"

"Very well," said Helen. "I can be there in twenty minutes."

She returned to her table. "Nancy, I'm so sorry ... I have to leave right now."

"When we're just about to start lunch? What's happened?"

"I can't tell you, I'm sorry."

"I knew it," said Nancy, tossing down her napkin. "It *is* a lover."

"Let me explain what I have been able to do," said Dr. Arcolio.

It was nearly two months later, the first week in April. Helen was sitting in the white-tiled conservatory of their Dedham-style mansion on the Charles River, on a white wickerwork daybed heaped with embroidered cushions. The conservatory was crowded with daffodils. Outside, however, it was still very cold. The sky above the glass cupola was the color of rain-washed writing ink, and there was a parallelogram of white frost on the lawns where the sun had not yet appeared around the side of the house.

"In your usual run-of-the-mill transsexual operation, the testes are removed, and also the erectile tissue of the penis. The external skin of the penis is then folded back into the body cavity in a kind of rolled-up tube, creating an artificial vagina. But, of course, it *is* artificial, and very unsatisfactory in many ways, particularly in its lack of full erotic response.

"What *I* can do is give my patients a *real* vagina. I can remove from a donor body the entire vulva, including the muscles and erectile tissue that surround it, as well as the vaginal barrel. I can then transplant them onto and *into* the recipient patient.

"Then, by using microsurgery techniques that I helped to develop at MIT, all of the major nerve fibers can be 'wired into' the recipient patient's central nervous system ... so that the vagina and clitoris are just as capable of erotic arousal as they were within the body of the donor."

"I've been too sore to feel any arousal," said Helen, with a tight, slanted smile.

"I know. But it won't be long. You're making excellent progress."

"Do you think I'm really crazy?" asked Helen.

"I don't know. It depends what your goals are."

"My goals are to keep this lifestyle which you see all around you."

"Well," said Dr. Arcolio, "I think you'll probably succeed. From what he's been saying, your husband can't wait for you to be fit for lovemaking again."

Helen said, "I'm sorry I made you betray your ethics."

Dr. Arcolio shrugged. "It's a little late for that. And I have to admit that I'm really quite proud of what I've been able to achieve."

Helen rang the small silver bell on the table beside her. "You'll have some champagne, then, Baron Frankenstein?"

On the second Friday in May, she came into the gloomy, high-ceilinged library where Bradley was working and posed in the center of the room. It was the first time that she had ever walked into the library without knocking first. She wore a long scarlet silk robe, trimmed with

scarlet lace, and scarlet stiletto shoes. Her hair was softly curled and tied up with a scarlet ribbon.

She stood there with her blue eyes just a little misted and the faintest of smiles on her lips, her left hand on her hip in a subtle parody of a hooker waiting for a curb-crawler.

"Well?" she asked. "It's four o'clock. Way past your bedtime."

Of course Bradley had known all along that she was standing there, and even though he was frowning intently at the land-possession documents in his hands, he wasn't able to decipher a single word. At last he looked up, tried to speak, coughed, and cleared his throat.

"Is it ready?" he managed to ask at last.

"*It?*" she queried. She had a new-found confidence. For the first time in a long time, she had something that Bradley seriously desired.

"I mean, are *you* ready?" he corrected himself. He stood up. He was a heavily built, broad-shouldered man of fifty-five. He was silver-haired, with a leonine head that would have looked handsome as a piece of garden statuary. He was one of the original Boston Ellises—shipping magnates, landowners, newspaper publishers—and now the largest single broker of laser technology in the Western world.

He slowly approached her. He wore a blue-and-white-striped cotton shirt, pleated blue slacks, and fancy maroon suspenders. It was a look that the Ellises cherished: the look of a hands-on newspaper publisher, or a wheeler and dealer in smoke-filled rooms. It was dated, but it had its own special Bostonian charisma.

"Show me," he said. He spoke in a low, soft rumble. Helen *felt* what he said, rather than heard it. It was like distant thunder approaching.

"In the bedroom," she said. "Not here."

He looked around the library with its shelves of antique leather-bound books and its gloomy paintings of Ellis ancestors. In one corner of the library, close to the window, stood the same flatbed printing press that Bradley's great-great grandfather had used to print the first editions of the *Beacon Hill Messenger.*

"What better place than here?" he wanted to know. She may have had something that he seriously desired, but his wish was still her command.

She let the scarlet silk robe slip from her shoulders and whisper to the floor, where it lay like a shining pool of sudden blood. Underneath, she wore a scarlet quarter-cup bra that lifted and divided her large white breasts but didn't cover them. Her nipples wrinkled as dark pink as raspberries.

But it was the scarlet silk triangle between her legs that kept Bradley's attention riveted. He tugged his necktie loose and opened his collar, and his breathing came harsh and shallow.

"Show me," he repeated.

"You're not frightened?" she asked him. Somehow she sensed that he might be.

He fixed her with a quick, black-eyed stare. "Frightened? What the fuck are you talking about? You may have been the one who suggested it, but I'm the one who paid for it. Show me."

She tugged loose the scarlet string of her panties, and they fell to the floor around her left ankle, a token shackle of discarded silk.

"Jesus," whispered Bradley. "It's fantastic."

Helen had bared her pale, plump-lipped, immaculately waxed sex. But immediately above her own sex was another, just as plump, just as inviting, just as moist. Only an oval scar showed where Dr. Arcolio had sewn it into her lower abdomen, a scar no more disfiguring than a mild first-degree burn.

Eyes wide, speechless, Bradley knelt on the carpet in front of her and placed the palms of his hands against her thighs. He stared at her twin vulvas in ferocious delight.

"It's fantastic. It's *fantastic!* It's the most incredible thing I've ever seen."

He paused and looked up at her, suddenly little-boyish. "Can I touch it? Does it feel just like the other one?"

"Of course you can touch it," said Helen. "You paid for it. It's yours."

Trembling, Bradley stroked the smooth lips of her new sex. "You can feel that? You can really feel it?"

"Of course. It feels good."

He touched her second clitoris, until it began to stiffen. Then he slipped his middle finger into the warm, moist depths of her second vagina.

"It's fantastic. It feels just the same. It's incredible. Jesus! It's incredible!"

He strode to the library door, kicked it shut, and then turned the key. He strode back to the middle of the room, snapping off his suspenders, tearing off his shirt, stumbling out of his pants. By the time he had reached Helen he was naked except for his large striped shorts. He pulled those off, revealing a massive crimson erection.

He pushed her onto the carpet and he thrust himself furiously into her, no preliminaries, no foreplay, just raging, explosive lust. First he pushed himself into her new vagina, then into her own vagina, then into her bottom. He went from one to the other like a starving man who can't choose between meat, bread, and candy.

Frightened at first, taken aback by the fury of his sexual attack, Helen didn't feel anything but friction and spasm. But as Bradley thrust and thrust and grunted with exertion, she began to experience a sensation between her legs that was quite unlike anything that she had ever felt before: a sensation that was doubled in intensity, trebled. A sensation so overwhelming that she gripped the rug with both hands, unsure if the pleasure wasn't going to be too great for her mind to be able to accept. As Bradley plunged into her second vagina again and again, she felt as if she were going to go mad, or die.

Then, like a woman caught swimming in a warm, black tropical swell, she was carried away.

She opened her eyes to hear Bradley on the telephone. He was still naked; his heavy body white and hairy, his penis hanging down like a plum in a sock.

"George? Listen, George, you have to get up here. You have to get up here *now!* It's the most fantastic thing you ever experienced in your life. George, don't argue, just drop everything and get your ass up here as fast as you can. And don't forget your toothbrush: You won't be going home tonight, I promise you!"

Just before dawn, she opened her eyes. She was lying naked in the middle of the emperor-sized bed. On her right side, Bradley was pressed up close to her, snoring heavily, his hand possessively cupping her second sex. On her left side, George Cartin was snoring in a different key, as if he was dreaming, and *his* hand was cupping her original sex. Her bottom felt sore and stretched, and her mouth was dry with that unmistakable arid taste of swallowed semen.

She felt strange; almost as if she were more than one woman. Her second vagina had brought her a curious duality of personality, as well as a duality of body. But she felt more secure. Bradley had told her over and over that she was wonderful, that she was spectacular, and that he would never think of leaving her, ever.

Dr. Arcolio, she thought, you would be proud of me.

Winter again. She met Dr. Arcolio at Hamersley's. Dr. Arcolio had put on a little weight. Helen was thinner, almost gaunt, and she had lost weight off her breasts.

She toyed with a plate of sautéed skate. There were shadows under her eyes the same color as the brown butter.

"What's wrong?" he asked her. He had ordered smoked and grilled game hen with peach chutney and was eating at a furious speed. "You've had no rejection, everything's great."

She put down her fork. "It's not enough," she said, and he heard the same dull note of despair that he had heard when she first consulted him.

"You have two vaginas and it's not enough?" he hissed at her. A bearded man at the next table turned and stared at him in astonishment.

Helen said, "It was wonderful to start with. We made love five or six times a day. He adored it. He made me walk around naked for days on end, so that he could stare at me and put his fingers up me whenever he felt like it. I gave him shows, like erotic performances, with candles and vibrators, and once I did it with his two Great Danes."

Dr. Arcolio swallowed his mouthful with difficulty. "Wow," was all he could say.

There were tears hovering on the edge of Helen's eyes. "I did all of that but it wasn't enough. It just wasn't enough. Now he scarcely

145

bothers anymore. He says we've done everything that we could possibly do. We had an argument last week and he called me a freak."

Dr. Arcolio laid his hand on top of hers, trying to be comforting. "I had a feeling this might happen. I talked to a sex-therapist friend of mine a little while ago. She said that once you start going down this road with human sexuality—once you get into sadomasochism or you start nipple-piercing or labia-piercing or tattooing or any other kind of heavyweight perversion—it becomes an obsession, and you never get satisfied. You start chasing a mirage of ultimate excitement that doesn't exist. Good sex is being exciting with what you've got."

He sat back and fastidiously wiped his mouth with his napkin. "I can have you in for corrective surgery early next week. Fifty thousand in advance, fifty thousand on completion, scarcely any scar."

Helen frowned. "You can get donors that quick?"

"I'm sorry?" said Dr. Arcolio. "You won't need any more donors. We'll simply take out the second vagina and close up."

"Doctor, I believe we're talking at cross-purposes here," Helen told him. "I don't want this second vagina removed. I want two more."

There was a long silence. Dr. Arcolio licked his lips, and then drank a glass of water, and then licked his lips again. "You want *what*, did you say?"

"Two more. You can do it, can't you? One in the lower half of each breast. Bradley will adore it. Then I can have one man in each breast, and three inside, and two in my mouth, and Bradley will adore it."

"You want me to transplant vaginas into your *breasts*? Helen, for God's sake, what I've done already is advanced enough. Not to mention ethically appalling and totally illegal. This time, Helen, no. No way. You can send all of your incriminating particulars about my transsexual surgery to the D.A. or wherever you damn well like. But no. I'm not doing it. Absolutely not."

Bradley's Christmas treat that year was to invite six of his friends for a stag supper. They ate flame-grilled steak, and drank four jugs of dry martinis among them, and then they roared and laughed and tilted into the bedroom, where Helen was waiting for them, naked, not moving.

They took one look at her and they stopped roaring. They approached her in disbelief, and stared at her, and she remained quite still, with everything exposed.

In drunken wide-eyed wonder, two of them clambered astride her. One of them was the president of a Boston savings bank. Helen didn't know the other one, but he had a ginger moustache and ginger hair on his thighs. They took hold of her nipples between finger and thumb and lifted up her heavy breasts, as if they were lifting up dish covers at an expensive restaurant.

"My God," said the president of the savings bank. "It's true. It's fucking true."

With gradually mounting grunts of excitement, the two men pushed their reddened erections deep into the slippery apertures that had opened up beneath Helen's nipples.

They forced themselves deep into her breasts, deep into soft warm tissue, and twisted her nipples until she winced with pain.

Two more crammed themselves into her mouth, so that she could scarcely breathe. But what did it matter? Bradley was whooping with delight, Bradley loved her, Bradley wanted her. Bradley would never grow tired of her now, not after this. And even if he did, she could always find new ways to please him.

He didn't grow tired of her. But then he didn't have very much longer to live. On September 12, two years later, Helen woke up to find that Bradley was lying dead, his cold hand cupping her original vulva.

Bradley was buried in the grounds of the Dedham-style house overlooking the Charles River, in accordance with that strange pretense that the dead can still see, or even care, where they are.

Dr. Arcolio came to the house and drank champagne and ate little bits of fish and artichoke and messy little barbecued ribs. Everybody spoke in hushed voices. Helen Ellis had kept to herself throughout the funeral and had been heavily veiled in black. Now she had retreated to her private apartments and left Bradley's family and business friends and political henchmen to enjoy his wake without her participation.

After a while, however, Dr. Arcolio climbed the echoing marble stairs and tiptoed along to her room. He tapped three times on the door before he heard her say, indistinctly, "Who is it? Go away."

"It's Eugene Arcolio. Can I talk to you?"

There was no reply, but after a very long time, the doors were opened, and left open, and Dr. Arcolio assumed that this must be an invitation for him to go inside.

Cautiously, he entered. Helen was sitting by the window on a stiff upright chair. She was still veiled.

"What do *you* want?" she asked him. Her voice was muffled, distorted.

He shrugged. "I just came by to say congratulations."

"Congratulations?"

"Sure ... you got what you wanted, didn't you? The house, the money. Everything."

Helen turned her head toward him and then lifted her veil. He wasn't shocked. He knew what to expect. After all, he had undertaken all of the surgery himself.

In each of her cheeks, a vulva gaped. Each was pouting and moist, a surrealistic parody of a *Rustler* center-spread. A barely comprehensible collage of livid flesh and composed beauty and absolute horror.

It had been Helen's last act of complete subservience, to sacrifice her looks, so that Bradley and his friends had been able to penetrate not only her body but her face.

Dr. Arcolio had pleaded with her not to do it, but she had threatened suicide, and then murder, and then she had threatened to tell the media what he had done to her already.

"It's reversible," he had reassured himself as he meticulously sewed vaginal muscles into the linings of her cheeks. "It's totally reversible."

Helen looked up at him. "You think I got what I wanted?" Every time she spoke, the vaginal lips parted slightly.

He had to turn away. The sight of what he had done to her was more than he could bear.

"I didn't get what I wanted," she said, and tears began to slide down her cheeks, and drip from the curved pink labia minora. "I wanted vaginas everywhere, all over me, so that Bradley could have twenty friends for the night, a hundred of them all at once, in my face, in my thighs, in my stomach, under my arms. He wanted a sex object, Eugene, and I would have been happy, you know, being his sex object."

Dr. Arcolio said, "I'm sorry. I think this was my fault, as much as yours. In fact, I think it was *all* my fault."

That afternoon, he went back to his office overlooking Brookline Square, where Helen Ellis had first consulted him. He stood by the window for a long time.

Was it right to give people what they wanted, if what they wanted was perverse and self-sacrificial, and it flew in the face of God's creation?

Was it right to mutilate a beautiful woman, even if she craved mutilation?

How far did his responsibilities go? Was he a butcher, or was he a saint? Was he close to Heaven, or dancing on the manhole cover of Hell? Or was he nothing more than a surgical parody of Ann Landers, solving marital problems with a scalpel instead of sensible suggestions?

He lit the first cigarette he had smoked in almost a month and sat at his desk in the gathering gloom. Then, when it was almost dark, his secretary, Esther, knocked on the door, opened it, and said, "Doctor?"

"What is it, Esther? I'm busy."

"Mr. Pierce and Mr. De Scenza. They came for their six o'clock appointment."

Dr. Arcolio crushed out his cigarette and waved the smoke away. "Oh, shit. All right. Show them in."

John Pierce and Philip De Scenza came into his office and stood in front of his desk like two schoolboys summoned to report to the principal. John Pierce was young and blond and wore an unstructured Italian suit with rolled-up sleeves. Philip De Scenza was older and heavier and darker, in a hand-knitted plum-colored sweater and baggy brown slacks.

Dr. Arcolio reached across his desk and shook their hands. "How are you? Sorry ... I've been a little preoccupied this afternoon."

"Oh ... we understand," said Philip De Scenza. "We've been pretty busy ourselves."

"How are things coming along?" asked Dr. Arcolio. "Have you experienced any problems? Any pain?"

John Pierce shyly shook his head. Philip De Scenza made a circle with his finger and his thumb and said, "Perfect, Doctor. Two thousand percent perfect. Fucking-A, if you don't mind my saying so!"

Dr. Arcolio stood up and cleared his throat. "You'd better let me take a look, then. Do you want a screen?"

"A *screen?*" John Pierce giggled.

Philip De Scenza dismissively flapped his hand. "We don't need a screen."

While Dr. Arcolio waited, John Pierce unbuckled his belt, tugged down his zipper, and wriggled out of his toothpaste-striped boxer shorts.

"Would you bend over, please?" asked Dr. Arcolio. John Pierce gave a little cough and did as he was told.

Dr. Arcolio spread his muscular bottom to reveal two perfect crimson anuses, both tightly wincing, one above the other. Around the upper anus there was a star-shaped pattern of more than ninety stitches, but they had all healed perfectly, and there were only the faintest diagonal scars across his buttocks.

"Good," said Dr. Arcolio, "that's fine. You can pull up your pants again now."

He turned to Philip De Scenza, and all he had to do was raise an eyebrow. Philip De Scenza lifted his sweater, dropped his pants, and stood proudly brandishing his improved equipment: one dark penis, like a heavy fruit, surmounted by yet another dark penis; and four hairy testicles hanging at the sides.

"Any difficulties?" asked Dr. Arcolio, lifting both penises with professional detachment and examining them carefully. Both began to stiffen a little.

"Timing, that's all." Philip De Scenza shrugged, with a sideways smile at his friend. "I still haven't managed a simultaneous climax. By the time I've finished, poor John's usually getting quite sore."

"General comfort?" asked Dr. Arcolio tightly.

"Oh, *fine* ... just so long as I don't wear my pants too tailored."

"Okay," said Dr. Arcolio dully. "You can zip yourself up again now."

"Over so soon?" Philip De Scenza flirted. "That's not very good value, Doctor. A hundred dollars for two seconds' fondle. You should be ashamed of yourself."

That evening, John Pierce and Philip De Scenza went to Le Bellecour on Muzzey Street for dinner. They held hands all the way through the meal.

Dr. Arcolio picked up a few groceries and then drove home in his metallic-blue Rolls-Royce, listening to *La Bohème* on the stereo. He glanced in the rear-view mirror from time to time and thought he was looking tired. Traffic was heavy and slow on the turnpike, and he felt thirsty, so he took an apple out of the bag beside him and took a bite.

He thought about Helen; and he thought about John Pierce and Philip De Scenza; and he thought about all of the other men and women whose bodies he had skillfully changed into living incarnations of their own sexual fantasies.

Something that Philip De Scenza had said kept nagging him. *You should be ashamed of yourself.* Although De Scenza had been joking, Dr. Arcolio suddenly understood that, yes, he should be ashamed of what he had done. In fact, he *was* ashamed of what he had done. Ashamed that he had used his surgical genius to create such erotic aberrations. Ashamed that he had mutilated so many beautiful bodies.

But as well as being painful, this surge of shame was liberating, too. Because men and women were more than God had made them. Men and women were able to reinvent themselves, and to derive strange new pleasures from pain and humiliation and self-distortion. Who was to say that it was right or that it was wrong? Who could define the perfect human being? If it was wrong to give a woman a second vagina, was it also wrong to repair a baby's harelip?

He felt chastened, but also uplifted. He finished his apple and tossed the core out onto the highway. Ahead of him he could see nothing but a Walpurgis Night procession of red brake lights.

In her house, alone, Helen wept salt tears of grief and sweet tears of sex, which mingled and dropped on her hands, so that they sparkled like diamond engagement rings.

THE SAD, NOT-SO-SAD, BALLAD OF GOAT-HEAD JEAN, AMBIVALENT DEVIL QUEEN

BY MICHAEL LOUIS CALVILLO

Not one idiot, cattle-minded, dim-fuck of a person believed in her. *Assholes, assholes, assholes.*

The world at large was overrun with idiot, cattle-minded, dim-fuck *assholes.*

Not one of them was cool with it.

Not one even *tried* to understand.

Well, maybe one.

But, Christ, her slutty, on-again/off-again friend, Karla, didn't really count. In fact, her enthusiastically positive opinion only made matters worse. Her acceptance and encouragement only served to reinforce everyone else's negativity. The whore's take only mucked things up.

But she *needed* this!

Jean even reasoned that she *deserved* this!

Before the awful, awful accident she was such a pretty, pretty girl. She had a mighty, mean walk. All sorts of men strained their necks to follow that sexy sashay.

Hubba, hubba! Yeah, baby! Woot-woot! You want some fries with that shake?!

Their horny brains went rock hard.

But now?

Now?

Now, Jean held her hands over her face and welcomed sobs.

Now?!

Now, those stupid, stupid men stared, but instead of leering and tenting their pants, their mouths formed tight, prudish lines and their nervous, suddenly guilt-stricken eyes jumped from her ruined pelvis to her straining forearms, to her clanking crutches, and eventually to another, *complete* woman with full, swaying hips and fully functional legs.

The grinding car accident did nothing to her face. It was as lovely as it had ever been—high cheekbones and a softly shaped chin. But a pleasant, symmetrical, bright-eyed visage did little for musky, animalistic sex appeal when the rest of her lady parts were twisted into savage ruin.

She figured a set of new breasts had to help. Mid-thirties. Unmarried. Shit was getting desperate.

Her original rack wasn't so terrible. She wasn't flat or anything like that. B cups. Decent. Not too bad. But a nice boost couldn't hurt, could it?

Jean hoped a new set of fun-bags would do the trick, distracting from the ebb and flow of her swinging crutches and her ever-flattening ass (no daily exercise equated no muscle and no butt). At the very least, she hoped they'd help her find a man worth a damn.

They did … and they didn't.

Men stared a little harder, but, as their eyes made the rounds, they invariably got stuck on the hollow aluminum and twisted bone. The only person who seemed to be thoroughly impressed by her pert, well-sculpted 38Cs was the same slutty friend who encouraged her to get them in the first place. Her family remained ambivalent (not that Jean was comfortable talking boobs with her mom or dad or brothers). Her coworkers half-smiled and looked at the ceiling when talking to her.

Jean was in the deepest throes of regret—five grand was a lot of loot—when Dan hit on her during Tuesday Night Karaoke.

Turns out, the wide-grinning suitor was a *genuine* Satanist, but, hey, he was tall, and, hey, he seemed to be into her, and, hey, beggars couldn't be choosers.

Besides, Jean really liked his pointy face and the way it looked like he was always on the verge of laughing. That she hobbled around didn't seem to shake him. He just smiled that near-exploding smile and treated her the way a lady needed to be treated.

After they made love for the fifth time, she even acquiesced and got a wicked goat-head tattoo on her right thigh.

All was well.

Now, when it came to this whole *Satan thing*, Jean kept quiet and feigned respect. She liked Dan too much to let silly religious belief get in the way of their burgeoning relationship.

He was into the devil.

So what?

Big deal?

She believed in Santa Claus until she was seventeen years old (for real, seriously).

Jean figured it was something they could definitely work around.

Dan was only twenty-five to her thirty-five, and impulsive, and super-eager to please. This devil-worshipping business was probably just a phase. Men were wishy-washy like that. Within two months' time, she got him to quit playing those idiotic video games. A little longer, and she'd get him to see that religion was nothing but babble invented before science to explain unexplainable phenomena.

When Jean felt comfortable enough in their relationship to demand Dan stop his ritualistic devil activity, her (*official!*) boyfriend put up a little fight. He claimed he needed his faith. It went deeper than social mores. It was a personal thing. If she wasn't down with the devil, then she wasn't down with him.

155

Jean argued that if he must worship something, why not pick God? Why go against the grain? Why not choose light over dark or whatever?

Dan shook his head and looked at her like a man millions of miles away.

Jean let it go (again) and even got a cute pitchfork tattooed on her left thigh.

Clanking crutches and rocky, weedy forests did not mix, but it was important to Dan, so Jean trudged on. He helped her when the going got too rough, and she appreciated his muscled arms and well-defined chest. Manly acumen aside, after an hour of thrashing through the foliage, Jean was ready to pack it in and head back.

"I'm all scratched up!" She hugged her crutches close to her ribs and rubbed at the tree scrapes striping her arms. It was far too hot out for long sleeves, but the summer dress she was wearing was not suited for serious hiking.

She wished Dan would stop being so damn cryptic!

When he picked her up, he failed to mention they'd be roughing it. He cooed sweet nothings (as usual), smiled brightly (as usual), and promised a surprise to surmount all surprises (which was sort of unusual—he was romantic, but not really prone to orchestrating surprises).

"You're fine, love." Dan dropped a bundle of blankets and picnic goods, and then wrapped his arms around her and pulled her close.

Jean lost her balance and fell into his embrace. Her crutches dug deep into her sides and rammed up into her armpits. The force sent little tremors of pain up and down her arms and into her chest, but Dan's lips pressed against hers before she had the chance to whimper or complain.

They kissed long and hard, the kiss of a fully maturing love, until Dan moved away and helped Jean steady her stance.

"Just a little further, I promise. I've got the perfect spot." That ever-laugh pushed at the back of his lips, vibrating his nose and quivering his eyeballs. Jean couldn't help but to nod and smile in accordance. Dan nodded back, swooped up their picnic supplies, and then resumed marching, clearing dry brush and dead tree branches so Jean had an easier time of it.

After another fifteen minutes of exasperating, sticky hiking, they arrived in a small clearing near a postcard-perfect stream that sparkled like a river of diamonds wherever the sun cut through and glittered upon its rolling surface.

At the far end of the clearing, a chunky formation of shiny black rock jutted from the soil. The strange stones arched and hung at odd angles. If you squinted just right, just so, they seemed to resemble the ruins of some ancient, sacred palace left to decay among the indifference of wild, wily wilderness growth.

Jean's eyes lit up when she saw the picturesque stream. This was more like it.

Dan dropped their supplies and held out his arms. "Well? Whadda you think? Not too shabby, huh?"

The hike was way grueling, but all things considered—the gorgeous stream, the flat, even ground of the clearing, the ample shade of overhanging tree branches, the cooling air bereft of muggy heat—it was well worth it. This was indeed an oasis. Its distance from civilization made Jean feel like the two of them were the only mortals on the planet, like the savagery of the piercing, poking, prodding forest had given up and bowed low, gifting them with their own private Eden, rewarding their struggles with the promise of luxuriant relaxation.

It was a good feeling and Jean was glad she had stuck it out. At that moment, she never wanted to leave.

But then she stared at the outcropping of those strange onyx stones and a cold shiver ran the length of her spine. She shook it off, propped her crutches under her chin, and hugged herself tightly.

Dan sensed her unease and moved in for another consoling squeeze. He moved the crutches aside, setting them on the ground, and then wrapped his arms round her. The warmth of his body banished the nervous chills. Jean hugged herself even harder, compacting her shoulders, an embrace within an embrace, and leaned closer into her man's warmth.

They kissed. Deeply. And though Jean wasn't the type to get freaky out in the open—she was generally much more modest than that—Dan ramped up the passion, spread out a fluffy den of blankets, and the two fell into each other.

The lovemaking was exquisite. Something about the small clearing and the cradling woods heightened the experience. Jean's body came alive. Her heart expanded. The devilish tattoos on her thighs seemed to glow a demonic red. The love she felt for her new boyfriend overwhelmed her. The notion that this might be the *ONE* momentarily tripped up her emotions. In that instant, electricity sizzling her from the inside out, she'd never been happier.

After they were done, Jean dressed and then wandered over to the stream. Dan laid out their picnic lunch, and then went about fashioning a large pentagram out of rocks and sticks at the opposite end of the clearing.

Jean gave him a look and he gave her one back.

"Come on?" Dan raised his arms and gestured at the beauty around him.

Jean nodded and waved her hands as if to say, *hurry up with it then.*

She wanted to put her foot down. This stupid Satan thing was a persistent bugger. She'd have her way in the end. If she learned anything before screaming metal stripped her of her womanly powers, it was that the fairer sex always got its way. Sometimes it took a little time, but in the end ...

Alas, a lot of Dan's mumbo-jumbo rhetoric was dependent upon the natural world. A clearing like this? It was Satanic gold. If this wasn't the most perfect spot to build a pentagram and worship whatever it was he worshipped, Jean didn't think he'd ever find one. If there was ever a time to go lax and let her man do his thing, it was now. Dan got it that she understood. He nodded appreciatively and started arranging rocks.

Jean turned her back on his religious preparation and wandered. She dug her crutches deep into the wild grass at the stream's edge and leaned over the crystal clear water.

Glittering fish—silver, and red, and orange, and blue—swam with the mild current. Overhead, birds of every variety chirped and rustled about the treetops. If there was a way to never go back to the peopled, concrete mess of everyday living, Jean would happily take it. This purity, this open wonder—there'd been nothing like it in her life.

Maybe before the accident, maybe when she used to be innately happy, maybe there were joys to equal the growing sense of rightness that now filled her, but at the moment she couldn't remember any of them.

Pushing upright, she swung around to watch Dan and whatever nonsense he was up to. While mucking their way through the woods, he chatted a bit about wide, open forces and pure pathways.

Shirtless, his muscles and golden skin looked awesome in the intermittent shafts of sunlight that punched through the thick canopy above. Jean felt her heart do a little somersault. She took a step and supported it with the proper crutch. The mass of black rocks glinted in the corner of her eye. Jean turned to her left and approached the odd formation.

The rocks projected this way and that and took about ten feet in diameter of clearing space. The formation continued into the lush wood for an indeterminate distance.

"What is this?" Jean called over her shoulder to her busy-beaver boyfriend.

Dan lugged a heavy gray stone near the apex of his nearly complete pentagram. He frowned, shrugged, and then went back to it, grunting while aligning the stone.

Jean turned her attention back to the rocks. She'd seen chunks of onyx and obsidian in displays at a number of museums. The massive black rock didn't look all that different from some of the more exotic minerals, but here, it looked completely out of place in this landscape of browns and greens and grays.

Struggling for the right amount of balance, Jean leaned on her crutches and reached a hand out to touch one of the smooth, black rocks.

Thought instantly swirled into a funneling mishmash of emotion. Jean felt like crying, screaming, laughing, raging, loving, embracing, fucking, killing, dying.

Her mouth went bone dry.

Her feet levitated a full inch off the ground.

She grasped her crutches with her armpits.

A little anal leakage seeped from a wildly clenching sphincter and absorbed into her silky panties.

No matter what Dan thought about natural energies and religious hot spots, Satan and God weren't real to her. Jean didn't think they'd ever be real to her. She liked myths and legends fine, they were fun and interesting. But she understood them for what they were—stories to fill in esoteric blanks. Nothing extraordinary had ever happened to her to make her believe otherwise.

But now ... with the strange black rock warming her palm ... and charging her brain ... everything ... *changed.*

She let her crutches drop to the ground and cradled the protruding rock in both hands. The warmth surging into her systems doubled. She floated another inch higher.

The constant pain that coursed the boney masses and muscle tissue of her right and left hip flickered in and out like a windswept candle.

The rock in her palms shifted. Its solid, glassy surface rolled like a rippling river and its sides went amorphous, gelling, leaking droplets of sludge-like ooze. The entire rock softened, then melted into a viscous pool. It thinned and began seeping into Jean's skin.

Everything inside hummed.

Suddenly, she believed in whatever it took. *God, Satan, Jehovah, Baphomet. Whatever.* Her soul unraveled and held its proverbial arms wide in loving acceptance.

That the pain was dissipating—that her pelvis, legs, knees floated in gauzy contentment—pried devotion from nonchalance and instilled a piety only possible in those that have actually seen *The Light* (or, perhaps in this situation, *The Dark*).

Jean reached under her dress and smoothed the black-gunk palms of her hands over her bare hips, massaging the dark tar-to-liquid-to-permeating mist deep, deep, deep, into the screaming hollows and crevices of her internal meat.

The creeping black wasn't partial to any one part of her body. It seemed not to care that it made Jean feel whole. Soothing aches and pains was not its mission. Filling in the cracks and strengthening weakened cells were all byproducts that happened to have a positive

160

effect upon its host. It supposed, or it would *suppose* if it could *suppose*, that this was all well and good.

A healthy host was ultimately an effective host.

But then, in the end, whether its latest incubator was howling in bloody pain or standing tall, shining with vibrancy—so long as it provided the right configuration of heat, bacteria, pus, and salt—the Dark could do its thing.

However, its *thing*—providing a stable conduit from which the transdermal, primordial ooze could be given a combative form—found an unexpected wrinkle in Jean's morphology.

If it could think, it would ponder, *why bother steering about one clumsy bag of bones when it could birth thousands of boneless wonders?*

But wait ... let's back it up a bit.

Whilst Jean luxuriates in pain-free wonder and her body accepts the new evolution, let's go way back ...

Before Light, there was Dark.

Sure, things always begin with the ubiquitous *in the beginning*, and then there's light, and life, and so on and so forth. Hundreds upon thousands upon millions upon billions of philosophical constructs and physical models prove as much.

But they always focus on the emergence of *illumination*.

What about *The Dark* that was and still is?

Shadows remind us of what once was, but there is little talk of the *Infinite Dark*—of its purpose, of its design.

In nature, say, in the very quagmire of hardened black at the edge of a familiar little clearing, deep in a dark, dense wood, the Infinite Dark manifests and entrenches itself within life like a stubborn cancer. It collapses and corrupts and waits for the opportunity to spread and flourish.

An oblong piece of gray-yellow limestone rounded off Dan's impressively large pentagram. He took a few steps back and regarded his work with pride. The clearing was comfortably shady, but lugging rocks and sticks had him perspiring. He stood still. A little breeze whispered through the trees and cooled the slick beads of sweat gathered under his arms, across his chest, and along the length of his shoulders. He rubbed his face, and then reached for the sky in a grunting stretch.

Jean was entertaining the beast. This is how it went with all of Dan's victims. Shannon, Krista with a "K," Christa with a "C," Lupe, and Angela all marveled over the Maker, allowing Truth to fill them in.

They still screamed and they still fought for their lives, but Dan liked to think they understood what he was doing. They didn't want to die for it, no matter the glories the beast showed them, no matter Dan's purpose, but deep down they had to know their deaths were anything but meaningless. This mattered somehow, right?

Dan made his way over to the picnic spread. This being sacrifice number six, he'd gotten pretty good at bringing along the essentials. The first few times out? Forget it. He forgot this and he forgot that, and any little miniscule mistake on his part brought on a potential for failure.

Though in his heart of hearts, he knew the Dark Lord wouldn't let him screw up. It needed the sustenance as much as he needed a rush of salty slut blood.

Rifling through the little cooler, he grabbed for the hefty steak knife. It was streaked with bits of hard cheese and French bread. Wiping it clean on his jeans, he stood and then approached his prey.

Technically, Jean wasn't a slut. Neither were Krista with a "K" or Lupe. Like Jean, they were nice girls who got caught up in his nefarious game. Sometimes Dan wasn't sure if the good girls he offered up counted. There wasn't any sort of rulebook or guide to walk him along. He just figured that the Dark Lord would want sluts.

Regardless, the black intermingling with his blood got as amped up over good girls as it did bad. Murderous intent blossomed. The urge pulled just as hard. It kept him awake and frenzied until he did the deed, and then once he gave the beast what it wanted, he got a little reprieve until the hunger began to gnaw away at his guts and the sacrificial courtship began anew.

Dan tightened his grip on the knife and took long strides. He found the faster he got it done, the better. Real feelings had developed between him and each of his girls, and it was no different with Jean. In fact, it was way worse with Jean. She was fragile. She needed him as much as he needed her. The end result was much, much different, but the developing love that brought them here followed similar paths.

Biting his lower lip until coppery respite filled his mouth, Dan held his knife hand high. He spun Jean around on her (floating?) heels with his free hand and then stabbed the hell out of her with the thick blade.

The very moment steel touched flesh, a number of things happened. Jean hadn't put two and two together just yet. She was still free-floating and marveling at the odd things happening inside her body. Dan got the same rush he got from stabbing the others. Like a potent drug, the blood savagery consumed him.

One hovered in oblivious bliss while the other labored with hot, animal force.

When a spray of blood followed Dan's knifepoint from flesh to the thick, forest air, misting and then splashing and cooling his face, all seemed right with the world (to Dan anyway). He continued the slashing motions and pushed the steel home again and again. Once the frenzy had left him, once he was spent, drained of murderous hunger, he'd pull his lady love close and let her lifeblood drench them.

Then, after a bit—just how long was hard to define, as it was different with each sacrifice—he'd lower her body into the center of the pentagram and make his offering to the beast. Once the ritual was complete, he'd feed her to the rocks and that was that—he'd be off to the bars in search of another flame.

Jean didn't even feel the knife plunge into her chest. The dark ooze coated her muscles and her inner tissues, and every time the blade tore her flesh and sheathed itself in muscle, nicking bone and savaging capillaries, the gunk amassed and filled in the empty spaces. It wasn't until the fourth or fifth strike that something in her brain rose above the ooze and noticed that her beloved boyfriend was trying to kill her.

The moment she noticed, a zillion tons of pressure compressed her chest, and pain—big and sick and bloody—welled. She burned from the tips of her toes to the top of her skull. At first, she couldn't tell if the murderous blade or the all-consuming gunk was to blame for

163

the growing pain. It seemed to be a combination of the two. Whereas the blade hit hard and fast, ice cold to blistering heat, over and over again, the Dark crept slowly, but had completed its circuit, and that fluffy good feeling that had filled her now dissipated and gave way to a disintegrating burn.

Her resplendent face lost all color and dropped. As Dan ground his teeth and drove the knife home, it dawned on her. She was in some serious shit.

While our human players struggled with the demons that devoured them, the primordial goo enshrining Jean's innards happened upon an unexpected wrinkle in its purpose and design. For millennia upon millennia, it sat where it sat and did what it did, inching its way through the crust, dead-dreaming about a new dawning and eventual eventualities. The sludge couldn't think things through or understand them like our fast-firing human brains, but it could *feel*. Inclinations came and went and came and went.

When Dan's brutalizing steel pierced Jean's right breast implant, the sharp point ripped the thick sack. The viscous saline solution ran from its shapely pouch. The second the black goo came in contact with the salty solution, a chemical reaction kicked the ooze in its ancient ass and dropped the transmogrifying process into high gear.

Vision expanded.

The ooze no longer needed eons to achieve dominion.

It no longer needed the minions it managed to infect and send out into the world to bring back paltry morsels of human blood and gristle.

Again, the *thing* at the thing's core could not conceptualize any of this, but it understood ... *opportunity* ... and it seized that motherfucker with everything it had.

Ropy strands of black absorbed the foreign fluids, and the massive amount of salt within the implant's malleable compound went to work shaping and invigorating *hungry*, toothy off-shoots.

Tadpole-like blobs of black leapt from the gaping hole in Jean's chest and wrapped themselves around Dan's knife.

Dan swung the blade back for his seventy-second grisly attack. The tadpole-things slunk up the steel. The unmarred black of their bulbous heads came apart in a razor-sharp yawn.

For a second in time, the world froze.

Dan's eyes, slits of bashing hate, narrowed further as he tightened his grip.

Jean's eyes widened as realization *and* confusion spun her mind.

The dark-manifest opened its new mouths, new jaws on the verge of unhinging, and then it slammed them shut on a nice, warm hunk of Dan's gore-soaked hand.

He dropped the knife, doubled over in pain, and screamed his throat bloody raw. Before his brain had the chance to switch from murderous to fearful, the dark mouths grew and grew and gnashed and gnashed and—just, like, that—as easily as Dan gave himself over to the idea of base, godly gratification; as easily as he craved carnal pleasures and masochistic release; his blood, bones, organs, and skin were pulped into mash, and then swallowed into nothingness.

Jean continued to levitate, rising a few more inches into the air, the overhanging sun casting her shadow over the inky mess that used to be her man.

The knife damage was of the mortal variety. Had things gone as planned, Jean's consciousness would have dwindled and disappeared like listless ash in a steady wind—but this new hiccup shifted the Fates. Destiny needed her.

Jean choked on a clump of coagulated blood obstructing her throat. She tried to get her bearings, but the black had worked its way into the folds of her brain. The ooze dampened thought until it was too soggy to hold together.

The black infiltrated every fiber of the gasping woman's being. It soothed this patch of brain matter here and pinched a particular cluster there until it got her to stop gagging, and then it went on filtering ooze through the implant's well of saline, producing an army of creeping, crawling doom.

The serene woman floating above the amassing army hung her head low and rested her chin on her chest. Warring trains of thought struggled in the quagmire of cerebration at the base of her brain. Things like *Me*, and *You*, and *Self Worth*, and *Belief*, and *The Unimportant Importance of Pert, Perfect Breasts* surfaced from the gray, swampy sludge before drowning in ambivalence, ready to rise and wash away the sins and faiths of the world in a devastating wave of cleansing, black death.

165

LOCKS OF LOATHE

BY JEZZY WOLFE

Alesha Aldopita's head resembled a butchered Barbie doll. Scant threads of dull brown gossamer barely covered her pasty scalp. Growing up, she envied men with comb-overs. Her peers in eighth grade nicknamed her "Alesha Alopecia" and it followed her through high school. The more her beautiful but vicious classmates ridiculed her, the more she grew angry and resentful. She'd missed out on sleepovers with the girls at school, staying up past midnight putting crooked braids in each other's hair. Prom was out of the question, along with every other dance and party the typical teenager begged to attend.

After graduation, she moved across the country to attend college, and never left her dorm room without a hat or scarf covering her cranium. Needless to say, she stayed as lonely as she was bald. A lifetime of poorly disguising her condition had passed, and she was tired of hiding.

Hell yeah, she was bitter.

"Have you considered wearing a wig?" This was her first therapy session with Dr. Wiston, a woman possessing more hair than the entire high school varsity cheerleading squad combined.

Alesha glared, regretting her choice of doctor. Taking advice from her would be the equivalent of a morbidly obese person taking nutritional suggestions from an anorexic.

"Hair salons donate hair to an organization that makes wigs for cancer patients and people with other illnesses," the doctor continued. "That would be an easy solution if you're so insecure about your appearance. Would you like me to give you their number?"

Alesha knew about them as well, but wigs were uncomfortable. They made her scalp itchy and sweaty, and she feared they would fly off her head at the worst possible moments.

"Wigs give me rashes. Isn't it bad enough that I have to wear sunscreen under my scarves? I'm tired of living like a freak!"

Dr. Wiston squirmed in her seat as she scrutinized Alesha's chrome dome.

Great. She's captivated by the drops of sweat covering it. They're probably reflecting tiny rainbows all over the room. I'm a human disco ball, whee!

"At the risk of sounding simple, many women flaunt a shaved head. Perhaps, rather than cursing your condition, you can turn it into an asset?"

Alesha practically hissed. "Absolutely not!"

"Okay," Dr. Wiston said calmly, "there are many advancements in hair replacement now. While the majority of patients looking for hair replacement are men, it is certainly not limited to them."

"If you are talking about Rogaine, it didn't help."

"There's also Propecia, Dithro-Scalp, cortisone injections, and hormonal modulators."

"You don't think I would've tried them already? I've seen four different specialists, and it's cost me more than a few years' salary. The only progress I've seen is the ability to have lots of sex now without getting pregnant, thanks to the contraceptives they told me would spur more hair growth." Alesha struggled to keep her voice steady. "But, hey, the pill works. Since it didn't make my hair grow, no man will touch me with a ten-foot penis."

"You're an attractive woman, Alesha."

"Right."

"Have you looked into hair plugs?"

"Have you *looked* at hair plugs? Don't I look weird enough?"

168

Alesha regretted her misdirected hostility, but she felt powerless to control the emotions dominating her reactions. She couldn't stop staring at Dr. Wiston's thick mane of spun gold. *She can't take me seriously because she doesn't understand how I feel.*

"How are your finances now?"

She didn't even listen to what I just said! "Uh, few years' salary, remember? I'm broke."

Dr. Wiston studied her again, eyes squinted and brow creased as she tapped her pen against her lower lip.

"I am not supposed to do this; it is a violation of policy. But if you promise to keep this disclosure completely confidential, I might be able to help you."

Alesha smirked. "How will you do that? Hair extensions and super glue?"

Dr. Wiston went over to her desk and opened a drawer, pulling a flat black box from under a stack of papers and laying it on her desk blotter. Resettling in a chair by the desk, Alesha watched as the therapist slowly lifted the lid of the box.

In the box rested only one simple business card.

Dr. Wiston started to hand her the card, but pulled back when Alesha reached for it. "Dr. Pift was disbarred six years ago, but he still practices from a private location. Some believed his methods were unethical and grossly negligent, and had his license revoked." She glared a warning at Alesha. "If I give you his number, you cannot tell anyone that you're seeing him. Should complications arise from whatever procedure you agree to, you will not be able to seek medical help from a hospital or outside doctor."

Alesha's heart pounded erratically and sweat rivulets raced down her temples.

"Because he has a humanitarian streak, his fees are reasonable. He continues his work because he believes in helping people like you, those who have tried every avenue they could afford without success."

Still not convinced, Alesha shrugged. "That's great, but is he any good?"

Dr. Wiston rounded the desk and squatted in front of her, eyes glittering above her twisted smile. She shook her head and a bounty of golden silk tumbled over her shoulders.

"You tell me. What do you think?"

Dr. Pift waited quietly behind an oversized steel desk as Alesha studied the sheet he'd handed her. It read like a menu, but rather than food, a list of surgical procedures and brief descriptions were laid out next to dollar amounts.

Her stomach dropped. *I can't even afford an appetizer ...*

"I appreciate you stopping in to see me. Dr. Wiston is a long-time friend. How is she looking these days?"

"Perfect," Alesha mumbled.

"Indeed. You know, there was a time her head was as bald as yours." He paused as Alesha's jaw dropped. "Unusually bad reaction to the chemo, I'm afraid. For many, the hair will return, but in her case ..."

"How did you fix her?" Alesha ran a hand across her scalp. When she looked at her palm, she saw four strands of baby-fine hair caught on her fingers.

"I'm sure you've heard of hair plugs." As disappointment registered on her face, he chuckled. "I'm not suggesting a traditional process of hair plugs, of course. You have no hair to re-harvest. But, after experimenting with a combination of techniques, I've discovered that healthy hair can be achieved on even the most barren head. What I'm suggesting for you is a full-thickness skin graft. We replace your scalp with the scalp of a healthy head and that hair becomes yours."

A vision of Frankenstein fluttered through Alesha's mind, complete with oversized metal sutures and neck bolts. "I ... I don't know, Dr. Pift. That sounds outrageous."

"Why? Successful skin grafts are performed all the time on burn victims. Hair plugs themselves are just smaller patches of transplanted skin."

"Yeah, but isn't the skin their own?"

"Most of the time, yes. But skin is an organ, Miss Aldopita. And organ transplants are hugely successful with the medications now available. Skin can be transplanted from a donor and treated just as if the recipient received a kidney or a liver. Once the body has successfully merged the new scalp into your system, the healthy follicles will continue to regenerate new hair."

"It sounds pretty fantastic, but I'm not sure I can afford this," Alesha said, dollar signs swimming in her vision.

Dr. Pift watched as tears welled in Alesha's eyes. Pity—or something close to it—poorly disguised his smile as he leaned across the desk and offered her a tissue.

"Usually, when patients come to see me, they've already exhausted their resources in an attempt to find a cure. I never refuse to treat a patient based on inability to pay." His smile warmed. "I came from a very poor background myself, but now I live a comfortable life. I'm not greedy."

He stood. He looked like a giant as he came around the desk and offered his hand to her. "Let me help you, Miss Aldopita. I promise, soon your bald past will be nothing more than a faint memory."

She was caught off guard when he explained the procedure in detail—but really, what did she expect? After all, you can't order scalps from a catalog, and how many women were willing to donate their entire head of hair to a stranger? They had to scalp someone. There'd be hell to pay if anyone found out what they were about to do. The agreement they made was unconventional, immoral ... criminal. But Alesha would sell her soul to the devil and tell him to keep the change, just to wake to the possible experience of bad hair days.

He warned her of all the usual risks—potential scarring, serious infections, and the possibility of tissue rejection if her medications weren't monitored carefully. But after twenty-three years of humiliation and insecurity, those risks were insignificant. Alesha's only real concern remained in finding the one head of hair that would be the envy of everybody she'd meet.

She found the hair sooner than she'd anticipated.

The sun bathed the sidewalks in an intense heat that bounced around the moving crowds in waves. Alesha stopped outside a tinted coffee shop window, debating on the purchase of a frozen beverage, as she studied the street at her back in the murky reflection. The glazing transformed the passing people into indistinct shadows that floated by. A sudden shock of glowing copper invaded the chiaroscuro—a manifestation of gilded snakes that slithered across the glass and disappeared into the door frame. Frappuccino forgotten, Alesha trailed the hallucination to an office building a couple streets over.

Perched on a bench outside the building, she searched the throng of executives and secretaries that flooded the sidewalk that evening. In a sea of carbon-copy grey suits and skirts, the lush sheen of long henna curls caught her eye. They bounced in the early evening breeze, beckoning her closer. Alesha hid in the crowd, following just near enough to keep her sights locked on the shimmering strands that fluttered like a flag at dusk.

When the young woman entered an apartment building less than a mile from Alesha's walk-up, she waited a beat and entered the lobby, just in time to see a door on the second floor landing slam closed. *This is it. She's practically in my own backyard!*

The initials on the mailbox read *A.A.* It was the only sign she needed.

Hiding under a stairwell, Alesha clenched and unclenched her fists to stop their shaking, fighting against a myriad of "what ifs." For instance, what if the woman fought back? What if the chloroform didn't work? What if her boyfriend happens to be a police officer who randomly stops by for an unexpected booty call, had his own set of keys, and bursts into the place after the woman is unconscious but before Dr. Pift arrives to collect her body?

She checked her watch. 1:30 a.m. Copper Curls still hadn't returned home. Alesha's stomach sank as another "what if" came to mind: What if she doesn't come home tonight?

The lobby door creaked as it swung open, and Alesha reached for the bottle in her jacket pocket. From the shadows, she watched as the woman checked her mailbox, and then ascended the stairs. Alesha tiptoed to a back stairwell that she had discovered earlier and climbed them two at a time, the soft soles of her sneakers muffling the sound of her steps.

Copper Curls fumbled with her keys, dropping them with a mumbled curse. Alesha prepared to sprint, cloaked in the dark doorway. *Okay, get ready now ...*

As Copper Curls pushed open the apartment door, Alesha sprang from the doorway, chloroform-soaked rag in her hand. In a fluid motion that could've been rehearsed, she cupped the towel over Copper's nose and mouth before she could struggle. Alesha leveraged her weight against the woman and pushed them both into the apartment. Shoved toward a squat sofa, Copper went limp and sprawled like dead weight over the cushions. Alesha rushed to retrieve the keys and close the door, locking the deadbolt as she fumbled for the light switch.

The woman splayed across the couch like she'd had too much to drink. Alesha pressed two fingers to her limp wrist. Copper's pulse was a little uneven, but strong. She pulled her cell from her pocket and called Dr. Pift.

While the doctor was enroute to collect the donor, she studied the woman's cascade of curls. They appeared wet to the touch, the color gleaming, shifting between penny-copper and fire-red. In direct light, the effect looked holographic. She slid her fingers into the silky weight, stunned by how cool it felt as it twined around her skin. Searching for the base of Copper's skull, she lifted the heavy tresses, breath caught in her throat as her fingertips caressed her skin. No clips. No weaves. Not even discolored roots.

My hair.

Clara, Dr. Pift's assistant, helped Alesha into her surgery gown. While they retrieved the donor, Clara had been prepping the operation room for the procedure. Heart monitors, I.V.s, breathing masks for the anesthetic, and several metal carts with various instruments and needles lined both beds. The doctor wanted to begin the transplant before sunrise.

"Are you allergic to shellfish, strawberries, kiwis, bananas, or poinsettias?"

Alesha climbed onto the gurney. "No ... why?"

Clara checked off boxes on a chart. "Standard questions. We need to know if you are allergic to iodine or latex."

"No allergies that I'm aware of," Alesha shrugged. After a moment, she cleared her throat and said, "You know, I probably should've asked before, but what is going to happen to the donor after the transplant?"

She focused so much on acquiring the donor that she hadn't thought about the aftermath. How would Dr. Pift keep them both out of danger once the transplant was completed?

"The doctor has a plausible explanation for her 'accident'. After the transplant, he will also monitor her recovery, but you will be in different wings of the building. She will have no suspicions of foul play." Observing Alesha's apprehension, she added, "Dr. Pift has performed dozens of these transplants and, so far, and they've been quite successful. You needn't worry. You're in the best possible hands."

Alesha nodded and tried to relax. *No backing out now.* She watched the second hand on the clock circle around as Clara started an I.V. on her arm and began adhering the electrode patches for the cardiac monitor to her chest. Once she was situated in the hospital bed, Clara placed a mask over her face and told her to count backwards from 20.

The scream was so distant, she thought she must already be dreaming.

Daily, she downed as much anti-rejection medication as she did food. Gengraf, Prednisone, Cytovene ... the names blurred together in a chemical cocktail designed to keep her body from killing the new flesh sutured above her scalp. The only medication she enjoyed was the morphine they administered in even higher doses to dull the crippling headaches. But her discomfort was outweighed by excitement.

Ten days after the transplant, Dr. Pift removed the bandages. Sitting with her back to a mirror, she kept her eyes closed tight. For the first time in her life, she would see herself with a full head of hair. Even as she faced her reflection, she didn't peek.

The copper curls were now just coarse waves, the color dull and greasy. She smiled regardless. They'd been wrapped in a turban of gauze for a week and a half—of course they were grimy. All that mattered was they were hers now. She met Dr. Pift's eyes in the mirror. He frowned.

"Is something wrong?"

He didn't answer, just circled around to inspect her scalp. His fingertip, though barely grazing the incision, felt like a razorblade slicing her open.

"Clara, take some fresh samples and send them to the lab, please."

He turned to leave as she grabbed his arm. "What's wrong? I see it in your eyes. What's happening?"

"Most likely nothing, but I need to make sure you're not in the early stages of rejection." As the color drained from her face, he continued, "Try not to be alarmed. Almost all transplants try to reject in the beginning. I expected this would happen. We will adjust your medications and monitor you, but I'm sure you'll be fine."

She faced her reflection, this time staring closely at the incision, practically indistinguishable from her new hairline. She almost didn't notice the slight puckering or the yellow stain that seemed to seep onto her forehead. Gently, she touched the ruched seam, wincing at the sharp sensation that squeezed her skull. Then, she noticed the faint odor of decomposition that reminded her of two-week-old road kill.

Deep down, she'd known the transplant was failing. The odor that grew stronger every day, the puckering that deepened around the edges of the incision ... to make matters worse, some of the hair started falling out. Dr. Pift upped the dosages of steroids, readjusted the Gengraf, but still it continued. Her head was decaying.

"You're in acute transplant rejection," Dr. Pift confirmed. "The only real remedy is another transplant."

"This is my hair, Dr. Pift." Alesha panicked. "I don't want another transplant. There has to be a way to save it!"

He shook his head, his eyes answering before he said, "Not with medicine, I'm afraid."

Dr. Laurie Middleton looked nothing like the woman Alesha pictured when she made the appointment. She answered the door with a tight smile and perfectly coifed hair, dressed in a floral sweater and tweed skirt. Alesha expected tribal gowns, and perhaps a bone piercing or two.

Dr. Laurie Middleton was a shaman.

As per the agreement, she avoided hospitals and doctors. But, after a few holistic attempts ended in heightening infections, she decided to look for a less conventional solution. Dr. Pift suggested she see a different sort of healer. "Sometimes, such a crisis can only be cured with faith," he said. During a brief telephone interview, Dr. Middleton agreed to meet with Alesha in her home office.

After a cool handshake, Dr. Middleton led her to the study. "Please have a seat while I ready the room for the ceremony."

Alesha watched Dr. Middleton place stone bowls filled with branches on either side of a chaise. As she lit the stems, they smoldered and caught flame, swirling pungent smoke into the air. She then turned on a small stereo resting on a nearby shelf. The faint sound of drums whispered through speakers mounted in the corners of the room. Once her ministrations were complete, she settled on the chaise and smiled at Alesha, then closed her eyes. They sat in silence for several minutes.

When Alesha softly cleared her throat to speak, Dr. Middleton's eyes opened and she smiled again. Her voice was calm, like she could drift off to sleep mid-sentence. "I sense you are missing a part of yourself. Something has been lost, and until it is brought back, you cannot be whole. As a shamanic healer, I can do several things to alleviate such situations. But, in your case, what would serve you best is what we call a soul retrieval."

"I don't know what that means," Alesha shrugged. "And I'm not all that religious. What am I supposed to do?"

"All I need is for you to remain quiet and open your mind. I will do the rest. This will require a spiritual journey, during which I will slip into a trance. Once I emerge, your healing will be complete. There may be instructions for your aftercare, but I will explain them to you before you leave. Do you have any questions before we begin?"

"How will I know it worked?"

"My dear, you will know without words. You will feel it," Dr. Middleton laid a hand over her heart, "In *here*."

"But I'm not sick there ..."

The doctor shot her a look that could quiet baying wolves. "When you are sick, you always need healing in your center. Now, if there are no other questions, are you ready to begin?"

"Sure, I guess," Alesha mumbled.

Dr. Middleton pulled her legs onto the chaise and reclined. Her eyes closed as she hummed a tuneless melody. The humming faded into deep breaths while the woman relaxed, her chest rising slow and even.

Alesha watched the woman sleep, her own eyes growing heavy. Between the acrid smoke and the soft, deliberate rhythm of ceremonial drums, it took all her will power not to doze off. She studied her nails, tried to read the titles of the books on the shelves, even tried to make a song from the drumbeats. But despite her most valiant efforts, sleep took over.

She hovered in a black abyss, her body numb and heavy, like an ocean buoy suspended mid-air, waiting to hit the waves below. When she opened her mouth, she couldn't speak. Couldn't scream. Couldn't even gasp. Confusion and panic gripped her, but, oddly enough, she didn't feel her heart race.

An electric current ripped through her. As it did, she was submerged into light and sound. Chills washed over her as she awakened, disoriented and overcome with vertigo. *Where am I?*

A quick glance around did nothing to ease her growing anxiety. She sat on an unfamiliar couch in a stranger's living room. *How did I get here? Shouldn't I still be at Dr. Pift's clinic?*

Then she remembered. *I'm at the shaman's house.*

But the room didn't resemble the traditional décor of Dr. Middleton's home. A widescreen television hung on a far wall, the furnishings pristine and contemporary. Various polished picture frames on the end tables held snapshots of people she'd never met. She searched the room for anything that would jog her memory, but nothing rang a bell. She ran her hand over a lush velveteen sofa cushion.

Come to think of it, she'd seen this couch before. But where?

The room was immaculate ... except for the dozens of empty yogurt cups that littered the floor.

Alesha's stomach rolled. She hated yogurt. The vile sour taste, the thick creaminess ... she couldn't eat as much as a spoonful without gagging. And yet, here she sat, surrounded by empty containers.

177

Including an empty cup in her left hand with a spoon resting inside. It had been licked clean.

Repulsed, she threw the cup down and stood slowly, immediately noticing a pain in her joints, similar to the aches she felt after rigorous exercising. Groaning, she dragged her feet through the sea of Dannons and Yoplaits, looking for her purse and her bottle of painkillers. No sign of either.

She located a telephone in the kitchen and dialed Dr. Pift's number. As she waited for an answer, she caught sight of her reflection across a polished refrigerator door panel. Her hair looked fantastic. So did her clothes.

Too bad they weren't hers.

Dr. Pift answered before she had time to end the call. "Yes?"

"Dr. Pift? It's Alesh—"

"Where the hell have you been?" He roared in her ear. "Have you broken our agreement?"

His reaction sent another chill through her. "What do you mean? I had the appointment with the Dr. Middleton, remember? I think I fell asleep."

"You've been asleep for three weeks? You need to come back to the clinic so I can monitor your recovery. Being off your anti-rejection meds that long will surely create dire complications."

Alesha couldn't speak; she was numb with shock. Her voice cracked when she found it again. "I've been gone for three weeks?"

His voice was tense, like he was speaking through clenched teeth. "Miss Aldopita, get back here at once. Your very life could be in jeopardy."

She ran a finger gingerly under her hairline, waiting for the jolt of pain. Nothing. She didn't feel as much as a scar. "Of course, doctor. I'm leaving here now. I should be there shortly."

If I can figure out where "here" is ...

She explored the rest of the apartment, finding a bathroom and bedroom. No sign of any of her belongings, other than her purse, which lay on top of a tall bureau. Reaching for it, her eyes fell on a picture in a small frame nearby.

Copper Curls. Or, as the diploma framed and displayed over the bureau clearly stated, Andrea Aimes.

"Oh god, I have to get out of here!" She looked around, making sure she hadn't left any other personal belongings behind. If Copper discovered her in the apartment, wearing the stolen hair, she'd have Alesha behind bars faster than she could blink. Hopefully she was still under treatment at the clinic.

Which is where I haven't been for the past three weeks.

She checked the bathroom once more, making sure there were no traces of her visit. Then a dark puddle in the tub caught her attention. Jerking back the shower curtain, she almost screamed. The clothes she'd worn to Dr. Middleton's house were heaped in the basin. Soaked in blood.

Sinking to the floor, she cradled her head in her hands, fighting a wave of nausea.

I'm in Copper's apartment, wearing her clothes, because my clothes are ruined. Why can't I remember the past three weeks? What happened at Dr. Middleton's house?

Dr. Pift might not have answers, but certainly he knew where Copper was. That little bit of knowledge was better than nothing. She would get back and let him finish her therapy so she could begin her new life.

A mile from the apartment, with her purse and a black garbage bag full of bloodied garments clutched in her arms, it occurred to her—for all the blood on her clothes, there was no blood anywhere else in the apartment.

Dr. Pift regarded her as if she'd laid a golden egg. Once he determined that her scalp had completely healed without the aid of repression therapy, he sat at his desk, looking dumbfounded.

She would have been amused were she not scared shitless.

"Dr. Pift, is my donor still in the clinic?"

"No." He looked away, busying himself with desk papers, and said, "I didn't want to tell you, but I suppose you should know."

"Know what?"

"While you were being prepped for your surgery, there was a bit of an accident. A freakish mishap, you might say. Your donor woke unexpectedly as we were getting her ready for the procedure. A struggle ensued before we could sedate her, and she thrashed about so much, her neck snapped." Both his face and voice conveyed no emotion. "It was an unfortunate situation, and by that time you were already under sedation. Don't worry though. We incinerated her remains. Neither you nor I will be implicated if she is reported missing."

Alesha was torn between terror and relief. Her palms were clammy, trembling so badly she kept them tightly clasped on her lap.

He seemed oblivious to her panic, instead hitting the button on the intercom. "Clara, can we get some samples from Alesha? I need to readjust her immunosuppressant therapy."

Clara responded quickly, entering the office with a tray of syringes, vials, and rubber tourniquets. "Wow," she said, "you healed better than anyone I've seen so far. Now, didn't I say you were in the best hands?"

Alesha nodded, unable to speak around the lump in her throat. She waited as Clara extracted three vials of her blood and left the room. "Dr. Pift, something is not right. I don't remember leaving Dr. Middleton's house. I don't have any memory of the last three weeks. When I called you, I had just woken up. In the donor's apartment."

Dr. Pift stared, speechless.

"Plus I seem to love yogurt now, which is weird, because the stuff usually makes me throw up. And that's not the worst of it ..."

"Yes?"

"These aren't my clothes. I woke up in them. My clothes were in her tub, covered in blood."

If he was worried at all, she couldn't tell. He rubbed his chin thoughtfully before replying.

"The Cytovene you're taking is known sometimes to cause changes in taste. Not unheard of. Just means we need to lower your dosage. Prednisone often comes with a host of complications, including confusion and a difficulty in your perception of what's real and imagined. I'm sure all this can be fixed with your medications. As soon as your tests come back, we'll see where your levels are and make the necessary changes. You are a very fortunate young lady. I suspect you'll be on your way much faster than anticipated."

But his unflustered optimism was clouded with concern when Alesha met to discuss the results of her lab work.

"The tests results came back with unexpected information. I'm not sure what to make of it, honestly."

Alesha braced herself for the bad news. Did they find a tumor? An impending aneurysm? Was she on Death's doorstep?

"Before the surgery, your records all indicated your blood type was A negative. The samples we just tested are O positive."

"Is that possible?"

"I wouldn't think so. Coincidentally, your donor's blood was also O positive, so most likely it was an error somewhere in our paperwork."

Alesha frowned. "But my blood type has always been A negative. I used to donate ..."

"That aside, everything looks good. I'm giving you scrips for the lowest possible dosages of your medications, and we can look you over in a couple weeks to see how you're doing. Meanwhile, relax." His demeanor was brisk, his smile tight and businesslike. "You finally got your dream come true."

"I love your eyes."

Alesha didn't realize the cashier was speaking to her at first. But the clerk smiled wider as she handed back her credit card. "Thanks. That's kind of you to say."

The woman laughed. "I'm sure you get compliments like that all the time. Men can't resist pretty redheads with big green eyes."

Alesha smiled nervously and shrugged. "I guess so." She took her bag of groceries and left without mentioning that her eyes were brown. *She'd have to be colorblind not to notice that!*

She was still adjusting to the attention she now received. While she expected people would stop staring at her like she was a freak, she never thought she'd get so many compliments. Men and women both seemed fascinated with her looks. Not used to all the praise, she found herself more often than not at a loss for words. Sure, she'd always had a pretty face, but adding a head of hair surely wouldn't transform her into a supermodel.

The cashier's comment really bothered her. Her eyes were so brown they were almost black. When she arrived home she headed immediately for the bathroom.

"Holy shit!"

They weren't green ... they were emerald. And for some reason, rounder. Not even the most expensive contact lenses existed to create the shade staring back at her. Those weren't her eyes.

She woke from her nap feeling heavy headed and drained. Standing up, she stretched, rubbing her eyes. Shuffling a few steps, her toe kicked something on the floor. Opening her eyes wide, she gasped. An empty cup of blueberry yogurt rolled across a designer rug. Copper's rug.

She crossed to a desk and brought up the screensaver on a laptop computer. She hovered over the time in the bottom corner. *Four days.*

The blackouts were continuing, sometimes for just a day or two, sometimes for weeks. Every time she woke, she found herself in Copper's apartment, wearing her clothes, eating her yogurt. But Copper wouldn't need it anymore. In fact, Alesha contemplated moving in permanently, especially when she discovered the checkbook to Copper's fat bank account.

It didn't hurt that Alesha discovered she could sign Copper's name perfectly.

She no longer panicked when people paid her unexpected compliments. Before her last blackout, a flirtatious waiter called her "freckle face" ... she discovered afterward that her pale cheeks had turned golden, sprinkled with sandy speckles. To her amusement—and delight—her breasts outgrew her brassieres by a whole cup size. Fortunately, Copper had extravagant taste in lingerie, and it all happened to fit Alesha perfectly. Almost everything about her changed in the months following her surgery, and for the better.

The only lingering concern was the bathtub full of bloody clothes that came with every blackout. She immediately dumped them in the incinerator, and would forget about them. *Out of sight ...*

Life was perfect now that Alesha Alopecia was history.

Copper's apartment proved a much better fit for her new life, as long as she remembered to check the calendar. Once, she forgot, and only discovered that she had blacked out when she went for a shower and stepped into a bloody tub. She only needed to make that mistake once.

She even remembered to respond when people called her Andrea.

Spring cleaning Copper's closet felt like an Easter egg hunt. Looking through boxes and drawers, she found photo albums, journals, budget planners, and keepsakes. Judging by the treasure trove of mementos, she gathered Copper accumulated a lot of frequent-flyer miles.

Humming a song she didn't know, she pulled a stack of hatboxes off a shelf and placed them on the bed. Most of the boxes contained hats. But when she opened the largest one, she found a jumble of mismatched sleeves.

There were different colors, different fabrics, different sizes. The only commonality they shared was that they were all men's sleeves. Some were torn off at the shoulder seam; others appeared to be hacked off with scissors. One by one, she laid them in a neat pile. Twenty three in total.

Underneath the sleeves was a metal lockbox, but the hasp was unlocked. She opened the box, half expecting to find, perhaps, a random collection of collars. Instead, she found a pile of newspaper clippings. She unfolded the clipping that rested on top and read the headline.

Body Found Believed To Be Victim Number 23 for Sioux City Slayer

She looked for a date on the article. It came from the previous day's newspaper. Thumbing through the other clippings, she discovered they were all about the same thing. They came from different papers, different cities, but each one detailed the killing spree of a psychotic murderer who slaughtered men without an apparent motive or agenda.

Her stomach started to cramp.

Twenty-three separate murders, six occurring in the past five months. She sank onto the bed, reading each article, absorbing the details of the murders. The killings started two years earlier, with no rhyme or reason. Investigators couldn't profile the suspect because the only consistent clues were that all the victims were male. And all were found missing one shirt sleeve.

Copper is dead. Dr. Pift burned her body. So why did the murders continue? Was Copper an accomplice? Did the real murderer have access to Copper's apartment?

Now that she knew about the killer, would he come for her next?

Waves of nausea seized her, and she ran for the bathroom. Dropping in front of the commode, dry heaves wracked her abdomen. Alesha rested her head on her arm.

And saw a puddle of bloody clothes in the bathtub.

An explosion in the living room pulled her away from the tub. Heavy footsteps stomping through the apartment amid shouts and commands in strange voices filled her first with fear, and then relief. She was saved!

Suddenly she was staring at the firing end of an automatic weapon, the man behind it screaming at her to lie on the floor.

"I don't understand! What do you want with me?" She couldn't make out exactly what he was saying because the bathroom quickly filled with officers, all angry, all barking orders that made no sense. She laid face down, hoping someone would explain what was happening.

"Andrea Aimes, you are under the arrest for the murders of twenty-three people—"

"No no no! That's not me! I'm not Andrea Aimes. I don't even know her! You're making a big mistake. She's still here!" Alesha pleaded with her captors as they cuffed her hands behind her back and forced her to her feet.

A voice at her back snarled, "Save it, you bitch. We got you on video this time."

"No!"

"Someone tell Forensics we have some evidence in here."

Over her shoulder, she could see a couple policemen leaning over the bathtub.

"I swear to you, I have no idea what's going on ..."

They pushed her into the hallway, where a photographer busied himself with crime scene photos. A flash of light bounced off a passing mirror, drawing her attention. The woman's face in the glass that stared back was not her own.

BY HOOK

BY ELLIOTT CAPON

Rarely does someone decide at an early age to become a pirate.

Such was the case of a medical student named Charles Breck, who, in October 1751, found himself in a situation where leaving his native London *immediately* was imperative; hubris had prompted him to try to reconfigure the damaged face of a member of the Royal Family. With a murder indictment against him and a howling mob almost literally at his heels, he paid a huge sum for an anonymous passage on the *Fair Wind*, bound for Jamaica. With only the clothes on his back and a satchel full of medical books, he reasoned that he could continue his medical education in the colonies; and, perhaps, ten or fifteen years later, return home.

The *Fair Wind*, a relatively small vessel carrying mostly manufacturing equipment, was targeted before it had even sighted Jamaica, overtaken, and easily conquered by one of the dozens of pirate ships stalking the Caribbean. Breck was obviously no seaman, and so sparked the pirates' curiosity.

"Well, lad," the captain of the pirate vessel asked him, "be ye worthy of ransom to some merchant or duke?"

Breck had to smile. The only people waiting for him back in England were the hangman and the headsman. "No, sir," he answered.

The captain glanced over the side, where several crew members of the *Fair Wind* were eagerly rowing away in the small lifeboat the pirates had deigned to give them. Several of their compatriots had been killed in the brief fight after boarding. The ones who had immediately thrown their weapons down had been spared. There was neither point nor profit in slaughtering fellow seamen—the purpose of piracy was to accumulate wealth, not souls. Ransom was as good a source of income as was the actual seizure of goods. But, since this young dandy was worthless ...

"Ye've missed yer boat," the captain said, pointing to the departing lifeboat. He withdrew a poniard from his belt. "I'm afraid we canna accommodate ye, and so—"

As a cold flash ran through his body, Breck looked left and right. He saw two of the pirates inexpertly trying to tie tourniquets around saber wounds they had received in the brief fight. Another lay on the deck, a musket ball in his belly. He saw a glimmer of hope. "Your men are wounded," he said, "have ye not a surgeon to tend to them?"

The captain froze his blade in midair. "No, lad. The bastard went and died on us last month." He tilted his head. "Why? Are ye a sawbones?"

Breck glanced at his satchel containing medical books, which was lying on the deck near the rail. "Aye," he said.

The captain, who replenished his losses of crewmen exclusively by the no-choice-volunteerism of prisoners, smiled. "And wish ye to be ship's surgeon, then, lad?" he asked quietly.

Breck swallowed hard. "Aye, sir," he acknowledged. "I would join your crew."

With a roaring laugh, the captain announced to all assembled that the gentleman was their new shipmate and surgeon. He then demanded that all extraneous debris on the deck—including that satchel full of—*faugh!*—books, be tossed overboard. Breck watched in horror as the rest of his education splashed into the water. Still, he was alive, and that was more than half the battle. Fate would have to look after itself.

Hubris. Arrogance. Cunning. Self-confidence. Megalomania. Charles Breck never fully realized he had these traits, but he did. After the first two or three nervous weeks, he gradually ingratiated himself with the crew to the extent that they thought they had known him since birth. And he knew so much! He would lecture them, singly and in groups, for hours about the mysteries of the sea and its creatures, of far-off lands they only hoped to visit when their pirating days were done, of the perceived (ah! to the trained eye!) mental and physical shortcomings of their captain ... all of which were lies. Breck assumed, and displayed, an intellectual superiority over his fellow buccaneers that had them at first in awe, then in worship. Illiterates the lot of them, they had all fallen into piracy as he had, by ill luck or impressments. They perceived him as a font of illimitable knowledge. The mortality rate among the wounded did indeed fall from previous levels. Others, who could have been saved by a *real* doctor, had their wounds surreptitiously embellished by the ship's surgeon, who would declare them as lost as soon as they were brought to the sick bay.

And thus it was that night in October 1753, when the captain, having another of his Breck-invented "dizzy spells," fell from the quarterdeck into the sea—and, by Davy Jones, right when the doctor was standing next to him!—that the crew unanimously voted Breck to be the new master of the vessel. He promptly demanded to be known as Captain Fear.

From having originally intended to delve into the mysteries of human blood, over the years Captain Fear, discovering how he enjoyed *power* over people, found himself thirsty for the red liquid of life. Thanks to the tales of the few survivors of his predation, Captain Fear and his renamed *Black Barracuda* became, in the truest sense, the "scourge of the Caribbean." The *Black Barracuda* was a swift boat, able to overtake any galleon or merchant ship.

After looting a vessel, the remaining crew and passengers, if any, were then subject to the dubious mercy of Captain Fear. If the captain found himself short of crew, he would see if any of the captured victims would care to join him—he often had more volunteers than he needed. Officers were generally put to death, with the added benefit of a little amusement for the crew by having them walk the plank. Ordinary seamen who were not taken on as *Black Barracuda* material were frequently set adrift in a lifeboat with minimal supplies. Passengers who were worth ransom were taken to a small town on Hispaniola that thrived on the illicit business of piracy—pubs and brothels, "guest houses" for unwilling detainees, even facilities where bulky merchandise would be exchanged for gold coin. But Captain Fear was not called the "scourge" because of his good business practices. Ship's officers who protested, who fought to the bitter end, who, even with their hands tied behind their backs, swore that they would see Captain Fear and his crew *hang! damn you, hang!* had special treatment. They were crucified to the mainmast, nailed three-quarters of the way up, hand and foot, so that they could spend the next two or three days enjoying the view and the wind and salty air and spray, until it was time to die and serve as food for the albatrosses and gulls. Others met fates similar, if quicker. One giant Irishman, for whom there was no room in the tiny boat set aside for his fellows' escape, thrust his chin out and said to Captain Fear: "Sure and I would serve wi' ye, Captain."

"Oh, aye?" asked the Captain, a smile on his face. To the Irishman, it was a good sign; to the Captain's crew, it was a sign of amusement to come.

"I'm a good seaman, a good fighter," the Irishman claimed.

"And would ye abandon your employer and your mates with such ease?" Captain Fear continued.

"Oh, aye," insisted the Irishman, "for what are they to me now but a dim memory?"

The Irishman had only time for a quick "Huh!" as Captain Fear's cutlass entered his pants right below where they buttoned and *ripped* up until the blade rested against his chin. The falling body extricated the sword with little effort from Fear.

"Ah, me lad," he said to the corpse as all of his men laughed and a few even danced a few steps of a spontaneous jig, "I value loyalty first among my crew, not seamanship." He couldn't resist laughing himself as he told his men to feed the sharks their Irish stew.

About a year after taking possession of the *Black Barracuda*, Captain Fear attacked a Portuguese ship that he knew was full of spices and sugar cane. Usually, ships under attack tried to flee; those that could not escape often merely surrendered in the hope of saving their own lives. Captain Fear did not know that this ship, the *Flor de Lisboa*, was family owned and to a large extent family staffed. The passengers and crew had no intention of surrendering their livelihood.

Captain Fear, having only a year of seamanship under his belt, was surprised that the *Flor de Lisboa* was turning *toward* him, apparently planning to ram the *Black Barracuda*. He scrambled about a third of the way up the mainmast netting, hoping to get a better view so that he

190

could direct his men. "Turn toward them, straight on!" he yelled. "Get those grappling hooks at the ready! Hook them, ye dungbies, ye damned freebooters!" The grappling hooks flew across the narrowing gap of water and caught on the Portuguese ship. With the ease borne of practice, the pirate crew turned the *Flor de Lisbon* sideways and brought it thudding into their hull.

A more experienced sailor would have known not to be standing on a rope netting, holding on with one hand, when two ships crunched together. Captain Fear was knocked off the ropes. He landed on his sternum, half-bent across the low railing of his own vessel, his arms hanging over the side.

The vagaries of the sea separated the ships for a few feet, for a few seconds. In that time, Captain Fear, stunned and unable to breathe, managed to get his left arm back to his side. But then the ships smashed together again, catching his right arm just below the elbow between the two vessels. The Captain choked a scream and managed to pull back a bloody, mangled mass of dripping flesh and ruined bone.

As was usual, the battle-experienced crew of the *Black Barracuda* eventually won the contest. This time, none of the opponents were permitted the succor of a lifeboat.

Some hours after the transfer of merchandise and the murder of the survivors, Captain Fear retired to his cabin. His crew heard screaming, but didn't dare enter. Two hours later, the captain came on deck, missing his right arm from about halfway down from the elbow, a bloody, bandaged stump defining the end of his arm. The crew saw him fling something overboard with his left arm, and then he gave orders to head to their town on Hispaniola. He retired to his cabin for eighteen hours and, when they docked, he came out clutching dozens of sheets of paper on which the crew could see intricate designs and drawings. He gave them three days' liberty among the rum houses and brothels of the town.

Captain Fear went ashore and sought out the surgeon who had been, for indiscretions that nearly had him dancing the hempen jig, expelled from the British Navy. This worthy now made his living in that godforsaken town, mostly performing abortions and amputations and treating the French Pox. Fear showed him his drawings.

For three days, people who passed the surgeon's house heard screams and curses ... which was not at all unusual. When Captain Fear emerged from the house on the third day, he sported a brand new hook on the end of his arm. But he also carried a large canvas bag that clanked as, pale but determined, he went back to his ship, collected his crew, and set off to sea again.

Captain Fear was not merely the owner of a hook on the end of his arm, his crew discovered; he had a *collection* of tools and utensils. For a good and proper fee, the disgraced surgeon had drilled holes in Fear's radius and ulna bones, cleaned them out, made nice little tunnels in them. He had then, with the assistance of the town blacksmith, made a variety of hooks, small spade-like tools, sharp pointed knives, and spoon-shaped utensils. Each of these ended in a round base that fit the stump at the end of Fear's right arm, and then had two long prongs that inserted into the holes he had drilled in the bones, making for a secure fit. He sewed a metal latch, something like a mousetrap, into the skin of Fear's arm that fit into slots on each of the addendum's bases, so that each tool slid into the bone, and, as added security, was latched onto Fear's arm.

Thus, the captain could switch from hook to spade to lance as the mood struck him. As he slid off and on the appendages, the pain was quick but intense, like the application of a branding—but it was a small price to pay for the versatility and the ability to increase his knowledge.

That vestige of a would-be doctor, the Charles Breck that still lived in the callous Captain Fear, had decided that the time was right to finish his medical education after all. Sometimes there were hostages who weren't worth ransoming, and whom it would be no fun just killing. These were the people Captain Fear took into his workroom to continue his anatomical research.

The narrow shovel, the thing that looked like a giant crochet needle, the pincer that actually grasped and tore ... he would unlatch whatever he was wearing, painfully slide off what he had on and painfully slide on the tool of choice. Once the burning sensation had subsided, he would begin to delve into the mysteries of human anatomy. There was rum and whisky in the workroom, but that was for him, to slake his thirst, not to dull in the slightest the pains of the objects of his experimentation.

The crew would gather at the other end of the ship and play hornpipes and sing sea shanties when the captain's curiosity was aroused. He was the captain and no one dared question Captain Fear, but still ...

There was not a cloud in the sky from horizon to horizon that April day in 1756 when they spotted the British man-of-war escorting a massive, low-in-the-water merchant vessel, headed northeast. That meant the ship was going back to England, doubtless loaded with raw goods.

The man-of-war put up a good fight. Captain Fear gave begrudging respect to the sailors on board, and to their morale and competence. That meant that the officers were probably decent men, so he considerately had their throats cut before dumping their bodies overboard.

Taking the merchant ship, of course, was as difficult as strolling through your aunt's tea-rose garden.

There were civilians on board, after all. A man of about fifty, well-dressed; apparently his wife; and a young thing of about fourteen who was likely their daughter. There were also three servants, but they counted for naught, at present.

The older man was shaking, whether from fear or indignation Captain Fear didn't know, nor care. "Pray, whom do I have the honor of addressing?" the captain asked him.

"I am Lord Ellington," the man said. "I am the Vice-Governor of the Royal Spice Conglomerate, to whom this ship and all its goods belong."

"Ah, sir!" Captain Fear chided him, waving his finger. "'Tis I, Captain Fear, to whom this ship and all its goods belong." He paused. "As do its passengers." The crewmen, who had gathered around watching the scene, chuckled in appreciation of their captain's wit. "And, speaking of passengers," Fear continued, "whom might these ladies be?"

Ellington turned red. There was no doubt but that fright was gone from him; he was angry now.

"My wife, the Lady Ellington, and our daughter, Miss Priscilla."

"Oooh, Miss Priscilla," Fear said in a high, lilting, feminine voice. This generated another, heartier laugh from his ruffians. "And, m'Lord," he continued in his normal voice, "has me fair wench yet to have been plundered, d'ya think?"

This got a hearty laugh from his men, while Ellington shook as if he had the ague. His wife and daughter looked like they were going to faint. Captain Fear joined the laughter.

"Worry, not, dear Papa! Ye are to be held for ransom, and it's the addled member of the brethren of the coast who damages his own merchandise!" He turned to look at his other remaining captives: servants, apparently of the Ellingtons. He pointed to a small, wizened man. "And who be this, m'Lord, your own dear papa?"

Ellington's indignation was now limitless. "Bounder!" he replied. "That's McTavish, my manservant."

"Ah," Captain Fear nodded in understanding. "T'will not return the cost of feeding a manservant, when ransom payment arrives, will it, m'Lord?" He took a pistol out of his belt and with absolutely no ado shot McTavish in the head. Two of his men matter-of-factly tossed the corpse overboard. "And this pretty lassie—" he got another laugh, for he was indicating another woman, also in the coarser garb of a servant, who by the looks of her had accompanied Noah on *his* inaugural sea voyage.

"My—my wife's maidservant, M-Mrs. O'Halloran," stammered Ellington.

"Tis *Mrs.* O'Halloran, it is then? Why then she be's not some blushing virgin, hah?" He turned to his men: "Who wants themselves a fair turn with this proud beauty?"

With a roar of laughter and exclamations of what passed for witticisms, the crew turned down the chance to cavort with the elderly woman. When the laughter had subsided sufficiently, the Captain made a small gesture with his hand and, while Lady Ellington and Priscilla screamed, two of his corsairs grabbed the old woman and dumped her over the side.

"And now ..." said the captain, approaching the last remaining hostage.

The woman was about thirty or so, black, black, black as the darkest night. Whether she was a second- or third-generation Jamaican or had herself come over on a slave boat direct from Africa, Fear couldn't tell. But there was one thing about her ... she held herself *proudly*. She stood tall and erect and looked him in the eye. She wasn't shaking, nor were her lips trembling, nor were there tears in her eyes. She was defiance personified.

Captain Fear couldn't take his eyes off her. "Take these three and make bilge rats of them," he ordered. Several crewmen grabbed the Ellingtons and forced them below.

Fear kept staring at the black woman. There was not only defiance in her stance, her posture, her expression, there was ... he searched for the word ... a *regalness*, a *dignity* ... a strength of spirit he had never seen in any *real* human being, much less a Black ...

And within him, Charles Breck, would-be man of medicine, decided that this manifestation of strength and haughtiness must have a physical basis. It had to be there, somewhere, inside that proud body.

He had her brought to his workroom. She was stripped and strapped spread-eagle to the table. The crewmen who had prepared her quickly left the room and headed for the foc'sle, where a loud musical soiree had been planned to cover up the anticipated noise. The captain fortified himself with a big glass of rum. He took out his book of notes and found a blank page. Then he went over to the wall where a dozen different appendages hung. Wincing, he removed the traditional hook he had been wearing, and pushed in a base that had a three-pronged fork.

He got to work.

The music was loud, the men sang as vociferously as they could, but they still couldn't drown out the screaming they heard when they paused for breath or for a drink. It seemed to go on for hours, and they themselves tired of the constant concertina playing, hornpipe dancing, and lusty song singing.

Eventually, to their relief, they saw the door to the captain's cabin open. He bore in his hands a ... monstrosity.

It was slickly red and it had no arms or legs. But it had eyes. From the other end of the ship they could see open white eyes in that mass of red. The captain slowly walked over to the rail, as if exhausted.

"I curse you!" the sailors heard, every one of them, as if the words had been spoken directly into their ears. "I curse you to hell!"

The crew saw no reaction on the captain's face as he threw the wet crimson mass into the choppy sea, where it hit with a splash. "I curse you!" each of them vividly heard. "I curse you to hell!"

The captain turned to where his crew were sitting, all gaping at him.

"Make sail, damn you!" he bellowed, and they all scrambled to their stations.

Men scurried up rope ladders and along the railings, untying knots and pulling on ropes. In moments, hundreds of square yards of canvas were unfurled. The captain walked up to the wheel.

And the wind stopped.

Hundreds of yards of canvas flopped down, limp and unmoving. "Becalmed," whispered forty voices. There was silence for a few seconds, the silence of shock and surprise, because never had the winds died just like *that*. There was no sound but the creaking of the wooden ship and the gentle slap of water against the sides. Until they all distinctly heard:

"I curse you! I curse you to hell!"

Everyone, including the captain, rushed over to the port side and looked down. Floating in the water, bumping gently against the side of the ship, was something red, something with no arms and legs but with big white eyes. "I curse you!" they heard from that floating thing. "I curse you to hell!"

The captain muttered profanities, though no one could hear exactly what he was saying. Finally he bellowed, "Sink that! Sink that damned thing!"

It took some time for the stunned crew to react, but finally the second mate took an empty barrel, leaned out over the railing just above the floating thing, and let the barrel fall. The object floated away from the ship and the barrel fell harmlessly between the ship and the thing. Then it drifted back, bumping into the wooden side of the vessel. "I curse you!" the crew heard, as if the sound were coming from the thing, "I curse you to hell!"

Other objects were thrown overboard to try and hit the thing. Each time it drifted away, to receive only the splash of whatever had hit the water, and then it was back, bump-bump-bumping against the side of the *Black Barracuda*.

Superstitious as only sailors can be, the entire crew, as if with one mind, backed away to the starboard side of the ship. No matter how much Captain Fear railed at them, they would not come back to portside and lean over and try to throw anything else at the floating thing. The captain uttered every profanity known to every seafaring man in the world at the time, but to no avail. He finally gave up and went back into his cabin.

For three days, the *Black Barracuda* remained motionless, as if anchored, with not a breath of wind to provide any motive power. For three days, it remained in one place, relative to the stars and the hot midday sun, while constantly, constantly they heard "I curse you! I curse you to hell!" from that red floating thing with the white eyes.

For three days, no one saw the captain. He remained in his cabin until at about noon on the fourth day, when he rushed out onto deck. "I can't stand it anymore!" he cried out to everyone and no one. "Is there no wind to free us from this damned thing?"

To his crew's astonishment, he began scampering up the ropes attached to the mainmast. He wore his plain hook, the one favored by pirates since time immemorial. He used this to climb the rope maze until he was in the crow's nest. Openmouthed, the crew stared at him. Captains did *not* go up to the crow's nest, not ever.

He raised one fist and one hook toward the sky and screamed, "Wind! Wind! Damn you, Neptune, Jesus Christ, whoever or whatever you may be, give me *wind!*"

Just then, an unusual swell suddenly lifted the *Black Barracuda* and tipped it over to starboard at an almost eighty degree list. Every man on board slid or fell against the starboard rail; everything not nailed to the deck followed them.

In the crow's nest, Captain Fear found himself suspended thirty feet over the water, the sides of the crow's nest becoming his floor and within two seconds of becoming his ceiling. With an instinct born of practice, he shot out his right arm and looped his hook over a stout piece of cross-rope. As the boat continued its list, he found himself hanging from the rope by just the hook—an uncomfortable position, but not an untenable one. He could hang there until the boat righted.

The hook's base separated from his arm with an agonizing shock of pain. He had a fraction of a second to look at his arm, to see that the latch that held the hook to his arm was still in the locked position, before he hit the water.

He went under, came up. He had removed and replaced his arm appendages a thousand times, and they had never bled; now his arm was gushing blood like a geyser. As he stared at the stump in disbelief, a gust of wind at gale force came up and filled the *Black Barracuda*'s sails to the breaking point, propelling the ship forward as if it were a horse with its tail ablaze.

As Captain Fear watched his ship sail away from him, he noticed a long shadow passing under him; left to right; right to left; left to right, as his blood continued to pour into the blue waters of the Caribbean. Then he saw the fin and, for the merest fraction of a second, was fascinated by the way the fin split the water into a slim channel.

It might have been an Oceanic Whitetip or a Lemon shark; Captain Fear did not care. All he knew was that there was a tremendous agony around his midsection, and he somehow knew that whatever there had been of him below the navel was now gone.

As the pain swept through him, he surrendered to death. But the pain was unrelenting. He opened his eyes and saw himself in a pool of red. *He was not yet dead.*

Through the waves of agony, he lowered his left hand into the water. He felt where his left thigh should have been ... there was nothing there. He crossed his arm in front of him, felt for the other thigh ... not there. Then he put his hand onto his belly, and moved it down. His hand went down under his torso, where his bladder and intestines should have been, and felt something hard and wooden. Something ... smooth. Like a ... polished wood. Like ... the base that was latched onto the end of his arm, to fit his tools into ... something that sealed his torn body and was not letting him bleed to death ...

He felt a bump at his back. At first, he thought, he prayed to the God he so often cursed, that it was the shark coming back to finish him. He turned his head slightly and saw something red, something with no arms and legs, but with big white eyes, rubbing against him.

"I curse you," the thing said. "I curse you to hell."

CREEPING DEATH

BY ARMAND ROSAMILIA

It was raining the first night I saw Angelika at the Limelight. I'd gone straight from work, a dingy café in Belmar, into New York City, dressing as I rode. By the time I walked from Penn Station to Avenue of the Americas and West 20th Street, I was drenched—my mascara running down my face, the black lipstick streaked, and my fishnet top weighing an extra ten pounds.

Ironically, I'd been to this location before, but for a different reason—although, if I was being honest, it was actually one of the same reasons. When this was Odyssey House, in the late '70s, I stayed for a month with a serious heroin addiction. My parents pretty much abandoned me at that point, and I never looked back. I kicked the habit, slinking into quieter ways to get high and drop out of society.

The weekend before, I'd been here to see Johnny Thunders with some friends from Jersey, the small clique of freaks that I trusted. Of course, most of them had gone off into different rooms of the Limelight to score drugs or sex, or just to get away.

I watched the band, watched the people, and got drunk on the overpriced drinks. With nothing else to do, I decided to make this my Friday night haunt until something better came along. Jersey clubs were so damn lame, with Springsteen or hair metal bands at the Jersey Shore. If another "soulful acoustic love" hit on me again, I was going to puke.

Boys back home were usually dirty, unemployed, and expecting to get laid because they carried a cheap guitar. I wanted nothing to do with any of them.

New York City was alive, armed and dangerous. Here I could meet a guy or a girl—as long as they were my type, who cared—and get to know them for a night, and then get back to my real, boring life by sunrise. I wanted to live the vampire dream, as they said in books and on the street. I also wanted to see how close I could come to heroin without partaking. Call it nihilistic, call it living on the edge, call it stupid, but I loved the high of being so close to the high.

Until I met Angelika. In a sea of soaking-wet goths and metal-heads, she alone was completely dry, as if she'd spent the day in the self-proclaimed Rock N Roll Church, sleeping in one of the dark recesses until the sun dropped below the tower.

Techno music was never on the top of my list, but when I watched her from across the main room, I was converted. She was flirting with a stoned metal dude, who was wearing his wet hair draped over his shoulders and his sleeveless denim jacket (with a menacing Black Sabbath depiction on the back) like a badge of honor. I immediately hated him and was jealous of the attention this low-life was getting from a chick I didn't even know. When she looked at me and grinned, I wanted to be with her—shit, I wanted to be inside her.

Without a word, she left the metal dude's side and approached me through the throng of bodies, swirling reds and greens and blues and yellows streaking across the dance floor. Two feet from me, she reached out her delicate hand. She was dressed in black, like ninety-nine percent of the crowd, but she wore the color like it was part of her. Her stomach was exposed under her half-shirt, taut and sexy, her legs were painted with black leather pants riding into her studded black boots. Black eyeliner, black lipstick, black nail polish, jet black hair, and arms covered in dark, swirling tattoos. I was in love.

"Do you want to get high?" she whispered, even though the room was deafening with the beat and the mindless chatter.

"I don't do that," I said, and wanted to cry. She smiled, her little pink tongue licking her black lips, before turning away. I caught a glimpse of her twice more during the night, but it was in passing, and each time I tried to follow her but she disappeared through the crowds and maze of rooms.

I wanted to meet her and be with her. I couldn't explain the feeling. I walked through the rest of my week like a zombie, going through the motions at work, staying in my apartment, and barely eating. I don't think the television was turned on once, and the Stephen King book I was reading went untouched.

Friday, I left work early, stuffing my clothes into my bag and heading to NYC. There was a sparse crowd hanging on the corner in front of the Limelight. The sun was dropping, the air was cold, and my stomach growled. The club wouldn't open for at least three more hours.

Then, suddenly, she was there, wandering through the crowd, touching and hugging as she went. Her all-black outfit had morphed into a red cat-suit, with tiny black felt ears on her head, and blood-red nails.

Suddenly I felt like a poser, with my mall-bought black boots and tight leather pants. I realized with a blush that I'd copied her outfit from last week, and it looked horrible on me. I turned to run back to the train station, tail tucked between my legs.

"Hey," she purred and placed a warm hand on my shoulder, spinning me around. "Hungry?"

We spent three hours, sitting side by side in a bagel store, talking and laughing and staring at one another. I knew that she was completely in control. I felt important in those three hours, like I was the only thing that mattered. I couldn't remember the last time I felt like that, and I didn't want it to stop.

My throat ached, and I realized I had done most of the talking, Angelika interviewing me with questions about my past, my dreams, and my fears. I opened up to her like I never had to anyone before. I knew nothing about her still, but my mind couldn't form a single question to ask.

"It's time," she said, and rose from her chair, taking my hand in hers.

"Huh?" I replied stupidly.

At this Angelika laughed. "The Limelight is opening in twenty minutes. You can go in with me, I know everyone."

I was elated and nervous. I'd be going in with her. I'd be *seen* going in with her. I felt like I'd finally made it.

"You know the story behind this place, right?" she asked as we approached the club.

When I shook my head, she smiled. "You can't experience the Limelight without knowing its history, now, can you?" Angelika stopped and pointed at the front of the building, ancient, dark and mysterious. "It was built in 1844 by Richard Upjohn, and it's considered a Gothic Revival brownstone by the State of New York. It was an Episcopal Church of the Holy Communion. When it was deconsecrated in the 1970s, it was sold to Odyssey House." Angelika smiled. "We'll skip that part for now."

I swallowed and looked away, back to the group of people standing idly around the front entrance, waiting to get in like the commoner that I had been last weekend.

We slid through a spot where the high, ancient fences didn't quite meet, the former church hovering over us in the dark, the spotlights drowned out by the blackness.

Inside, we stepped into a small antechamber, and I imagined priests and altar boys waiting here for the crowds to amass.

Three figures emerged from the corner shadows, the effect unsettling. They wore garish outfits of black and leather and spikes and makeup. The closest wore corpse-paint and had so many body-piercings on his face that I stopped counting. His naked upper torso was covered in strange tattoos. The other two were females and looked like twins, with matching dominatrix outfits and the same exact tattoos on their exposed flesh.

"Newbie?" the man said, spitting out the word as he stared at me.

One of the twins suddenly gripped my wrist tightly and pulled my arm close to her black lipstick. She smiled as I tried vainly to pull away. "Heroin?" she asked and finally let me go. I was sure I would bruise where she'd grabbed me.

"Not anymore," I muttered.

All three looked at Angelika, who only smiled.

The other twin pulled up her shirt, exposing her tattoo-covered chest. I looked away instinctively. Everyone laughed. When I looked back to her she was still flashing me, but I controlled myself and looked. On each breast, around the nipple, was the symbol for anarchy that I'd seen all the punk kids using—a letter 'A' in a circle. Other tattoos went up and down her sides, but they seemed to start at the nipple tattoos.

The guy put his wrists together, forming the anarchy symbol there as well.

I looked to Angelika, confused, but she simply lifted her dark hair from her neck and showed me her own anarchy mark at her nape.

"I have six of them," the first twin said. "She only has five."

"One more, tomorrow, and I'll be caught up. There's a tattoo dude we use in the Village." She glanced at Angelika. "We all use him."

"What's his name?" I finally asked when no one said anything.

"Ask for Carlo."

"Where?" I asked.

"Greenwich Village. Everyone who is anyone will know Carlo," the guy said.

"I'll do that," I said, having no desire to. I was tattoo-free and wanted to stay that way. Even though I'd used a hundred needles for drugs in my time, I didn't want the permanence of tattoo ink staining my skin.

Without a word, Angelika opened the door to our small vestibule and we were inundated with blaring techno music, swirls of dancers, and the stomping of feet.

Angelika quickly disappeared into the crowd with her three apostles and I ran to catch up, but they were already gone into the bowels of the Limelight. Tonight the club was packed, and it took me several hours to get my first drink and calm my nerves. I watched an all-female metal band pump the crowd up, shatter some eardrums, and then scream their way off stage.

The rest of my night was spent looking for Angelika, but she'd become a ghost. Finally, at the last possible minute, as the crowd thinned out only slightly, I trudged back to the train station and back to my un-life in Jersey.

My week was spent at work, pulling a couple of doubles because I needed the money. My trips to New York were costly, once you factored in train tickets, food, and the proper clothing. Now my rent was a week past due and I was struggling to make it up.

On Friday, despite still being a hundred bucks short on the rent, I was back in front of the Limelight. It was coming into late October and the wind and the chill were getting to me. Wearing only a short skirt and fishnet stockings wasn't helping, either.

A metal-head approached me cautiously. I did my best to ignore him but he stood in front of me and smiled. He was actually cute, with piercing blue eyes and a thin goatee, his dirty blond hair pulled into a ponytail. I played the bitch and stared at his leather jacket and various band insignias. I'd never heard of most of the bands, and the logos were so damn hard to even read.

"I'm Bruno."

I ignored him and moved to the fence.

Bruno didn't take the hint. "I saw you with her last Friday, but not on Saturday."

"What?" I blurted.

"You were at the L7 show but not here the next night."

"So? I have a life," I said defensively. I was hurt to think Angelika hadn't bothered to invite me to the Saturday show, and then realized how stupid and childish that sounded.

"You went?" I asked.

"Yeah." He pulled up his sleeve and showed me a new tattoo, a very familiar one. "I got it yesterday."

"Where?"

He eyed me skeptically. "Carlo."

"Can you take me there?"

Bruno took a step back. "I don't know."

"What do you mean, you don't know?"

"You need to find Carlo on your own."

"Whatever." Now I was pissed at this waste-of-time dirtbag. "I'll do it myself."

I walked away and hailed a cab, heading for Greenwich Village. I had no idea what I was looking for, which street to stop on, or who to ask about Carlo.

The night was a bust. I made it to the train just in time, and spent so much money on cab fare that I was even further behind.

Elena and I had been roommates in Odyssey House and had kept in touch for the last few years. I hadn't seen her in six months, when she suddenly was there, sitting in the corner of the café and ordering a coffee.

I took my break, we hugged, and I sat with her. Elena had fallen off the wagon a number of times since Odyssey, but she looked clean right now.

"You've been back?" she asked over her coffee mug.

"Back where?" I asked.

"I saw you in line Friday night at the Limelight."

I laughed. "Yes, every week. I can't help it, the place is so freaking cool. You were there?"

"Yes. It's so weird being back there, after being ... there. Our old rooms are now a bar, which is ironic."

"Remember the time we snuck in that Mad Dog 20/20 and got ripped?" I asked.

"Good times."

"It's funny, but I've been there three Fridays in a row but never bothered to find the rooms. It's so different in the dark, and with the lights and noise."

"I saw Nikki and Cindy."

"Where?"

"Where do you think? Last Friday, hanging around with the cool crowd."

"That's weird. I took those two for complete dweebs. How'd they get with the cool crowd?"

"I didn't talk to them. You should have seen Nikki, though. She was covered in tattoos. Remember, she was the one who used to shit on you for using needles, saying she'd never stick herself?"

"No kidding?"

"Covered. All kinds of weird shit, too. Sayings from the Bible, band names, punk symbols, animals ..."

"What kind of punk symbols?" I asked, but the hair on my neck stood up and I knew, I already knew.

"That dumb anarchy thing you see graffiti idiots spray-painting on the sides of buildings. You still a cutter?" she asked.

I shriveled when she said that. Elena put a hand on my arm and frowned. "I'm sorry, that was so rude."

"No, it's alright." I put both arms up and showed her my healed marks. "I haven't done it in years." Besides being a heroin addict, I'd been a cutter, slicing into my forearms, legs, and torso and bleeding. Odyssey had cured me of drugs and the self-mutilation.

"Going to the Limelight on Friday?" she asked, to change the subject.

"Yes."

"I'll pick you up at six and we'll go in together," she said.

I wanted to punch Nikki in the face. We stood near the stage, waiting for some local band to start the night, pushed and prodded by way too many people in the club.

Nikki was proudly showing Elena and me her third anarchy tattoo, the ink still drying.

"Where'd you get that? Better yet, why?" Elena asked.

"Carlo did them."

"Where?" I asked, trying to remain calm.

"You need to find him," she said slyly. I balled my fists and refrained from swinging and getting thrown out before I'd talked to Angelika. I needed to see her.

"What, do you want one of those stupid things?" Elena asked.

I ignored the question and moved away, into the crowd, in search of Angelika or someone who might be able to help me. There were quite a few people there with the tattoo, but they mostly looked me over to see if I had one, and when they didn't see it, would ignore me like I was a leper.

By the time the headline band was up and blasting out their techno/metal hybrid, I was defeated. I then set out to find Elena so I could get back home to Jersey, back to my shitty job, shitty apartment, and shitty non-life.

Elena was still with Nikki, laughing as I approached her. I saw Cindy as well as the metal dude I'd talked to last Friday, and a dozen others.

And, right in the middle of the circle, was Angelika, looking positively angelic in all white. As I approached, Angelika suddenly stepped away from the others and hugged me, gripping me tightly. "Where have you been? Your friend Elena is so charming."

I was jealous. Elena had spent the night with Angelika while I spent the night on a wild goose chase. I faked a smile and joined the group, but it was already breaking up.

"She is so cool. Why didn't you tell me you knew her?" Elena asked when we walked away. Once again, Angelika had disappeared.

"I need to go find someone," I murmured.

"Carlo?" Elena asked.

"How do you know?"

"I think the two of us can find him."

I followed her outside and straight into a cab. Once again, I found myself being led by someone else through life, but I had no idea how to change the course of events. Instead, I walked a step behind Elena in our search for Carlo, asking random people in Greenwich Village about tattoos.

We almost passed a homeless man cradling a worn backpack in a dark doorway. I stopped and asked him bluntly, "Any idea where Carlo can be found?"

He smiled, his two remaining teeth bright white. "The tattooist?"

"Yes," Elena and I said much too loudly. In the middle of the night, with the cold creeping into my bones and my hooker-ish outfit, I realized that we were very vulnerable.

"My thoughts are always fuzzy when I'm sober, for some reason," he said.

Elena pulled a single from her pocket and handed it to him. The bill was sucked into his clothing but he still smiled.

"Well?" I asked.

"You gave me a dollar, which I appreciate. Good luck in finding Carlo."

I gave him a ten dollar bill and watched it vanish. He simply pointed at the doorway behind him. When we didn't move, he shook his head and laughed, a dry, two-packs-of-cigarettes-a-day cough. "Carlo."

We gingerly stepped over him and his possessions, entering the hallway. It reeked of cat urine—I hoped it was only cat urine—and mold. As quickly as we could manage, we found another door and Elena knocked on it. When no one answered, she jiggled the door handle and it swung open, revealing bright light.

The room was large, with walls painted white, and at least a dozen fluorescent lamps illuminating the rows of television screens mounted haphazardly on the walls, piled on tables and counters, and stacked on the floor three and four high.

"Hello?" Elena called out.

A wiry man dressed in a white lab coat and fingerless gloves stepped out of a side room and smiled. "Can I help you ladies?"

"We're here to see Carlo."

"That would be me. Are you here to pick up or drop off a television set?" he asked.

"We're here about the tattoos," Elena said.

He frowned, clearly puzzled. "Sorry, I only do TV repair."

We'd been had? Was this some elaborate joke to make me look stupid? I finally took charge, something I never do, and stepped forward. "Let's cut the games, Carlo. I know what you do, and I want the anarchy tattoo that everyone who knows Angelika seems to have."

Carlo smiled. "Why?"

I stared at him. Nothing solid came to mind. Why did I want a tattoo, when I'd never wanted one before? "I need it." That was as good an answer as I could think of right at that moment.

Carlo looked at Elena. "You?"

"Same as her."

He put his hand on his stubbly chin and stared into a corner for a full minute. I was about to clear my throat and bring him back to Earth when he turned and asked us to follow him.

The room was smaller than the previous but equally bright, with a single tattooing chair in the middle of the room and a wheeled cabinet holding his tools. The walls were bare, and no tattoo art covered the walls, no pictures, no stray pieces of dirt, no scraps of paper.

I was shaking as I sat down in the chair.

"One hundred dollars," Carlo said.

My heart nearly stopped. "I think I have eighty," I stammered.

He pointed at Elena. "One hundred dollars."

She fished through her small pocketbook and pulled out a thin wad of cash, counting out five twenties. She hesitated, holding her last twenty in her hand, before handing it to me.

I smiled, gave him my money, and then tried not to pass out or shake myself to death while he gave me the tattoo on my left shoulder.

While I stood in the corner afterwards, nursing my bruised and bleeding arm, Elena got hers in the same spot.

"Will you be returning soon?" Carlo asked.

"I'm not sure," I said. "Why?"

"Many of Angelika's friends get multiple tattoos from me." He dropped his smile. I was suddenly reminded of a wolf. "Only I can give this tattoo."

I ducked my landlord for the rest of the week, picked up as many shifts as I could at work, and pawned my radio, TV, and some of my clothes I would never wear again.

Elena popped into work Friday morning sporting a new matching tattoo on the other shoulder.

I was pissed. "You went without me?"

"Nah, I got this one in Point Pleasant."

"That doesn't count."

Elena laughed and ordered coffee.

"It really doesn't. Carlo was very specific about not getting one from anyone but him."

"I don't remember signing an exclusive contract with him. Besides, he does so many of these. I'll wait a couple of weeks and get another one then."

"How many are you going to get?" I asked, trying to keep my voice from pitching higher. I knew I was going tonight to get another one, thinking she'd stop at one. I remembered seeing people at the Limelight with six or seven of them.

"As many as it takes. One chick had seventeen of them."

I was stunned. I also needed to get more money, and get it fast.

"I'll pick you up at six."

Three weeks and three more tattoos later, I was in serious danger of being homeless and eventually going to jail. I'd begun skimming a few dollars from the register at work, then not claiming a few customers each night and pocketing the money. Finally, I was thinking of staging a holdup so I could get a few hundred bucks in one shot and get four or five tattoos at once.

I'd sold almost everything I owned except for the two outfits I alternated each Friday night. Elena, who had played it cool and not gone with me to see Carlo, finally decided that it was time to go back and get another tattoo. I'm sure she was quite envious of my four.

I'd seen Angelika around the Limelight, but we'd never been able to connect. Several of her followers said "hi" to me, smiling when they saw my tattoos. I was now on the edge of their little clique, I could feel it. Almost all of them had more tattoos than I did, however, and I felt like I was running out of time. I knew I was running out of money.

We stopped at Carlo's and he greeted me with a smile, asking where I wanted the next tattoo. I now had both shoulders and both ankles done. I decided to be daring—and desperate—despite Elena in the room with me. "I want one just above my pussy. How does that sound?"

Carlo nodded absently. "You should really get them where you can see them. How about on your neck? Or your shoulder blades?"

"How about both?" I said, trying to be casual. I was no whore, but I knew what I was about to try and I was terrified. "Can you give me some discount on two at a time?"

Carlo went to his tools. "No, one hundred dollars each. No discounts."

"What about if we strike some type of deal?" I said, licking my lips seductively when he turned back to me.

"One hundred dollars per tattoo."

I glanced at Elena. "What if we both ...?"

I noticed that Elena didn't complain, just stared at Carlo.

Carlo grinned and shook his head. "One hundred dollars per tattoo."

Without another word, he took my hundred dollars and immediately started to prep the left side of my neck. I was going to protest and tell him that I wanted it near my crotch, and that my boss might not take kindly to a bright red tattoo on my neck, but I said nothing. Once again.

It hurt like a bitch, but I never made a sound.

When it was Elena's time she proudly announced that she wanted the same spot. Carlo shook his head and tapped her right shoulder. "Not my work."

"Sure it is." She waved the hundred dollars in front of him.

Carlo turned away. "It is time for you to leave."

Elena looked stunned. "You can't be serious."

He turned to her and I thought he was going to attack her. "I am dead serious. You are no longer welcome here."

I never saw Elena again, but I didn't care. In the weeks between that fifth tattoo and now I did some bad, bad things: I began playing loose, hitching up with losers in the bars of Belmar and Sea Bright and having sex with them for a place to crash for a day or so. Then, when I'd gained their trust, I'd simply rob them and sell all their stuff and move on to the next loser. I couldn't go back to the job since I'd taken the deposit my first night back, and I was sure the cops were looking for me.

Now I was back in NYC.

Carlo was waiting for me at the door with a smile.

I dropped $4,982 on the tattoo chair. "What can I get for this?"

"Ever heard of scarification?"

The Limelight had a line wrapped around the building, even at three in the morning. I didn't know what band was playing, but I knew I was trapped here for the day since the last train back to Jersey would be long gone. I thought on that and smiled—although doing so made my mouth hurt, and my face, and my eyes—about never having to go back to Jersey again. There was nothing that I needed there. I stared at the church before me and knew I was home.

The line was moving quickly, and as I got near the front I saw why. There were five people letting people in or rejecting them. Most of the line was being turned away, but I knew I wasn't going to be.

211

When I got to the front, two of the guys, whom I'd seen with Angelika before, smiled in awe and let me pass. Inside, everyone was openly staring at me as I made my way slowly to the main room and the stage area.

There was no band tonight, the house lights were low, and there was a sea of candles on the stage and in the alcoves and catwalks above. Angelika, completely nude, stood on a raised platform on the stage, surveying the hundreds before her.

Her body was covered in small anarchy symbols, of varying colors and sizes, but none bigger than six inches. They seemed to be taking over her other, older tattoos.

When our eyes met she gasped with delight and had me escorted to the stage to stand with her.

It took me nearly fifteen minutes to get through the crowd to the stage. I thought I was going to pass out, but I made it, my sweat mixed with all the blood.

"Behold, the true believer!" Angelika exclaimed, quieting the crowd.

I noticed Nikki and Cindy among several other familiar faces I hadn't seen in years, all former friends from Odyssey.

"I thank you for coming to the last night some have on this vile Earth. Former drug addicts, alcoholics, and the insane, rejoice! The outside world as we know it will soon be gone, and in its place a new civilization will emerge," Angelika shouted. "There are those that believed enough to mark themselves and prove their worth in the coming apocalypse, and I thank you. There are those that went above and beyond and strove for a better place in the new world order."

Angelika turned to me. "There are those that went so far beyond where I thought it would go that they have proven to me their love."

I held back the urge to pass out or puke. I could feel the bruises and blood pumping in time to my rapid heartbeat. I looked down at my arms, slit open and weeping, my skin sizzling from the scarification. Six brutal hours strapped in the chair while Carlo worked on every inch of my body. I'd passed out several times, especially when I first saw the jagged branding irons.

My cheeks were branded, my forehead, both breasts, up and down my thighs, my stomach had several different-sized anarchy symbols branded, and my back was on fire with pain.

212

I didn't know what exactly was going on and whether I was going to die, but I could feel my life's blood slowly draining away. Already, there was a puddle forming at my feet, a mixture of blood, mucus, and fried skin.

There was a rumble like thunder out in the street and Angelika held her hands above her head. "It is coming. I need you to stand fast and true. Those that swear fealty to my cause will survive this night. We are the new messiahs, the new gods of a new age. Like Moses before us, who painted doors in lamb's blood, so, too, we have painted our bodies with a mystic symbol so that Death will pass us."

When the green mist began leaking through the walls and doors, sweeping past the gathered, I smiled, even though it twisted my scarred flesh and my eyes fluttered from the pain.

I was home.

PARAPHILIA

BY LISA MANNETTI

"Geri? This is Felicia from What's Your Fetish. You want to work tonight or what?"

"What's the deal?"

"Two slap-happy drunks in town for a convention. They're at the Helmsley New Yorker. They want a redhead with a stump."

"Yeah?" Geri lit a cigarette. It never hurt to pause a little, give herself some maneuvering room. The redhead part was easy. She could do a quick temporary dye job on her sandy brown hair or throw on a wig. The wigs were slightly riskier because some johns grabbed your tresses, but the dye job would take a couple of hours. "They give you a time?"

"Midnight."

Geri looked at her watch. It was just going on ten now. "What else?"

"They want the amputation just above the ankle—like the chick who married Paul McCartney—but they'll settle for any part of a leg."

"What's the pay out?"

"Twelve hundred for two hours for both."

That meant Geri would collect four hundred if the johns came through. Geri's left leg had been amputated just above the knee. "You tell 'em I'm low-thigh and collect up front. Then we both get paid."

215

"Shit, Geri, I already got the Amex card."

"It checks out?"

"It checks out."

Geri had been with What's Your Fetish long enough to know it showed up on Amex, Visa, and other credit company statements as Taylor Steakhouse—a sort of courtesy to the stupider johns who hadn't gone paperless and whose wives and bosses had access to snail mail. Felicia was just the receptionist; Maive Saunders owned the business and Maive was savvy. Smart enough to hire accountants who knew how to rig books, how to launder money. But credit card charges were easy to cancel. One phone call and presto, the debt was in contention. Maive was good about fronting some of the money to her girls, but if the jerks didn't pay, Geri would be looking at less than a hundred.

"They seem like tippers?" A tip on top of the fee would compensate if they didn't come through on the payment to Maive.

"They're from Texas."

"Call me back when they okay the low-thigh cut."

"Ten minutes."

In her bedroom, Geri looked into the mirror and adjusted the auburn wig. It had taken Felicia a hell of a lot longer than ten minutes to call back with the okay from the johns. She had to nix the dye job; but, what the hell, she looked pretty good. Even with the wig and the cut just above her left knee they might give her a decent tip.

More details had come in from Felicia. They didn't want Geri showing up in a wheelchair or on crutches. They wanted her to come in with the prosthesis—but it had to be hidden by slacks or a coat.

No biggie there. They wanted to fantasize that they didn't know she wasn't whole, strip her and find it. Then, as Geri knew, they'd "confess" they'd always had a "thing" for amputees. Whatever. It was a lot easier to handle guys who wanted to hump a stump than guys who wanted to be beaten, guys who wanted to watch girls take a shit on glass coffee tables while they lay on the carpet below, guys who wanted to dress up as women and pretend the two of you were having girl sex—until they whipped out cock.

216

She checked her watch. 11:45 p.m. She shrugged into her black mink coat and headed down the elevator to the waiting taxi below.

She was still in the cab heading downtown when her cell phone rang.

"Geri. Hey. This is Felicia."

"On my way."

"Yeah." Felicia inhaled sharply. Geri caught on to the anxiety before the receptionist explained. "There's a slight wrinkle."

"What wrinkle?"

"Ah, you know how these out-of-towners at cons are. The johns trade info and connections like insider stock tips. They got a number for What's Your Pleasure and they hired a chick named Missy who's *got* the cut just above the ankle."

Stupid. She should have known. Unless there was a Knicks or Rangers game in town the johns wanted to see, the jerks almost always insisted you show up at their hotel immediately—while they still had the nerve and weren't completely drunk under the table—yet.

"I know Missy," Geri said evenly. Fucking Missy. She was a twenty-something blonde who had gotten *her* amputation as a badge—the way ten years ago straights hit a tattoo parlor. Geri thought back to the last time she heard about a john asking for a bad girl with tattoos—1995? Tattoos were not unique to bad girls; they were strictly middle class. Welcome to the suburbs, baby. "What's the split?"

"Technically we're—you're—up first. But Missy's got the goods."

Geri wasn't born yesterday. These guys figured she was the throwaway. They could cancel the charge in a minute and have Missy—she of the diminutive tapered calf that ended in a delicate curve. Maybe it would cost them a little more, because if they bailed, they'd still have to pay the booking fee—a couple hundred. But if Felicia could talk Geri into the gig, the agency would collect close to the entire fee. Fucking What's Your Pleasure. And Missy wasn't the only one-legged whore in town. There were dozens now. Geri said nothing and Felicia went on.

"We get six, they get nine—that's as high as the schmucks would go. That's two-fifty for you, two-fifty for Missy. She's cool with the halfsies."

Instead of four hundred with a tip, Geri was looking at a long hard night. Once both girls were there, everything could go south in a minute. The johns could bail on both services and suck up the booking fees. God only knew what shenanigans the johns would want—and hell, no matter how you added up the cash, with or without tips, she wasn't getting paid nearly enough to fuck Missy.

"Give it to the young lady."

"Geri—"

"Not tonight, Felicia."

A few ticks past midnight, Geri was uptown, back in her apartment. Should she? She'd given up the money. So yeah, she needed to know. She picked up the coal-gray phone, punched in the speed-dial number 1, leaned over and took off her right high heel.

"Fatima? It's Geri."

"Oh, Missus, I am so glad you called tonight. Roberto—Robert is okay, but he had the little bit of fever. I gave him St. Joseph's ... the baby aspirin. Now he is sleeping. But I was so worried. I was going to call you, but I thought, let's wait and see if the aspirin works. Miss Geri doesn't like me to phone at night unless it's emergency."

"He's all right?"

"Yes, the fever has broken. A little cold, I think. He's sleeping good. Do you want me to show on the videocam?"

"Yeah."

Geri booted up her computer and waited patiently while Fatima got everything set on her end.

There he was. Robert. He was lying on his stomach in the crib. He was wearing yellow footie pajamas. One arm was stretched out straight by his side. The other was crooked and his small pink fist lay near his mouth, which was slightly open.

Every few seconds, there was a huffing sound—a plug-in vaporizer emitted a wisp of steam barely visible on Geri's monitor.

Fatima was there, it was all right.

218

"I'll stop by in the morning." She stopped by almost every morning.

"Of course." Fatima petted Robert's head, smoothing down his curls.

Gerri cupped her hand to her mouth and blew a kiss.

"Goodnight," she said.

"It used to be called apotemnophilia—what we now term body integrity identity disorder—BIID."

"Yeah, Doc, I know." This was all stuff Geri—or anyone else who cared to—could look up on the Internet. Hell, there was even a shrink right here in the city, according to the *Times*, who treated people who craved amputations. That shrink—not this one—wanted to be carved up, too. This one, Doctor Williams, had come recommended by Robert's pediatrician when Geri told her she was feeling low and needed to talk to someone.

"It's an erotic fantasy with two components, undergoing amputation of a limb, and subsequently overachieving despite a handicap," Williams said.

"Uh-huh," Geri said. Had he consulted with the pediatrician or her ob-gyn? Did he know about the tricks? She knew how to dress like a straight, and now she tugged the hem of her navy skirt over her knees. Her intuition told her this guy wasn't getting why she was here.

"Some people feel they will be more beautiful, more desirable—sexier—with a missing limb," he said. Williams leaned back in his chair; the top of his head grazed one of the hanging plants in the window behind him.

"I don't think that's the case here," Geri said. "It's not why I came to talk with you." The curtain of plants swayed gently. His eyes were closed, maybe he *was* listening.

"It's difficult for the average person to understand." He sat forward now, eyes open, and looked directly at her. "Technically, it's not all that different from sex reassignment. Guy wants to be a chick, gal wants to be a guy."

"Sure," Geri said. How could she explain that a sex change was unimportant to her? He wasn't shocking her; his idea of epiphany was no epiphany.

"At one level, it's not even that different from wanting cosmetic surgery," Williams said. "Nose job. Breast implants. Penis enlargement." In his attempt to connect, he leaned forward further and the point of his paisley tie had flapped and now lay folded—an arrow sending her directions—onto the mahogany desk. "Liposuction," he added.

"But—"

He clasped his hands. "No one is sure if those are even the correct models—this dysmorphia could be more like anorexia—a wrong-headed perception of one's body—skeletal girls who still feel fat." He swung sideways in the black leather chair, one knee crossed above the other.

"It's not like that," Geri said.

"Studies have been done. The least common site people long to have amputated is a finger or toe. The most common fantasy is above the knee." He swiveled and faced her. "Four inches above the left knee to be exact," he said. "They'll do anything to get the amputation. If they can't find a surgeon, they shove their 'offending' limb in a wood chipper, or blow their legs off with a shotgun." He picked up a folder from a stack on his desk.

"Well ..."

He handed Gerri a blue flyer. At title at the top was "Amputation: DPWs—Devotees, Pretenders, and Wannabes." Shit. The last time she checked, DPW stood for Department of Public Works. She stifled a giggle; the sound that erupted became a half snort.

"There's no shame involved." His dark brown eyes widened. "I don't make judgments. You can tell me anything you want."

For the sake of protocol, she glanced at the flyer, and then folded it in half and put it in her purse. He didn't want the truth; he was more interested in trends. This latest trend would make his fame and fortune. He could publish articles in magazines, he could write monographs—maybe even a book.

"Nothing you say will surprise me."

Geri had a feeling that wasn't the case.

220

"So." He was leaning back again, his eyes closed so that the big revelation could be uttered by the patient more easily. "What happened?"

Geri stood, pressing the heel of her right foot down, pushing up with her right knee and thigh, and using both arms for leverage. Her handbag was already on her shoulder.

"I had bone cancer."

Geri was back in her apartment before three o'clock. The twice-weekly cleaning service had come and gone, and she could see the tracks the Oreck upright had left on the oyster carpets. All the rooms smelled faintly of lavender.

She thought about making a drink, but steered toward the kitchen to make herself a cup of tea. She had gone to the shrink because she was trying to understand where she had gone wrong, and where someone like Missy had gone right.

She had better find out soon, she thought, because today was the 26th and she didn't have the rent money for this place or her real home where her son lived. Cleaning services and fresh flowers and scented linens were going to be a thing of the past pretty soon if she didn't do something. Taking care of Robert the way she wanted to take care of him was going to be an even bigger problem.

But how could Missy and all those other whores—and straights—want an amputation? Geri had been twelve when the cancer was diagnosed. She had been terrified and depressed for years—was maybe still depressed—after they'd taken her leg. Crying herself to sleep at night because kids made fun of her at school, on field trips, at the beach, in gym class. She could get away with skirts, but there were all the years of not wearing shorts because the black or gray tights she wore to hide the ugly, jointed prosthesis looked stupid with shorts. There were all those years adding up to right now, when she was thirty-eight, that her left shoe never had a crease in it. It always looked as if it had just come from the display shelf. She had seen the eyes of observant men and women staring. A dummy shoe for a dummy leg.

She poured the tea into a thin cup, took a lemon from the refrigerator and cut a slice, laying it on the edge of the white china saucer. She got her handbag and took out the flyer, and then sat down at the wooden gate-leg table with her tea to read.

- If I can't have my amputation right away, is thinking about it preventing me from doing the other things I need to do in my life?
- What obstacles (dangers of self-mutilation, finding a willing surgeon) prevent me from getting my amputation?
- How do I remove the obstacles to getting my amputation?

That last wouldn't be so hard, Geri thought. Anything—*anything*—could be bought on the black market. Missy and the others who were raking it in probably had no problem finding a backstreet medical student or two.

She skimmed down to the bottom, to a quote set off in curlicue brackets that seemed to be a reminder that beauty was in the eye of the beholder:

> "Since the late 1800s the medical literature has described men and women who are sexually attracted to amputees, those who limp, or use crutches, braces, and wheelchairs, as well as individuals who pretend to be or who actually want to become disabled."
>
> *Richard L. Bruno, Ph.D.*

Geri picked up the phone. What's Your Fetish and What's Your Pleasure weren't the only specialty whorehouses in town that commanded top dollar. She spent a long time scrolling through the huge list of contacts, some of them coded. Finally she dialed the number for a place called Kinkettes. It took a few minutes to get past the receptionist and on to the madam.

"I'm working with Maive—for the most part," Gerri said.

"Yeah?"

"And here's my question ..."

"Shoot."

222

"What are the johns paying—the ones who want an amputee—what are they paying for a girl," she said, "a girl with both legs gone above the knee?"

INDEPENDENCE DAY

BY P. I. BARRINGTON

Barneby Cottrich inspected his visage with approval. The long-desired transformation was complete. The hands he once considered too effeminate had been replaced by a stranger's hands, rough and hard, and the legs he thought too weak, thin, and spindly from a hated illness had been replaced by another stranger's. His face, eyes, ears, nose, and mouth had also been replaced by even more strangers' appendages and features. The scars healed instantly, miraculously, as if by magic, just as with every time he went into the laudanum-laced dreams during the mysterious procedures.

Now, the last and most important piece of flesh transferred onto him would give him a new lease on the world, a new lease on life, and fulfill his deepest wish to buy even perfection itself! Only a little while now and he'd be perfect, the way he wanted to be, not as he was. Everything would change now that the process had been completed; he only had to heal from the last ministrations. Over the past year, he'd undergone many surgical and seemingly mystical transformations, determined to recreate himself with the help of a strange yet effective physician who promised the world for a price—and who had not disappointed him so far.

In 1898, the type of surgery Cottrich required and sought was unimaginable. He prided himself on the fact that he was both rich and daring enough to undertake such risky medical procedures. Yet, every physician and surgeon he'd approached scoffed at his intention, thinking it impossible, regardless of his money.

A year ago, when he'd opened the door of The Dr. Animus Shoppe of Commodities, heard the enchanting tinkle of chimes, and saw the apothecary drawers of every size imaginable, he had been both intrigued and inspired. Rumors surrounded the doctor, that he could perform medical miracles, so skilled was he with the scalpel. Some even said he possessed skills beyond man's limited knowledge, possibly even acquired by dark arts. Cottrich cared not for such wives' tales and lunacies. His only concern was his quest for perfection.

"Hello," Cottrich said in a bright tone when the doctor made his appearance from behind thick, cream-colored denim curtains. The doctor wore a full suit, expensively cut, and a waistcoat with elaborate embroidery. His hair and beard were trimmed in the current style, and he exuded a genteel charm. "I presume you are the Doctor Animus of this Shoppe?"

"That is correct, sir. What may I help you with today?" He smiled. He checked his gold pocket watch and nodded as if an expected appointment had arrived.

"I've heard of your Shoppe and that you sell ... well ... perfection. Physical perfection, if you know what I mean." He leaned over the counter with a conspiratorial expression and lifted his cane high enough to be seen. The doctor stared at it as if he'd never seen one before and, for a moment, hope hung suspended. Then the doctor smiled knowingly and turned to a roll-top desk, opening it to the letter slats. He took several sheets from within and turned back to Cottrich.

"If you'll just list all the areas you'd like to be perfected, my dear sir, we can get the procedures under way." He handed the paperwork over with another smile, and then provided Cottrich with a quill pen and a small inkwell jar. "I'll just be preparing my surgery while you do so."

"You mean to start this day?"

"I'm sorry, sir. I assumed you were anxious—"

"Oh, not anxious at all, my good doctor! I did not think it could be done at such short notice."

"I can make preparations now, if you like."

"Please do."

Dr. Animus disappeared behind the curtains into a back room.

When the doctor returned, he looked over the list of "improvements" and "perfections" listed and glanced up.

"This is a rather extensive list, sir. The price is quite high for such a large ... purchase."

"No matter," Cottrich said with a shrug. "I will pay any price."

"Are you sure, sir?"

"Yes. Quite sure."

"Well, then, you must sign here at the bottom, sir." The doctor pointed to a signature line at the bottom of the list, just below several paragraphs. The doctor looked up and smiled yet again. "Just an agreement—a formality, you understand—to ensure both parties get what they want"

"Why, of course I understand!" Cottrich exclaimed. "I am a businessman myself, used to handling contracts and deals! That is how I come to afford this 'purchase,' as you call it." He gave the contract a cursory read, ignoring some of the Latin and legalese that he didn't understand. No matter. He grasped the pen again and bent over the papers to sign. A stiff, sharp prick from a barb on the quill feather drew a large, red bubble of blood, quivering on his fingertip, and he jerked, causing the drop to land at the line just at the edge of his name.

"Damn it all, man!" he said, putting the finger to his mouth for a moment. "Be sure to nick that barb before the next person uses it!"

The doctor apologized profusely, and then directed Cottrich through the curtain for the first "perfecting."

Cottrich no longer bothered with the walking stick he'd needed since the age of fourteen; he would never use it again. For the first time after his final surgical procedure, he walked out of the penthouse and exited through the palatial foyer of the New Dakota building, built twenty-nine years before and still the most impressive apartment building in all of New York. At last, he was worthy of living in such a striking place, a worthiness valued beyond any amount, regardless of the cost.

As he walked, he made gentlemanly salutes to women, children, and other men passing by, tipping his hat to everyone. A few gave him odd looks, as if he perplexed them, and in some cases the women returned frightened glances at him, while their children stared at him with open curiosity. At first puzzled, he soon realized that they most likely didn't recognize him, despite his clothing and voice.

"Hello, my dears," he said to everyone, using his familiar voice in his most jovial tones. "How are you today? Fine? That's splendid, splendid!" Again, the strange looks, often from those he knew socially, if not personally. He wondered if his close friends might have the same reaction upon seeing his perfected body. He was newly transformed, he assured himself. In time, they would acclimate themselves to his new persona. By the time he'd walked home from the park, exhaustion set in—expected from this, his first extended physical exercise in seven weeks.

As the days passed, his personal assistant assumed a pale and concerned expression, but said nothing of use to him. Cottrich grew tired of the worried silence that surrounded him.

"I say, what is the problem? I'm recuperating, that's all. There isn't cause for concern."

"Um," was all the man would say, apparently afraid to comment further.

"Come out with it, man!"

But his servant merely hung his head in silence.

"Ugh, you're a foolish manservant! Why, I can find a hundred—no, a thousand—more like you in a minute! Take care you do not upset me further!"

Cottrich rarely berated his assistant, but the man's lack of response was curious and near repugnant. He wondered at his own unusual attitude for a moment, and then shrugged. It did not matter in the least. In the morning, he would take himself out again for a Central Park promenade, this time introducing himself to people who did not yet recognize him. Yes, that was a plan all right, a perfect plan. He fell asleep dreaming of the world's response to his new life.

At first, he dismissed the problems as the quirks of new body parts becoming accustomed to his body and to each other. Dr. Animus warned that some adaptation and adjustment would be required. Minor setbacks, he assured Cottrich, nothing more.

Cottrich was determined to continue with his plan of an afternoon stroll. He knew that most of the populace would take refuge from the sweltering New York City heat in the Park—older people on the wooden and iron benches, younger women and children sitting on quilts or playing under the trees for the relief of the shade. Against the protests of his manservant, he chose his best clothes and found himself struggling to tug them on, relying on the assistant to shrug on his waistcoat, knot his tie, and button up his boots, something he'd always found easy to do on his own. He walked down the street, smiling at the people passing who now stared at him agog, as if he were some alien thing. What the devil was this, he thought.

As he stepped across the street toward the park, he tripped slightly over nothing—not a crack in the pavement or an uneven stone. He righted himself and tried to continue on his way. Several things happened at once. His legs jerked out from under him, each moving at right angles and knees bending oddly. His feet twisted nearly backward, making his gait freakish and his movements strangely mechanical. He struggled forward, determined to control himself—no one and nothing dared defy him, and his body would not either. He stumbled into the park, heading for a bench that vacated as soon as he veered toward it, the woman with the little girl rising to run away, hiding the child's face in her skirt as she dragged her screaming youngster away from him.

"Oh, for God's sake," he tried to say. But his mouth was no longer his own.

He approached the bench and reached out to grasp the iron arm to steady himself and lower his body into a sitting position, but the new hands that he prized now spread wide, the fingers curling and uncurling on their own. In frustration, he snapped the hands in the air to clear the spasms, their response a brief respite. He sighed in deep gratitude when he managed to sit, although his feet still faced the wrong way and his legs stuck out in even weirder angles, jerking and twisting. He now wished that he'd brought his manservant along with him. He cursed his dullness in silence. Silence! He would soon lose the ability to speak at all. The thought both perplexed and angered him. Then, with a flash of insight, Cottrich knew what he had to do.

He stood slowly, waiting for each movement and compensating as best he could, and began to walk. Young women, walking with parasols over their shoulders, stopped and squealed in fright as he walked by, and gallant young men seized the opportunity to shield and save the maidens from whatever they perceived him to be. Yet even those young men turned their faces from him, sickened by what they saw. He made his way to the one place that would solve it all, make it all go away for good.

Like a half-blind man, he read the street signs through a glazed view, as if through the stained and leaded glass windows of his penthouse. Words that were normally easy to read were now blurred and slanted, impossible to decipher. At last, he came to the street block he sought and with slow, careful steps, he scuttled up the stairs like a crab, wishing for the discarded walking stick that now appraised priceless in his estimation.

Cottrich felt his way along the door, fumbling with the doorknob and forcing his hand to grasp and turn it through sheer will. The familiar tinkle of chimes now grated in his ear. He clambered to the counter, slapping his hand uselessly on its top.

"Doctor! I must see you immediately! Doctor! Doc-*tor!*"

The doctor reappeared through the heavy curtains and gazed at him blankly.

"What is your complaint, sir?" he asked.

"What ... what is my com—plaint?" Cottrich screeched at the man. "Loo—*look* at me! I cannot control this new body that you have given me! My legs bend out sideways ... my feet turn backward and my fingers twist this way and that as they please!" He stopped speaking for a moment, trying to regain control of his mouth and tongue. "It is as if they are acting independently of one another! In fact, I believe my ... manhood ... my *organ* ... may have a mind of its own as well!"

"Humph. Most customers find that an advantage," Dr. Animus said. "The terms of the agreement are quite clear about restitution policies. It was clearly stated in the contract when you signed the papers, sir."

Fury overtook Cottrich and he tried to scream out in rage, but only managed a strangled sound from his tongue-filled mouth and snarled lips.

"I will sue ... sue you for every ... everything you ... you own!" His right arm swung out toward his back and stayed akimbo and stiff.

"Now, sir, that is not prudent at all, not at all," the doctor said. "The court would not be disposed toward recognizing you at all. Not to mention the extreme humiliation you would be face."

"Humi—humiliation? *Look at me!* People run shrieking away from me in fear and disgust! Humiliation is the least of my concerns, Dr. Animus!" Cottrich managed to walk awkward strides to a low couch opposite the counter, richly appointed in red velvet and ebony wood, and tried to sit while one leg bent at the knee and the other locked itself from his hip into a right angle. "Argh ... ugh ... I can barely move now! You must do something and do it immediately!"

"I'm afraid that is not possible," the doctor said. He smiled, then added, "But there is a clause in the contract, a provision should a customer be dissatisfied. But I must first inspect you to make certain recompense is duly warranted here."

He approached Cottrich. He grasped the hands and pressed his thumbs against pressure points, and then did the same with the face, arms, legs, and knees. The doctor straightened, his face wearing a look of slight surprise.

"Well, it appears as if the connections I've made to your nervous system, to your brain, have somehow run amuck," he said. "That happened once before to a man for whom I replaced an arm."

"Wha—what did he do? You—you maim—maimed him!"

"Sir, the man was a *criminal*—an escapee whose arm was severed as he escaped his prison cell! He should have been grateful to even sign the contract that released him from that hell!"

"And wha—what of me? I—I am no cri—criminal! I do not belong in this hell I am in, as he surely did!"

"Possibly not, sir, but you did sign the contract." Doctor Animus rifled through the papers in the roll top until he came to the one he wanted. He looked down through the glasses balanced on the tip of his nose. "Ah, yes. Here is the clause in your particular contract! Every ... patient, shall we say, signs an individual agreement. It clearly states here that if said patient feels dissatisfied with the results of his

231

'perfectioning,' he agrees to accept all the conditions of the contract. Ah! There it is, sir, signed in your own signature and with a dot of your own blood to seal the agreement."

"What are you telling me, you charlatan?" Cottrich screamed. *"If you did this, you can undo it! I want my body back! I don't care what black magic you have to perform! I will pay you any price—any price at all!"*

"You already have paid," Animus said. "The price, unfortunately, is far greater than the worth of the merchandise, I'm afraid."

"But, you have yet to charge me. No money crossed hands—no bills or notes of credit."

"Surely you did not believe my services were free."

"Damn you, man! What is the price?"

Animus merely smiled.

"Animus, you bastard—*what is the price?*"

Animus looked down at the contract again, sighing heavily as if he'd dealt with unhappy customers many times in the past. "According to the contract—a contract you have signed, sir—" he paused for effect, "there is a clause concerningthe return of the merchandise—a reshelving stipulation, one might say. The contract dictates that your original body parts may be returned, should you not be satisfied."

"Oh!" Cottrich said, relief raising his shoulders. "Is that all? I was afraid you would tell me you could not reverse the processes—what?" Fear crept back up over his shoulders.

"Well, under the current circumstances—"

"What circumstances? Why can you not fix me?"

"Not only am I bound by the terms of the contract, which I cannot break, even if I desired so," his smile turned sardonic, then evil. "Did I forget to mention I have a partner in my shop? A silent partner ... at least for the most part." He snorted out a cruel little snicker. "He reserves the last say in a contested contract. Oh, and he has a little, oh, quirk, you might say. He fulfills the wish, but only for an instant. I told you the price was steep, yet you insisted upon entering that agreement yourself. As I was going to say, when the original removed tissue, flesh, and bone has become atrophied and decayed, it must be ... destroyed. That is common law, despite any contractual determinations. I cannot break the law, sir."

"What have you done with me?"

The physician looked at him as if he should know the answer.

"I've put you in the incinerator."

Slowly, so slowly it was almost imperceptible, the bag rolled down the long, steep metal chute, gathering momentum to launch it into the furnace. The heat of the flames singed and desiccated the skin and muscles until they grew tight, then charred and blackened. The fingers, toes, arms, legs, eyes, and finally the lips burned as living flesh, twisted and roiled and bubbled. Finally, all living and dead tissue melded into one, one complete body, united in death as it never could in life; one body without mind or life or soul, united in final eternal uselessness.

MARVIN'S ANGRY ANGEL

BY JONATHAN TEMPLAR

"Is simple procedure, yes?"

Doctor Gregori grinned at Marvin, exposing nicotine-yellow teeth. This was not a face you would trust to serve you a fast-food burger, let alone operate on your flesh. His eyes betrayed the bloodshot evidence of too little sleep and too many narcotics. There was a slight slur in his speech, detectable even above the guttural accent of some obscure European region where medical training was cheap and easy to acquire, if not exactly legitimate.

"We not even need to give you anesthetic general. We just numb you, let you watch as we put her onto shoulder."

"Have you done many of these procedures before?"

"Ha!" Gregori barked. "Dozens and dozens! Is popular, people want their own angel. Angels are the answer to the modern malaise; this is what they say, yes? The world is more impersonal, there is no family unit no more, everyone lonely and need love. You are never alone with angel on your shoulder."

"That is what they say," Marvin agreed. It was what his friends said anyway. When they actually spoke to him. Once you had an angel, it seemed you didn't need friends anymore. You were *never* alone, company wasn't something you had to go and look for. Marvin's circle of friends had been growing smaller and smaller.

So here he was, ready to have his own angel. This was the cheapest surgery he could find, the fastest turnaround. That was Marvin's way. If he was going to do this, he was going to do it fast and he was going to pay as little as possible.

"Okay," he decided.

The surgeon clapped his hands in glee.

"Do I get to choose my own angel?"

"Is not possible, we have to take one that flesh banks give us, one that is ready for implant. But no to worry, my friend, all the angels is good!"

Marvin hoped this was true. He had heard stories that suggested otherwise. Dr. Gregori dismissed them with a wave of his hand.

Within half an hour, Marvin was on an operating table, the left side of his body numb. The surgeon stood over him with a scalpel in his hand, a facemask on, and a bored nurse assisting him—she simultaneously fed something feline she had sewn into a flesh pouch on her abdomen.

"Is that appropriate hygiene for a sterile theatre?" Marvin tried to say, but the anesthetic turned the question into a wet, drooling garble.

The doctor gave Marvin the thumbs up. "Is all good!" he said, and then started to cut.

Marvin lost consciousness.

There had been a lot of stuff on the Web, whispers and rumors, but it was obvious that the angels were losing their appeal. They had been the must-have accessory for a year or so, and everyone who was anyone had one grafted to them. There were places where you wouldn't dare be seen unless you had an angel glowing on your shoulder—clubs and eateries where they'd never be so obvious as to say you *had* to have your own if you wanted to enter, but they would still make it clear in their never-quite-subtle manner that you were below the standards they expected if you didn't.

But, like all things, the allure faded and a new trend exploded and suddenly the angels weren't quite as desirable. Celebrities who had clamored for the prettiest the flesh labs could produce were now retreating back to private Beverley Hills surgeries to have the angels removed, often against the angels' wills.

And where celebrity goes, society follows.

At the start of the year, the flesh farms worked overtime to generate new creations. By its end, they were struggling to cope with the rush of returns, screeching creatures three inches high that had been torn from the shoulders of those they had come to depend on. The most damaged, physically and psychologically, were melted back to their constituent flesh to be reformed. Others were sold at a huge discount. Secondhand dealers flourished. The angels being grafted onto shoulders were no longer fresh from the tank. They were pre-owned. Tainted.

But suddenly very affordable.

It didn't take Marvin long to realize that he and his new dependent were ill-suited to each other.

He woke after his surgery with a shoulder that felt as if it had been dipped into lye, the agony of his flesh screaming at him. Then he realized it wasn't his flesh screaming, it was her. She could open her tiny mouth and make a sound that would render a dog unconscious. And, for hours, it proved impossible to stop her, until they had doped her into unconsciousness and sent Marvin on his way with his angel drugged and slumped across his neck.

"Will be fine, Marvin," Dr. Gregori said. He sipped a "purely medicinal" glass of something with an alcohol content strong enough that the fumes alone could blind you. "Is normal! Angel wakes up on shoulder of stranger, is tough thing to do, yes? She does not know you, why she be happy? Give her time to get used to you, to find out what lovely man you are, all will be fine." He patted Marvin on his empty shoulder.

Behind him the nurse continued feeding the cat-thing in her pouch with milk from a baby bottle. The thing mewled with bliss as she stroked a strange protuberance on its face.

Marvin meekly accepted the situation, left the surgery with a shoulder still burning, a hazy head from the anesthetic, and an angel snoring into his right ear.

By the time he got back to his apartment, he was barely conscious. He hit his sofa with a thump and slept for fifteen straight hours.

When he awoke, she was staring at him.

The gauze over his shoulder had come loose and he could see the flesh was puckered and red where she had been attached. Her legless body was firm, upright, her arms crossed over her perfectly engineered breasts, her blonde hair loose over her shoulders, her lips pouted in an aggressive manner. She had been designed to be impossibly beautiful, but the quality of the flesh couldn't disguise the disturbing eyes, the madness that shone from them like torchlight onto an empty stage. She made Marvin nervous, and she was only an inch away from his face.

"Who the fuck are you?" she asked in a voice laced with venom.

"M—M—Marvin."

"Well M—M—Marvin, get me the fuck off your shoulder NOW!" she screamed. Marvin recoiled, although this did him no good whatsoever—she was, after all, attached to him.

"I don't know if that's possible, you've just been implanted," he said.

"Do you know who I am?" asked the angel.

"An angel?"

"Yes, Einstein, I am an angel. But do you know *whose* angel I am?"

"Mine?"

"No, I am not yours. I am Mimi Fedhora's angel. I am supposed to be on Mimi's shoulder. We have a very special relationship, Mimi and I. What the fuck am I doing here?"

Who was Mimi Fedhora? The name rang a bell in Marvin's mind, but it was a quiet one simply overwhelmed by all the others that were clanging loudly in alarm.

The angel screeched and had a tantrum until Marvin agreed that they could go online and look up this Fedhora woman. He had to determine why the angel believed she should be anchored to Mimi.

Of course. That Mimi Fedhora! She was a soap star, a devastating beauty fading away into late middle age and fighting off each passing year with a warrior's arsenal of plastic and collagen that had turned her face and much of her body into a surgeon's playground. She looked like a stranger wearing a Mimi Fedhora facemask, there was so little of the original left.

Mimi was notorious as the worst of the New Hollywood dames, a woman with a personality so rank, a manner so poisonous, that there were more people who hated her in Hollywood than there were aspiring screenwriters. She had retreated down the ladder to soap operas and the warm embrace of the gossip columns. And then, just recently, she had fallen even further out of favor.

"I don't remember any of that," the angel said in a hushed whisper. They read the story about Mimi being accidentally introduced to her replacement in the series *Hopes and Dreams*, in which she'd been plastic matriarch for six seasons, before the producers had the chance to tell her that she was on her way out. They read about how she'd taken the champagne flute she'd been holding and rammed it into her successor's face, shattering the crystal into shards and slicing the aspiring actress' face into so much tattered flesh. There were pictures of Mimi being led away by security people, the thick makeup that hid the sins of her flesh melting down her face. On her shoulder was a screaming angel, the one now stitched into Marvin's shoulder.

"That's you," he said quietly.

"I don't remember any of this. Poor Mimi, they were always against her. Always plotting. She had to fight them, you know, every day. They hate powerful women. They'll do anything to put them in their place. She stood up to them, stood tall and told them to go fuck themselves. Why don't I remember this episode in her life?"

Marvin had remembered something he'd read when he was researching angel implants. That there were cases where hosts had been convicted of crimes and had their angel severed before their sentence began, as the law had no authority to incarcerate angels unless they, too, were considered to be guilty of an equivalent crime.

"They would have removed you. The trauma must have caused some sort of amnesia."

"Well, fuck amnesia. I need to get back to Mimi, she needs me."

"Too late for that. You're my angel now."

"I am not your angel. You are a nobody. I belong to Mimi Fedhora and I demand that you take me to her this instant."

"No. You're mine now. Get used to the idea, darling. My shoulder, my rules."

239

The angel, of course, had other ideas and made her objection clear straightaway.

There was the screaming for a start. Marvin tried to put a stop to that by covering her mouth, but she bit him, so he learned to ignore it.

She had more subtle tactics, however.

On his first night in bed with her (after the difficulty of finding a way of sleeping comfortably with her protruding had been overcome with the aid of a complicated arrangement of pillows), she'd asked to see him naked. She'd never seen a nude man before, she said coyly.

Marvin obliged—the sensuality of the angels was one of their big selling points, and the one that had finally swung Marvin to the idea of getting one for himself. She made approving noises, asked him if he could play with *it*, show her what *it* did. This Marvin needed little encouragement to do, but she gave him some anyway. She whispered things into his ears that made his blood rush and his mind boggle.

And then, at the exact right/wrong moment, she screamed again, and cursed and said the most demeaning things to dampen his ardor. And she told him she'd do this every single time, that he'd never ever again enjoy a moment of pleasure or peace. That she would ruin everything he enjoyed for as long as she was stuck to him, destroy every aspect of his life unless he freed her. And she promised that she could be patient and determined in her endless assault.

So Marvin surrendered to the inevitable.

They had read online that Mimi had been incarcerated at a private mental institution in California, but had been released just days before into private care in the comfort of her own home.

Marvin and the angel headed for Hollywood—with just one small stop along the way.

Mimi's house was not a house. It was a *castle*, a sprawling complex kept spotlessly clean with barely a sign that anyone actually inhabited any of it—a sterile show home, something to be displayed in the lifestyle magazines of the rich and infamous.

Mimi was sedated in her bedroom suite, a massive chamber that could have housed a dozen refugee families. One sheer glass wall faced the swimming pool and the grounds of the estate; others led to a walk-in wardrobe larger than some department stores and a bathroom that you could play tennis in.

All this space was currently of little use to the frail and agitated figure writhing on her bed, $10,000 sheets crumpled beneath her.

Her three visitors waited impatiently for the sedative to wear off and Mimi to regain a measure of consciousness. Her nurse and the court-appointed guardian stationed at the door had been rendered prone by injections from Dr. Gregori. Marvin hoped the injections would have no permanent effect (he suspected that Dr. Gregori had just plunged the first syringe he could find into the unfortunates and was hoping for the best).

"Is no good, none of this," Gregori muttered while smoking another of his potent black cigarillos.

"Shut it, quack," the angel hissed at him, waving away a cloud of tobacco smoke.

Slowly, Mimi returned to consciousness. She looked her age. The implants and injections that had promised to maintain her youth now made her face look as if it had been taken apart and then reassembled by a short-sighted monkey with clumsy hands. Without her heavy makeup, she was a ghoul, and the sedatives had clouded her eyes and slackened her jaw, so she drooled onto her pillow as she tried to speak.

"What are you ... where?" she mumbled as if through a mouth full of cotton.

"Mimi!" the angel said with rapturous adoration. "It's me! I've come back! They tore us apart, but even that couldn't keep me away. I've found you again! I'll get you out of this nightmare. We'll be together forever, just as we were always meant to be."

The aging diva started to focus. There was first recognition in her eyes, and then they darkened with the shadow of fear.

"You? Oh God, not you!"

"Mimi!" said the angel, a hand to her chest. "I've come halfway across the county to find you. I woke up stuck on this loser's shoulder."

"Hey!" Marvin said. The angel hit him with a tiny hand.

"I've been running back to you ever since, Mimi darling. Aren't you happy to see me?"

"They tore you off me. I begged them to take you away and they tore you off. Why are you back? Oh God, please take her away from me!" Mimi writhed on her giant bed, trying to get uncooperative limbs to work.

"It's all going to be fine, Mimi darling. We'll find a way to get beyond this. That bitch deserved everything she got, people must realize that."

Mimi looked to Marvin. "You've got to help me. She's a devil! They told me I'd be having an angel on my shoulder, but they gave me a devil! She whispered such terrible things, made me do such terrible things. She forced me to hurt Olivia. She kept telling me to push the glass in her face over and over again until I just couldn't help myself. Oh, she made me hurt that poor woman!"

The angel tutted. "Now that's hardly true, is it darling? You didn't do anything you didn't want to. I just helped you actualize your anger, and made sure you put your money where your mouth was. That's why we're so good together. I know how you think. I know what's really on your mind, the things you whisper when the rest of the world can't hear you. I'm the one that can make those things really happen."

"No, please just leave me alone. I want to be alone!"

"Nonsense, darling. I've brought a doctor with me, a good one."

Gregori moved forward and waved a yellow-stained hand. "Is good evening, nice to meet you, yes?"

"He's going to put us back together, Mimi. We'll be one again, you and me against the world. What do you say?"

Mimi Fedhora raged. She screamed. She bellowed obscenities that even made Marvin blush. "If you get stitched back in, I'll rip you out with my bare hands. I'll stamp on you until there's nothing left. I'll kill myself before I have you anywhere near my shoulder."

Her tirade went on in this manner for quite a while.

Eventually, the angel just turned her head to her new host. "Kill the bitch, Marvin," she said dispassionately.

Marvin took one of Gregori's operating instruments, which was still smeared with the remnants of its previous procedure, and attacked the helpless woman on the bed. He did this without hesitation and wasn't sure why. On his shoulder, the angel encouraged him, her face practically orgasmic with pleasure as she wiped the blood of her previous host away. When Marvin was finished, Mimi was little more than a smear over the expensive silk covers. The angel leaned over and kissed him in the cheek, and he felt a sense of incredible well-being.

"I believe they call this bonding with your host," he said.

"The beginning of a beautiful friendship." the angel agreed, licking her gore-splattered lips.

Dr. Gregori had fled the room, but they managed to chase him down before he could escape the building. They performed a procedure of their own upon him. When they had finished, Marvin used Mimi's shower to clean them both and found some fresh and rather grand clothing in one of her closets, a remnant from the days when she still entertained guests of the opposite sex. He felt good. He looked good. The angel agreed.

"What do we do now?" asked Marvin.

"You know, I've always wanted to take a ride on a Harley," the angel purred.

Marvin rolled up his $2,000 sleeves.

"Then a Harley it is," he purred back.

CHANGE OF HEART

BY ROB M. MILLER

Tara slammed both fists against the tabletop. "Swear to God, Jerry, I wish your mom had knocked herself off instead of your dad."

Jerry just stared at her.

Silence.

"I'm sorry. I shouldn't have said that."

Jerry walked over and hugged his wife. "Sorry, too ... and I'd be pretty pissed if the thought had never crossed my own mind." He pulled away and looked in Tara's eyes. "But my dad is dead. Besides you, mom's all the family I got, nuts as she is. And now, well, all she wants is a visit. A chance to make peace."

"No goddamned way." Tara brushed her blond hair back over a shoulder, and then glared at her husband with her chin jutting forward. The chin was key. Whenever Jerry saw that particular tell, he knew the fight was over. "And we're still not pregnant."

"What?"

"Pregnant. Pregos. Bun in the oven." Tara took a seat at the dining room table. "And it's not in the budget to figure out why, either. Furthermore, what if it's true?"

"If what's true?" Jerry gave his wife a playful wink. "That we might just have to keep working at it? We've only been married five years, and've only been trying for three. We've got time."

245

Tara's hands flew up in frustration. "Your mother, dork? She's a witch, right? I mean, that's been her bag since you were a kid, since your dad passed, and then, even after you got taken away: black magic, tarot cards, potions, wands and crystal balls—the whole shebang." An ugly pause. "What if it's true? Her curse? You heard her, and at our own wedding for Christ's sake: 'Lookee here, my son has done gone and married himself an ugly duckling ... a cheap, infertile whore that'll never sprout the fruit of life.'"

Jerry took a seat next to his wife. "Don't be ridiculous. The woman's mental. Always has been—and she's got a monthly disability check to prove it. The last thing we need is her sickness infecting the two of us." He tried to take one of his wife's hands—and failed. "C'mon, hon. Since when did you become superstitious?"

"Don't patronize me."

"'Sides, truth be known, the real curse came from my dad, and obviously on me, not you."

"How's that?"

"About an hour after coming home with mom from one of their séances or whatever, back when mom was just starting to dabble, the man pulls me aside and says: 'Movies have it all wrong, son; whatever, you do, don't have any children.'"

"Creepy. You never told me that."

"Yeah, it is. He even made me promise—and no, I've never told anybody until now. Anyway, a few minutes later, he went out into the garage and did it. Rode a shotgun right out of my life forever, the bastard."

"You're right."

"I am?"

"Yeah, I'm being silly. It's all a bunch of superstitious nonsense."

"I wouldn't be too quick saying that. Look at what you did."

"What?"

"With mom ... you're the one that told her she needed to stop being such a child, all obsessed with her Halloween bullshit."

Laughter.

"And it looks like it worked. She wants to come and visit and make things right. Says she's changed. And hell, it has been five years. What if she's telling the truth?"

"Whatever. I still hate the woman. It's that simple."

"Dinner?" Jerry half-said, half-asked. "One meal, hon. That's all I'm saying." He reached for Tara's hand, this time succeeding. "A dinner her first night into town, and it'll be pleasant. She'll be nice, or we'll give her the boot."

"The boot, yeah. I like the sound of that—the boot, right upside her head."

Jerry understood his wife's vehemence.

"Fine." Tara stood and went to move out of their living room and into the hallway. "But one mean act, and I swear ... in front of God-'n-country, on our front lawn, I'll burn that woman at the stake."

"Deal." Jerry decided not to follow his wife into the bedroom just yet. Instead, he stared at his mother's letter resting atop the table, and then gave it a sniff. Things sure smelled different with his mom. Used to be everything she touched got scented with her nasty patchouli oil. Her latest mail, however, smelled like it'd gotten sprayed by something sold at Nordstrom's. *A good sign.* Whatever, the one thing he couldn't afford right now was another disaster with Tara. He also needed to figure out what to say to the woman on the phone. They hadn't talked in ages. And then, of course, was the biggie: *When in the hell are we gonna get pregos?*

Tara gave the place a final once-over. Everything seemed easy-peasy-nice-and-cleanzee. She wasn't that concerned about impressing mom-in-law, but at the same time, she'd be damned before giving the old cow any ammunition by showing an ill-kept home.

"Everything's fine, sweetheart," Jerry said, walking up beside his wife, giving her a playful slap on the backside. "Don't be so antsy. And don't forget, we've got a baseball bat ready in the coat closet, just in case."

"Very funny. Maybe some wolfs bane is be in order."

Jerry laughed. "A better idea would be to drive down to The Majestic, raid their motel rooms for a bunch of Gideon Bibles, and then—you know, put them, like, everywhere."

Tara turned and slugged Jerry on the shoulder. "*Now* you think of something good. Too bad we're running out of time; she's going to be here any minute."

"Hope so," Jerry said. He turned toward the kitchen, smiling. "Ummm! That smells good. If she's not here soon, we're going to have to start without her."

"That reminds me, I better check on the roast. It's almost done." Tara started to turn and almost made it, when the doorbell rang.

"I'll get it," Jerry said.

"It's all right, go ahead. I'll stand with you. We can get shocked together, seeing what kind of black cape she's wearing now." Knowing her face was bunched into a hardened pinch, Tara did her best to relax. *God, I hate the cow, but if I don't want her coming in and starting trouble, at least I can slap a smile on.*

Jerry clasped his wife's hand and led the both of them to the door. Jerry was already surprised. The bell had only rung once. Not like mom. She always pushed and prodded and stabbed until somebody got the damn door open. *Hmm*, he mused. *Maybe things are going to work out, after all.*

He opened the door.

"Good evening," Joan Bannan said from the flower-bedecked entryway. "Can this ashamed, ugly woman come inside and begin her apologies?"

It was all Tara could do to keep her eyes from exploding from their sockets. She knew Jerry was just as surprised, could feel it in the way he squeezed her hand. Joan *wasn't* standing in her doorway the way she'd been expected—black hair, maybe a cap, an oversized upside-down cross around her neck.

Instead, Joan looked the way a fiftyish woman of maturity and class was supposed to—an imploring smile on a face wearing only the most modest of makeup, low-heeled black dress shoes, tan slacks, white blouse, and a small right-side-up cross resting across her bosom. The dyed black hair was gone, replaced now with the woman's own natural brown, slightly sprinkled with silver strands, pulled back and pinned in place.

"Come in," Tara managed to say, beating her stunned husband.

Jerry—keeping ahold of his wife's hand—stepped back and to the side, opening a path for his mother. As Joan walked by and into their home, a subtle hint of perfume greeted his nose. *Is that Escada?* he thought, thankful for the confirmation that mom's patchouli-wearing days were over.

Coming full into the center of her son and daughter-in-law's comfortable-but-not-cramped living room, she turned and faced her estranged family. "The new me," she said, turning slowly, full circle. "The old version caused nothing but grief, and, for me, one heck of a lot of shame. Thanks so much for letting me stop by. I have so much to answer for."

"Mom, the witch thing, you're—"

"All gone, Jerry," she said, holding her head down, embarrassment clearly showing through her posture and reddening cheeks. "Stupid and childish stuff, that was. Crazy stuff. A big reason why I was such an evil bitch, and why," Joan raised a hand and gestured toward her son's lady, "Tara has every valid reason in the world to hate my guts. I'm just happy I eventually got the therapy and medication needed to not have my brain all wonky."

"Joan, don't talk that way! We're happy to see you," Tara said, the lie slipping out easily, almost as if even she believed it. She wanted to believe it.

"You're saying that, and if you're not being overly polite, you're certainly being too gracious. I deserve to have your door shut in my face, not stand here in a lovely house with the smell of perfect steaks coming out of your kitchen."

"Speaking of which ...," Jerry glanced at Tara.

"Yes. Thanks ... it's a roast!" Tara started moving toward the kitchen. "I'll be right back with dinner. We're going to feast."

"Wonderful," Joan answered. Her son showed her to a place-setting at the table. "I haven't had a feast in a long, long time."

What a nice home, Joan thought, unpacking the suitcase Jerry had brought in from the car. She placed her purse on the bed. *A three-bedroom townhouse, digital cable, two full baths, gorgeous kitchen complete with island. Everything. Only thing missing ... the patter of little feet.*

She'd already opened the room's empty dresser drawers; all that was left was the putting away of a few things. "Here you are," she said, voice low. She smiled and picked up a lidded glass jar from her suitcase. Inside, floating in a clear, viscous fluid, was what looked like a piece of misshapen coal.

She stepped over to the room's cushioned rocker and sat down. For a few moments, she stared at the jar, looking intently at the fist-sized lump of rock, before setting it atop a nightstand.

Unbuttoning her blouse, she sighed. She felt that things had gone well. The binding hex placed years before was still in full effect, but would be gone come midnight. Soon, very soon, Tara would be in a state of conception. *Oh, boy*, Joan thought. *Jerry and wife are going to be happy then.*

Dinner had been a sweeping success, too. Joan had to admit, that bitch could cook. The roast had been superb, along with all the rest—the red wine, the baked potatoes, the homemade rolls, mixed vegetables, cheesecake dessert, everything.

She had won them over. They had about tripped over each other's tongues when they'd started telling her, *begging* her, to stay. At least for the night, but the weekend, at least, if she would. They had no idea, as of yet, that she was going to be staying for a lot longer than that.

She had a grandson in her future, prophesied so many years before—a bright, handsome boy with a curious glint in his left eye. He would be needing his Grams.

Blouse wide open, Joan undid her front-clasping bra, exposing the five-inch long zipper running between her breasts and just to the left of her precious third nipple.

She grasped the zipper and pulled down, opening up her chest cavity. A rose-smelling draft poured from the opening. Joan whispered a cant into the air and, on the nightstand, the jar's lid unscrewed itself. Then, reaching inside her chest, Joan pulled out a robust, healthy heart from within. The muscle pulsated in her hand, its four valves still pumping away.

Joan was glad to be rid of it for the night. The thing pained her, but she needed it, at least during the day and the early evening hours, at least for the time being.

She switched the heart for the coal and whispered the cant again, sealing the heart in the jar, and put the coal into her chest. Immediately she could feel her internal organs begin to desiccate nicely, her body becoming infused with energy of a different sort.

She zipped up and put on her nighty.

She had lied, yes. And she wasn't done—not by a long shot. There would be plenty more lies coming. The heart made them believable. But she hadn't lied about everything.

She smiled.

It is true that I no longer mess with the childish stuff.

HEARING MILDRED

BY WELDON BURGE

Mildred Mayfield died of a ruptured aortic aneurysm on the cold eve of Easter. She'd left her Easter Sunday best spread out on the bed in the guest bedroom. Harold, her husband, figured she'd been thinking of him, not church—what better clothes to bury her in? Mildred was always so thoughtful, Harold thought. If she didn't tell him what to do, she did it for him.

"Dad, we need to talk," William said. He sat on the couch opposite Harold's recliner in the living room. The TV, as always, was tuned to an old cops show.

William was a respected tax attorney, a man who had political aspirations in the state. He had helped Mildred and Harold with their retirement planning, setting up their estate. But he had spent less and less time with his parents over the years as his career took off and he had his own family to support.

Harold never called his son, his only child, William. He would always be Billy to him. But, it didn't seem right to call a fifty-five-year-old attorney Billy.

"I already know what you're going to say, Billy."

Harold smiled a bit when he saw his son wince at the name.

"Dad, you're eighty-two. Mom's been gone for six months. You can't stay in this house by yourself."

"Why not? I've lived here for five decades. Your mother would not want me to leave our home."

"What if something happens to you? Jen and I live an hour away."

"There's always 911."

"What if you can't get to the phone?"

"Then I can't get to the phone. So what? I just want to sit in my comfortable recliner, occasionally with a good Scotch, and watch TV."

"All day long?"

"Of course. What, am I going to go play tennis? Go drag racing? Chase skirts? I'm eighty-two. Meals on Wheels keeps me fed. I see no reason to leave the house, Billy. None."

William sighed and shook his head.

Harold loved watching police TV series and old mystery shows, when he could find them, typically late at night on three-digit cable networks. He spent hours watching shows like *Mannix*, *Ironside*, *Perry Mason*, *Hawaii Five-0*, even the old *Dragnet* episodes. His favorite was *Matlock*. He'd been told, more than once, that he looked like Andy Griffith, and he could easily imagine himself in the scenarios Matlock found himself in during each episode.

One night, an episode of *Baretta*, starring Robert Blake, was scheduled for two a.m. on channel 306, whatever network that was. Harold had no TV-watching routine, other than stalking the channel scroll for viewing candidates. He didn't care much for sitcoms (just *I Love Lucy* and *The Honeymooners* plots regurgitated ad nauseum), so it was often difficult to find anything of interest.

As the theme song for *Baretta* began, Harold turned up his hearing aids. He couldn't hear a damn thing without them, even when the TV was at full volume. This time, his hearing aids were filled with static, so much so that he couldn't hear the dialogue on the television. It wasn't so much static, he realized, as murmuring, distant conversation with no discernible words. Unintelligible chatter. "What the hell!"

Harold switched off the TV with the remote and listened. Yes, there were voices. He could hear voices, talk of some kind. But he couldn't make out the words.

He pulled out the hearing aids, placed them on the coffee table. Nothing. He couldn't hear a thing. He put the hearing aids back in. He again heard the same noise, like a radio program just out of range. Voices, but not voices. Something else ...

"Damn things are defective!"

He tried adjusting the volume on the hearing aids, to no avail.

Then, he distinctly heard his name, *HAROLD*, spoken with clarity through the mindless chatter. It was so sudden, so unexpected, that he yanked out both devices and tossed them on the table.

He definitely heard his name spoken.

And it was definitely his dead wife who'd spoken it.

The following day, soon after getting out of bed, Harold made a cup of coffee, turned on the TV in the living room, settled into his favorite recliner, and put in his hearing aids. No static, no murmuring. The hearing aids worked perfectly—the Weather Channel came through loud and clear.

Harold shrugged. He must have been hearing things before.

A week passed before Harold heard his wife's voice through his hearing aids again. He was watching the latest iteration of *Hawaii Five-0* (not the same without Jack Lord!) when the static began. This time, he turned down the TV volume, closed his eyes, and just listened.

Whispering. Not quite intelligible, but almost, coming through the noise.

"Mildred?" he said aloud.

The noise became louder, more intense, irritating.

hear

Harold kept his eyes closed, kept silent.

hear

hard

He was pretty sure it was Mildred's voice.
hard to
"Is it you, Mildred?"
hear me
"I can—"
hard to get
"—hear you."
hard to get through
"I can hear you, Mildred. I can hear you! Where are you?"
The static was getting too loud.
here
And then he heard nothing but white noise.

William spread a number of pamphlets and brochures across the kitchen table in front of his father.

"What's this?" Harold asked.

"I just brought them for you to look through. They're from retirement homes I'd recommend. We really should visit a few, get a feel for what they offer."

"Not interested."

"Dad, you need to seriously consider your options."

"I have."

"Well, I particularly like Shady Oaks. The facility is clean and the folks there are very nice. Plenty of activities. The food is great. I really think you'd like it there, if you gave it a chance."

"Not interested."

"Dad, you can be so stubborn at times! Well, I'll leave these here for you. Maybe you'll want to read them later."

Harold
"I'm here, Mildred."
it's hard
"What's hard?

0

getting through ... takes all my strength
"Where are you?"
here with you
"I've missed you so much."
I know
Her voice was barely a whisper. Harold turned up the hearing aids, but the static made it difficult.
"Do you miss me?"
I've been here
"Why can't I see you?"
can't ... manifest
"What?"
not strong
"I don't understand. Manifest?"
mani ... ong enough
"I don't understand, Mildred."
weak
"You know that I love you."
know
Then there was only static.

Harold had no idea how she had made contact with him. He was only pleased that she did. Was she actually haunting the house? Or was she talking to him from the other side? She said she was "here"—but where is "here"? No matter. He was happy to have Mildred in his life again.

They had talked off and on for days, and she seemed to be getting stronger and better able to communicate with him. He did not understand the barriers, what made it so difficult for her, and wished he could help in some way. He'd never believed in the paranormal, yet now it had become a mainstay in his life.

"Mildred, are you here?"
right here
"Can you see me?"
yes
"Why are you here?"

You need me

Harold nodded. He did need her.

why do you watch television so much

"I enjoy it. Now that I'm retired, I just want to kick back and relax. You know, I started working on my Dad's farm when I was fourteen. I worked hard every year after, supporting our family over the decades. Now, I finally have time to do the thing I enjoy most. Watching TV."

The noise in his hearing aids was dissipating, usually a sign that she was losing her strength and could no longer communicate with him. Her voice became a whisper.

but there's so much to do

"Do?"

around the house

"I wish we could go out to dinner together, like old times."

that would be nice

"I wish I could see you again."

I know

"Are you happy where you are?"

I'm here

"Are you happy?"

I'd be happier if you didn't watch TV so much

"But I do vacuum the house, Mildred."

every week

"No, not every week. Maybe once a month. I don't see a need to do it more often."

you must vacuum every week

"Mildred, I'm watching an episode of *McCloud*. Do you have any idea how hard it is to find an episode of *McCloud*?"

not important

"It's important to me."

there are more important things

"Such as?"

the kitchen won't paint itself

"I'm watching my show now."

why must you disappoint me

"I'm not doing that right now."

the trash needs to go out

"I'm watching TV. I'll do it in the morning."

you'll forget to do it in the morning ... do it now

"Leave me alone, Mildred."

do it now

nothing is getting done around this house

look at the dust ... can't you see the dust

you are the most lazy, inconsiderate man I know

After tolerating several weeks of endless nagging, Harold took another tack.

"Mildred, we were married for fifty-two years. More than half a century. You were my high-school sweetheart, the love of my life. But, darlin', you have to understand. You're dead. You died over six months ago. It's time for you to move on. Go to the light. Go get your heavenly reward. And, for the love of God, leave me the hell alone!"

At first, Harold thought maybe she'd left him; the quiet was almost oppressive. Maybe she understood, finally. Maybe she had moved on after all. A minute went by, then two.

Mildred whispered.

there's so much to do around the house

Harold sighed.

the kitchen needs to be painted ... you promised me that you'd paint the kitchen ... the dining room chairs need to be varnished

Harold's sigh was even heavier.

and the carpet in the living room needs to be—

"Mildred, I just want to watch my TV shows. I'm eighty-two years old. I just want to watch TV. I don't need to paint the kitchen. I don't even use the dining room anymore."

but Harold

"It's only a house. Wood, plaster, and stone. Fifty years from now—hell, ten years from now—it won't matter one iota if I've painted the kitchen or not. If the house hasn't been bulldozed, it will be owned by someone else who will likely repaint and remodel everything anyway. Those green drapes you spent days deciding on? The next owner will rip them down and put up purple ones. It's just a house, Mildred. I refuse to waste what little time I have left toiling over a house."

He wasn't quite sure, but he thought he heard Mildred crying. Can ghosts cry? If they could talk, Harold assumed they could cry.

it's our home

He nodded, frowned. Can you hurt a ghost's feelings?

"Yes, it *was* our home, and we kept it well. It was a beautiful, loving home" he said. His voice was calm, soothing. "And, when you lived here, I did things around the home to make you happy. I always wanted to make you happy, Mildred. But, doing those things did not make me happy in the same way they did you. Do you understand? Now that you're not here, I don't care about those things. When you were here, it was our home. Now, it is my house, and I have no desire to paint anything. It is only a house. It is a home when someone lives in it. When I'm gone, none of this will matter."

paint the kitchen

Harold shook his head. He removed his hearing aids, placed them on the coffee table, and promptly fell asleep in the recliner.

"I'm sorry, Mr. Mayfield, but our technicians have tested your units and have found no malfunction. In fact, they pass every standard test with flying colors."

"Flying colors my ass! Did you actually *listen* to them?"

"We could not duplicate what you described. Static, you said?"

"Irritating static." Harold nodded.

"Hmm ... well, here's the situation, Mr. Mayfield," the twenty-something salesman behind the counter said. "The company will not allow me to replace fully functional devices. The warranty clearly states—"

"To hell with the warranty. I want new hearing aids!"

"Dad, don't be so rude to the young man," William said. "He's only trying to help."

"I can order a new pair, no problem," the salesman said. "But your insurance and your Medicare doesn't cover it at all. You would have to pay out-of-pocket for the new hearing aids."

Harold sighed. "Fine. I just can't wear those any more. The incessant noise will drive me insane."

"I'll cover the costs," William said to the salesman. "Do you need a down-payment?"

The new, sleek hearing aids only made Mildred's voice more distinct and shrill.

why must you be such a slob

Harold ignored her. It was becoming more difficult for him every day to do so. But, to hear the television, he also had to hear her. He had no options.

He flipped through the channels using the TV remote.
when was the last time you washed those windows
He then happened upon a show about ghost hunting, on that science fiction channel that he usually avoided. He stopped scrolling. He was never interested in these shows before, believing them to be bunk—just a bunch of supposed researchers wandering through spooky houses with flashlights and other contraptions. But now he had a different perspective. He settled back to watch the show.

"Billy, I was watching one of those ghost-chasing shows last week. Do you ever watch those shows?"

"You shouldn't watch that junk, Dad. It's all fake. There's no such thing as a ghost."

don't tell William about me

"Well, on this show, the guys looking for ghosts were using all kinds of gizmos—videocams, gadgets that could detect electromagnetic fields, and recorders that could pick up sounds and voices that the ghost chasers couldn't hear with the naked ear. They could record voices of spirits, Billy."

"Really, Dad. It's garbage."

"They're called EVPs. Electronic voice phenomena."

"It's not real. They're probably just recording fragments of radio broadcasts or CB radios or something."

"I don't know, Billy. It seemed legit to me."

"Dad—"

"I think I'm picking up EVPs through my hearing aids."

William stared at his father.

"Your mother has been talking to me, Billy."

"Oh, Dad—"

I told you not to tell him ... I told you

"Where's the friggin' remote?" Harold said aloud to the others in the room. No one seemed to hear him, which didn't surprise him in the least. He'd been largely ignored at the Shady Oaks Retirement Home, ever since Billy had left him here the week before.

will you stop worrying about the stupid television

Harold sat on the couch in the TV room, facing the big-screen television fastened high on the wall.

why did you let William put you in this place

The remote wasn't on the coffee table in front of him, just a pile of old magazines. The end table nearest him was piled with hardback books—no remote.

is William selling our house

"Yes, Mildred, Billy is selling our house. Do you see the TV controller anywhere?"

you can't let William sell the house

"Sure I can. I'm no longer living there. And you're no longer living."

why are you being so cruel

"Just stating the obvious. So, do you see the remote or not?"

don't you care about our home

"Fine. Don't help me then."

A large woman slept at the other end of the couch, her head tilted back, drool pooling at the corner of her mouth. Her snoring was cavernous. The remote was buried between her clenched thighs.

"Dammit," Harold said. He reached for the remote, careful not to touch the woman and wake her.

you need to get on the phone immediately and call William

Harold gingerly extricated the remote; it was slathered with the woman's thigh sweat. "Dammit," he said again.

call William and tell him not to sell our house ... call him now

He started flipping through the channels, trying to find anything of interest. Anything to take his mind away.

I want you to move back into our house and ... and ... fix things

There was an episode of *Matlock*. Thank the stars and all that was holy! He cranked up the volume on the TV.

Harold, are you listening to me

He closed his eyes. It was time. Long past time, actually.

don't ignore me

He twisted the hearing aid from his left ear, rolled it in his palm, contemplating ...

263

Harold, don't you dare

... and then dropped the tiny device to the floor. He crushed it under his heel like a walnut.

"I love you, Mildred," he whispered.

He reached for the hearing aid in his right ear ...

NOOOOOOOO

... dropped it to the floor and crushed it as well.

The silence was immediate, welcome relief.

Harold looked around the room at his fellow Shady Oaks denizens, all in varied degrees of conversation. A group of old codgers played poker at a card table in the corner—maybe he'd join them tomorrow night. He glanced at the sleeping woman slouched on the couch next to him. No one seemed to have noticed his actions. He reached down to the floor and gathered the hearing aid debris in his hand, and then placed the ruined devices in his shirt pocket. He'd flush them down the toilet when he returned to his room later in the evening.

Harold stared for a time at the television, hearing nothing but a low growl, even with the TV at full volume. The episode of *Matlock* was one he'd seen so many times that he didn't have to hear the TV to know what Andy Griffith was saying.

He abruptly realized just how boring television reruns were.

Harold sighed. What now? Thumb twiddling?

Then, he remembered the pile of books stacked on the end table, all hardbacks. The book on the top of the pile was Mickey Spillane's classic *I, the Jury*.

Why had he never read any books by Mickey Spillane? Or Dashiell Hammett? Or Raymond Chandler? Or Ed McBain? Or any number of other crime and mystery novelists? He always meant to read the classics, but had never gotten around to it. Shady Oaks had a large library downstairs, just waiting for exploration.

He picked up the Spillane book. With a smile, he opened it, turned to the first page.

And began to read.

THE WRITERS

MICHAEL BAILEY

Michael Bailey is the author of *Palindrome Hannah*, a nonlinear horror novel and finalist for the Independent Publisher Awards. His follow-up novel, *Phoenix Rose*, was listed for the National Best Book Awards for horror fiction and was a finalist for the International Book Awards. *Scales and Petals*, his short story collection, won the same award for short fiction. *Pellucid Lunacy*, an anthology of psychological horror published under his Written Backwards imprint, won for anthologies. His short fiction and poetry can be found in various anthologies and magazines around the world. He is currently working on his third novel, *Psychotropic Dragon;* a new short story collection, *Inkblots and Blood Spots;* and is tossing around ideas for a second themed anthology, as well as rereleasing a special edition of *Palindrome Hannah.* You can visit him online at www.nettirw.com.

P. I. BARRINGTON

After a detour through the entertainment industry, P.I. Barrington has returned to her roots as a fiction author. Among her careers she counts journalism and radio air talent. She lives in Southern California where she watches the (semi-wild) horses grazing in the hills behind her house. Her series of science fiction novels, the Isadora DayStar trilogy, includes *Book One: Future Imperfect: Crucifying Angel, Book Two: Future Imperfect: Miraculous Deception,* and *Book Three: Future Imperfect: Final Deceit.* She can be contacted via e-mail at pibarrington@yahoo.com. Her Web site is www.thewordmistresses.com.

WELDON BURGE

Weldon Burge, a native of Delaware, is a full-time editor, freelance writer, and creator of Web content. His fiction has appeared in *Suspense Magazine*, *Futures Mysterious Anthology Magazine*, *Grim Graffiti*, *The Edge: Tales of Suspense*, *Alienskin*, *Glassfire Magazine*, and *Out & About* (a Delaware magazine). His stories have also been adapted for podcast presentation by *Drabblecast*, and have appeared in the anthologies *Pellucid Lunacy: An Anthology of Psychological Horror*, *Don't Tread on Me: Tales of Revenge and Retribution*, *Ghosts and Demons*, and *Something at the Door: A Haunted Anthology*. He has a number of projects under way, including a police procedural novel and an illustrated book for children. He also frequently writes book reviews and interviews for *Suspense Magazine*. Check out his Web site at www.weldonburge.com.

MICHAEL LOUIS CALVILLO

Michael Louis Calvillo writes lovely, dark fiction. His works include *I Will Rise*, *As Fate Would Have It*, and *Death & Desire in the Age of Women*; the collection, *Blood & Gristle*; and two novellas, *Bleed for You* and *7BRAINS*. Visit his Web presence at michaellouiscalvillo.com for more information.

ELLIOTT CAPON

Elliott Capon's novel, *The Prince of Horror*, has sold well on Amazon Kindle and other e-book sources. Several of his stories have appeared in *Alfred Hitchcock's Mystery Magazine*, one of which was reprinted as title story of an anthology (*Fun and Games at the Whacks Museum and Other Stories*); one other story was reprinted in Signet's *Mystery for Halloween* and was read onto books-on-cassette. His stories have also been published in *Amazing Stories*, *Fantastic Science Fiction*, *The Horror Show*, and *American Accent Short Stories*.

CHARLES COLYOTT

Charles Colyott lives on a farm in the middle of nowhere (Southern Illinois) with his wife, daughters, cats, and a herd of llamas and alpacas. He is surrounded by so much cuteness it's very difficult for him to develop any street cred as a dark and gritty horror writer. Nevertheless, he has appeared in *Read by Dawn II*, Dark Recesses Press, *Withersin* magazine, *Terrible Beauty Fearful Symmetry*, and *Horror Library* Volumes III, IV, and V. You can contact him on Facebook, and, unlike his llamas, he does not spit.

A.J. FRENCH

Aaron J. French, also writing as A.J. French, has appeared in many publications, including *Abandoned Towers*, *The Absent Willow Review*, *Golden Visions Magazine*, the upcoming issue #7 of *Black Ink Horror*, the *Potter's Field 4* anthology from Sam's Dot Publishing, and *Something Wicked* magazine. He also has stories in the following anthologies: *Zombie Zak's House of Pain Anthology*; *Ruthless: An Extreme Horror Anthology* with introduction by Bentley Little; *Pellucid Lunacy*, edited by Michael Bailey; *M is for Monster*, compiled by John Prescott; and *2013: The Aftermath* by Pill Hill Press. He recently edited *Monk Punk*, an anthology of monk-themed speculative fiction, and *The Shadow of the Unknown*, an anthology of nü-Lovecraftian fiction.

ADRIENNE JONES

Adrienne Jones is the author of the novels *Brine*, *Gypsies Stole My Tequila*, *The Hoax*, *Backbite*, and *Seeded*. She lives in Rhode Island and is currently at work on her next book. Her Web site is www.adriennejones.net.

MICHAEL LAIMO

Michael Laimo's novels include *Atmosphere* (nominated for the Bram Stoker Award in the category of "first novel"); *Deep in the Darkness* (nominated for the Stoker in the "novel" category); and *The Demonologist*, *Dead Souls*, and *Fires Rising*, all of which were published in paperback by Leisure Books. His dark science fiction/suspense novel, *Sleepwalker*, was published in Limited Edition hardcover by Delirium Books. His short fiction has found its way into the pages of *A Walk on the Darkside*, *Lost on the Darkside*, *Hot Blood XII: Strange Bedfellows*, *Lipulse Magazine*, *Inhuman Magazine*, *The Best of All Flesh*, *Portents*, plus many more anthologies and magazines, many of which have been collected in *Demons, Freaks, and Other Abnormalities*; *Dregs of Society*; and *Dark Ride*.

LISA MANNETTI

Lisa Mannetti's debut novel, *The Gentling Box*, garnered a Bram Stoker Award and she was nominated in 2010 both for her novella, "Dissolution," and a short story, "1925: A Fall River Halloween." She has also authored The *New Adventures of Tom Sawyer and Huck Finn* (2011); *Deathwatch*, a compilation of novellas—including "Dissolution"; a macabre gag book, *51 Fiendish Ways to Leave Your Lover* (2010); two nonfiction books; and numerous articles and short stories in newspapers, magazines, and anthologies. Her story "Everybody Wins" was made into a short film by director Paul Leyden, starring Malin Ackerman and released under the title *Bye-Bye Sally*. Lisa lives in New York. Visit her author Web site at www.lisamannetti.com, as well as her virtual haunted house at www.thechanceryhouse.com.

GRAHAM MASTERTON

Graham Masterton made his horror debut in 1975 with *The Manitou*, the story of a three-hundred-year-old Native American shaman who is reborn in the present day to take his revenge on the white man. A huge bestseller, it was made into a classic movie starring Tony Curtis. Since then, Graham has written over a hundred novels—horror, thrillers, and historical romances—as well as numerous short stories. Before he took up writing novels, he was editor of *Penthouse* magazine. It was there that he met his late wife Wiescka, who became his agent and sold *The Manitou* in her native Poland even before the collapse of Communism—the first Western horror novel to be published in Poland since the war. Apart from five *Manitou* novels, Graham has also published the Rook series, about a remedial English teacher who recruits his slacker class to fight ill-intentioned ghosts and demons; the Night Warriors series, about ordinary people who battle against apocalyptic terrors in their dreams; as well as many other supernatural thrillers, including *Family Portrait, The Pariah,* and *Mirror*. He recently finished *Voice Of An Angel*, a crime thriller with a tinge of the supernatural, and is now working on a new Rook novel and many other projects. Graham's Web site is www.grahammasterton.co.uk

ROB R. MILLER

Born and raised in the hood of Portland, Oregon, over the years, Rob M. Miller has been victimized by violent attackers; thrashed violent attackers; enlisted in and honorably mustered out from the U.S. Army; taught martial arts; and worked in security, video store clerking, window washing, tire retreading, and store stocking. After two years of freelance stringer work and a number of publishing credits, he tired of nonfiction and turned to use his love of the dark, his personal terrors, and talent to do something more beneficial for his fellow man—*scare the hell out of him*! His work can be found online at the TheHarrow.com, as well as in American and British horror anthologies. He moderates a writer's site at www.writers-in-action-spruz.com, and his own Web site can be found at www.robthepen.pigboatrecording.com.

CHRISTOPHER NADEAU

Christopher Nadeau is the author of *Dreamers at Infinity's Core* published by COM Publishing, as well as over a dozen published short stories in such august publications as *The Horror Zine, Sci-Fi Short Story Magazine, Ghostlight Magazine,* and more anthologies than one could take out with the toss of a single hand grenade. He was interviewed as part of Suspense Radio's up-and-coming authors program, and collaborated on two "machinima" films with UK animator Celestial Elf titled *The Gift* and *The Deerhunter's Tale,* both of which can be viewed on YouTube. His novel *Echoes of Infinity's Core* is slated for a 2012 release. An active member of the Great Lakes Association of Horror Writers, Chris resides in Southeastern Michigan.

SCOTT NICHOLSON

Scott Nicholson is the author of more than twenty books, including the bestsellers *Liquid Fear, Disintegration,* and *The Red Church.* He's also written seventy short stories, six screenplays, four comics series, and three children's books. "The Shaping" originally appeared in the anthology *Unspeakable Horror,* edited by Vince Liaguno. Scott's Web site is www.hauntedcomputer.com.

ARMAND ROSAMILIA

Armand Rosamilia is a New Jersey boy currently living in sunny Florida, waiting for the zombie apocalypse to come. And it will come. His extreme zombie novellas *Highway To Hell* and *Dying Days* are now available, as well as two short story collections: *Skulls* and *Zombie Tea Party.* He loves horror, heavy metal, and the Boston Red Sox. Check out his Web site at armandrosamilia.wordpress.com.

JOHN SHIRLEY

John Shirley is the author of numerous novels and books of stories, including the best-selling *Bioshock: Rapture* and the urban fantasy novel *Bleak History*. Among his many books are the novels *Demons, Wetbones, City Come A-Walkin'*, the *A Song Called Youth* trilogy, and the story collection *Black Butterflies* (which won the Bram Stoker award and was chosen by *Publisher's Weekly* as one of the best books of that year). His new story collection is *In Extremis: The Most Extreme Stories of John Shirley*. He was co-screenwriter of the film *The Crow,* and has written scripts for television series, including *Deep Space Nine*. His latest novel is *Everything is Broken*, published by Prime Books. Visit John Shirley's fan-created Web site at www.darkecho.com/johnshirley.

J. GREGORY SMITH

Prior to writing fiction full-time, Greg Smith worked in public relations in Washington, D.C., Philadelphia, and Wilmington, Delaware. He has an MBA from the College of William & Mary and a BA in English from Skidmore College. His first published novel, *Final Price*, was originally self-published, before being signed by AmazonEncore, and released in November 2010. He is also the author of the psychological thriller *A Noble Cause*, published by Thomas & Mercer, January 2012.

L. L. SOARES

The fiction of L. L. Soares has appeared in such magazines as *Cemetery Dance, Horror Garage, Bare Bone, Shroud,* and *Gothic.Net,* as well as the anthologies *The Best of Horrorfind 2, Right House on the Left, Traps,* and the one you're holding in your hands. His first story collection, *In Sickness* (with Laura Cooney), was published in the fall of 2010 by Skullvines Press. He also cowrites the Bram Stoker-nominated horror movie review column *Cinema Knife Fight,* which now has a whole site built around it at cinemaknifefight.com. No matter how many times he forces radioactive arachnids to bite him, he just can't seem to get the amazing abilities of a spider. To keep up on his endeavors, go to www.llsoares.com.

JONATHAN TEMPLAR

Jonathan Templar lives in Cheshire, England. He has worked for local government, raised a child, and is now a full-time writer of speculative, horror, and children's fiction. His work has been published by Open Casket Press and Wicked East Press, among others. He can be found at www. jonathantemplar.com.

JEZZY WOLFE

Jezzy Wolfe is an author of dark fiction, with a predilection for absurdity. A life-long native of Virginia Beach, Jezzy lives with her family and quite a few ferrets. Her stories have appeared in such ezines and magazines as *The World of Myth*, *The Odd Mind*, *Twisted Tongue*, *Support the Little Guy*, and *Morpheus Tales*. She has also been published in a variety of anthologies, such as Graveside Tales' *Harvest Hill*, *The 2009 Ladies and Gentlemen of Horror*, *The Best of the World of Myth: Vol. II*, Library of the Dead's *Baconology*, and the Choate Road fun book, *Knock, Knock ... Who's There? Death!* She was a founding member of Choate Road.com and at one time cohosted the blogtalk radio shows "The Funky Werepig" and "Pairanormal." Currently she writes reviews for Liquid Imagination. In addition to her brand of humor and horror fiction, she maintains both a blog and storefront for ferret owners and lovers, known as FuzzyFriskyFierce. You can visit Jezzy Wolfe on her author's blog at jezzywolfe.wordpress.com, on her ferret blog at FuzzyFriskyFierce.wordpress.com, or at her storefront at www.cafepress.com/3fmerchandise.

THE ILLUSTRATOR

SHELLEY EVERITT BERGEN

The magnificent book cover graphic was created by Shelley Bergen, who was born and raised in Winnipeg, Manitoba, Canada. She still lives there today with her husband of nearly thirty years. They have one son.

"I have always been artistic to some degree, dabbling in painting with acrylics, poetry, tapestry, and, finally, digital photomanipulation," she said. "Discovering digital photomanipulation in 2000 opened a whole new door artistically for me. I now specialize in dark/macabre portraits, but am not limited to just that. In 2003, I was invited to join an online art community called Twisted Realmz, which is where I met fellow artists Antti Isosomppi and Matt Shealy. Great friendships ensued as well as collaborated artwork. This led to the launch of our company, Groundfrost Illustration & Design, in 2004. In the years since, we have had the privilege of creating artwork for projects for The Black-Eyed Peas, Kanye West, John Legend, God Forbid, Fragments of Unbecoming, The Killers, Dead Eyed Sleeper, Cutting Block Press, and Telus Publishing, to name but a few. In 2008, we created the artwork for the graphic comic *Lobster Girl*, story written by Jon Morvay. The comic went on to become the best-selling independent comic of that year. We are still going strong to this day, with no end in sight!"

Groundfrost can be found at www.groundfrost.net, or Shelley can be contacted personally for commissioned work at gbergen3@shaw.ca or on Facebook under her full name.

23994065R00161

Made in the USA
San Bernardino, CA
07 September 2015